HONEY POT

AUBREY TAYLOR

Book Cover by Aurora McGaughey

Editing and Proof Reading by Becky Clapham

Illustrations by Aubrey Taylor

First Edition 2025

Contents

JUST KEEP REMINDING YOURSELF
THAT YOUR WORTH ISN'T FOUND
IN THEIR RECOGNITION.

-MK

TO EVERYONE WHO FEELS IT ALL
& TO THOSE WHO FEEL
LIKE THEY'RE TOO MUCH.

CAEL CODY IS FOR YOU

AND TO JAS, BETH & NETTY

TWO HANDS ON THE HEAD BOARD
BECAUSE CAELY NEEDS TO CUM

OFFICIAL PLAYLIST

BOY VIOLET - **DEZA**
KILLED THE KID - **HAIDEN HENDERSON**
FEELIN' GOOD - **THE ORPHAN THE POET**
PETER - **TAYLOR SWIFT**
DEEPLY STILL IN LOVE - **ROLE MODEL**
MORAL OF THE STORY - **ASHE, NIALL HORAN**
BREATHE - **FAITH HILL**
BAD LUCK - **NOAH KAHAN**
ODE TO A CONVERSATION STUCK IN YOUR THROAT - **DEL WATER GAP**
I REALLY WISH I HATED YOU - **BLINK-182**
ALL I WANT - **KODALINE**
THE NIGHT WE MET - **LORD HURON**
LAVENDER GIRL - **CAAMP**
WAIT - **M83**
ALL THESE THINGS THAT I'VE DONE - **THE KILLERS**
I LOVE THIS PART - **THE WRECKS**
CELLULAR - **THE GLORIOUS SONS**
TRIBULATION - **MATT MAESON**
JAPANESE POSTERS - **REBOUNDER**
QUITTER - **CAMERON WHITCOMB**
HEAVY - **BIRDTALKER**
SUN TO ME - **ZACH BRYAN**
IN THE LIGHT - **MICHAEL MARCAGI**
I'M STILL HERE - **JOHN RZEZNIK**
PUT ME IN MY PLACE - **MUSCADINE BLOODLINE**
DEAR ARKANSAS DAUGHTER - **LADY LAMB**
REPENTANCE (REIMAGINED) - **GABLE PRINCE AND FRIENDS**
PLEASE PLEASE PLEASE - **SABRINA CARPENTER**

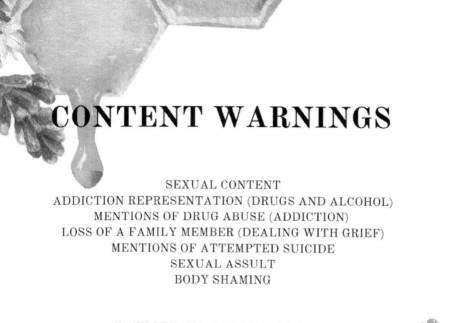

CONTENT WARNINGS

SEXUAL CONTENT
ADDICTION REPRESENTATION (DRUGS AND ALCOHOL)
MENTIONS OF DRUG ABUSE (ADDICTION)
LOSS OF A FAMILY MEMBER (DEALING WITH GRIEF)
MENTIONS OF ATTEMPTED SUICIDE
SEXUAL ASSULT
BODY SHAMING

TAKE BREAKS, GET SOME WATER,
SNUGGLE YOUR LOVED ONES AND PETS.

**BE KIND TO YOURSELF,
BEING A HUMAN BEING IS TOUGH.**

MATTHEWS

"Cael, don't," I warned, putting my hand up to stop him from coming any closer. He stalked me, his white t-shirt sticking to his biceps and abs, covered in mud and leaves from the creek, with the devil's smile on his face. "I swear to God, if you touch me, I will kill you!"

I screeched, stumbling backward as he chased me up the embankment, away from the rushing river of the creek that ran between our properties. My feet slipped in the wet dirt beneath my toes. I slid down before I could get to the top and crashed into Cael. His legs flew out from beneath him as he collided with me and wrapped his arms around me to protect me as we rolled to the base of the hill and back into the creek.

"Cael!" I gasped as I broke from the surface. My whole body curled up from the frigid temperatures and I barely made it back to the shore before my toes and fingers began to feel stiff and numb from the water.

"That wasn't even my fault!" He helped me out of the water and we rolled onto our backs, sopping wet and breathing heavily.

His head lolled to the side, the sun bathing his tanned skin in the warm light that peaked through the covering of trees above us. His hair was so light from the summer sun that it was practically bleached blond, and I had the insane urge to brush the streaks of mud that clung to it around his forehead and ears.

We lay there like that in the grass, with only the sound of heavy breathing and the wind pushing through the trees filling the silence.

1

"Momma said you're leaving early." I used all the courage to say the words that had settled heavily between us in silence for the last three weeks of August spent together.

"The job in Rhode Island at the University needs him up there before the season starts," Cael inhaled sharply. "I don't wanna go, but..." he trailed off into silence.

"You don't have much of a choice." I shrugged. I wound a piece of long dark hair around my finger, trying to avoid the devastating look that swam around in the glassy color of Cael's eyes.

I could count the random flecks of green that stared back at me, heartbroken and already so tragically lonely. Cael and I had never been apart. Not in our entire seventeen years. We had been born three hours apart, in the same hospital. Our mothers best friends, our houses on the same land in backwater Texas and two hours outside of Austin, our hearts beating to the same rhythm.

Cael was a part of me and, in the most bittersweet way, I was a part of Cael.

"What's going to happen?" I asked him, terrified of the answer.

Distance and time didn't apply to us. It never had.

"We'll talk daily on the phone," he said, rolling over onto his stomach and inching closer to me. "We can email, and I'll even send stupid letters."

At this distance, I could count every freckle on his face and trace them until I found all my favorite constellations. The most noticeable was the cluster that decorated his left cheekbone. Sharp and smooth, I was tempted to reach out and touch it. Curious to the point of being in agony over whether or not Cael felt the same about me.

If he loved me like I loved him.

"Clem." My name rolled from his lips. "Did you hear me?"

I knew that the pain was written all over my face. It wasn't something I would be able to hide much longer, if at all anymore, and Cael had always been able to read me like an open book.

"Letters," I said softly, dropping my stare and focusing on the tie around my dress. "I want letters."

"Every day," he promised, brushing his finger beneath my chin and raising my gaze to meet his. "Mama will get sick of buying stamps. I'll send so many."

"We were supposed to leave together," I whispered, so softly it was barely recognizable over the breeze.

Letters wouldn't be enough. Words on paper couldn't satiate the sadness I felt. Cael would go off and charm every pretty girl in Rhode Island. He would fall in love, find himself, and never think of me again. The thought of slowly fading out of his existence was terrifying and heartbreaking, but he didn't seem to care.

"Now I'll be alone." The words left my throat, choked and clumsy, as I felt a tear slip down my cheek.

"You won't be alone, Clem. You got other friends. I'm just one lame guy," Cael suggested, trying to bring my mood up. "You'll be okay."

"I don't have any other friends, Cael," I said as I sat upright in the grass.

His grip on my chin suddenly felt too hot and I needed space. He moved with me, sitting up, the fabric of his dirty white shirt tugged against his skin and crumpled around his hips.

"You have other friends. Everyone loves *you*! I'm just the chubby girl you take pity on because we grew up together. They don't see me as a friend. They see me as your little sister, and so do you!"

I swallowed so tightly that it hurt my throat.

"I'm just your shadow."

Cael flinched like I had slapped him.

I did everything in my power to hold the wave of tears at bay as they pricked the corners of my eyes and formed a lump in my throat. He would never love me the way I loved him. I pushed from the grass when he didn't say a word, his blue eyes glossy from fighting his emotions. He simply watched me walk away. I stomped along the path, taking out all my anger and agony on the trees and moss around me. When my house came into sight I inhaled a long breath to calm myself down before breaking out into the backyard.

"Hey, Lovebug," Momma cooed from the porch as I straightened myself out and wiped away the tears. "What's wrong? You're all covered in mud, Baby."

My mom stood from the garden and wiped her hands on her overalls, making as if to stop me before I entered the house through the back door, but I just brushed past her, avoiding her gaze.

"Nothing, Momma, I just tripped." I couldn't look at her. My mom would see through the façade and lies, furthering the breakdown that edged closer. "I'm going to go shower. Tell Cael I went to the library... if he comes looking. I don't wanna talk to him."

As the back door swung shut, I heard Mom call out for more explanation, but I kept walking up through the house to my loft where the world couldn't hurt me, and Cael couldn't come.

Once I was inside, I clicked the door closed, making sure the latch was tight and no one could bother me, before climbing into bed in my muddy dress and muffling my sobs with the soft, clean fabric of my pillow.

I cried myself to sleep, my shoulders sore and head pounding, every part of my body in pain over preemptively losing my best friend. The reality that he was leaving had finally sunk in, but the truth that the distance would change everything about us had hit me like a freight train.

When I woke, the sun had gone down and my pillow was damp from the tears I cried, making my face sticky and clammy. I groaned, pushing from my bed and stripping from my dress, leaving it in a puddle on the floor near the foot of my bed. I wandered to my bathroom, still painted sky blue from my sixth birthday, when my dad let me pick whatever color I wanted. I ran warm water, briefly staring at my pale, freckled face and stringy dark hair in the mirror.

The girl that no one could love.

Cael Cody's shadow.

The water seemed to ease the tension from my shoulders but only made my headache worse and, after a while, made me dizzy enough to sink to the floor of the tub and put my head between my knees. I had been so stupid to think that Cael would ever see me as anything but a friend.

I distinctly remembered the moment I saw Cael as something more, the exact day to the hour the sun casted differently on my image of him. He had stepped down from his porch, baby blue button-down undone at the top to show the gold necklaces he had stacked up on top of each other before the party. His hair was longer than usual, and chunks of dirty blonde had fallen against his forehead. He smiled at me that day, and I felt my chest open up and swallow the feeling of being loved by him whole.

I climbed out of the shower, trying to focus on anything, but my mind kept slipping back to his face. A year ago, somewhere between being kids and turning into teenagers, I had forgotten how to be his friend and started to become a lovesick puppy. I just hadn't realized it until that moment.

I rummaged through my drawers for shorts and a tank top, changing into them and drying my hair, before chucking the towel back into the washroom. Quickly, I changed the dirty sheets on my bed, kicking the muddy ones into a pile and crawling back into my fresh-smelling bed. I pulled my journal from the dresser beside me. The top was carved apart and painted on with tiny little doodles that I couldn't get out of my head.

I kicked around under my sheets until my feet hit the tiny knit bag full of pens, and I dragged it up to myself, picking out my favorite black one before throwing the bag somewhere into the void of my messy room. I could hear my parents in the house below, dancing in the kitchen to Tim McGraw like they always did.

I sighed. I had been taught that love is forever. It's like cement. Once you're in it, there's no getting out. I craved it, longed for it, and it seemed to always pass me by in the form of watching Cael pull girls into his lap or flirt with the cheerleaders during lunch hour in the cafeteria. I had a list as long as my leg of the girls Cael had loved that weren't me.

Time seemed to creep by, and as the sun set in the sky, a soft knock came on my door, scaring me into hiding my journal beneath my pillow. I padded across my ugly, thrifted floor rug and turned on the small, dingy lamp on my desk beside the door before popping the latch and opening it.

"Mrs. Matthews said you didn't eat," Cael stood before me, his eyes cast to the ground like he was in trouble holding out a plate of my favorite fries. "I went and got them from Duke's."

"Why?" I asked like I didn't know the answer, my door still half closed like it might protect me or even stop me from letting Cael come in.

"Because I made you sad, Clem, and I didn't mean to," he looked up at me through his thick lashes, and I could see that he had been crying too.

"You didn't make me sad, Cael," I bit. "I made myself sad, wishing for something I couldn't have."

"What do you want? I'll go get it for you," he said without hesitation, and I felt my heart shatter like a piece of china inside my chest.

"What I want, you can't just go get," I said, strained and twangy.

"Just tell me what it is, Clem, I won't leave until I know. Your Momma and Daddy went to a movie, you're all alone in this big house, and I sat outside for two hours until they let me in. And Mr. Matthews threatened me with a gun before they left, so you better tell me what you want before he comes back and shoots me."

"Stop!" I yelled louder than I ever had before, and Cael's head cocked to the side in surprise. "I can't tell you."

I said each word with purpose and intent so he understood that it wasn't something he could buy from a store and it wasn't something he could fix with his pretty smile and perfect jokes.

"You can tell me anything, Clementine," he said, pushing his foot against the door, "and you're gonna tell me right now what's making you so sad."

"What if saying it out loud makes *you* sad?" I asked, backing away as he made his way into my room.

His flowery blue eyes scanned his surroundings and, for a second, I forgot that this was the first time he had ever been here. My daddy was strict about boys being in my room. Even having known Cael from diapers didn't give him special privileges.

"I'm already sad Clem; I have to leave you."

If my heart wasn't already cracking in two, Keith Urban started to play over the radio in the kitchen below, and the lyrics to *Making Memories of Us* cascaded up into the loft.

His soft voice made me want to cry. "Don't do that."

"What?" he asked. He set the plate of food on the dresser as he explored further into my room. "Tell you the truth?" he shrugged, his jaw flexing as he looked around and avoided my stare. "Come into your room?" He asked with a soft smile. "It smells like lavender in here."

"Cael!" I said, my emotions bursting, "Don't force me to tell you."

"We don't keep secrets from each other." He played with the threaded friendship bracelet on his wrist that I gave him... It was sun-bleached and frayed, but he never took it off.

"This isn't a secret," I replied, walking back until my heels pressed tightly against my side table.

"Then tell me," he begged now, a sound I had heard from him so often that I thought myself immune. But his eyes seemed bluer, his voice pleading, and all resolve in my body cracked under the weight of the sound. "Is this about him? Did something happen?" He asked.

"I want you," I whispered just to get him to stop talking, cheeks red and tears rolling down my face. Everything had been ruined by that day, all my worst fears, but it made it clear that all I had ever wanted was Cael.

"My first kiss, my first time," I swallowed the cotton ball in my throat. "I wanted you—"

When I looked up, the tension snapped like a rubber band. Cael closed the space between us, and his hands were tangled into my damp hair without hesitation. His fingers pressed into the back of my neck as he collided with my mouth, his lips tracing my own shape. Breathlessly, he pushed into me, begging silently to come closer, but I was paralyzed, my hands gripping the table, my toes curling into the carpet.

MATTHEWS

I stared in surprise for a long moment at the freckles on his nose before finally closing my eyes and sinking weightlessly into the soft feeling of his mouth. My hands came up around his waist and gripped tightly into his shirt, my fingers tugging at the fabric. He pulled back, and a slow whimper dripped from my lips, following his path as he peppered more delicate kisses along the corners of my mouth and up my jaw to my ear.

"Your daddy's definitely gonna shoot me now," he chuckled, nibbling at my ear lobe.

"Wait," I said, pushing him back. My head was dizzy from his kiss, and my heart was beating faster than I had ever felt it move, "are you only doing this because I'm sad, Cael, because—"

"Clem, for once in your life, *please be quiet*." He hushed me with another long kiss that felt like flying.

He gripped the back of my neck as his hand raked down my side and cupped my thigh, lifting my leg until it was wrapped around his waist, and he rolled his hips against mine. I could feel every inch of him through my pajama shorts, and suddenly, everything felt too natural and too warm.

"Hey," Cael tugged back without me even opening my mouth and moving his hands to cup my face as he looked at me. "What's wrong? Was the kiss that bad?"

He laughed, and I felt the shift in my anxiety from the sound.

"No, no," I shook my head in his hands. "Of course not."

"It's too fast," he said, rolling his tongue over his bottom lip. I could see him jumping to conclusions, cursing himself quietly that he was no better than...

"I'm sorry." He severed through my thoughts.

He took a whole step back, and before I could even think about what I was doing, I followed him, linking our fingers together in the soft light that peered from my bedroom lamp. "I'm not..." I stopped, looking away from him, trying to collect myself when he hooked a finger around my chin and pulled me back. "Experienced like the other girls."

Cael's pouty lips curled at the corners, "Clem," he laughed, his nose scrunching up and his eyes catching the moonlight, "do you think I slept with all those girls?"

"Well, you—" I started and then realized how horrible I sounded, "I just thought—"

"I'm never opposed to a little heavy petting, but Plum, I've never slept with any of them." His finger slipped absentmindedly between the strap of my tank top and skin as he talked, his eyes drifting down to my shoulders and collarbones.

"That seems like a secret, Cael," I said, not trying to start a fight, just wanting to shift the embarrassment away from my jealousy.

"You never asked."

I gave him a sharp look that only made him laugh, but he roped his fingers through my hair again, moving slower. This time, he kissed my bottom lip, tugging it into his mouth. My hand tangled into the collar of his shirt, brushing against the buttons and pulling him closer as he took his time kissing me.

"How come you never told me you wanted to kiss me?" Cael asked, his breath hot on my neck.

"You never asked." I smiled against his mouth as his tongue slid between my lips and tangled with my own, sending all my senses haywire. I felt his fingers play at the hem of my shirt, tickling a line across my stomach to my hips before he wrapped them tight and tugged me closer.

"I'm asking now," he said in such a sober tone that all the thoughts in my head went fuzzy, and all I could focus on was how nice it felt to have his hands all over me and his lips on mine. "Clem, don't make me beg," Cael whined against me as his hands moved further under my shirt, tickling my ribs slowly as he worked his way up.

"I think you should," I giggled, skirting away from his touch to steady my pounding heart.

I pushed back and sat down on my bed, staring up at him with stars in my vision and butterflies in my chest. I had forgotten how tall he had grown over the summer, towering over me with built-in waves of slim muscles from farm work and horse riding.

I watched him roll the blue button down over his shoulders, dropping it to the floor and showing his toned muscles beneath. I had been around him more naked than he was now a thousand times, but the sight of him made my breath catch in my throat. He flicked the heavy metal latch of his belt buckle and slipped the leather from its loops, the sound echoing through my room. Without a second to breathe, he shucked from the jeans and stood in front of me in nothing but a pair of loose boxers, his white tank, and the golden pendant necklace I had given him for his birthday. I dug my fingers into the sheets beside me to balance myself as he dropped to his knees before me.

"I think I like you best on your knees," I found the courage to say, watching him with hungry eyes. He laughed, his head dropping to look at the floor and then back to me with a smirk.

"Clementine," he stepped forward on his knees, slipping from his undershirt and chucking it into the pile of his clothes. "Mary," he crawled forward a little more until his fingers were within reach to brush a line up my calf. "Matthews," he whispered, and his breath hitched, causing his stomach to flex as his fingers roved over my thighs and dug into the meaty outer muscles.

"Yes, Cael Cody?" I answered with tight, sticky words that I barely got out.

"If you'll let me," he kissed the inside of my knee before positioning himself between us carefully, his hands daring to rake up under my shorts to my upper thighs. "I will spend whatever time we have left kissing every inch of your skin until the feeling of my lips is burned so brightly into your memory that you never kiss another boy again without thinking about me."

I had never been talked to like that, and I had certainly never heard Cael speak to anyone like that, so I must have turned the color of a ripe tomato because Cael just smirked at me.

"Is that a yes, Plum?" He asked, kissing my thigh, "You have to say it out loud for me."

"Yes." For such a tiny word, I managed to stumble over it as I said it, but Cael didn't seem to mind as his fingers found the band of my shorts and began to pull them down over my thighs.

I felt warm, but I loved the way his eyes traced over all my bare skin as he exposed it slowly. He set the pajamas next to me, and as I went to remove my tank top, he stopped me.

"Just wait," he said, "I want to do it."

I felt giddy at his authority; I had never seen him so serious. The light-hearted, playful boy I had grown up with had receded behind the walls of a grown man. I dared to touch him again and realized I could, lifting my hand to brush it through his dirty blonde hair. I momentarily raked them back through the soft locks and tangled them there when I realized he was staring at me in awe.

"What?" I huffed lightly.

"You're beautiful," he said so quietly that if the wind had wanted to steal the sound, it could have.

There was no stopping him once he had declared what was on his mind. I had seen that look in his eyes a few times before. It was determination and want, and Cael never stopped until he had what wasn't his. The problem was that I had been his from the beginning, and I was worried he might get bored without the chase.

"Why'd you get sad?" He pushed up onto his knees, brushed his nose against my jaw, and kissed a soft, wet line down my neck to the swell of my breasts in my tank top.

"No reason," I whispered, wrapping my hand around his neck and leaning back onto the bed.

Cael followed my touch, crawling over me until his legs framed my thighs. With so little fabric between us now, I could feel the hardened length of him against my thigh. A fire burned in the pit of my stomach like I had never experienced before as he pressed a hand between us and brushed against the damp fabric of my underwear.

11

He looked up at me, blue eyes shining in the moonlight, and smiled. "If you need to stop, want to stop," he paused and kissed me, tugging my bottom lip between his teeth as gently as he could. "We stop, no questions."

"I thought you said you had never done this before," I pressed my hands against his chest. It was so warm beneath my palms that I nearly got distracted from my worry.

"Clem, this is still second base," he kissed me, and I could feel his boyish smile on my mouth. "Do you want to stop?" He asked me.

I shook my head no and stole another long, much-awaited kiss from his lips. He smelled like fresh grass and the fruity cologne he swore he hated but wore because he loved his momma, and it was a gift from her. I loved that smell. It reminded me of home, safety, Cael, and everything I had been lucky enough to love about him over the years. It was a smell that I would hold on to after he was taken from me. Soon, it would be the only thing I had left of him. It was bittersweet to be consumed by it only to know how quickly that moment would end.

He held his promise and kissed me until he could no longer, smiling against my skin like he savored the taste of it. For the longest time, I had felt awkward in my skin, like it was too tight and worn in for someone who had only lived for seventeen years. But Cael proved every thought that swirled around my head wrong with every kiss of his lips, every pinch of his fingers around my thighs and tummy. He honored me for who I was, not who the world told me I should be.

"I'm going to take this off," he informed me, "you look so pretty in the moonlight, and I want to remember all of it." He smirked, rolling the hem of my tank top up until he needed me to lift my arms. But he didn't throw my shirt away. He wrapped the fabric carefully around my crossed wrists and left them above my head.

"Cael," I huffed, wiggling a little as he did so. My mouth was so close to his chest that every time he shifted, his skin brushed against my lips, eventually tempting me to kiss him there over and over until he directed his attention back to my face. "I can't move my hands now," I whined.

"Good," he said, "I don't want you covering up," he chuckled and kissed a hot line down my collarbone to my breast.

My hips lifted from the bed as his tongue licked a slow circle around my nipple. My body lit up in clusters of fireworks that only seemed to spread as he continued to work his tongue over all my most sensitive spots. His fingers hooked into the sheer fabric of my underwear and tugged them down over my thighs, sinking his head between them and kissing a pattern against my skin.

I wiggled against the ticklish feelings. "Do something," I groaned impatiently, "anything."

He didn't respond with words as his tongue brushed against my thigh. "Cael, if you take any longer to make me feel good, I'll let Daddy shoot you just for good measure."

That produced a laugh from him, but it was short-lived and drowned in the sound of a sharp gasp that dripped from me as he licked a trail through me. The fire in my belly seemed to rage as his fingers dug into my thigh, and he worked his tongue deeper. The bit of stubble he had managed to grow rubbed against my skin and tickled me as he moved in light circles. I wanted to touch him, but he had tied my hands to the rungs above my head, so instead, I raised my hips to meet his face and curled my free leg up against his shoulder.

My back arched against the feeling of his fingers slipping into me. I was too tight and unready for the sensation. It burned at first but slowly faded to a dull heat as he moved them in and out of me.

"Cael," I said, pressing my leg against his shoulder tighter in an attempt to control the cord that wound as tightly as it ever had within me. If he didn't stop soon, it would snap before we even had sex. "I'm not going to last to third base if you don't quit," I warned.

"Oh." His breath was warm and tickled against my sensitive clit as he spoke between nibbles and licks. "I don't want you to last," he said. "I want you to come for me now and then again when I finally get inside of you."

"Cael Cody!" I gasped at how dirty he was talking to me. "I thought you were a gentleman."

"You never thought that," he laughed wildly, his blue eyes glimmering up at me like he had stars trapped behind them. "Besides, I am being a gentleman." He kissed my clit. "Ladies first."

His hands started to move faster, his tongue working in time, and he began to rub soft circles with his thumb against all the sensitive spots. I couldn't form a thought to argue with him. Stars exploded across my vision, and heat rose through my neck and consumed everything around me. Shockwaves of pleasure rolled through my body in an overwhelming way I had never experienced before. Like flying and falling at once, his touch tingled every nerve ending in succession. The world seemed to be hazy except for Cael, who was in perfect focus as he kissed his way up my stomach to my breasts.

Cael's thumb brushed over my nipple, followed by his tongue and a trail of soft kisses back to my mouth. I leaned into the taste, chasing the high that my body was coming down from as he pushed my legs apart with his knee.

"There she is," Cael whispered as my eyes finally focused on him. His chain hung between us and slowly brushed against my hot skin.

"Again," I pushed up to him, nipping his bottom lip, making him laugh excitedly as his hands came up to frame my face.

"Patience, Plum." He kissed my nose gently and then worked carefully to untie my hands, kissing and licking the few spots that had imprints from my tank top. "It was too tight." His pretty smile turned down at the corner.

"It was perfect," I insisted, kissing the corners and, finally free of my bindings, able to touch him the way I wanted to. I pushed him back, ready for a sense of control, and flipped him onto my mattress with a giggle as his hands raked up my back. "Thank you," I said, peering down at his dumb, pretty face and big idiot grin.

"Anything for you, Clem," he said, the words hanging between us. "Now kiss me before your daddy comes home 'cause I ain't looking to find the end of a shotgun between my legs tonight."

"Shut it." I kissed him a little longer that time, savoring every tiny twitch of his hands and legs as I pressed down against him, still separated by his boxers. His hands kneaded my ass and helped me find a rhythm as we made out until our lips were sore and we couldn't breathe any longer.

"What do you need?" Cael asked as he buried his mouth into the curve of my neck. "Tell me so I can give it to you," he begged. "Please, Plum."

"You," I huffed, dragging my hips along him until I felt him catch on my ass with a long groan, "I just need you."

"That I can manage." He smiled against my skin as he wiggled free of his boxers. I felt him bounce free against my ass, and I practically whimpered as he raked and handed me over in preparation. He hesitated just for a moment, the wet tip of his cock pressed at my entrance. "If it hurts, tell me." He kissed my jaw. "We'll go slow."

I nodded and buried my face against his neck to brace for it, and he was right. As he pressed deeper, stretching me around him, it burned for a moment, just like it had with his fingers, but over time, it faded, and all I could feel was the pulse of us moving together.

"That's my girl." He raked his hands over my hair, tangling into it and gripping my neck as he rocked deeper. I pressed my hand up around his back, curling my fingertips into his shoulders, and kissed my way across his neck as he pumped and brought us closer together than we would ever be.

"You okay?" He asked quietly when I paused, but the cord was rewinding, and my breath was caught sticky in my throat. "Clem, you gotta talk to me. I don't wanna hurt you," he whispered to me.

"Don't stop," I choked out as he pushed all the way in, bumping every sensitive spot within me. "Cael, I'm not gonna make it." I could feel myself spiraling. Before I could beg further, he picked up his speed, and all the pain turned to an intense wave of pleasure that seemed to crash down over me.

His breathing became labored, and his grip around my body tightened as he pushed us both closer to the edge. "Almost there," he kissed my sweaty temple, rocking into me as the cord snapped. It wasn't at all what I had been expecting, it was a tricky combination of pain and intense vibrations that made my fingers and toes tingle.

Cael groaned and pulled from me, quickly shifting away as he finished, his warmth spreading over my stomach as he did so. "Sorry," he whimpered breathlessly, sounding embarrassed.

"Don't," I said, brushing his sweaty hair away from his forehead.

I pushed from the bed on weak knees and padded to the bathroom to clean up. I stared at myself in the mirror and, even though nothing was different about my thick thighs, belly, or swollen breasts, I felt different. I felt alive, like every inch of my skin was sparkling, and for the first time, I felt seen.

I returned and handed him a clean cloth, tugging my shorts on and climbing into bed beside him. I felt him wrap me up in his arms, and his lips found home against my neck as he buried himself into me again. "I'm sorry if you're sore," he apologized, looking up at me.

"I'm not," I lied.

"That feels like a secret." He narrowed his eyes at me and kissed the corner of my mouth.

I was a little, but it wasn't anything that would ruin all the good things about that night. "I am, a little, but you were gentle and perfect," I kissed him, pressing our foreheads together when I pulled away. "And I will never kiss another boy without thinking about you."

He stared at me with those sad, indigo eyes and whispered, "I wish you would have told me how you felt. Sooner, I guess. I've gone my entire pitiful seventeen years knowing one thing." He brushed a piece of hair from my face and ran his thumb across my bottom lip.

"I could die a thousand times over loving you, Clementine Matthews, and it wouldn't hurt for a second."

I wanted to tell him it was true, but I was afraid to let the sadness creep back in. I tried to tell him how much I loved him, but I couldn't without crying, so instead, I curled into his arms and closed my eyes, giving us a few spare moments to be Cael and Clementine one last time

CODY

2024

I rolled out of bed and away from the girl I fell asleep with. Her dark hair fanned out over my pillow like she owned it. I groaned, digging around on my floor for a pair of clean shorts with my eyes closed. The migraine that woke me dug at the base of my neck and rattled my spine under my skin.

Between the lack of sleep and crippling bad dreams, I couldn't remember how she got there, but I hated the fact that my bed sheets smelled of fake roses and cinnamon. I would have to wash them later to bring back the lavender smell and get some sleep.

I slipped from my room and down the stairs to the kitchen, my eyes half open, to find my Peachy sitting on the counter reading a book in her pajamas. I rubbed out the knots that formed along my shoulder and rotated it in a lazy circle as I tried to ignore the sharp pain that radiated across the healed incision.

"You look like shit," Ella chimed, without even looking up from her book. "Is your shoulder bugging you?" Her blonde hair was curled around her pretty face, but she wasn't hiding her scars with makeup anymore. It made my chest lighter in a way only she could.

"Good morning to you too." I pulled the fridge door open, deflecting her question, and grabbed a water. I looked up at her, twisting the cap off and throwing it in the garbage can. "Why are you up so early?" I asked her.

"It's noon, Cael." Her big brown eyes flickered up over the top of her book at me so she could mock me. "Why are you up so early?"

"Sleeping sucks when you aren't doing it black-out drunk," I sighed.

17

"Yeah." Ella smiled. "It's a little harder when your brain has time to dream."

"Nightmares is more like it." My Texas accent slipped out just a touch with the laughter.

Ella slipped from the counter, pouring me a warm cup of coffee. "It'll get easier. Maybe Silas can prescribe it for you—"

"No," I stopped her. "I don't want anything, I just need to get through this."

"Sorry, I wasn't thinking..." Ella gave me a sad look as she handed me the mug. "I'm learning too. I guess it'll be harder than we expected to navigate this. I'm here, though. I can't promise to give the best advice, but I'm here." The ring on her left finger sparkled in the sunlight and I felt genuinely happy for the first time in a long time that my best friend had found someone so special.

Jealousy wasn't the word.

I wasn't jealous of them. I was sad, and it consumed all my other logical feelings. Which is precisely what got me into drugs. The need to feel something other than miserable. Rehab had been long and exhausting. I'd spent a month in a facility outside of campus and nothing felt right. Coming out and back into the Nest was tense. Dean avoided me the entire first week back, and that piled the anxious feelings on top of resisting temptation, Arlo leaving, and my shoulder injury. The nightmares started to flood into all the cracks that drugs and booze had previously filled.

I shuddered. I'll never forget the way the stitches pulled at my skin, lying in that tiny rehab bed, my feet hanging off the edge, staring at the ceiling with the urge to pick each one out.

"Earth to space cadet," Ella wiggled the cup at me. "Where'd you go there?"

"Nowhere important. Thanks, Peachy." I winked, holding up the cup and shoving away all the nipping thoughts of addiction to smile for her.

"Good." She leaned in, giving me a tiny kiss on my cheek. "You have a meeting tonight at seven. Arlo can't take you, he's in Dallas for an interview with the owners of the Rangers. I'll pick you up at six forty-five."

I hated that I needed to go to the NA meetings and hated that I needed to be escorted, but I was grateful that Ella was willing to take me. I was thankful that Arlo still had hope for me. The selfish little kid in my heart silently hoped his meeting went horribly. Then he'd come home for good, and the spaces between my family wouldn't feel so impossibly empty.

"Six forty-five," I repeated the time to her, so she knew I was really listening, and watched her shuffle from the kitchen to prepare for her day.

Instead of returning to the booty call I had so desperately used for a distraction the night before, I slipped on a pair of running shoes and threw on my headphones that hung on the hook by the back door. The worst thing I could do was go back to bed. Two weeks after the accident, Aunt Riona insisted that I start therapy with someone outside the Hornet family. A therapist detached from the situation.

The rehab facility had a few options. I went with Doctor Harson. He was younger, with funny glasses that never stayed on his nose as he took notes. He was nice enough and had been training me to put my energy into things that make me feel better.

Arlo ran to feel better. So I tried that. And it usually worked. It made me feel like shit in the moment. Every mile I ran closer to campus made me wanna puke. Each droplet of sweat that poured between my shoulder blades reminded me that I was a piece of trash without direction. But at least it was productive and, by the time I slipped into a shower on the main floor of the Nest, Maddison...Mykayla, or Mckenzie, whatever the fuck her name was, had disappeared from my bed.

I was shoving my sheets into the washing machine when Dean found me.

"How are you doing?" He asked but didn't want the answer. His blond hair had gotten longer and grew in honey curls around his thick neck, ears, and jaw, but his blue eyes remained bright as he watched me.

"Exhausted." I rolled my eyes and dumped in the soap and a handful of the lavender beads I bought from the grocery store once a week. Staring inside, I shrugged and dumped in a little more.

"That's why they never leave." Dean pointed to the container. "Your bed doesn't smell like a frat boy's. If you let it sit for a week, you'll never wake up to anyone."

"You love how my bed smells," I teased and watched his strong jaw tighten.

We weren't in a place for those jokes, not after what had happened with his mother. He was still tip-toeing around his conservative family like they might disown him for being gay.

After the ball season, we sat down and concluded that what we wanted and needed from each other was very different. I was using Dean as a distraction from my issues. That wasn't to say I didn't love him. I always had. I knew the moment I saw his stupid boyish face at warm-ups. But that's not enough. I couldn't run in circles pretending he would ever be ready to be out. It wasn't healthy for me, and I would never force his hand. That wasn't my story to tell.

Dean shrugged. We were having a hard time finding our way back to being friends. Every conversation was a chance to pick at old scabs.

"I figured you wanted to go for a run, but you did that without me." He sounded annoyed. "So how about some lunch? My treat?"

He was trying to be a friend, and I couldn't deny his pretty smile.

"Hilly's," I demanded, my stomach betraying me. I could use a plate of their french fries right now. They had never been and would never be as good as Duke's, but they were hot and close enough to the real thing. "Pretty please, Big Guy."

"I'll bring the truck around." Dean started to walk away from me when I sighed.

"I'll drive," I offered, with Dean raising an eyebrow at the suggestion.

I never drove because I was always drunk, and when I did drive, I was usually drunk anyway, but I was turning over a new leaf. For Ella and Arlo, but I'd never admit to that. Tying my recovery to other people was a big no, no. But I needed the anchor, and they were the most stable part of my life.

Dean shrugged, seemingly convinced, and turned on his heel to grab his wallet before we climbed into my car. The Supra still needed hours of work. In typical fashion, I had gotten bored listening to Arlo preach about car mechanics. It was rusty, and I couldn't even begin to explain the state of the engine under the hood, but I didn't care. Momma had helped pick this car out, and I wasn't giving it up without a fight.

"Cael," Dean groaned about the leg space in the passenger seat. "I get you wanna live out some sick *Fast and Furious* dream, but this is cruel."

20

"I don't know." I stared over at him. His head brushed the ceiling of the small car and his muscular thighs were practically tucked up to his stomach in the seat.

"Looks hilarious from this angle." I laughed, threw it in reverse, and whipped from the garage. His hand flew to the handle above his head as I took every corner too fast.

When we arrived, Hilly's was empty. During the lull between Harbor sports, the small two-story brick building that housed the old-school diner-style hangout was dead. Once hockey began, the service would skyrocket again, and people would crowd around the entrance to get in so they could watch the game.

"Hey, Kayla." Dean waved to her as we passed through the main floor.

It was dark inside; dim lighting hung over rich-colored cushioned booths and sizeable round scuffed-up tables. The shabby floors had just enough shine left to reflect all the neon signs on the walls.

"Boys." Kayla leaned over her desk, pretty red hair cascading down over her trim shoulders. I turned in a half circle, climbing the first couple of stairs up to the loft backward. I leaned back, holding onto the railing, and opened my mouth.

"Never going to happen, Cody." She rolled her eyes and waved me off.

"You'll surrender one day," I said.

"The day you start wearing full shirts, I'll let you take me out." She pointed to the ratty navy blue crop top that hung across my belly button. The Hornets athletes' logo faded from the sun.

"And hide this adorable tummy? Never." My smile mirrored hers as I shrugged, turning back and taking the stairs two at a time to catch up to Dean.

He slid into the booth and leaned against the cushion with an exasperated sigh. "You know Kayla would absolutely—" I paused, tracing my eyes down his massive, muscular frame. "Go for that. Your mom would give you a medal for bringing her home."

"You think?" Dean opened one eye to look at me. I would never let him bring a girlfriend home just to placate his mother.

"Not a chance." I smiled at him and licked my bottom lip. "She's so far out of your league she might as well be space, Elon Musk."

"I don't—" He started to talk his way through the confusion but stopped. By far, one of my favorite pastimes was contributing to Dean Tucker's constant state of bewilderment with obscure pop culture references from the dark holes of the internet.

"Besides, she's not blonde enough for you."

"I don't specifically date blondes," he argued.

"You have to in order to keep the genes alive. A baseball team of little blond Dean look-alikes." I laughed, but Dean just scowled at me. Kids and legacy were a sore topic around the Hulk action figure. "What?... You can adopt. Or get your sister to be a surrogate. She loves having kids."

That made him laugh. God I loved his smile.

"It's terrifying how good she is at it."

"I'm just saying you have options when it comes time to build the army of vanilla Hulk action figures." I smiled and nudged the tension out of his flexed muscles.

We ordered and, just as expected, the addition of warm, salty french fries unknotted all the tense feelings that hung between us. There was something fucking magic about french fries. A cure-all.

I moaned when the salt hit my tongue and devoured them way too fast.

"Don't." He slapped my hand away as I reached over to steal a few of his.

"Ow!" I shook out my stinging fingers. "You're in a foul mood today. What crawled up your ass?"

"No one, just give me five minutes of silence, Man. I know it's hard for you, but—"

"You invited me for lunch, Ponyboy," I argued, but he just stared at me for a long moment.

"You're reading into it, and it's nothing." He ignored me and shoved another fry between his lips.

I scrunched my brows up.

"No, seriously," leaning forward on the table, I said, actually concerned when his frown didn't loosen. "What's going on?"

Dean was typically sunshine. Sure, he had his moments of weakness, as we all did, but he was built differently. Raised from the ground in a nuclear family, he was the golden child, and he worked hard to protect that image of himself in the shadow of his older brother and sister, who were both genuinely and weirdly incredible in their own right.

I was always a little jealous of his life and all for surface reasons.

Professor Tucker was a headstrong jerk, but he was a decent dad. His mom was a retired doctor who had stayed home and raised the kids from the moment his older sister was born. She moved on to be a grandma to a handful of kids that his older brother kept popping out like rabbits. He had a family—a big, loving family that wanted him to succeed.

The problem lay in how his family viewed him. His mother refused to acknowledge his sexuality, and it was a sore spot between them. Homophobia ran deep, and it made the love they extended to Dean feel like sandpaper on his skin.

I supposed that was the problem.

Love only got him so far when he spent half his time hiding who he really was. They played happy family in public, with smiles and jokes, but behind closed doors, it was barrages of text messages laced with passive-aggressive comments about his love life and his career. It was tiring to watch from the sidelines; I couldn't imagine how exhausting it was to live through it.

"Anna is in town with her stuffy political husband." He rolled his eyes at me. "I can't do this again, Cael," he groaned and pulled away from me as I went to rest my hand on his. "I won't."

"Hiding isn't healthy either." I shrugged.

"I'm not ashamed to be gay, Cael," he snapped at me. "I just know it doesn't matter what I want or need."

The golden boy.

Stuck forever in the position he was carved into.

"We tried," he continued, "really hard, a few times, and I love you." He finally looked at me, and it hurt more than I expected it to. My fingers itched to rub the corners of his chiseled jaw and calm the storm that brewed behind his gray-blue eyes, but I didn't because it was not what he wanted or needed. I might have been an idiot, but I listened well.

"But you can't love me back. You tried, and I love you for the effort. But..." He sighed, his finger reaching out from under his plate to brush against the frayed friendship bracelet around my wrist. "You hid behind the drugs and booze to forget that you already gave your heart to someone else, and I'm not going to play second string to a ghost."

She wasn't a ghost.

She was a daydream.

"I'd offer to join you for Thanksgiving, but I don't think that will go over well with your mother." I tried to ease the tension and erase the lavender smell of her hair from my nose before it made my eyes water.

"Didn't you hear?" He cleared his throat and inhaled. "The Shores are hosting Thanksgiving up at the cabin. Silas has been planning it for weeks."

Focusing on my recovery has left me out in the cold in ways I could have never imagined.

"I guess you'll be okay then," I forced a smile.

"My treat." He waved Kayla over to pay.

I slid down against the booth and sighed as my stare became unfocused and the emotions I fought so hard stirred beneath the surface. I was trying my best to be the Cael Cody they all knew and loved, but it was hard, firstly and most importantly, without the drugs, but even more so sometimes when I realized they didn't need me as much as I needed them.

"Let's get you to therapy before Silas kicks my ass." Dean slapped me against the shoulder.

CODY

"*Plum.*" I kissed a line down her neck to her shoulder and hooked my finger beneath the strap of her tank top. "*I missed you,*" I whispered against her warm skin. "*Where have you been?*"

"*I'm always right here.*" She shivered beneath my touch as her hands cupped my face and brought us together. The kiss was languid and filled with heat as her tongue slipped into my mouth and my hands tangled into her dark brown hair.

"*You're only here when I close my eyes.*" I kissed the corners of her mouth and ran a hand down her back to her ass, grabbing as much of her as I could and tugging her up to straddle my legs with her own.

I wanted to stay there forever, staring into her dark brown eyes. I could die there and know true happiness. I brushed a thumb over her round jaw, plump bottom lip, and across her rosy cheek, taking in every delicate, goddess-like feature she bore.

"*Your eyes are wide open, silly.*" She smiled at me, her shoulders bouncing as she giggled.

Her dark hair draped across the dark purple lace bra she wore and tickled my skin as she leaned down. She rolled her hands over my chest and kissed a crooked line across my skin, sucking and nibbling on my neck. Heat pooled in my stomach, but the icy feeling of distance sparked at my fingertips, and I knew she was slipping away.

"*You're too far away,*" I groaned as she leaned away from my touch. "*Don't go,*" I whined as she rolled over into the darkness.

"Kitten." Arlo's sneaker dug into my ribcage and I clawed at him in the hazy light of sunrise.

"This is a nightmare. You're supposed to be in Dallas." I rolled over.

"That was two days ago, Cael," Arlo snapped. "Let's go for a run."

"No, Asshole." I pulled the pillow over my face. "You ruined a really good dream and, for that, I hate your guts and will not be partaking in your five a.m. torture session you describe as a run!"

My body was still sore from the day before with Silas, and the therapy, though doing its job to rehabilitate my shoulder, was exhausting and frankly dull. Silas had been slowly taking over my sessions from Ella because, according to Grandpa, together we never got anything done. That was just a lie. That fun vampire wouldn't understand enjoyment if it slapped him in the face.

"I got news," he said, and I peeked out from behind the pillow to see him standing awkwardly beside my bed with his hands in the pockets of his black hoodie. "Ten minutes. *Outside*. Don't make me come back up here."

He left my room, and I rolled back into the pillow, inhaling the lavender scent as deeply as possible before straightening my arms and pushing from the bed. I tugged a sweater on to block out the cold air and laced up my sneakers with one eye open.

"Have you seen—" Arlo handed my baseball cap to me as I bounded down the stairs of the Nest toward him.

"Cool," I flipped it up and over my overgrown hair. "I still hate you." I looked him up and down. "But curiosity will *always* kill this cat."

"I'm pretty sure you have more lives than any cat I've ever met," he groaned and led the way.

"So, news?" The burn from the chilly morning air started to sink into my lungs as we rounded down the hill toward the stadium.

"Dallas offered me a position as a pitching coach for the season."

The silence was pulled so tight I could look at it wrong, and it would snap.

I had known this day was coming. Arlo wasn't going to stay at Harbor forever—that was a foolish little dream that sobered me up, held onto like it would save my life.

"Breathe, Cael," he laughed, slapping my chest. "It's an interim position, a trial run. I'll be gone a lot, but not permanently."

"You say that now," I shook my head, desperately fighting the selfish monster that wanted to make it about me. "But they'll love you, and then we'll never see you again. Dallas isn't close."

I knew the distance to Texas down to the inches.

I had spent nearly seven years measuring them with my heartache.

"No," he agreed, "it's not."

It's one thousand eight hundred and seventy-two miles.

"And Ella?"

"She has her job here."

"You're going to leave her?"

You're going to leave me? I stopped in my tracks with a heaving chest because I couldn't run and sort through all the thoughts in my head.

"I'm not leaving either of you. Enough," Arlo barked and stopped, turning around to look at me. He walked back to where I stopped, hunched over with my palms braced against my thighs.

"Going to Dallas sounds like leaving," I huffed, looking up at him. The attempt failed, and the monster was loose. "What? Is the team not offering you enough money to stay here? I'll talk to Dad or Silas. Someone has to be able to offer you what you want!"

"Don't be a brat." Arlo stomped back toward me. "It's not about the money. It's about the experience."

"This is bullshit. No one just ups and leaves across the country for experience."

"That's exactly what they do! Are you listening to yourself? If you want everyone to start treating you like an adult, you have to start acting like one, Cael. Pouting when things change isn't the correct response."

"I don't want things to change," I confessed. "Aren't you happy here? With us! This is our family, and you're leaving for some stupid job?"

I watched as all the pieces clicked into place behind Arlo's dark eyes. *Shit.*

He had knitted together the real issue faster than I had, and I walked right into a scolding.

"I'm not your Dad, Cael," He dropped the tone of his voice. "Ella *isn't* your Mom."

"Please keep talking to me like I'm an idiot." I clenched my jaw and deflected his statement even thought he was right. I was being selfish, acting like a child.

My fingers were itching for release and my heart was racing. Arlo watched on patiently, waiting for me to regulate myself as I counted to ten, bringing myself back to reality. "I'm sorry," I said. "I'm figuring out how to regulate without the drugs, and it's harder than I thought it would be."

Arlo gave me a sympathetic smile.

"I'm not going to leave you for a job, and she won't get sick. This will be hard and different, but we aren't abandoning you." Arlo had read me like a book, and I hated that it made me feel better when he did.

"It *feels* like you are." I chewed on the inside of my mouth to control the tears that threatened at the corners of my eyes.

"I can't change how you feel. I can only show you that I mean what I say."

He pressed two fingers to his chest, and I mirrored the gesture even though I was still tripping over the anxiety inside me. Like a cruel joke, every time I finished the race, ten more hurdles were set up for me to jump.

"Besides, I need someone here to handle our girl while I'm in Texas. Do you think you can manage that?" He clapped a hand against my face and took off running again.

"I'm telling her you said 'handle our girl' the minute I see her." I shook my head. She was going to love that.

"Please don't," Arlo groaned. "She'll give me the speech, and then I'll spend my entire weekend groveling."

"All the more reason." I picked up my pace, letting my long legs do the work as we circled the path down around the stadium.

Lately, it has been quiet. After the win, all the press died down, leaving only a few reporters who thought they might be able to get an exclusive.

Today was the day that the one reporter lucky enough to be awarded the privilege arrived to interview all of us. Dad said she'd be here for a few weeks as she got through the entire team and staff. They wanted both a print piece and a television piece. It felt like overkill, but the Shores wanted the press, and we didn't have a choice. I wasn't looking forward to their questions about my shoulder or the accident. It was healing from surgery, but it was sore, and I couldn't play for a little while. The timeline was completely up in the air, and ultimately it was Ella who decided on it.

Our sessions were going well but it was still tough to watch most of the guys on the team be able to practice like normal while I was stuck in the medical wing, rolling my arm above my head like a toddler.

Ella did her best not to remind me why I was stuck in that position but sometimes, when the whine dropped from my lips about the situation, she cocked her eyebrow at me and waited for the guilt to sink in. I had brought myself to that point and needed to work to get myself out.

They gave me the space to figure it out but Arlo leaving felt like punishment when it should have been something to celebrate. I sighed, slowing my pace to a walk as we approached the side door.

"I'm happy for you," I said with a tight smile that I knew he'd deem as such. When he scrunched his brows together, I knew he had seen right through it. "I am," I admitted. "You're basically my brother, and I don't know how to function without you around. I need a new brick wall to talk to in your absence."

Arlo punched me in the arm. "I'm a great listener." He rolled his eyes.

"Let's agree to disagree on that one."

"I'm going to go talk to Silas, you'll be okay?" Arlo asked as I swiped my player's card against the black box for us.

"That was always the plan." I nodded, to be okay.

Arlo gave me a sharp, concerned look, waiting for me to force a smile on my face. I did it only for him. He stared for a moment longer before deciding he could trust me. Two fingers raised to his chest, he tapped, and I followed in unison. I'm fine.

He nodded, taking it to heart, and wandered toward the medical wing of the stadium.

Fine with the decision he made, but not fine with anything else. I needed to fix this.

Maybe there was something I could do. I ground my teeth together and turned tail to my father's office. The little monster within me screaming for justice, for blood. I didn't bother knocking. I walked through, past his messy, unused secretary desk, and into his main room.

"What the hell is wrong with you, letting Arlo just leave? Offer him a long-term position, more money, something. You can't just let him go to Dallas!"

Dad stared at me with a morose expression. He was dressed in a brand-new, button-down shirt, and his hair was washed and combed back. He looked put together for once, and it was unsettling.

"Cael." He swallowed tightly. "It's not a good time."

"I don't give a shit," I said, stepping into the room further, only then noticing the girl sitting on the couch out of the corner of my eye. "Sorry," I look at her properly, nodding, and then back to my Dad.

"Cael," he said again as my head snapped back to the girl on the couch.

Short, dark brown hair brushed against her round jaw. Gorgeous, voluptuous curves covered in a tight shirt that framed her entire chest and painted-on jeans that extenuated her full thighs sank into the couch. Her lips were pressed into a thin line, but her eyes watched me with a tight, agitated expression.

"Clementine?"

MATTHEWS

2012

"Stop dragging your feet," Daddy warned.

The cool air nipped at my skin as we walked down the path toward the Cody house. The trees were bare and the little snow that fell that morning had already melted. Typical Texas. I would give anything for the white Christmas they have in the movies. Just once.

"At this rate, Ryan will have the bird carved and eaten before we even get there," Dad grumbled, the ends of his reddish brown hair had started to turn gray and his attitude grumbly.

Momma laughed under her breath at him and I didn't understand why. Dad wasn't that funny, he usually just complained about everything.

"What's eating at you?" She slowed down to match my pace.

"Nothin'," I mumbled, and she reached out to tug on a stray piece of my dark hair to get my attention. "I couldn't find anything fancy for Cael." I stared down at the small box and scowled.

"I know for a fact that boy will love whatever is in that box. He's never hated a damn thing in his entire life, Lovebug." She tapped the top of the box and smiled. "You could stuff it with dead bugs, and he'd still find a reason to love it."

"That's silly." I laughed and brushed my thumb over the box.

"But it's true," she cooed at me, stopping us just before we got to their steps. "Christmas isn't about how fancy a gift you got, Clem. It's about spending time with the people in your life that make every day feel like a gift."

31

"I spend every day with Cael, it was supposed to be special today." I didn't mean to, but a small whine slipped from my lips.

"I can assure you, little Lovebug, today is special. He will treasure whatever you've brought him," Momma said.

"What if he doesn't?" I asked her.

"Then he's a silly little boy with a silly little brain and, one day, it will catch up to him and he'll realize just how much of a gift you are." She cupped my jaw in her hand and kissed my forehead, leaving a small, warm tingle on my skin.

Before I had time to argue again, the front door swung open and a lanky, twelve-year-old Cael stepped out on the porch in the ugliest pajama pants I've ever seen.

"You like them? Ma found them at the thrift store." He spun in a circle, nearly falling over sideways in the process, and smiled at me. They had dogs or cats on them, all wearing cute little red hats. "She found you some too!" He held up a bundle of fabric from behind his back. Similar to his own but bright green.

"They're ugly." I laughed but took them from him anyway. I looked down at the box in my hand and held it out to him with a shake. "Here."

Cael smiled down at the box, his ruffled blonde brows pinching together as he took it from me. He popped the lid quickly and unwrapped the tissue paper that I had spent hours trying to fold nicely. The crumpled edges were a testament to my struggle.

Cael chucked the paper aside, lifting from the box the small bracelet that I had threaded for him. Shades of blue, teal, purple, and gray. All of our favorites wound together in a flat, lined pattern. It had taken me forever to get the knots just right and tight enough to hold in a flat line. It was the most frustrating thing I had ever created, and I cried over it at least four times but had decided the shed tears were worth it until this morning when I had second-guessed everything.

I had never been so nervous I wanted to puke before.

I'd never hear the end of it if I puked on Cael on Christmas.

I swallowed the bile.

He was so silent for so long, but then a smile spread across his face, and he dropped the box to the ground, rushing forward with the bracelet held up to the December sun.

"It's so cool, Plum!" He gasped and extended his wrist to me. He had called me Plum since our eighth birthdays, I never understood why. At first it had made me feel silly, but now it made me feel special. My cheeks felt so warm.

"Help me?" He asked and gave me his wrist. Momma gave me a small wink, took the ugly pants from me, and disappeared inside the house, leaving just the two of us outside.

"Did you make this?" Cael asked me.

"There was a book of patterns in the school library...and-" I paused, looking around and leaning in closer to him as I tied a knot in the thread. "I took the colors from the corner store."

"You stole them..." he gasped. "Tie it tighter I don't want it to come off."

I double-knotted the thread and stepped back from him.

"It's perfect." He looked up from his wrist to me, and I understood what Momma meant. That Christmas wasn't special because of the gifts; it was special simply because of the way Cael made me feel. "Mama made sweet potatoes without the marshmallows the way you like, and Dad threw a fit. You just missed it."

"The marshmallows make it too sweet," I scoffed and followed him into the house without another thought.

MATTHEWS

"Mary," Bobbi's voice chirped over the barrier between our desks. "Boss called a meeting. What do you think it's about?"

Occasionally, I forgot that I went by Mary Matthews in the office, dropping the Clementine from my name for some semblance of privacy and safety.

"Probably nothing." It was always nothing. I ran my hands down the dress pants I had slipped into this morning after stumbling around in my loft like an idiot, still half-drunk from the night before. "If we're lucky, there'll be coffee," I groaned.

"One of your buttons is undone." She laughed, wandering closer to me and fixing the mistake with her delicate, warm brown fingers. Bobbi was too pretty to be wasting away in a cubicle, but I wouldn't have survived all these years without her big smile and brilliant brain. Her bundle of thin, long, mixed blonde braids hung down between us as she focused on the buttons with a giggle. "You're a mess. Where did you end up last night?"

"A bar downtown." I shrugged.

"What about that guy... Did you take him home?"

He was tall, with ruddy hair and empty eyes. The complete opposite of the ghost that haunted me, his blue eyes like the brightest lights on the darkest of nights.

"Yeah," I shake out of the daydream, "he was great."

"That was enthusiastic."

"He wiggled his fingers around inside of me like some sick rendition of a cheer from *Bring It On* before he pretended to eat me out, and then sat there staring at me from between my legs for praise." I looked at her as we walked down through the office toward the boardroom. "I need to get a bag of treats for my side table drawer for all the men that act like dogs."

"Roll over, sit, good boy," Bobbi giggles beside me.

"Who knew *spirit fingers* would haunt me into my twenties." I wiggled my hands at her with an annoyed grin on my face. "I need one man to give a shit, just one."

It was busy for a Friday morning—too busy. The office lights were making my head spin, so I blinked the sleep out of them and rolled out my neck in an attempt to center myself.

"Mary," Bobbi waved a hand full of rings in front of my face, "did you hear me?"

"Sorry." I blinked my eyes a few times to focus.

"You need more sleep." She shook her head, not bothering with her previous question, as she pushed backward through the office door and into the room.

The long table was full of other reporters and junior journalists just looking to get that one piece that might propel their careers, not realizing they were only there because their superiors needed someone to take meeting minutes.

"Did you hear Tony is sending Lacey to New York to cover the World Series?" Bobbi slid into the chair next to me with a coffee and smoothed out the collar of her tangerine-colored button-down.

Of course he was. "That's what happens when you grow up a nepo-baby," I groaned and sipped on the scalding coffee like it might save what few brain cells I had left from drinking so hard the night before.

I tried to pretend I was upset. It's not like that mattered to anyone anyway. I was trying to break into sports, but it seemed impossible to get my foot in the door when Lacey French had it out for me. I wasn't even sure she knew what a baseball was, but it didn't matter because she knew I did.

She paraded into the board room as if on cue, her perfect body draped in a tight yellow mini skirt and crisp white dress shirt she left untucked. She flipped her long blonde hair over her shoulder and slammed her bright yellow leather purse to the tabletop as if she didn't have all the attention in the room before making an unnecessary amount of noise.

Bobbi stifled a snort and looked at me with wide eyes. "She's like some demonic version of Big Bird, and we're stuck in *Sesame Street* hell."

I covered my mouth to stop the laughter that tumbled from it but still received more than one dirty look from the table. Tony French, of course, was late to his own meeting, and we sat in waiting, sipping on coffee when he slumped through the door half-dressed. The sleeves of his dress shirt were rolled to the elbow, and he looked like he hadn't seen sleep in three days.

At least that made two of us.

He poured himself a coffee despite his daughter holding out a fresh cup to him; he waved her off and ran his hands through his fluffy, salt and pepper hair. "I need someone in Rhode Island." He looked around, skipping all formalities. "Matthews, you're up."

Rhode Island.

My heart raced, and the nausea in my stomach built.

"No, anywhere else."

Bobbi looked at me in shock. All the news I covered was local but the moment the location had left his lips, I felt my heart clenching in my chest for the first time in nearly seven years. "I won't go there," I said again, louder when he didn't respond.

"You will," he insisted..

Lacey narrowed her eyes at me from beside him, her head cocking to the side in suspicion.

"What's it for?" Bobbi asked when I didn't.

"College baseball. The team that won after a three-year losing streak."

There was that unfamiliar thumping in my chest again.

This was not how I wanted to get my foot in the door.

"I don't want it," I said as the bile climbed in my throat and my hands became clammy.

"You don't want it." Tony leaned over the table on his hands and stared at me with venom. "Miss Matthews, I will remind you that you are not in charge here."

36

"Give me grunt work for a month. I don't care."

"This is grunt work." His jaw ticked. "You go cover this or go home for *good*."

We sat there for a moment longer, the tension in the air ticking like a clock as everyone waited to see what we would do. I swallowed the pride that threatened to destroy my career. I ate the fear and the pain I felt clawing at my chest at the thought of what awaited me in Rhode Island. I would not let him take this from me like he took everything else.

"When do I leave?" I asked because all of the other details could wait.

"As soon as you can, they only offered this to a handful of outlets. We were lucky to get our horse in the race. *Do not* screw this up, Matthews." He looked at me, and I could feel how serious he was, but I had been waiting for a job like that my entire life and I hated that it would be attached to him.

"Lacey," he barked, and she jumped from beside him at the sound.

Her heels clicked against the stone floor as she rounded the table with a folder, slapping it onto the table beside me. She stared at me for a moment longer. Whether or not she was trying to be intimidating, it didn't matter. My heart was in my throat. I couldn't speak even if I wanted to.

Bobbi pushed her chair back, hitting Lacey in the stomach with the back. "Oh shit!" She faked surprise as Lacey groaned and stumbled back dramatically. "I'm so sorry I didn't see you there."

I pressed my lips into a thin line to keep from laughing as Lacey smoothed out her skirt and wandered back to her spot at the table. Tony went on with the rest of his meeting as the noise faded out, and I flipped open the folder of information. Bobbi snuggled closer to look as I flipped through the profiles of each team member.

"There you are," I whispered as I found his photo.

His bleach-blond hair was shaved close to his scalp, and his skin was paler than I had ever seen. His face had slimmed out and became sharp without baby fat. He wore a bright smile that pushed up to his eyes and showed off his pretty, white teeth. It didn't hide how worn out he looked. New lines around his eyes made them look hollow and distant.

He was exhausted.

That was not the boy I remembered, the sun-kissed lover with ocean-blue eyes, but I could see him hiding behind whoever was in that picture.

"Is that?" Bobbi's voice dropped as she slid the folder closer to herself. "Mar." She looked up at me after taking the time to read over the information. "Are you sure?"

She was the only person that had ever heard about him. Drunken, crying fits that happened in moments of weakness. She knew exactly what I was doing. I nodded.

I had never been so unsure about anything.

I locked the door to my loft behind me as I wandered through and tossed all of my belongings on the island in the large industrial kitchen. A massive bouquet of flowers sat on my island, and I plucked the card from within the roses, pricking my finger on a stray thorn.

"Ow," I sucked on the pad of my finger as I flipped the card open.

I miss you

Of course, they were from Julien.

"How the hell did you get in my house?" I said out loud to no one but the roses before hauling them off the counter and chucking them into the garbage. "I don't miss you, Julien."

He had been what I thought I wanted for a long time; tall, with dark hair and big brown eyes. He was a lawyer who worked under some big political names here in Austin. He was sweet and attentive, and the ring he proposed with still sat on my nightstand. But...

He could never erase how Cael had made me feel, which wasn't fair to him. It wasn't fair to anyone. So, in the three weeks I had asked for space from Julien, I had slept my way through the rougher population of Austin and still didn't feel anything.

Or at least I hadn't until I saw Cael's photo in that folder.

Bobbi had proclaimed loudly how bad of an idea it was to go to Rhode Island with the hopes and dreams that Cael might still harbor feelings for me after all these years, but I had to know for myself, and I'd earned a viable reason to go.

My phone rang on the counter and, despite seeing his dumb, pretty face, I answered. "Hello, Julien."

"God, I love it when you say my name like that," he mumbled on the other end.

"I thought we were taking a break?" I flicked the card from him across the wood top island and watched it fly in the air.

"It's our third anniversary, Clemmy," he said with a sad whine in his voice. "I know you asked for space, and I'm willing to give it to you, but that felt special. We should still celebrate it-celebrate us."

I tried to remember the list I made of all the things that made me want to be with Julien, but when I closed my eyes, Cael was staring back at me. His sweet, lopsided smile and big blue eyes knelt over me in my bed, hands all over my body. *You will never kiss another boy again without thinking about me,* he whispered.

Fuck Cael Cody.

"It was a nice sentiment, Julien," I forced.

"How about I come over and cook you dinner?" He said, I could hear him shuffling around, preparing for my inevitable cave-in, but I couldn't be bothered this time. I needed this break, I needed the time alone to get my thoughts straight.

"No, I don't think so. I need to pack."

"Pack?" His tone dropped. "Where are you going?"

"Rhode Island. It's a placement piece for work. I'm not sure how long I'll be gone." I offered, just trying to get him to drop the issue.

"That's vague, Clemmy," he groaned. "I don't like it."

I don't like when you call me Clemmy, but here we are.

"It doesn't matter what you like, Julien. We're on a break, remember?"

There was a long pause, but finally, he spoke again. "Yeah, I remember. I'm sorry, Babe, I just miss you so much."

"I'll call you when I get home and maybe we can meet for lunch." *I need to bring you the blood diamond sitting on my dresser*, I said in my head as I rolled my eyes.

"Do you need a ride to the airport? When do you leave?" He asked.

"No," I said. "I'll call you."

I hung up before he could say anything else that would embarrass him.

I rubbed the sleep from my eyes with the heels of my palm and sighed.

MATTHEWS

I had managed the first weeks of interviews from my hotel's board room downtown; mostly stuffy general managers and old white men who never played baseball but enjoyed the money it made them. I had been grabbed, pinched, hugged, and sexualized, but I had yet to see Cael Cody.

I knew today would be different the moment the car drove me out of the city and down toward the Harbor campus. Switching hotels had been a hassle, and it seemed like I would still have to drive an hour into the city every night after I was finished at the stadium. It was annoying but I'd manage.

Rhode Island was gorgeous; large oak trees tangled together and rained down red, orange, and brown throughout the wide paved roads that led up to the University. I'd tucked into a tight pair of jeans and a form-fitting dark blouse that showed off the swell of my breasts. I'd thought about wearing something more formal, but it struck me that most of the people I would be meeting today absolutely would not care how I was dressed.

They'd all be in sweats and gym clothes anyway.

The feathery edges of my freshly cut brown hair rubbed against my jawline as I stepped from the car and carried my belongings to the front entrance. The stadium was massive, bigger than I had ever expected and it was incredible in design. Long, swooping architecture collided with strong navy blue steel beams and frosted glass. It was beautiful.

I snapped a photo of the Hornets' blue and yellow logo painted on the main door and texted it to Bobbi.

Welcome to Hell.

I hit send and pulled it open stepping into an empty brick hallway. It was early as hell, and rolling out of bed before five was not something I had wanted to do, but when Ryan Cody, head coach, emailed me instructing me to arrive early, I listened.

I had a bone to pick.

Looking around and attempting not to appear too lost, I wandered into an empty office to my left that was labeled 'main' and hoped to at least find a person.

"Well, aren't you a pretty thing?" An older lady walked out from a back office in a Harbor hoodie and a pair of jeans. "What can I help you with?"

"I'm here to see Ryan Cody? My name is Ma—"

"Clementine Matthews."

His voice sounded just as scary as it always had and, when I managed to turn myself around to face him, I felt all the angry resolve leave me. He looked so old and tired, his dirty blond hair had started to gray and curl around his ears, tangling into a messy beard. But his eyes were the same, mossy green and kind. It was hard to stay mad at him when he was looking at me like that.

"You look more like your Mama everyday," he said, trying to break the tension, but his words burrowed into my chest and left a stinging sensation. "Thank you, Susanna." He looked over my shoulder, waving off the old lady, and directed me toward his office.

"How did you know it was me?" I asked.

"They sent over your picture for press tags." He handed me a navy blue lanyard with two cards on it, one my ID and the other a scan card. "You can use that to get into the building," he instructed.

"How are you?" I asked him, not even sure I wanted the answer.

"Small talk feels weird, Clementine. I used to watch baseball with you in the living room each Saturday since you and Cael were in diapers."

The mention of Cael made my heart race.

It was inevitable that he'd be brought up and, to my knowledge, I had prepared myself for that moment. Turned out I had been lying to myself.

"Small talk is a formality."

He stopped, swallowing whatever he was going to say, and opened the door to his office. It was a mess, which I assumed it would be. He had never been good at keeping things together; that had been Lorraine's specialty. Towers of boxes created a tunnel into his main office that seemed much tidier than the previous. He had a small ratty couch in there that he swept blankets off of and tucked into a cabinet behind his large wooden desk.

He offered me a seat and I set my bag down beside the couch, waiting for him to say anything that might make me feel a little better about everything.

"Do you want coffee?" He asked me after a beat of silence and I shook my head.

"Mr. Cody," I said, trying to sound polite. "I'm here in a professional capacity to interview your team on their incredible win after such a drought. I'm not here as Clementine Matthews; I am not the girl you watched run around in diapers. While I'm here I would appreciate it if you upheld that level of professionalism."

He cocked his head at me, mulling over my words.

"You certainly are not."

"Thank you." I swallowed tightly. "I'll need an office space to conduct the interviews and if you know of any hotels in the area that would be wonderful. The drive into the city is nearly an hour."

"I thought you were staying in town." He licked his bottom lip. "If I had known you were traveling in, I wouldn't have asked you to meet me this early."

"Why did you?" I asked, ignoring his half-assed apology.

I'd been curious since the email came through about why he wanted me here long before any of the other players would arrive.

"I'm here to interview the players, Mr. Cody, and if it was to prevent us from colliding—"

The door to his office swung open wildly and all of the air was sucked from the room.

"What the hell is wrong with you, letting Arlo leave? Offer him a long-term position, more money, something. You can't just—"

Whatever he said next was muted.

My ears rang and the corners of my vision grew dark.

Cael stood, mere feet from me, in a sweater and shorts; he had grown. His frame was at least a foot taller than the last time I'd seen him and he had developed nicely into all of his chiseled features. He had to be at least 6'3 now. His jaw ticked when his father didn't answer him. He hadn't even noticed me sitting there.

"*Cael,*" Ryan clenched, "it's not a good time."

"I don't give a shit," he said, stepping further into the room.

His hair was longer than in the photo and stuck out in dirty blond chunks from beneath his backward hat. He stared at his Dad, ready to fight, and I'd never seen him so aggressive. It was intriguing and terrifying.

It made me curious and I shifted on the couch, making the fabric strain loudly in the silence.

"Sorry," he lobbed an apology at me with a curt nod, not even taking the time to process what his eyes saw.

"Cael," Ryan warned as his head snapped back to where I sat, ankles crossed, staring at him.

Fire burned behind those exhausted blue eyes and my heart came alive at the sight.

"Clementine?"

My name dripped from him like it pained him to say it and he blinked at me for a moment before closing his eyes and shaking his head. When he opened them again it was like he expected me to be gone, as if I was nothing more than a ghost.

Cael pushed his hat off and ran a hand through his hair, confusion and shock vibrating from him as his eyes flickered over me. He opened his mouth to say something and then closed it again into a tight line before he cocked his head to the side and left the office.

I made to get up and go after him but Ryan stood first.

"Don't," he said. "Let him go."

"You knew it was me and you didn't tell him I was coming?" I asked.

"Now you understand why I wanted you here early." He picked up the phone, dialing an extension and, within minutes, there was a knock on the door.

I had been so unfocused I hadn't even heard who he had called. My fingers itched against the fabric of the couch, begging me to get up, to go find Cael. That invisible string wound so tightly around my neck I could barely breathe.

"Silas," he introduced us.

I stood and shook his hand. He was older than me, but not quite as old as Ryan, and had the prettiest gray-blue eyes I'd ever seen. He was tall and his hair was dark and short, pushed back off his face, but everything about his demeanor spoke to his softness as he shook my hand.

"Silas Shore," he tried again when I didn't introduce myself.

"Mary Matthews." I used my mother's name and I could see Ryan flinch out of the corner of my eye. Silas looked between us like he could sense the tension and nodded.

"It's wonderful to meet you." He was more than polite, which I'd expected from the only male grandson of the Shores. He had been born with a weight on his shoulders to uphold the family name.

It wasn't a simple task, carrying around that kind of wealth, but the politeness he extended wasn't fake like most of the men I had met recently. It was genuine.

"I'm head of the medical staff here at the stadium. I primarily work with the baseball team but I oversee the care for another six professional teams on campus."

"The women's fastpitch, basketball, and soccer, as well as the men's hockey, basketball, and lacrosse," I said and he looked impressed.

"She did her research," he said to Ryan, who was still staring at me like I might crawl out of my skin and become the monster under his bed.

"Research is my job, Mr. Shore."

"Silas," he corrected. "Mr. Shore is my father, who I assume you met."

"I did have the pleasure, yes," I nodded.

The resemblance was there; the same ashy-brown hair and expressive eyebrows. His father was clean-shaven whereas Silas sported a trimmed beard and mustache. Rebellion in the form of facial hair. His father had been polite, but handsy.

"She's staying in the city," Ryan said finally.

"Ah! That's why I was called. Seems lately I'm just a landlord..." He laughed tightly. "There's a guest room at Dansby House that's yours for the duration of your stay. It's cozy but it'll do, and then you aren't driving two hours every day." He explained. "Luckily for you, it was just cleaned out."

"I couldn't do that." I shook my head. I wanted to keep my space from their personal lives. From Cael.

"I insist, and Dansby has a sitting room with a couch which will be much more comfortable for conducting interviews."

"That's very kind of you but—"

Ryan cleared his throat. "Ms. Matthews." He struggled to call me that, it was written all over his tired face. "Please, stay at Dansby. Interview the boys. I promise you that you'll get better results in a space where they feel at home."

"You make them sound like gremlins, should I be scared about getting them wet?" I smiled.

"*Yes*," Silas answered for Ryan. "And definitely don't feed them after midnight."

"Alright." I laughed gently and turned to look at Ryan for a moment, considering the softness of his usually demanding voice, and nodded. "I'll have my bags brought over."

"Perfect, now if you'll excuse me..." He left his own office and Silas clapped his hands together.

"Lucky you." He wiggled his eyebrow at me. "Getting to witness a famous Cody family blow up so early in the morning."

He had no idea who I was. I wasn't sure if I was relieved or offended that I had never been mentioned. Maybe a little of both.

"They seem at odds with one another," I said.

"Not sure I should be talking family politics with a reporter," he retorted.

I completely understood his cautious approach. Over the last year, the Hornets ball team had been put through the wringer more than once.

The local papers, as well as the NCAA circuit, seemed to love the drama that surrounded the team; from Arlo King's messy life on and off the field, to the coaching staff and team record. The Hornets have been a nest poked more than once. I would have to be gentle with them to get anything of interest for the piece on them, and I wasn't leaving until I did.

"Off the record," I said with a soft smile.

"Something about the look in your eyes tells me you are never off the record, Mary."

I stifled a laugh, shifting in my high heels, and nodded. "I suppose you're right to assume that. How about we start with the house? Dansby?"

"The gremlins call it the Nest."

CODY

I ran up and down the hill four times before collapsing on the stairs of the Nest. Sweat dripped between my shoulder blades and my lungs burned so severely I thought for a second that I might stop breathing.

Clementine.

The next breath I took was shaky and shallow.

I sat up on my elbows and stared down the driveway. For the last seven years, she had been too far away to reach, and she had been less than five feet away from me this morning.

I ran away.

I fucking ran away.

"Shit."

I climbed the steps into the Nest and stripped out of my clothing along the way to the shower. There were very few people in the house that hadn't seen my ass and, frankly, I didn't care much.

"Cody," Silas called from behind me. "Why are you butt naked?"

I don't turn around, "because I'm going to shower, Grandpa."

Silas cleared his throat.

"What?" I grumbled, facing him without hesitation, and crossed my arms over my chest. "Of course," I huffed under my breath, finding Silas and Clementine standing there with her bag over her shoulder, smiling. I covered myself with my hands as her brown eyes trailed down the expanse of my naked body and back up to my face as her head tilted to the side.

Anger, heartbreak, loneliness.

The need to numb it.

No.

"We have a guest," Silas choked out between clenched teeth and nodded to the trail of clothing I had left down the hallway from the front door.

"Yes, Shore. I noticed." I shifted on my feet, gathered all my courage, and bowed. "Enjoy the show." The words were clipped as I dropped with both hands in the air, completely exposed.

The satisfaction I felt as Clementine's cheeks turned bright red was enough to make my chest hot and tight. I winked at her because if I was going to protect the complicated emotions that were crashing inside of me at that moment, I would do it in the most Cael Cody fashion I could.

I could hear him apologizing to her as I closed the bathroom door and let my head fall against the heavy wood. I ran the water hot and climbed in, attempting to wash away all the urges to go out and find something to make me feel numb. My fingertips scratched at the tile, and my heart raced beneath my chest.

After all this time, why the hell was she there? She was just as pretty as the night I left her, with dark hair and round chocolate eyes, staring back at me, expecting me to have all the answers. I rolled my thumb across that stupid threaded friendship bracelet and wondered if she still wore hers.

"Get it together." I rubbed my hands over my face roughly and tried to snap myself from the daydream that was Clementine Matthews.

Years spent in a fantasy chasing her, laughing with her, fucking her.

I needed a release.

I climbed out of the shower and dried my hair with the towel before loosely wrapping it around myself and wandering back out into the empty house.

Scanning my surroundings, I looked to the right and then to the left briefly before stepping out directly into another body.

"Jesus Christ." I fumbled to stay upright and my damp arms wrapped around Clementine as our bodies collided. Her skin was soft and the smell of lavender exploded up into my nose without warning. I recoiled from her, my skin too hot and too needy to be that close to her.

I just wished I had been immune to the hurt in her eyes at my reaction.

"Sorry," she clipped. "I was just looking for..." She pointed to the bathroom behind me.

"Clementine," I huffed as she moved around me to enter the room. I had eight hundred different questions I wanted to ask her.

Why did you never write me?

Why did you stop answering the phone?

Who did you become?

How did you get even more beautiful?

"What, Cael?"

My name on her lips sent a shiver rolling down between my bare shoulder blades.

Her lips. *Can I kiss you?*

"Why are you here?" I asked her instead, like the tried and true idiot I am.

"I'm writing a piece on the Hornets for my job." She was professional, curt, and polite as she pulled her wrist from my hand. I hadn't even noticed that I had grabbed her, but the thread of her pale pink friendship bracelet brushed against my skin as she did.

She caught my eye as I noticed it and tucked her hand into her pants pocket. *You're still mine.*

A new fire lit beneath me, one that I'd only felt around her.

One that only she could ever fuel.

"Is that all, Clem?" I lowered my voice and leaned in closer, testing the waters.

Clementine's brown eyes flickered between my lips and eyes as she tried to devise a suitable excuse. When she pushed up on her toes to meet my challenge I nearly moaned, her lips so close to mine that I could feel her breath on my skin.

"Maybe I came back to ruin your life," she whispered, and a sick smile spread across my lips, curling at the corners. The shock in her eyes was delicious.

"Too late." I dared to brush my nose against hers and watched as her jaw tensed in response. "I managed to do that just fine on my own. Why are you really here?" I asked her again.

A tiny huff left Clementine as she lowered back down away from me. Her head tilted to the side as her brows pinched together, watching me, always watching.

"You don't get to call me Clem anymore," she warned. "You don't even get to call me Clementine. It's Mary now."

50

"I'm not calling you Mary," I said, without hesitation.

"You'll call me what I tell you to call me. You don't run my life anymore, Cael Cody." The hostility that blanketed us was thick and weighed down on my shoulders like an anvil and I couldn't understand why. "I can ruin your entire career if I want." She was bluffing, but it made my heart race. She was so confident, unafraid, and loud.

"Threaten me, Clem," I said tightly in an attempt to ignore the arousal. "It doesn't matter." I stepped closer and our chests brushed together. I looked down between us and ran my fingers across her chest, stopping to feel her heart beating beneath so rapidly.

It was clawing its way back to me.

"You're mine, and I'm yours."

For a moment, I saw her, that girl I loved. She was there with a Texas spirit, a big heart, and even bigger dreams, hiding beneath whatever hardened version she portrayed. She was fooling herself if she thought calling herself Mary would protect her from us. Hurt and heartbreak flickered across her face for a split second before the fire returned.

"I haven't been yours for seven years, Cael."

"Oh see—" I pulled away finally, gasping for air as I teetered on the edge of a breakdown. "That I don't believe, not even for a second. How many have there been, Clem?"

She bristled at my question. "That's none of your business."

"The number doesn't matter." I tilted my head to the side and smiled at her, wide and bright—enough to make her shift on her feet, and I knew that I was under her skin. "It doesn't bother me either. How many have made you forget?"

There it was, her defense crumbling when she realized what I was getting at.

"And I'm talking really forget, Clem," I searched her eyes for the answer, counting the freckles of gold that danced in her irises. "When they were buried inside of you, making you feel good, how many of them made you forget how I made you feel? The touch of my skin on yours?" My reach was long enough to brush a finger against her jaw, even at the distance.

I was playing a dangerous game with our emotions, when all I really wanted to do was lift her around me, carry her to my room, and never see the light of day

51

again. But she didn't feel that way, it was loud and clear. Something had cracked in her in my absence and I couldn't help but feel the guilt that seeped in.

I swallowed tightly, waiting for her response, and tried to ignore the anxiety that feasted on my insecurities. I expected her to lash out, maybe cry. I was cruel and rude, but I needed to know how deep her resentment for me ran. Evidently, her anger was still loud, but had the memories of us slipped too far from our reach?

"You are so different." She stared at me, her fingers twitching at her side like she wanted to touch. "What happened to you?"

The response drove the knife in my chest home. The blade burned and twisted at my sensitive skin like it was truly buried there. I bit down hard on my tongue to keep my eyes from watering. The way she stared at me broke down too much, too fast.

I could feel the angry, bitter monster climbing out from where I had shoved it the day I got clean, and before I could stop the vile shit it threatened to spill, I choked out, "You."

She flinched at the response.

"Ms. Matthews?" Silas turned the corner, and I took another full step back. He looked between the two of us.

His gray eyes landed on me. "Everything alright?" He asked. I couldn't be sure if accusation or concern settled behind his gaze.

"I'm just getting to know Mary," I said with a clenched jaw. I saw the praise flicker in her eyes. "I'm going to get dressed; I have a meeting with Ella."

A stupid lie. Silas narrowed his eyes at me. I didn't have a meeting, but it was better than being in this suffocating situation.

"Alright, we're having dinner here, tonight, to welcome her into the Nest."

The muscles in my neck and back tightened as I turned to him. "She's staying here?"

"It's easier for her to conduct the interviews if she's not driving to and from the city," he explained, but the reason alone wasn't enough to justify letting her stay here. There were hotels in town. "Your Dad insisted." Silas tapped his fingers to his chest, searching for an answer to the tension that suffocated us, but I didn't respond. I wasn't okay.

52

I didn't dare stifle the groan that vibrated up out of me.

Silas chuckled tightly. "If you have issues with it, take it up with him."

"I'll add it to the list." I ran my tongue against the inside of my lip and nodded, trying to understand why Dad would send her here, knowing what he knew.

Taking one last look at Clementine, I turned and went to find Dean instead of going to my room. Luckily, he hadn't left his.

CODY

"What's up?" Dean turned, half inside of his t-shirt, with a surprised look on his face. His blond hair was messy around his strong jaw, and he was only wearing a loose pair of sweatpants that did nothing to hide what lay beneath. My cock throbbed at the sight of him, in need of release from everything that had happened that morning.

Dean wasn't drugs, but he sure was close.

"I need you."

I slammed the door shut and closed the distance between us, enveloping his face with my hands. He resisted for a moment, his hands pressed against my chest to shove me away, but I kissed an apology for the bluntness across his lips before slipping my tongue into his mouth.

His fingernails dug into my skin, trying to resist what was happening but, just like always, his primal need to consume me took over and his hands freed the towel from my waist before he shoved me back against the bed. Dean kissed me all down my bare, damp chest, past my stomach, and along the hardened lines of my hip bones. My fingers raked through his messy hair and tugged lightly on the root to garner the attention of his big blue eyes. He returned to me, sloppy and hungry, because no matter how hard we fought to keep our distance from one another, we always ended up back here.

I helped him from his sweatpants and rolled him over on the bed so I could lay on top of him, my knee pressed gently against him to separate his legs and allow me to settle down between them. I dragged another deep kiss from his lips, our breathing becoming short and fast before I rolled down over him and molded us together. Every curve, every muscle, pressed tightly together as I ground myself against him.

"Cael," Dean growled, grasping at my skin with his fingers as he grew harder beneath me.

I kissed a wet line along his collarbone before his finger hooked beneath my chin and pulled me back to him. I could feel his body relaxing against mine, finding the fragile corners of our relationship and settling against them like he belonged there.

It's what he wanted but not what I needed.

"Too sweet," I groaned against his mouth as our cocks rubbed against each other.

I could feel the heat building in my stomach and, as Dean attempted to break again, no doubt telling me how much we shouldn't be doing this, I growled low and deepened the kiss so he couldn't.

"Roll over," he ordered as he grabbed the lube from the top drawer of his nightstand.

I rolled over without a word, pushing up onto all fours as he ran a slicked-up hand against the length of his hardened shaft. The bed dipped as he settled behind me, lining us up, and pushed his tip inside. Dean gave me a moment to inhale and prepare myself before grasping my hip in his strong hand and shoving deep inside me.

It wasn't soft, not even close. As he thrust hard again, Dean ran a hand between my damp shoulder blades and pushed me down into the mattress. A low guttural growl left me and I braced myself against the wall as Dean's thrusts became rougher. He couldn't hold back; each unrelenting slap was a short, fleeting release from everything happening outside these four walls. It was making my head dizzy and my breath short. I couldn't get enough.

A long, dirty moan dripped from Dean as he pounded my ass. The pressure built in my core and created sparks of fire over my skin.

"That's it," he whispered between breaths. "Give in to me," he demanded.

Despite his previous hesitation, I could feel how much he enjoyed it. My ass clenched around his dick as he rolled his hips against me. Dean wrapped his arm around me and pulled me back so I was pressed against his chest as he shoved into me even harder than before.

"Fuck, Cael." His entire body tightened as he began to suck at my skin.

I dug my fingers into his hips hard enough to pierce his skin and leave delicious little bruises that no one would ever see. Dean moaned softly as I pushed back against his thrusts. The laugh that dripped from me was strangled and turned into a groan as his movements became just as needy as mine.

"How could you ever deny us this?" I growled and wrapped my hand around my cock, rubbing my thumb across the tip as I continued to roll back and force him deeper. My dick leaked for him, and the sound he made at the sight proved he fucking craved it just as much as I did.

Our skin slapped together as my hand pumped at my cock faster, dragging myself to the edge with him. His entire body shuddered in time with mine as hot, sticky cum spilled into my hand, and it was enough for the cord to snap within him as he released deep inside of me. It was like fire tearing its way up through every single muscle in my body. The waves of pleasure were intense enough to make my head spin. They licked at my fingertips like live wires, and I couldn't catch my breath.

"You good?" Dean asked as he shucked free from me and rolled onto the mattress. I shoved him back against the pillows, crawling over him. I nodded, eyes trained in the distance as I collected my breath and my thoughts. "You're an asshole," he sighed, rolling over the bed and sitting on the edge with his shoulders slumped over as he pulled on his sweatpants.

"You can't switch one addiction for another, Cael." He stood to look at me, sex worn and ready for a nap.

"You seemed to be enjoying it just fine." I rolled my eyes and rested my arms beneath my head. "I'm sorry I forgot that everything has to be at your behest." I offered what I thought was a half-assed apology, but he didn't smile at me.

"I'm not a medicine cabinet for your issues. I'm a fucking human being. Wash my sheets." He pointed at the stain forming, grabbed his shirt, and left the room.

I stared at the ceiling as the door slammed shut and closed my eyes.

Even without the drugs, I was managing to run everything into the ground.

MATTHEWS

ilas and I stood in the kitchen over two mugs of coffee when a massive blond kid I recognized as Dean Tucker, the first baseman, stomped through the kitchen. His enormous frame swayed out of the way, just barely avoiding slamming straight into me as he made his way to the fridge. He reappeared from behind the door with a bottle of water and, when he finally made eye contact with me, he popped the cap, watching me for a moment as his head tilted to the side.

A tiny venomous-filled laugh ripped from his chest and he nodded.

"Mary, this is Dean Tucker." Silas introduced us.

"The first baseman." I held my hand out to him.

He stepped forward, leaning over the island so we were closer than before, and inhaled sharply. His eyes dropped to my wrist before finally taking it.

"Mary's going to stay in the guest room for the duration of her visit, and she's going to conduct her interviews from inside the Nest," Silas explained as Dean leaned against the counter, his eyes flickering back and forth as he listened.

"Oh." Dean nodded, and I watched as he masked the discomfort on his face. "You're the fancy reporter."

"I am," I said, knowing he recognized me fully. *You're close to Cael.*

"What's for dinner?" He brushed it off and looked back to Silas.

Dean Tucker was a specimen in his own right. If I had to guess, he was nearly six-three and what had to be close to two hundred fifty pounds. He was pure muscle from head to toe. His jaw ticked tightly as my eyes ran down over his strong neck, traps, and broad chest to his taut, excised stomach, where his sweats hung on his hips just low enough to create a sliver of tanned skin between the band and his shirt.

His blue eyes studied me as I drank him in, but his expression never changed.

"A list." Silas swiped a piece of paper from the counter. "You and Cael are on duty tonight."

"I switched my day with Van," Dean said without skipping a beat. "I have therapy with Ella in an hour, I'll text him this."

"Seems Ella is a hot commodity this morning." Silas narrowed his eyes before pressing his lips together in question but didn't seem to sense the tension in the air. "Go and tell her about dinner, please."

"Mmm," he hummed and turned to look at me again. "Mary." He nodded and left the kitchen with not a single *'it was nice to meet you'* in sight.

"If you'll excuse me, I just need to make a phone call," I said to Silas before following Dean's route toward the front door. He was walking out onto the porch as I caught up to him. His long legs carried him much faster than I could walk.

"How do you know me?" I asked, causing him to turn with a sigh.

"You smell like lavender," he said, jaw tense as he looked me over with disapproval. "It's his favorite."

"Cael?" I asked, and hurt flickered across his face. He didn't say anything more before climbing down the steps toward a truck parked along the curve of the driveway.

I lifted my fingers to my mouth and my teeth found my nails, worrying them as I spun out with thoughts. I couldn't figure out if I had screwed this up. Heat licked at my chest and my heart still raced from my run in with Cael.

It was hard to ignore the way he made me feel.

Even worse was the idea that it wasn't anger that bubbled up.

It was longing.

"Shit," I swore under my breath and wandered back into the house to find Silas.

"You ready for the rest of the tour?" He asked as I entered the kitchen and I gave him a polite smile and quick nod, unable to think past the image of Cael's damp naked body.

The rest of the day was spent on the phone with the hotel as I set up in the corner of the Nest that Silas had organized for me. The house was like nothing I had ever seen, and it outdid any other frat house on campus. *Not a frat house*, Silas had grumbled when I made a comment, brushing my fingers along the dark wood of the banister that led to the upstairs rooms.

He explained that a female medical intern had previously occupied the room I was staying in, so it was cleaner than any other room in the house. He left me to organize but it wasn't long until he circled back, standing in the archway with his arms crossed.

"Excuse my intrusion," he said, as I set my laptop on the couch beside me.

The light from the grand window behind me made the chunks of ashy, nearly gray pieces of his beard and hair stand out more. He rolled his slim shoulders back in his shirt and danced around his question like it pained him to hold onto it.

"What can I do for you, Mr. Shore?" I asked, setting down my phone and giving him my full attention.

"You know the Codys, don't you?" His brows kissed in the center and created worry lines across his forehead.

"I do," I answered honestly.

Silas clicked his tongue at me and sighed.

"Do you know the term '*baby gloves*', Ms. Matthews?" He asked me, his tone dropping from polite to serious in a matter of seconds.

"It's a common term," I said, and he raised a brow at my sass. "Yes."

"Use them," he said curtly, the muscle in his jaw ticking as he ground his teeth together.

"How did you know?" I asked him as he turned to leave me again.

"First of all, don't insult my intelligence." He laughed but it was tight as he stepped forward. "You'll come to figure out that this..." He waved a hand around to signify the house. "...is much more than a baseball team. It's a family."

"Vague," I said.

"Protective," he corrected. "Be gentle, please. They've struggled enough this year, they don't need anymore character growth."

I bit my tongue to keep from saying something I shouldn't but desperately wanted to. The Codys were *my* family first. This team, this house, took them from me. I was alone.

I finished setting out my things and grabbed my cell phone from the table.

"Hey, Lovebug." Momma's voice nearly made me cry every time.

"Hey, Momma." I leaned back on the couch and looked around at the dark green wallpaper and fancy, mahogany crown molding.

"How are things going?" She asked. I could tell she was mucking around in the garden because I could hear the birds in the background chirping circles around her head.

"This might have been a mistake," I said, picking at the hem of my shirt. "I thought he would at least want to see me, or even talk like adults."

"And he doesn't." She sat in one of the rickety steel lawn chairs; the squeaky sound of the old metal echoed through the phone. "So much like his Daddy," she groaned. I know that tone in her voice. She had predicted this but had kept her thoughts to herself so I would learn something.

"He's so different," I whispered, trying not to let my emotions get the best of me.

I had come here with a plan. I'd held on to the idea that Cael was the monster under my bed for so long. My loneliness had turned to resentment over time. He had ruined so much of my life because, no matter what I did, he was there, tainting it and reminding me it would never feel as good as I felt when he smiled at me.

He was the sun and I sat in darkness when he'd left. I became a person no one would recognize, because if I wasn't his Clementine, he wasn't my Cael.

But I was wrong.

And he had proven it in one conversation.

"You're mine, and I'm yours."

He hadn't changed as much as I had hoped, and now I was left disappointed.

"Do you remember that summer when you found that injured bird?" She asked me, and I said yes. I remember every summer with Cael. "You were so young, maybe ten. Do you remember what Ryan said to Honeybug when he declared he would make the bird a bed with hay and blankets?"

I hummed at the nickname. It had been a long time since I had heard it. It was a pair of names given to us when we were young: We were both bugs; I was love and Cael was honey.

"He told him it was foolish because the bird would never fly again." I bit down. I could picture the defiance that had flickered in Cael's pretty blue eyes, even then, butting heads with his Dad.

"And do you remember what Cael said back to him?" Momma asked.

"He—" I stopped to laugh. "He put both hands on his hips and said..." I inhaled tightly, the fuzzy feeling of the memory flooding my chest.

Momma repeated it back to me. "You misunderstand how powerful love can be."

"I don't even know where he learned the word misunderstand, but the look on Ryan's face had been priceless. That man walked out to the barn, dragging Honeybug with him, and not an hour later, you had a brand new bed made from wood and filled with blankets for that bird," she said.

I stayed quiet for a long time, unsure how to respond to her story.

"Here's what I know about Cael Cody," Momma said over the phone. "And no matter how different he may be, granted, he's been through a lot, Lovebug," she added, as if I could forget the hole that his mother had left.

"His love has the ability to move mountains."

I chewed on the inside of my lip for a moment before responding. She wasn't wrong. Cael had and always would be a force of nature, but I used to be the breeze, the birds, and the sun. Now I am the mountain, hard and cold.

"What if I forgot?" I asked her. "How to love."

"It's like riding a bike, Baby," she cooed.

Once she hung up, I set the phone down on the couch beside me and tried to sort through the thoughts she had left me with. She had forgotten one crucial detail of the story.

The bird never flew again.

It became dependent on Cael and, like a typical child, he grew bored of it.

Ryan had to kill it two weeks later because it couldn't feed itself.

Love hadn't been enough.

CODY

Most of the day was a blur. I spent a few hours training out the kinks in my shoulder with Silas watching my every move. The recovery had been hell so far. Without drugs to dull the burning roar that vibrated through the stretched and bruised muscle, it was healing slower than we had initially estimated.

I'd be lucky if I were confident enough to play during spring camp.

But I wasn't going to give up. I had made a promise.

New season, new Cael.

That was before Clementine smashed back into my life without remorse. Now, my thoughts strayed from healing, training, and school. All of a sudden I could only think of her, and it was going to drive me insane. As we pulled back up to the Nest, the truck engine dying was barely enough to distract me from the walking nightmare I'd suddenly found myself in.

The smell of lavender burned at my nose.

The sun felt too hot and the breeze was sticky on my skin as I wandered around to help Van bring the groceries in. He lifted two bags from the back of his truck in unison with me. We had gotten the stuff to make lasagna because it was one of the only meals the two of us knew how to make that was appropriate for a family dinner.

I shifted uncomfortably in my skin at the thought of sitting across a table from Clementine, with her thick brown hair, big doe eyes, and pouty smile. I sighed and bit down on my tongue to ground myself in reality as my mind wandered into dangerous territory.

I've dreamed of that night with her for seven years, never trying to replicate it with random partners but always chasing that high. I never found it. I came close with Dean, but there was still something missing. Longing, maybe? The explosion of young love that I had been so blind to until it was too late.

Mama had said it was for the best that it took us so long to realize, because it would have been a lot harder to leave her if we had. It was hard anyway.

My mind might not have been aware of it, but my heart had been in love with Clementine Matthews since we were born. Connected by a rough, invisible string, we had always been two halves of one whole.

I rubbed at the frayed bracelet on my wrist. Over the years I had patiently waited for it to fall off, for it to succumb to the abuse I put it through, but it never did. The small strands of thread held strong and outlasted every binge, every blackout, and every game.

"You alright?" Van asked, and when I looked over at him, we were standing in the kitchen.

I'm sleepwalking, I wanted to say to him.

"Do you ever..." I stopped trying to find the right words—ones that wouldn't have him running to Ella or Arlo to tell them I was slipping or losing my mind. "Do you ever feel like you aren't fully awake?"

He set the bags on the island and started removing the boxes from inside, his boyish face confused. Van was pretty, simple as that. He had shaggy brown hair that he kept tight on the sides and long in the back, massive honey-brown eyes, and a soft, inviting smile that made it impossible to hate him.

He licked his bottom lip as those too-kind-for-his-own-good eyes flickered up to me. His half-baked inner therapist was slipping out as he watched me with caution.

"Today has felt like one long nightmare or maybe a dream?" I slide a jar of sauce across the island, trying to organize my thoughts. "No matter what I do, I can't jolt myself from it. It's like I'm trapped inside without the option to wake up."

"Maybe you just need a push?" He mumbled, dark strands of his hair falling against his forehead as he rounded the island toward me.

I laughed and shoved him off as he attempted to jostle me around.

"Seriously," I said. "What do you do when things get too much?"

I couldn't ask Dean these questions because he was what I *did* when things got too much, but after our interaction today, I felt that I was the last person he wanted to see or sympathize with. On occasion, more often than not... I felt bad for using him the way I did. Guilty feelings and shame crept in like they belonged there, but there was also so much love for Dean. It was messy, complicated, and ours.

"Talk to Zoey," he sighed.

"I don't have a Zoey." I rolled my eyes and ground my teeth together. "No one has a Zoey," I added with a smile when Van scowled at me.

The truth, for once, was that no one was like her, and Van was the luckiest bastard in the Nest next to Arlo. I rolled my tongue against my teeth and slid onto the counter, letting my feet swing lazily over the side.

"I've never seen you so *doom and gloom*." Van shook his head and wiggled his long fingers in the air to look menacing. "What the hell is wrong with you?"

A pitiful, defeated laugh fell from my lips.

"Aside from the usual?" He added between turning the oven on.

"The reporter." I stared at the bracelet on my wrist. "I know her."

Van stopped what he was doing to look at me. "That's right, Texas. So?"

"I *know* her," I repeated, and leaned back against the island to stare at the lights hanging from the ceiling above.

"Holy shit," Van swore under his breath and slapped my slack thigh a few times as he figured it out. "She's *that* girl. *She's* lavender girl."

Lavender girl. I couldn't help but giggle at the nickname. It had never been a secret that there was a girl back home; it was just a topic they all tip-toed around. It took nearly four years for me to turn her into a ghost and, when I finally did, she was nothing but a whisper between them.

But somehow she was still a poltergeist with the power to uproot my entire life with a flash of her smile. Frustration rumbled from me. I hadn't thought I would ever get the pleasure of chasing the chaos and high she created ever again.

And now I didn't know what to do with myself now the opportunity had arisen.

"Why is this a bad thing? Talk to me," Van said, poking me with the end of a wooden spoon.

"I don't know." I shrugged, rolling my head to the left so I could see him.

"Cael Cody, at a loss for words. I never thought I'd see the day that anyone could make you silent." Van laughed, but I didn't find the statement very funny.

Clementine had my tongue all twisted and my feelings in knots like they hadn't been in a very long time. I didn't know where to start untying them as the emotions flooded me like a tidal wave. I was drowning in the past and the present all at once. My hope of rescue dwindled with every second she remained at arm's length from me.

Having her inside the Nest was going to kill me.

"I just don't know if she..." I sighed. "...wants me like that anymore?"

That was a lie.

I could still feel the electricity that licked like a live wire at the edge of a pool of water from our conversation earlier that day like it was fresh. There was so much left unsaid between us.

So much heartbreak, anger, lust, and need.

The confusing aspect was where to start.

"So talk to her, man. I've seen you talk your way out of, and into, about a thousand different situations with partners. What's different about this one?"

"She sees through it." I sat up. "Through all of it."

There was no hiding from her, not really. She could feel the shift in the room between my father and me the second she laid eyes on us both. Clementine had always been intuitive to the people around her, as if she were feeling what they were feeling. I used to think she was reading my mind when I was a boy, but I realized how much of a a burden it was for her as we got older; to feel what everyone else was feeling so heavily all the time. I tried to hide those dark feelings from her on occasion, to protect her in whatever ways I could, but it never worked. She always saw right through my fake smile and mass-produced responses.

Van nodded and slapped a hand to my face. "Then you, my friend, are screwed."

"Thank you, Mitchell. You've been so fucking helpful."

MATTHEWS

"Happy Birthday to you," everyone sang in the kitchen. Momma carried a piece of cake across the mix-matched tile and slid it toward me.

"Make a wish, Lovebug," she cooed and Mrs. Cody clapped in excitement.

I wish to spend the rest of my days as happy as I am today.

I looked around at them all, landing on Cael last, who was beside me with a cheesy, braces-filled grin on his face. He jokingly threatened to blow the candles out on me, but I knew he wouldn't actually. His candles would come later, and it would be his chance to turn thirteen.

I exhaled, blowing out the candles, and Cael's hand whipped out, sneaking some of the icing before popping it into his mouth.

"What did you wish for?" He asked, licking the traces of icing off his lip.

"An MP3 player." I shrugged as Momma started to slice up the cake for everyone.

"Lame," Cael scoffed, twirling in a circle to get free of his sweater before sneaking another bit of icing

"It's not lame just because you don't like it." I shook my head and pushed his shoulder, tipping him off balance just enough that he tumbled back into the stool.

"We can share mine, why do you need your own?" He challenged.

"Because we don't have to *share* everything, Cael!" I groaned. He was always so annoying about it, like we were twins or something that had to share instead of being our own people.

"I thought you liked listening to music with me?" Cael scoffed and took a step back.

"I do but... I'm *sick* of sharing. I want my own." I was mad, mad over something I hadn't even wished for. Mad that he was ruining my birthday by being a jerk.

"Fine," he snapped. "You don't have to share with me anymore, not anything. You can keep it all to yourself!" He said, crossing his arms over his chest before storming from the kitchen out onto the back deck.

Momma looked over at me and raised her eyebrow. I knew if she wanted to scold me, she would. She'd tell me it wasn't very polite to yell at Cael, but he could just be so frustrating at times.

We ate cake and I never got an MP3 player, but Daddy got me a new blank journal, and Momma knitted me a new sweater with pretty orange yarn that sparkled. I thanked them both and took it all up to my room, sitting on my bed.

On the dresser, under the light of the dimming thrifted lamp, was Cael's stupid MP3 player, mocking me for being mean. I looked over at the clock that said nine-thirty and crawled into bed, pressing my head tightly into the pillow. When I finally stirred, the clock was flashing twelve-nineteen and I hustled from bed, pulling on the sweater Momma had knitted me, and swiping the MP3 player from the dresser.

I quietly snuck downstairs to see that Momma had left a piece of cake on the counter. I smiled and carefully picked it up before sneaking out into the dark and down to the creek. Even though he was furious with me, I knew he'd be waiting. Sitting in a beanie and a sweater, he stared up at the sky.

I sank down into the grass beside him and leaned in close to his face, practically resting my chin on his shoulder as I whispered. "Happy Birthday, Cael."

He turned to look down at the cake in my hands and smiled softly. "Thanks, Clem."

I tugged out the player and wiggled it at him.

"Wanna share?" I asked. His blue eyes reflected back the stars as they flickered from my hand to the sky again as he nodded.

"I didn't get to give this to you," he said, digging something from his pocket. It was a small box, almost identical to the one I had gifted to him over Christmas.

"Is it an MP3 player?" I teased and he laughed with me.

"Don't be mean." He shook his head and pick at the cake with his fingers, popping pieces into his mouth as I pulled apart the box to find a small threaded bracelet in all sorts of pinks. I could have never imagined that he would take the time to make me one. I smiled down at it so hard that my cheeks hurt.

"It's so pretty, Cael. Did you make it yourself?"

I could tell he had even before he nodded. It was sloppy, and some of the knots were loose, but it was perfect, and *he had made it for me*. He set the cake down and helped me tie it around my wrist carefully, his fingers brushing against my skin, warmer than the breeze blowing around us.

"I'm never going to take this off," I said to him and stole a bit of cake as he picked the plate back up.

"Now we match," he said with a mouth full of cake, holding out his wrist.

CODY

I fought to keep my eyes in my head as Dad wandered through the front door of the Nest, with Silas at his side. He rarely stepped foot in the house anymore. It reminded him too much of Mama. She was in the walls of this place, and it made him sick to his stomach.

It was written all over his face.

But this wasn't about his feelings; it was about putting on a show for Clementine.

That alone made me angrier than it should have.

"Interesting." Arlo approached from behind me. "I don't remember the last time he came for family dinner."

"He never did," I said.

"Not even once." He braced himself on the island beside me, dressed in a clean black shirt and jeans. We both knew well enough what was going on. Arlo had been there through all the blow ups, he was tangled in our story as much as Clementine was.

His hair was getting longer, and he had it pushed back off his face. He had shown up an hour ago with Ella on his back, giggling and smiling. For the first time, I understood the level of jealousy that others felt. *I wanted that.* I could hear Clementine's laughter deep inside the sweet sound of Ella's, and it bothered me. I curled my fingers around the edge of the counter.

"Gimmick," I said to him. "That's all this is."

"Maybe he's turning a new leaf." Arlo sank onto his elbow to catch my eyeline. "Kitten," he warned softly. "Behave tonight, blow up tomorrow."

"Have you met her yet?" I asked him, ignoring his wise guidance.

"No." he shrugged. "Ella said she saw her this morning visiting the stadium. Silas took her on a tour."

It felt like I was stuck inside a tank that was slowly filling with water and had no way out.

The water pooled around my feet, warning me of what would come.

"Behaving isn't an option," I said, scooping Mitchell's bowl of salad into my arms and backing away from the island. "Sorry."

"Cael," Arlo growled, but followed my lead into the dining room we never used.

I leaned down, pressing my lips to Ella's forehead. She had dressed nicer than usual, wearing a dark blue button-up and jeans. "Hey, Pretty," I whispered, before I started toward where I usually sat.

When she was able, Mama had forced us all to partake in a family dinner once a week. She called it team bonding outside of baseball and, for all the groaning that happened when she started it, it quickly became a coveted pastime between us all—until she died.

We ate in the dining room, but never together.

And no one ever sat in her chair.

I dropped the bowl to the table. "Move, please," I said to Clementine, who sat with her phone in her lap. Her brown hair was tugged back into a messy, short bun that left chunks of brown hair around her face.

"Excuse me?"

I held my breath as she looked up at me.

"Pick a different chair," I said in a more polite tone as more eyes drifted to our end of the table. "Any chair but that one."

Her head lolled to the side as she inspected me, but she made to rise and move.

"Cael." Dad's voice floated over the table, and I already knew he was standing in her defense. "Mary, you stay put," he said to her in a gentler tone.

"Father," I clipped, turning my head to look at him.

"It's just a chair."

Arlo groaned loudly from behind me as I straightened my posture. He knew better than anyone that the switch had been flipped, that behaving had gone out the window like a hurled brick.

"To you," I said.

I could hear Arlo stopping Ella from rising to get between us. The legs of her chair slid against the wood flooring, but the whispers were louder than they should be, and everyone was staring.

"To *us*." I looked around at the table full of sad-faced players. "That's *her* chair."

I didn't have to say Mama because his face tightened, and he knew exactly who I was talking about.

"It's just a chair, Cael." He ground his teeth together after he reiterated. "She's not here. That's not her. Sit down and have dinner."

"You never came to a single one of those dinners. You were always too busy in your office."

"Cael," Arlo tried then, as the entire team watched us reach a tipping point.

"Watch your mouth," Dad warned.

"Now you wanna play house for *her*?" I pointed to Clementine without looking away from him. If I looked at her, if I gave her that moment, it would make her real and my heart couldn't take it. I wanted the anger, knowing sympathy was the only thing I'd find in her eyes. "Why?"

"Ms. Matthews is a guest of the University." His hands flexed on the table, turning his knuckles white. The angrier he got, the further a piece of his dirty, graying-blond hair fell into his face.

"Ms. Matthews?" I mocked. I stood silent momentarily, mulling over his words until I inhaled and shook my head at him. "You and *Ms. Matthews*," I hissed at him, "can enjoy your lasagna. It's Mama's recipe."

I stormed from the house, emotions high and tangled together, creating a monster of anger and grief as I slammed the front door behind me and sunk down onto the front steps of the Nest.

Pretty shades of dark purples and pinks danced through the streaky fall clouds, casting a blush hue over the entire world. I chipped away at the peeling paint on the steps, letting the paint slivers slide under my nails just to feel the stinging rather than the sadness eating me alive.

My body tightened when the door creaked open and her footfalls came across the deck. I knew those footsteps. They echoed in my dreams anytime there was a threat of forgetting her.

"Go back inside," I snapped. "I don't have the energy to be nice to you."

"Is that what you've been doing?" Clementine paused on the porch. The sound of her inhaling filled the air.

"I've never been mean to you a day in our lives, Clementine." I tugged at the strings of the bracelet on my wrist, the tangled shades of teal and lavender easily falling apart.

She scoffed and then got quiet.

"Alright, maybe just now, but..." I chewed on the inside of my mouth. "That was her spot at the table. She never used any other place, and it was a lot to see you sitting there. I'm sorry."

"I'm sorry too," she said, settling down on the step beside me, wrapping her arms around herself in the cold breeze that had fallen over the house on the hill. "I didn't know."

I couldn't bring myself to look at the sunset, it would hurt me too much. Clementine could outshine the sun, and cool its heat, so the sunset didn't stand a chance against her beauty and I wasn't ready to be that sad. Not yet.

"You didn't know what? That it was her chair, or that my Dad had turned into a raging asshole? A lot happened while you weren't around, Plum."

She flinched away from the use of her nickname. "You say that like I was the one to leave."

I closed my eyes, letting her voice wash over me, and ground my teeth together because I knew she was right. Our being apart had never been her fault. It was easier to take it out on her because I had been beating my fist against the brick wall of my father's office for seven long years.

"You didn't come to the funeral," I said.

"I didn't know about it until after it was finished," she sighed. "That should have been the first sign that something was wrong. Mr. Cody called Momma a week after the funeral to tell her it had happened."

I turned to look at her and, as I'd predicted, the world's colors were mute compared to the blush of her cheeks and those big, devastated, brown eyes.

Please don't cry.

If she cried, all bets on what I might do next were off the table. It had forever been my weakness. I would cave—I always did.

"Don't," I said out loud, as the water welled in her eyes.

I caught the tear that rolled down her cheek before it hit her jaw and sighed.

"I'm sorry you and your Mom didn't get to say goodbye to her," I said, trying to control my own volatile emotions. Keeping them in check with the smell of lavender suffocating me was proving difficult.

"It wasn't your fault," she said quietly, pushing my hand away. "You can't do that."

"Do what?" I could feel myself leaning into her. That invisible string tugged so tightly that it left raw abrasions in my throat.

"Pretend like there aren't still thousands of miles between us. Even now."

"You're sitting in front of me, Clem." I bit down on my tongue.

"Mary," she corrected, and the string went slack.

"I already told you I won't call you that," I said slowly. She wasn't that fake persona she wanted so desperately to hide behind. She was Clementine, and she was mine. "Especially not when we're alone."

"You've changed," she noted *again*.

I chuckled quietly. "I'm exactly the same, Clementine."

I wiggled my fingers at her and her eyes caught the frayed bracelet on my wrist. Her brows scrunched together in confusion as she looked from it to me.

"Is that?" She danced her fingertips across the disgusting thread.

"Same boy," I confirmed. "Same bracelet."

"No." She shook her head as she dared to let her palm press against mine.

They fit together like they were made that way: two halves into one.

Together again.

"Same *bracelet*, different boy."

"You're wearing yours too," I said.

"Same bracelet, different girl."

"I don't think you're that different," I whispered, inching closer to her. I just needed to feel more of her skin. "Sure, you're louder, but you were always loud.

You were just never loud for yourself. It was always in the defense of someone else."

"For you," she corrected me. "Always for you." Her voice was tight as she spoke. She looked down at the bracelet like it was made of thorns.

"I was selfish back then." I swallowed tightly thinking about Dean. "I'm selfish now. I'm sorry."

I just wanted to kiss her, to feel her lips on mine again and remember how sweet they tasted. Leaning closer she breathed me in, her eyes trailing to my lips with slow precision as my fingers cupped her chin and tilted it toward me.

But that was selfish, too.

"Just one kiss," I whispered, my breath hot on her lips. "Be mine again, Clementine."

Even though I could feel her want, her need, she pulled away from me as I brought us together for the first time in seven years. Hurt danced across her soft brown eyes.

"Was I really that horrible?" I asked, folding my hands into my lap to keep from pulling her back to me. It was clearly not what she wanted or needed.

"You were never horrible, Cael. That's the problem."

"So what is the problem? You're here, I'm here." My hands flexed at my sides in a pathetic attempt to avoid brushing her hair behind her ear.

The sunset glazed her cheeks in warm pink tones and highlighted all the soft, freckled patterns that ran across the bridge of her nose. She looked like an angel.

"Our problem has never been us being together, Cael. It's the 'apart' that destroyed us."

My brows kissed at her words. She was so sure of everything she said.

"That wasn't our fault!" I pinned my shoulders back, feeling cornered. The hair on my arms rose, but I couldn't take my eyes off of her.

"But everything else was."

MATTHEWS

"I feel like I'm listening to a phone sex line," Bobbi laughed in my ear. "That's the hottest shit I've ever heard. *Just one kiss?*" She mocked, in a voice that made her sound ridiculous.

"It was nearly impossible to say no." I brushed out my hair with my free hand and made sure my makeup looked good. I had two interviews today before I could explore the campus more, but all I wanted to do was run into Cael.

I had barely slept after our talk. My mind had spun itself in circles before I closed my eyes, and my alarm had gone off an hour later. The Nest was nice enough, with high ceilings, dark wood trim, and carpeted runners on all the hardwood floors. I had been in a lot of frat houses during my two years at Texas University, but none had ever given old-money architecture quite like Dansby House.

"I don't understand why you did. I was watching playback clips," Bobbi sighed dramatically. "That boy is a tree. A tall, muscular, blond, should-be-in-a-boyband, tree. I'll climb him for you if you're scared. I'll take one for the team."

Bobbi moaned loudly in my ear.

And then the faint humming of Backstreet Boys track *Everybody* floated through the receiver. *"Am I sexual..."*

Even thinking about his hands on me had heat crawling through my body and I turned the faucet to cold and ran a hand under it as she talked.

"Aren't you in the office?" I asked, laughing wildly at her nonsense. God, I missed her.

"Yeah, but moaning pop songs in my cubicle is a constitutional right," she laughed, and I could hear someone giving her grief in the background. "Shut up, Peter," she barked from the other end. "Are you okay though? I know this is hard."

"I'm fine," I said, drowning the bracelet around my wrist under the stream of water. Lately, it felt like it was burning my skin.

"That was *so* convincing, Mar," she scoffed through the receiver. "Take two, and this time don't lie to your best friend."

"I'm horny," I admit, "and I'm heartbroken," I sigh.

"I think that's a Shakespeare play," she joked.

"Ha, ha." I shook my head and wandered out of the bathroom into the quiet hallway. I was still trying to find my way around the Nest. At times it felt like I was getting more lost the harder I tried.

I turned to the stairs and cautiously wandered up to the second floor to admire the stained-glass window at the end of the hallway. It was one of the most beautiful things I had ever seen and must have cost a fortune, with all its tiny floral details and glass hornets.

"So what now?" Bobbi asked me.

"More interviews. I can't tell if I want to ignore his existence or fuck him in the closet," I mumbled as I turned back to the stairs. I only stopped when I noticed one of the doors was open a crack, and I knew instantly it was his room.

"Do I get a vote?" Bobbi said.

"Absolutely not," I whispered.

"Why did your voice get quiet... what are you doing?" She instantly became more invested. "Are we snooping? Turn on the camera you stingy bitch," she whined.

"Nothing," I cut her off and pushed open the door with the toe of my shoe, peering inside to find it empty. "I might have found his room?"

"You're in his room!" She yelled, and I hissed into the receiver to get her to shut up. "Sorry, what the hell are you doing?"

The walls were covered in horror movie posters from all different countries, and stacks of horror manga were piled by his unmade bed. The lamp on his cluttered dresser was covered in a shirt that made the light in the room hazy and dark. There were piles of shoes on the floor and his rings were neatly placed in three different bowls balanced on the windowsill. I inhaled a sharp breath to quell the suffocating anxiety that rushed through me. Just like his Dad, everything was a mess but had a place, and it made my heart ache to see how his room exposed the seventeen-year-old boy he was trying to stuff down and hide.

"It's all the same," I whispered. I rubbed my fingers over his comforter, pulling the blanket to my face and laughing when the lavender laundry soap hit my nose.

"What's the same?" Bobbi asked in a hushed, hurried voice.

"His room, *him...*" I sighed, letting the blanket fall back to his bed. "It looks exactly like his old room."

I looked around my feet at the dirty laundry and scooped up one of his shirts, bringing it to my nose. It smelled like sweat, sweet, sticky gummy bears, and that dried-out scent of a shirt that spent too much time in the sun. I rolled it in my palm and tried not to cry.

"You need to get out of his room, M.," Bobbi urged, and it clicked that I was standing frozen, staring at the walls.

I nodded and backed out, closing the door like it had been before. The shirt was still tangled in my fingers and I was not ready to let go of it yet. I hurried back to the guest room and shoved it under my pillow for safekeeping.

"So, we're fucking him in a closet, right?" Bobbi snapped. "Because that was some weird shit you just did for a boy you supposedly hate with your whole body, Baby. I cannot stress this enough: *you are screwed.*"

"Fuck," I swore under my breath, barely able to get my head straight. I had interviews, but all I wanted was to search him out. "I gotta go," I said, hanging up before Bobbi even got a chance to respond.

I shoved my phone in my pocket and stepped back out into the hallway, looking around, trying to remember which way would lead me to the sitting room. Then a loud chorus of rough banging echoed from my left. The sound led me to the kitchen, where a tall, blonde girl was slamming around a drawer beside the fridge, her grunts of frustration loud as they echoed against the cabinets.

"Do you need help?" I asked over the racket.

She turned to look at me and I realized it was the same girl from dinner the night before. She was pretty, with wide, brown eyes that glowed warm under the lighting, in contrast to the white scar that split her delicate features in half.

"Ella?" I said, hoping I didn't fuck it up. "You were at dinner last night."

"And the stadium. I saw Silas giving you the tour. Ella Miele." She wiped her hands on her pants and extended one to me.

"Mary Matthews." I pointed at the batter on her fingertips.

"Sorry." She pulled back when she realized there was still a mess. "I'm attempting to bake cupcakes for my best friend's boyfriend, but—" she sighed, "the liners are in that drawer, and I can't get it open."

"Can I try?" I scooted around her, set my phone on the counter, and shrugged off my dress jacket. She raised both hands in the air and backed away from the fingerprint-covered drawer.

"So you're here to interview the guys?" She said, hitting the faucet with her elbow and washing the batter away.

I opened the bottom cupboard, slinking my hand beneath and feeling around for the back. "Yeah, I have two today."

Gripping the drawer's base, I rattled it around until I could hear the utensil unhook. "Try again," I told her, backing away.

She smiled over at me, tucking a piece of blonde hair behind her ear and pulling on the drawer. "That's impressive," she praised, when the drawer slid open without resistance.

"We had a drawer like that, and the utensils got caught on the wood inside. Just needed a little wiggle."

Ella watched me for a moment longer before speaking. "Keep that in mind when talking to the guys today. Sometimes, they need a little wiggle to pop loose. Especially the grouchy one. His bark is worse than his bite." Ella laughed, grabbed the muffin liners from the drawer, and waved them in the air. "Thank you."

"You're talking about Arlo King." I leaned against the counter and she nodded. "And the cupcakes are for?"

"Van Mitchell." She looked up from where she was popping in liners. There had to be at least six tins on the counter.

"Second base," I said, trying to remember what positions they all played.

"Left field, you'll get it straight eventually." She smiled at me and it warmed the room. "You should come to the party at Hilly's tonight. It's a sports diner off campus. I'm going down early to decorate with Zoey and Cael."

I had almost declined, but the opportunity to see him gnawed at me.

"That would be nice." I smiled. "I should get to it, wouldn't want to keep the Captain waiting."

"He's cranky today." Ella laughed, grabbing something from the cupboard. "Take this."

I stepped back into the kitchen and grabbed what was in her hand. "A chocolate chip muffin?"

"Trust me." She smiled, and it crinkled delicately at the edges of her scar. "A favor for a favor."

"Thank *you*, Ella." I waved it in the air and made my way through the house to the sitting room where Arlo was sitting on his phone in a dark Hornet's athletics t-shirt and a pair of jeans.

"Mr. King," I announced myself as I rounded the corner into the room and held out my hand to him. He stood, slipping his phone into his pocket, and laughed, looking down at the muffin in my palm.

"Did she say I was cranky?" His thick eyebrow raised, and mischief danced across his dark brown eyes. "I'm not cranky!" He hollered back over his shoulder and I heard Ella laugh in the kitchen.

"You two are cute," I said as he took the muffin and shook my hand. "I'm Mary Matthews, we met briefly at dinner yesterday."

"I don't recognize you from any channels," he practically interrupted, waiting for me to sit on the couch across from him before he settled back down.

"Am I not famous enough for *The Arlo King*?" I smiled and grabbed my book from the bag at my feet.

"That's not what—" He stopped, his brows furrowed. I could tell he wanted to ask the question, so I remained quiet and gave him the chance. "You know the family then? Is that why you took the job?"

"The Codys?" I said, as if there was anyone else he could be implying. He nodded. "I do. But I'm not here for them. I was sent here to interview the team on their win. Starting with their Captain."

He waited a moment, staring me over with his lips pressed into a thin line, and then plastered on a smile that could only be described as a 'Press Smile.'

I hit record on the tape.

"Congrats on the win. It was hard fought, and many people didn't believe you could make anything out of the team last season. Your last season." I said, and he narrowed his eyes. "From the very beginning, the Hornets were at a disadvantage."

A tight, frustrated form of rage flickered over his face.

"At any time, did you question their ability as a team to take them to the World Series?" I asked him and, without hesitation, he ripped out a chunk of muffin and tossed it between his teeth.

"Their ability? Never." He said carefully, leaning back on the couch, and he seemed relaxed. "Did I question my leadership? Regularly. A team is only as good as every working part. I..." He paused and thought about his words. "Unfortunately, I had been working at half speed the last few years."

"What changed?" I asked him.

"Everything." He was quick to answer.

"Are you comfortable elaborating?" I brushed a piece of my hair behind my ear and shifted on the couch as the air in the room became dense. "That felt *personal*."

"That," he pointed at me, lifting his hand from the back of the couch to snap, "right there is the problem." He nodded. "Reporters all separate the game from the emotion when in reality, the emotions drive the game. If you aren't feeling everything, you aren't playing the game as hard as you can."

"Interesting." I nodded, urging him to continue.

"I'm not going to pretend I'm perfect, I'm not." He sat up. "I let my anger fuel most of my decisions until," he looked over his shoulder toward the kitchen, the movement smooth and almost involuntary, "I was given a new outlook on the team and on myself."

"Behind every great man." I smiled at him.

"Exactly," Arlo sighed. "We all had growing to do, and we did it together. The team is on the right track to continue those wins."

"So you are leaving?" I asked.

He swallowed hard and set the half-eaten muffin on the table in front of him. "I am."

MATTHEWS

H illy's was massive.

When Ella described the building, I was expecting a small diner. The two-story brick building that climbed into the soft, cloudy sky of Rhode Island was not a tiny neighborhood diner.

A flashing deep blue neon sign hung over the massive set of double doors and flickered *Hilly's* at me as I slipped from the rental car and huddled into my sweater. It had started to get colder in the evenings than I was used to from Texas weather, and a chill had settled against my bones.

I slipped into a pair of jeans and a tight black tank top that ruched at the sides of my belly and pushed up my chest. The sweater was simply there to keep me warm until I was safely inside. I pulled the door open to a different world. Long brick walls were adorned with sports memorabilia, most of it highlighting the athletes of Harbor University. It was a shrine.

What was behind the bar to my left brought a smile to my face. A life-size cutout of Coach Cody stood propped against the wall. He was in good shape for an old man, and when the girl behind the counter caught me inspecting it, she raised an eyebrow in my direction.

"Do you want a picture with it?" Cael's honey-like voice rolled down my neck as he came up behind me. "We could ask him to recreate it for you, get the real thing if that's what you're into."

I spun on him and pushed him away from me with one finger. "I've never been one for fucking dads."

He was wearing a tight white tank top and a short-sleeve button-down that glowed orange in the bar's black light. Rings decorated his hands, which clinked together as he scratched his eyebrow and stared at me.

Cael's Cheshire cat smile grew. "What about their sons?"

"Been there, done that." I clicked my teeth and slipped from my sweater as his icy blue eyes narrowed in on me. They raked down my chest and over the curves of my hips. "Eyes up here, Loverboy," I said, and his gaze snapped to mine.

"I like that," he purred.

"I'm not flirting with you."

"Are you sure?" Cael cocked his head to the side, and the light bounced around in his blue eyes. "Feels like flirting."

"One apology doesn't undo a past as tangled as ours, Cael. You can't just—" I stopped. "Words don't mean anything."

You promised me so much.

You never sent a single letter.

"Clementine," he sighed.

You promised.

"Mary."

A frustrated huff left him. "I'm not good at apologizing." Cael's shoulders rolled back tightly and stuck his knuckle between his teeth as he thought. "And given your stance on words..."

He stepped forward, inching closer and suffocating what air I had left to breathe. His hand dropped and flexed at his side. I could tell that all he wanted to do was touch me. It took everything in my body, every tense, scared muscle, not to let him.

"Let me show you how sorry I am?" He asked and ghosted his lips over mine.

"Where is Ella?"

"Upstairs." He whispered.

I left him standing there, turning toward the stairs and ignoring how his body leaned into mine, begging quietly for more. Every inch of me wanted it, needed it, every inch except the unsteady beating of my heart that warned me not to get close.

Everything at Harbor was temporary.

In four weeks, I would be home.

I would have to deal with Julien. With my job.

If I let Cael Cody wrestle his way back into my life, then history would surely repeat itself.

"Mary!" Ella popped up from behind a table with a banner in her hands. "Help me with this?"

Grabbing the other end we hung the happy birthday banner against the wall with a few pieces of tape and stood back to admire our handy work.

"I'm glad you came," she said with a smile. "Zoey!"

A petite brunette appeared from the stairs with a box in her arms. Struggling to carry it, she grunted and slid it against the floor, kicking it the rest of the way to us.

"Zoey Novak, this is Mary, the journalist interviewing the guys."

"It's nice to put a face to the name. Van said he's never had so much fun in an interview." She shrugged, not an ounce of venom in the girl. Zoey smiled, and it lit up the room, her big brown eyes full of life even in the dim lighting.

"Van is an incredible liar," I laughed. "It went well though. He's very..."

His interview had been a shit-show. He was sweet enough but getting him to focus on the topics at hand was torture. His mind wandered like a rubber ball bouncing trapped in a tiny room. It was hard to believe that he would be a fully licensed therapist in one more year. But maybe that was the point. He was welcoming and bright; even I had a hard time not telling him every single one of my problems.

"Polite?" I finished.

Both Ella and Zoey burst into laughter.

"So he ran you in circles, and you ended up talking about his comic book collection?" Zoey tilted her head.

"Weirdly accurate."

"I'm pretty sure Van talked Zoey in circles until she agreed to date him."

"Homecoming, freshman year."

"You two have been together that long?" I asked, almost in shock.

"Van Mitchell with braces, bad look." Zoey laughed. My mind couldn't help but wander to Cael with braces, his stupid, sharp grin covered in metal. He had worn them for two years and wore them like they were cool. Every kind in our grade wanted them by the time he got his off. It was the Cael Cody effect.

"The buzz cut was worse." Ella rolled her eyes, and Zoey agreed.

"You'll be going to law school next year?" I asked her. Van had mentioned briefly that she was studying.

"Yeah." The mood dropped in the room.

"Are you being depressing up here, Sour Patch?" Cael yelled from the top of the stairs with a tray of shots in his hands. "I strictly remember saying that no one was allowed to be whiny today!"

"Says the king of complaints!" Zoey laughed. "No, we're just getting to know Mary."

Cael flinched. I had never seen a man hate a name so much.

It only fueled my need to hear people say it around him.

"Shots for the pretty women." He lifted the tray dramatically in the air.

"You could at least wait until the party starts, Misery," Ella scolded with a smile as she took a shot. I looked at him, and he wiggled the tray at me.

"Because I'm not drinking, by proxy, I need the three of you as drunk as possible tonight," he cooed. "I want you so loaded I can get drunk off your sweat."

His eyes flickered to me.

"Ew." Zoey rolled her eyes and took a shot.

Ella took her shot, smelling it with a dirty look on her face. Cael smirked at her and shrugged his shoulders as she shook her head. He turned to me and shifted his feet so I could reach it, but I didn't take one.

"I don't bite, *Mary*," he said, showing off his pretty white teeth.

"Don't believe him." Zoey shook her head. "He bites."

I smiled and the air shifted in the room again. I shrugged and wrapped my fingers around the shot glass, not caring what either Zoey or Ella thought.

The three of us took back the shots, and I was naive enough to think they would slow down.

MATTHEWS

The party was much more than I had expected. With the cupcakes and banners, both Ella and Zoey made it seem like it was for a child, but when the bodies started rolling in, so did the chaos. It was a true frat experience. That's what I was having. It was like a booze-soaked fever dream.

It wasn't just the baseball team. There were people from all the facilities and teams. I even noticed Silas and Arlo tucked into a corner, laughing and watching over everything. Ella rested in his lap with her hand around the back of his neck, playing with his hair and chatting with the people around her. The lightness of their relationship made me jealous. Even when Julien was being a gentleman, it was always uncomfortable.

He was afraid of what people thought of us. Of what they thought of me.

An actor at heart, he was damn good at pretending, but it showed in the way he looked at other women. Leaked out in his comments about how much I eat and how little interest I had in the gym. But the mistake was in his ignorance. I loved my body. I hadn't when I was younger. It was hard being around the athletic girls, seeing them move and fit into clothes that I couldn't.

None of that mattered. Not after that night.

I loved my body, and Cael Cody showed me just how much he did, too.

My soft belly, my pillowed curves, and my beautiful thighs. There was so much of me to love, and it was Julien's loss that he couldn't see past the scale to understand that.

My eyes scanned the crowd below, my hands wrapped around the railing of the loft as I searched for him. The booze tingled in my fingertips, and the music thrummed through my limbs. The urges coursed through me, unable to resist just seeing him.

Eventually giving up, I wandered past a tight crowd playing darts and chanting *Mitchell* into the air as Zoey stood up against the dart board with a cupcake on top of her head.

"Do it, Baby!" Zoey laughed, balancing the cupcake and moving her hand away.

I stopped, turning my head just in time to see the dart slide clean through the cupcake.

They erupted into screaming and clapping as Van scooped her in his arms, and she smashed icing all over his face. Everyone at Harbor seemed so at peace with who they were, and it was weird to see such dynamics. I had come down expecting to find turmoil and heated secret fights in the locker room. But they weren't that, and I shook my head, remembering what Silas said to me that first day. They were a family.

The sentiment should have brought me comfort, but the idea that I was right—that Cael had left Texas only to be welcomed into the arms of another family—made my stomach churn bitterly. I was glad he had found that, but he had done it without me.

Not a care in the world for his Clementine.

I pushed through the crowd in search of the bathroom, finding a line into the girls I turned and shrugged before pushing into the men's room. *Cleaner than expected and empty.* Dark blue subway tiles covered the bathroom from floor to ceiling, urinals lined the back wall, and there were a few stalls to my right across from the long counter of sinks.

The door closed with a click behind me and I steadied my hands on the side of the bathroom stall, closing my eyes. When I closed them he was there, staring up at me with those ocean eyes that screamed for undivided attention—the boy who had given himself to me that day, sitting waiting for me to welcome him back.

It was going to hurt.

But the fall would feel so good.

My mind wandered to him, the buzz of the alcohol taking control. It tangled with all the luscious, delicate memories from the night I offered up my girlhood. The memory of his body rolling into mine was forever burned into my memory. There hadn't been a day gone by in the last seven years that Cael Cody hadn't gotten me off.

I chewed on my lip, knowing I probably shouldn't but I was so ridiculously pent up that I didn't trust myself not to find comfort from someone at the party, or worse from Cael himself.

I unbuttoned my jeans and slid my hand into my pants between my underwear and skin, feeling the wetness engulf my hand. Cael Cody was running through the collection of underwear I brought. All having been dirted without his knowledge or his assistance.

The sheer thought of him had me sinking my finger deeper.

"Can I help?" his voice rolled through me, keeping my eyes screwed shut. I had been so consumed with my thoughts I hadn't even noticed his arrival. Not the sound of the stall clicking open or shut, not the overwhelming smell of sweat and gummy bears. Nothing. He wasn't there and then he just was.

His hands crawled down my ribcage and over my hips, fingertips begging to be let in. Warmth spread over me as he snaked down in the tight space between my hand and core.

Cael's body tensed as I leaned back against him and wrapped my hand around his neck. His teeth finding my neck, he nibbled at the hot skin and sunk deeper. "Have you been walking around the party soaked all night?" He whispered.

His hand raked over my body, cupping my jaw in the palm of his hand.

"Answer me, Clementine." The words were strangled as he bit down on my shoulder and sent shockwaves through me.

"All night," I groaned as he dipped a finger into me, and I removed my hand to let him work. His lips roved over my hot skin, sneaking closer to my mouth. "No," I turned away, "No kissing."

A barrier to protect what shred of dignity and willpower I had left.

A boundary set to keep me from losing myself again.

Cael pulled his hand from the front of my jeans and flipped me around, pressing my back against the cool metal of the stall.

"Open your eyes," he demanded. "Look at me and tell me no."

I opened my eyes. He was so close that I could smell the difference between the sweat that rolled off of him and the laundry soap from his shirt. Little pieces of his dirty blond hair stuck to his neck, and the collar of his shirt was wet from all his dancing. Cael's blue eyes followed me as I traced over those features, trying to find the boy I knew buried beneath this cocky, rude man that stood before me.

"No." I cocked my head to the side. "Either follow my rules and finish the job or get out, Cael, and I'll do it myself."

"You'll do it to the thoughts of my tongue in places that used to make you blush." He tucked his mouth against my throat and sucked gently, whispering the words just loud enough to hear them over the muffled sounds of music and screaming.

"I don't blush anymore." I leaned against the stall, pushing my hips toward him. "Better hurry before we're interrupted."

"I want them to hear you," he moaned and returned the friction with his own hips, rock hard beneath his jeans.

A rough growl left my lips in protest, the thought of someone walking in making my temperature rise. *Two can play the game you've started, Cael. I'm not that nervous inexperienced girl you used to know.*

"Scream for me?" He teased.

"Earn it." I let my leg fall open and he smiled. "And do it before I get bored of this."

"Patience, Plum." The nickname made my toes curl in my shoes, and I swallowed down the urge to break my only rule. "I know she's in there, you know," he said quietly, pressing his hand back into my jeans. "That scared little girl, too afraid to take what she wanted. But I'll admit, I do like the version of you that *bites*."

"Liar," I moaned.

Cael's fingers curled into my core and brushed all the nerves deep inside. He pumped his hand faster, working the sensitive areas with a smirk on his face. He worked hard to keep to himself, ghosting over my lips but never touching them. He was enticing and intoxicating.

His hand raked over my throat as the main bathroom door swung open, and two guys stumbled in. Mischievous thoughts flickered across his blue eyes, and he rubbed the pad of his thumb over my bottom lip before slipping it into my mouth.

Cael worked me open, sliding in another finger and dragging a rough whimper from my throat that echoed into the open bathroom.

"Do you hear that man?" One of the guys mumbled.

"Give them a show, Plum," Cael demanded, and I couldn't deny the violent lust that dripped from his words.

Crying out in pleasure, begging him to move faster, he listened.

"You can do better than that," I mumbled and sucked his thumb into my mouth.

"Holy shit, man," one of the men whispered, and feet shuffled around in the bathroom.

Cael reacted to the challenge instantly. Thrusting faster, his grip on me became feral. His thumb worked at my clit and pulled a stream of moans and begging from me. My cheeks burned as my body pushed up against the bathroom stall and onto my tip toes.

"Cael," I panted as he sank even deeper. The rings on his fingers rubbed against me, sending a thousand tiny sparks into my stomach where a fire had already raged. "Cael, don't stop," I begged louder.

"Atta boy, Cody!" A hand banged against the door.

Cael laughed before kissing a line down my neck. His tongue lapped at the sweat that beaded in the hollow of my throat. He circled my swollen clit with his thumb and bit down on the swell of my breast.

"Come for me, Clementine," he mumbled, his thumb still pressed flat against my tongue as he kissed the sore spot where his teeth had marked.

My walls fluttered around his fingers, and the coil that wound deep in the pit of my stomach snapped at his words. I gripped his hips, digging my nails into whatever skin I could find to keep myself steady as he worked every last drop of pleasure from my exhausted body.

Cael pulled his hand from my mouth, snaking it around my back to support my wobbling knees, and slipped his hand from my soaked underwear. I watched as he popped the drenched fingers into his mouth and sucked.

"Some things never change," he said when he removed them. "Still sweet as a plum."

As the orgasm rolled through me, tickling at my fingertips and toes, the reality of what had just happened sunk in.

I was in so much trouble.

CODY

"*No, not like that,*" Clementine pointed to the paper and shook out her brown hair from the pigtails it was in. It had gotten long over the summer, and I wanted to put my fingers in it. "Cael, are you even paying attention?" She smacked me with her pencil.

"Yeah, you said I have to carry the six and divide it by eight," I mumbled, removing my stare from her face. Failing freshman math hadn't been my brightest move, but conning Clementine into tutoring me? That was the smoothest move I could have ever made.

"We aren't even doing division," she laughed and leaned back against the couch.

Clementine's entire house smelled of roast chicken and sweet potatoes. It was a mess of patchwork furniture, too much art, and brightly colored walls. My Dad called it a fun house, not a home, but it felt warm and welcoming for reasons I couldn't understand at fourteen. Mrs. Matthews was in the kitchen with my Mama, singing as they cooked dinner and giggled in bouts of hushed whispers and gasps.

"Cael." Clementine pinched my thigh and stared at me with her soft chocolate eyes and rosy cheeks. "If you wanna get this credit, you have to pay attention. No girl is gonna wanna date a loser who can't pass basic math."

"Correction, Plum, *you* wouldn't date a loser who can't pass basic math. You're too good for that." I scrunched my nose up and extended my legs across the old carpet.

Clementine slammed her textbook closed as Mr. Matthews wandered in through the back door with a bundle of flowers in one hand and his lunch kit in the other. Mrs. Matthews tucked the flowers away with a quick kiss and told him to go wash up for dinner. Thinking back, there wasn't a day when Mr. Matthews hadn't come with flowers for her, always different, always beautiful. Their house smelled of nature and was littered with petals from old bouquets that Mrs. Matthews hadn't gotten around to tidying up. Clementine loved those petals. She'd collect them and press them into books. All over the house, there wasn't a book without petals tucked carefully inside. I even found them in my textbooks, leaving them there for the next student to find. Little pieces of Clementine.

Now they'll last forever, she would whisper and press a few more.

Standards that would no doubt have to be met for a lifetime.

I hoped whoever was lucky enough to buy Clementine flowers for the rest of her life understood that. I huffed gently, unable to bear the idea of bare books.

"Let's go for a walk," she declared, pushing off the floor and straightening out her yellow sundress before she held out her hand to me. She wiggled her fingers when I didn't take it right away.

"Fine, stay here, see if I care, but don't complain to me when they start making you peel carrots," she said.

That got me moving. I pressed my hand into hers, and she mocked a grunt as she pulled me off the floor.

"I'm going to have to start threatening you with peeling carrots more often," she laughed under her breath and gave my palm a squeeze as we wandered through the kitchen.

My current favorite thing about Clementine was how she never let go first. Her fingers tangled in mine as she dragged us toward the back door. Her skin was soft and warm and fit perfectly in my palm. Our stupid bracelets rubbed together as she pulled on my arm to make me move faster.

"Come on, slowpoke," she whined and slipped her shoes on. I sighed under my breath and uncurled my fingers from hers. My sneakers were harder to get on, and I silently cursed every second of lacing them before jogging out the back door toward her.

"You're so fast. Where are we going?" I asked her, tugging on the fabric of her dress to slow her down a bit.

She swatted my hand away and looked over her shoulder, "Anywhere we don't have to peel carrots!"

We walked down around the creek and, with each flower I passed, I scooped it into my hand, collecting a bundle before Clementine even noticed what I was doing. "Hey, Daydream," I called out to her.

When she turned to look at me, the wind kicked up her soft brown hair, and the setting sun seeped through it in thick rays, framing her in the most glorious way. My breath caught in my throat at the sight of her, and my chest tightened in her presence like it never had before.

"These are for you." I handed her the flowers and watched her bury her nose in them. "You can press them into your books."

She stared down at them, her fingers brushing over the petals softly. "Just like Momma's," she smiled, "but these are mine. I'll have to find a special place for them."

Anything she said after was mute, the smile on her face creating a pocket of warmth deep within me that I hoped never cooled.

CODY

"Mary is nice." Ella walked her fingers along the expanse of my bicep with a steady, painful pressure.

I sat on the floor as she hovered above me. With our height difference, most of the time I did my therapy cross-legged while she moved around me making sure that my shoulder was healing properly.

"Am I going to be able to practice soon?" I asked her, avoiding the conversation of Clementine.

I could still taste her on my fingers and smell her on my skin. I fucking hated every second of it. She was sitting in the kitchen in tiny satin shorts and a sweatshirt when I crawled from my bed the morning after the party. The shorts did nothing to conceal the soft skin of her thighs. My thoughts wandered to my hand between them and how wet she had been for me before even touching her. Her bright brown eyes engaged in an email on her laptop, and her perfect long fingers wrapped around a mug of coffee.

I wanted to bury my face in the space between her shoulder and neck, but I left her alone, sneaking out the front door without breakfast.

The conundrum of why she didn't want me to kiss her still wracked my every waking thought. At the time, I couldn't tell if she was just playing hard to get but the more I laid awake staring at the ceiling thinking about it. It was the second time she had denied me. I realized that she wasn't playing a game. She was protecting herself.

She was scared of me, of us, of whatever was coming.

A collision of stars.

"When you stop," she tugged on my arm, and I winced as the sharp pain vibrated up through my neck into my jaw, "doing that when I move your arm. Sure."

"Everyone is getting antsy, Peach," I said.

"They're always antsy. I've never seen Coach relaxed. Not once."

Strands of blonde hair tickled my cheek as she leaned in to work out a knotted muscle.

"I just wanna get into the batting cages," I groaned as she found a cluster of tense muscles. "I'm antsy, too."

"It must be hereditary then." She nudged my head with her elbow. She hummed and moved around me to sit across with her knees up against me. "But it's not the schedule bugging you, so what *is* eating at you?"

Her brown eyes stared at me, urging me to spill my guts, but it was too hard. There was too much to explain.

"Oh, we aren't playing this game, Cael Cody," Ella warned. "You're worse than a tongue-tied cat sitting in a bathtub of cold water."

"We're spending too much time together. That made no sense but was somehow the most southern thing you've ever said." I laughed, but my mood was still tight and sour. "What if I never play ball again?"

"That's dramatic."

"What if my *happy* came back, and now I don't know how to hang on to it?"

"Ooh, a callback." Ella narrowed her eyes at me. "Spill."

"She's here, my *happy*." Clementine.

Her face changed, "Are you talking about Mary?" I flinched at the name.

I don't answer for a long moment, trying to figure out how much of my heart I want to expose here in the gym. But it's Ella, and I could tell her anything. So I did. I told her everything.

"So her name is Clementine?" Ella sunk back on the mat with a soft expression. "That's tragic." She chewed on her lip. "The story, not her name."

I offered her a pity laugh.

"Fingering her in the bathroom at Hilly's probably wasn't the best idea," she scolded, the golden flecks in her eyes catching the light as her brows came together.

"You're just jealous, Peach." I rolled my eyes at her.

"I know whose fingers I like, and he wouldn't dare do it in a shabby sports memorabilia bar." Her smile was bright and made her scar scrunch up around her nose.

I shrugged. "Pretty specific. Where *have* you been fingerbanged then, Ella?"

"There's a list, *Cael*," she responded with a sneer. "It's extensive, you want it?"

"Kind of." I sighed, relaxing a little under the ease of our banter. I sighed again and closed my eyes. "She ignored me in the kitchen this morning, but we have an interview this afternoon, and I don't know how to act."

"It's cheesy, but you could try just being you," Ella suggested.

"Hah," I huffed. "She has this preconceived image of who I am, but it's stitched together with memories of who I was. I'm not seventeen anymore."

"You aren't?" Ella's head cocked sideways. "That's the most shocking statement to leave your mouth today."

"I'm not that kid from Texas," I rephrased. "Any trace of that kid she clings to is gone."

"Are you sure?" Ella sat up and scooted forward to take my face between her hands. "When I first arrived at Harbor things were volatile, my life had zero stability. Zoey did her best to help, and Van was there when he could be there, but do you know who made a difference?"

The gold ring, Arlo's mother's ring, dangled from her neck in a soft rhythm.

"Arlo," I said, knowing it was the answer. He had become her diffuser, the one person who could step through her combustible thoughts like he was fireproof.

She scoffed. "The egg came before the chicken."

"Did you just refer to us in a biblical fashion?"

"No, can you open one book this semester, just one..." Ella groaned and looked at me like I was insane. "It was you."

"Well, now you're just lying to make me feel better."

"We don't do that, remember?" She shook her head, "You were so kind to me even when I was shoving back. I fought you every step of the way. If you asked me what I thought of the Cael Cody I met at the party, I would have told you he was cocky, rude, a show-off with a need for validation. Nothing but a pretty smile. But you didn't care how everyone else perceived you. You don't now. So why do you care so much how this girl sees you?"

"It's going to complicate things." I swallowed tightly, scared of what would come if I continued being me.

"It's already complicated. How much worse could it get?"

"Cael." When I didn't answer, she pressed our foreheads together. "If she doesn't love you for who you are now, after everything you've been through, how hard you've fought to be here, then maybe she's not your *happy*."

"Easy enough for you to say," I grumbled, and she pinched my cheek.

Ella scowled.

"Right." I pulled back from her grasp, thoughts whirling around at a top speed.

I scratched the top of my head and rolled back onto the mat into the pile of sweat that formed from working out as we talked. "I just don't know what to do."

"You do what you do best, Misery." Ella cupped my cheek in her hand. "You grovel."

The door to the rehab gym popped open, and Silas wandered in. "I warned you two!" He shook his head. "You can't be goofing around in here."

"Yeah, Silas, because that's what we're doing," Ella rolled her head to the side to look at him, "*goofing around.*"

Silas huffed in response and handed her a clipboard full of papers.

"It's always what you're doing," he slapped me across the back of the head softly and sunk into a squat beside me. "How does it feel?"

"Like I crashed a car and ripped a bunch of fancy muscles in it then had surgery and am now recovering with no pain medication." I looked up at him and met his icy gray stare. "It's better." I changed my answer when he found little amusement in the first response.

"What do you think?" He asked Ella, who hadn't looked up from the papers she was scowling at.

"He's getting better, I'll have him ready by spring training."

"Spring training!" I growled. That was months away.

Ella's brown eyes lifted from the papers and stared a hole through my outburst.

"To play, I didn't say anything about batting cages," she added.

"What she says, goes. You chose her, which means that you're stuck with her authority." Silas offered me his hand. "Come on, we have interviews to do."

"Have fun, boys," Ella called out to us and went back to flipping through her papers.

MATTHEWS

It was cold in the Nest. I tucked down into my sweater as Silas got comfortable on the couch across from me. He was wearing a Hornet's ballcap with a matching polo shirt and a pair of jeans. It wasn't every day I got to interview a team doctor. I had been through six other players between Arlo and Van. They were all normal, some of them second string. I just wanted to get a good feel for the team dynamics, good or bad.

Sometimes, it was the ones forgotten that gave the most information.

Silas Shore was a watcher.

Even when they thought he wasn't around, he seemed to be. He had their backs. He kept their secrets, fostered their growth, and kept them healthy. Some might say he was the reason most of them were alive.

"From the dugout, as the chief medical staff for the Harbor Hornets, how do you think the season went?" I asked him after a few warm-up questions.

His gray eyes flickered up to meet mine. "That feels like a trick question."

"A coach cares about wins, the players care about the series final. What is it that the team doctor cares about?"

Silas paused and ran his hand over his scruffy jaw before answering, "I care about the health of the team."

"Diplomatic." I shifted and tapped my pen against my notepad. "You've had a lot of injuries this season, some related to the game, *some not.*"

"Ask the question, Ms. Matthews." Silas's brow raised at me.

"The accident, that's all anyone has been talking about. What happened?" I had known that asking Arlo about that day would have been met with a meltdown. He wasn't going to answer my questions, but Silas looked like someone who was willing to shut down rumors, even if it meant getting in trouble later on.

"You didn't ask him?" Silas leaned back against the couch.

"*Arlo*? No." I shrugged.

"Smart," he scoffed. "It's exactly as the news relayed it. Cael got high at an after-party and crashed his car into a ditch."

"You make it sound like car accidents are something that happen often at Harbor." I scrunched up my face in concern.

"They're not," he confirmed. "What happened was, in fact, just that, an accident."

Not only a watcher but Silas Shore was the only Hornet with media training. *Annoying.*

"So there's no underlying issues with the team that brought the star pitcher and his shortstop best friend there?" I asked.

"A lot happened that night, I'm sure you've seen the videos."

I shake my head at him.

I didn't make a habit of searching out Cael; it always had the ability to make me sad.

"I wasn't in the car," Silas said, pressing his lips together in a thin line, "but if you want to dig that deep, you're going to have to ask him yourself."

Ask Cael.

I stuck my pen in my mouth, chewing on the cap, thinking about him. His hands down my pants, the smell of booze, bathroom cleaner, and sex wafting over me and glazing my thoughts with lust. It was hard to focus on Silas in front of me when I knew I'd be seeing Cael later. I had every reason to stay away from him, yet here I was, impatient to ignore every single one.

But first, I needed to finish with Silas, who was clearly growing annoyed with my prying. His gray eyes narrowed in my direction, and his hands rubbed over his jeans. He was uncomfortable but hiding it well.

"Were Mr. King's issues with his hands because of the accident?" I asked him.

"Those issues predated the accident." His voice was tight. That was a sore spot that I didn't partially feel like digging my nails into just yet.

"And Mr. Cody's shoulder?" I slipped in.

"Ms. Matthews." Silas cleared his throat. "The health of my players is the end of the line for me. It means everything. As I've stated before, we're a family, and when one of us hurts, we all hurt. I suggest you don't bring up the accident to the rest of the players. You won't be met with the openness I've offered today."

I was readjusting the lighting in the living room, stretched onto my toes, when Cael swooped in to help. Long fingers wrapped around mine to twist the screw tightly in place so the pole didn't wiggle.

"Hi," he whispered against my ear as I lowered back to the balls of my feet.

Memories tangled together from Hilly's, flashes of his body pressed against mine that made me squeeze my thighs together as he pulled away and wandered around to the couch.

Cael looked good today. His hair was still damp, and little pieces of his natural blondness licked at his forehead. He shifted in his gray sweatpants, that hung low on his hips, and loose navy blue crop top that showed off his taut stomach. His muscles strained as he wrapped his sweaty arms across his chest. I was starting to think that Cael didn't own a real shirt but, at that very moment, I was glad. His big blue eyes watched as I collected a few supplies from my bag and joined him in the sitting room. I sat on the couch across from him and counted to ten in my head.

My heart was racing.

A smirk formed on his face, and I knew I was done for.

"Are you okay, Ms. Matthews?" He asked, dragging the end of my name over his lips as he cocked his head to the side and stretched out his body. His shirt rose around his chest, forcing me to press my tongue to the roof of my mouth to keep from making any illicit noises. "You seem flustered."

"You seem sweaty," I countered with a shaky tone, just doing my best to shield myself from the charming blows he hurled my way.

"I ran from the stadium. It clears my head." Cael sat forward and rested his elbows on his knees. "I can go shower if I smell," he offered. "You can come with me and make sure I'm extra clean."

"The camera is recording." I pointed to the red light on the camera beside me.

"Good," he said, sitting back, mischief twinkling in those ocean eyes as he got comfortable.

"The interview shouldn't take long." I ignored the excitement in his tone.

"Guess I'll stay sweaty." His tongue ran over his teeth as his smile grew.

"Baseball suits you, Mr. Cody." I gave him a tight smile and, without warning, started. "Was it always your dream to play at college level?"

"No." He shrugged. "Next question."

"Then why play?" I asked.

There was no flicker of amusement on his features. I knew the answers to these questions because I was there. I knew how much he hated ball. Ryan had a habit of reminding Cael that if he hadn't come along, Ryan would be further in his career. Like his son was a mistake that cost him a run at the major leagues. Every Sunday, we would watch hours of baseball, and Cael spent it outside with his mom in the backyard in the sun. But any chance Ryan had, he'd make a joke or mumble under his breath. It was never vicious, always teasing, but it made Cael indifferent to baseball. He never wanted to end up like his father.

And now look at him.

"I was bored." Cael shrugged.

I pressed my lips together into a thin line and nodded. He was going to make this harder than I expected. "Alright," I laughed under my breath.

Back to playing the game.

"Your father, Ryan Cody; the head coach of the Harbor Hornets grew up playing baseball. He was the star player on his high school team, married his high school sweetheart, and went on to have a decent career in the minor leagues until you were born," I snapped, and Cael flinched, almost unnoticeable, but his eyes flickered from me to the floor and back again. "He went on to coach high school baseball until his sister, your aunt, called him with an opportunity to coach at a NCAA level."

"Do you always give history lessons during your interviews?" His smirk faded.

"I'm just curious." I shrugged. "Baseball seems to be a family affair and you joined a record-winning team because you were *bored*?"

He swallowed tightly, his shoulders rolling back as he sat forward again.

"There's no one in the house," he said, instead of answering me.

"Answer the question," I urged him as heat licked at my neck.

"They're all at practice for another two hours." His head lolled to the side and his eyes raked up my legs as his tongue darted out over his bottom lip.

I crossed my legs to quell the soft pulse that tickled at my core from his gaze.

"Mr. Cody," I said, trying to control the situation. "This is a professional setting, please behave."

"Mr. Cody is my Dad," he quipped lightly.

"Answer the question," I responded.

"If I answer the question, can I kiss you?" He said, eyes flickering up from my legs to meet my eyes.

"No," I said coldly. I'd have to cut that out later.

"I got into baseball because I had nothing else," he said flatly. "No friends, no interests. I was bored and getting into trouble. Dad gave me an ultimatum when I graduated: school and baseball, or I could leave. So I joined the team at an entry level, but you already know that." He raised an eyebrow at me. "It wasn't a shock that I was good. Really good. I'm one of the top-ranked shortstops in the entire league." His voice was low and tight, darker than I had ever heard from him.

"That was before you ruined your shoulder," I baited him.

"That was an *accident*. I never meant for Arlo to be in that car, and if the reporter in you wants the sob story of the nepo-baby baseball star, you're gonna have to do your research because I'm not giving it to you for free," he snapped, but the playfulness still danced behind his eyes. "I'm done talking about me."

"This interview is about *you*, Cael," I reminded him.

"This interview is done." He clicked his teeth together and slid from the couch to his knees. "I'm *bored*."

"Cael." I swallowed tightly. "The camera."

"Leave it on." He leaned over, moving the remote out of my reach, and lowered his voice to a whisper, "for *research*."

"This isn't a game," I warned him. In a pathetic attempt to stop him, I put my hand up and pointed at him. "Cael." His name left my lips as a growl.

"This is how you like me, isn't it? On my knees, or did that change?"

He tugged off the sweaty shirt and chucked it away from him. His muscles were still flushed from his run, and beads of sweat clung to his tan skin as he walked himself across the carpet on his knees toward me. My traitorous pussy clenched at the sight of him.

Some things never change.

"That's what I thought," Cael laughed. "You'll always be my girl."

His confidence was infectious, and it drove me mad.

The closer he got, the harder it was to breathe, and when his hands slipped over my knees, pulling them apart so he could slink between them, I forgot what air was altogether.

"Presumptuous," I huffed as his fingers trailed further up my thighs and looped into the elastic band of my tights.

"You can try to hide it, Plum." He kissed a line down my bare skin as he pulled each leg down, nipping at my calf. "But I can *feel* how much you miss me every time our skin touches."

I couldn't fake the reaction I had to his touch, no matter how much I tried. He left a scorching trail in his wake as he worked his way back to my core.

"And if we get caught?" I lifted his chin so he'd look at me and was met with a raging fire behind those ocean-blue eyes.

"Even better," he hummed and dropped his chin. Using his tongue to catch my fingers, he sucked them into his mouth and bit down just enough to hurt.

I practically melted into the couch from his words, and the sensation of his lips wrapped around my fingers as his other hand tickled a path toward my underwear. I couldn't stop my muscles as they contracted around his shoulders. Laughter dripped from his lips as he let my fingers go and sunk back between my legs.

"You're always so wet," Cael whispered, blowing cool air over my cunt. "Is it always for me?"

Blue eyes flickered to meet mine and I nodded.

"Good girl," he praised and slid the soaked underwear to the side.

"Fuck." My hand flew into his hair as his tongue darted over my folds and circled my throbbing clit delicately. I heard the fabric rip before I could stop his teeth from tearing through it, leaving it in tatters on the couch and leaving me exposed to the entire sitting room. "Cael," I scolded, but it only drew a throaty laugh from his lips.

"They were in the way," he teased.

"Seriously?" I scowled down at him.

"I'll buy you new ones," he purred and dove back in.

With careful, broad strokes, he worked the pleasure from my core and spread it out over every muscle in my body. I raked my fingers over his scalp until he was trembling beneath my touch. Gasping for air, for any sort of release, his fingers dipped into me without warning. My cunt fluttered at his touch as my toes curled into the carpet, searching for something to hang onto as Cael dangled me over the ledge.

Knuckle deep, I pleaded for him to move faster.

"Greedy," he teased.

Cael's tongue lapped over my clit, his teeth caught skin, consuming me with pleasure as a breathy moan dripped from me. His pace was affectionate and he took the time to pause and rework each spot that drew a sound from me.

My muscles tightened as he sucked at my swollen clit and snapped the cord deep within my stomach, his fingers plunging deeper to coax the orgasm from my soaked center.

"That's it, Baby," he purred as I tightened around his fingers. "Come for me."

He didn't have to ask twice.

Strangled noises flooded the room as I dissolved into pleasure, my head falling back against the couch. I let the orgasm drown out every thought I had as Cael cleaned me with his tongue, lapping up everything and leaving no trace behind.

"I'll never get sick of that." He licked his bottom lip and kissed my thigh.

His eyes were brighter than I had ever seen them, so proud of himself.

"That was a good distraction," I hummed and sat up, wrapping my hands around his face. I brought my mouth to hover over his. "But this interview is not over, Cael Cody," I whispered before pulling away.

Cael groaned, falling back onto the carpet as I unhooked myself from him and pulled on my tights. His face tightened with disappointment.

"I'm not *your* girl anymore, Cael." I looked down at him. "Sweet talking and a few decent orgasms won't make anything better."

"Keep fighting it, Clementine," he responded.

Pushing off his knees, he brushed his hand along my thigh as he straightened out and hovered over me. I could tell he was thinking about stealing a kiss, despite the rule I had set. His eyes darted to my lips, and his throat bobbed slightly before he stepped back and collected his shirt from the floor with the swoop of his long, muscular arm.

"And that orgasm..." He leaned in close, teeth finding my ear lobe and biting down before he spoke again. "...was better than decent."

"You're full of shit," I bit back.

"You're *trembling*."

The words sent a shiver down my spine as he pulled away and left me standing in the sitting room, staring at the blinking red light of the video camera with shame.

MATTHEWS

I emailed off the current interviews I had finished to Bobbi to look over, except for the tape that Cael and I had made the week before. It mocked me on the dresser across from the bed, a physical reminder that, no matter how hard I tried, staying away from Cael was going to be much, much harder than anticipated.

He hadn't done much talking since, avoiding any subject that surrounded our past with distraction. I'd never seen a man so obsessed with eating pussy. *It's a hobby*, he whispered the last time I asked.

Cael would wander into my room, announce his boredom, and satiate it all in one go.

No talking, no kissing.

Just Cael silently apologizing for seven years worth of absence.

Had anyone asked me back then, before I lost my virginity to him, if I ever thought that there was a future that existed that looked like this, I would have died from embarrassment. Now? Now, I was taking full advantage of what Cael considered an apology, even if he wasn't sure what exactly it was for. It felt like flying.

My phone rang at my side. Bobbi's pretty smile lit up the screen, and I set it up so we could talk. "Hey." I typed more notes into my document.

"Where's Cael's tape?" She asked without pleasantries.

"It's—" I swallowed, "tainted."

"What does that mean? Did the recording mess up?" Bobbi said, not really paying attention to the conversation as she worked at her computer on the other end of the FaceTime.

"No." I leaned back in my chair and waited for her to look at me.

Her brown eyes widened in shock when she took in the blush on my cheeks and the smirk on my face. She set down her hands and leaned closer to the camera.

"Oh my god, you filthy slut," she whispered.

Both of us broke out into laughter and I told her everything that happened in a hushed voice so that it didn't float out of her cubicle. "So I have to schedule him for a new interview."

"I'm actually very offended you didn't send me that tape." Bobbi crossed her arms and sat back in her chair. "I'm so lonely here." She pouted.

"I'd never be able to look you in the eye again." I shook my head, and her eyebrows rose in shock.

"So what now?" She posed the question I was dreading trying to answer. "Does that mean Clem and Cael are officially back on?" She said, dramatically whispering the Clem with her hands cupped around her face.

"No," I said. "Absolutely not."

Bobbi scowled and teased me. "Boo, I need the *romance* portion of this Shakespeare play, Juliet."

"It's a distraction." I shrugged.

"Yeah, I would be distracted with his tongue down my throat too," Bobbi huffed.

"I haven't kissed him. I won't," I admitted.

"You haven't..." Bobbi looked confused. "Why the hell not when the boy's been knuckle deep?"

"Cael doesn't know what he wants and, frankly, neither do I. I don't know who he is anymore, and I can't just blow up the life I've worked so hard to create just because he's really good at eating me out. Kissing him would only remind me of all those feelings. It's too intimate. I can't do it."

"But you can if the spark is there," Bobbi suggested. "Maybe it's time to ask yourself what you want because I know it's not that stuffy white-collar douchebag you call a fiance."

"Ex," I corrected. "But now that you mention him."

"You haven't thought about Julien the entire time you've been there, have you?" Bobbi's smile was vicious.

"Is that cruel?" I asked.

"It would be if you'd left him with the possibility of the two of you reconciling, but you made it pretty clear that you weren't ready to seal your fate in a blood pact."

Bobbi was anti-commitment and strongly believed that marriage was a ritual, cult process and that signing papers meant signing your soul over to the devil, or the government as most called it.

"It just shows where your head's at, M." She sighed. "Have you tried, I don't know... having a conversation with him?"

"Every time I think about it, I just get upset."

"Over what, the past indiscretions of two teenagers forced apart by their parents?" Bobbi scoffed. "You want to blame him, but you both stopped trying. Now he's there trying, and what are you doing? Complaining about being eaten out three times a day by a man with the prettiest blue eyes I've ever seen."

"Okay, okay, I surrender!" I put my hands up to stop her from berating me.

"Give the baseball edition of Justin Bieber a chance, he might surprise you. I haven't seen you this happy in a long time. He's clearly doing something correct."

"It's not what he's doing now that scares me." I pinned my shoulders back and brushed my fingers through the short brown locks around my face.

"No way." Bobbi raised her hands in the air and got close to the camera. "I've known you since we were nineteen, and from the day I met you until the day you left for Rhode Island, you have wanted one thing." She put her finger up to emphasize it. "And that one thing is Cael Cody."

A knock on the door frame of my room scared me off my seat, and I hit the end of our phone call when I saw who was standing there. Cael leaned against the frame, in a cropped gray t-shirt with *FUCKBOY* scribbled across it in yellow letters that showed off his taught lower stomach and hardened V-lines, with his arms behind his back and a shit-eating grin on his face. He was in a pair of wide-legged jeans and a green ball cap that looked older than the both of us combined. His cheeks were red with blush and his tongue brushed out over his bottom lip. *Okay, now I was definitely convinced that handsome idiot didn't own a proper shirt.*

"How long have you been standing there?" I asked him, and he just shook his head and looked away. *God dammit Bobbi.* "What do you want, Cael?"

"You haven't eaten today," he said, his eyes raking over me.

"Yes, I have," I protested, pointing to the half-drank cup of coffee on the small working desk at the end of the bed.

When I looked back at him, he was holding a paper bag out in front of him. The smell of warm fries wafted from it and filled my nose.

"Are those?"

Dukes.

"Hilly's, but the taste is close," he answered. "It was the only thing that I ate when we moved here. Turns out french fry grease is brutal on the complexion of a teenager—Mama had to bribe me to eat a vegetable after six months."

The mention of Lorraine had his brows furrowing.

"Take them." He wiggled the bag at me and forced a smile back on his face. "Before they get cold."

I grabbed the bag from him and unrolled the top to let the smell out. They were still hot. He had come straight here with them, and he was right. They did taste like Dukes. It almost made me angry that he had found something so similar here.

"Did you bring sneakers?" He looked around my room.

"Why?"

"We're going down to the stadium."

When I didn't move he rolled his eyes and stood up. His tall stature filled out the door frame and he used his arms to lean toward me. "If you're writing a piece on the Harbor Hornets, I expect you to actually get to know them. No more of this interrogation bullshit."

I hated how much pure compassion flowed from him. He loved the team even if he pretended it was forced. Somewhere along the way, he had found himself a family.

"Aw, but those have been so much fun, Loverboy. You should see how many *interrogations* I have." I cocked an eyebrow at him and popped a fry into my mouth, reveling in the jealousy that flickered across his face and tightened his jaw.

"Watch out for Dean," he recovered quickly. "He bites."

"I have a feeling he learned that from you." I waited for him to get mad but he just smirked at me.

"I have scars to prove the legitimacy of that statement, Plum. Get your sneakers."

"If I do this, you have to finish your interview," I said, passing the bag of greasy goodness back to him.

"I never leave a job unfinished." His blue gaze raked down my body, catching on the hem of my tank top where a sliver of skin was exposed.

"Turn around," I said, pulling out a clean pair of tights.

"If you think I'm turning around, you're delusional." He didn't hesitate in his response.

"At least shut the door. I don't need half the nest seeing my ass."

"But what about the tapes?" He mocked as he kicked the door closed behind him.

For a short moment, I thought he might take advantage of my privacy but, instead, he gave me one more look, popped a fry between his lips, and turned around to face my bed so I could change.

The softness of his behavior caught in my throat, unexpectedly tender and unlike the man he had been up until now. It was such a young Cael movement that, for a second, we were back in my room, and I was still hoping that he'd notice the look of love in my eyes.

Please don't notice the look of love in my eyes, I begged quietly now instead. Bobbi had gotten in my head. Was it so wrong to *want* to give Cael a chance?

His shoulders tensed as his eyes dropped to my bed. The shirt I had stolen from his room was untucked from beneath my pillow. I waited for him to tease me. To say something about it, but it never came. He just dug in the bag for another fry as he waited.

"You ready?" He asked as he turned around. I sat on my chair and started to pull on my sneakers, tucking my face down to hide the pink color my cheeks had turned with embarrassment.

He walked over, dropped to one knee, and patted my calf softly to encourage me to raise my foot.

"Always on your knees for me," I cooed quietly. Cael smirked as he tied each shoe, careful to double-knot them before helping me stand.

His sweet, citrusy cologne filled my nose as he wrapped his hand around my back and pulled me close to his body. Goosebumps covered my arms, locked in by his as I worked to control my beating heart, resisting the feral urge to run my thumb over his pouty bottom lip and kiss him until he begged for air. Those endless blue eyes ate away at my resolve to keep him at arm's length and I could feel the barriers crumbling as that boyish, lopsided smile formed to the left of his face.

"You smell pretty," Cael whispered, pulling away but lingering on my wrist and rolling the bracelet there between his fingers before letting go.

I stood there for a moment longer as he disappeared down the hall toward the front door, unable to catch the breath that he had stolen from my lungs without remorse. I was treading water, trying desperately to keep my head above the surface, grasping onto the memories of that smile like a life preserver.

I had missed Cael Cody more than I could have ever imagined. I'd just barely learned how to swim on my own, and now I was paying the price for underestimating his intoxicating ability to pull me back beneath the surface.

"Move it, slow poke," he whistled from the front door.

I followed him around the house to a path that led down the back. It was well worn, all the grass eroded away from them using it to get to the stadium. When it broke out from the tree line to the highway, Cael skirted around and put himself on the outside without breaking his train of thought as he rambled on about the muggy weather.

As we entered the stadium, he stopped to talk to a group of people who were painting a new mural on the west side.

"Hey, Tess! It looks amazing." He looked up at it and nodded. "Arlo's nose is bigger, though." He pointed, and the girl covered in paint laughed. "I'll give you ten dollars to paint a mustache on Dean." He pointed to the man a little further down, who had just shaken his head.

I felt like I was watching a movie as he interacted with everyone around the stadium. Everyone he saw, he treated like family. He knew something about each of their lives that caught me off guard, and I couldn't help but lean into him as he led us down to the field. It was weird to see him at ease, there was no tension in his shoulders, no tightness to his jaw. Just that light-as-a-feather nature that he carried around.

Cael stopped, poking his head into what looked like a gym but was empty except for Ella, who was working with a player I didn't recognize.

"Hey Peach," he called to her, and she looked up with a smile on her face. "Jensen has a meeting with his counselor. Would you mind substituting for dinner tonight?"

She nodded and went back to work.

"You call her Peach?" I said as he closed the door.

He looked back at me for a moment, confusion on his face. "You jealous?"

"No," I said, but I looked back over my shoulder through the glass at her, talking softly to the player she was working with, and wondered what I was missing between her and Cael. Or maybe it was just a stupid nickname, and I was reading too much into it.

"Down here." He opened a door that led to the field where players tossed balls back and forth. "Stadium has a retractable roof so that we can keep in shape during the off-season."

The Shore family had spared no expense to give the team a top of the line stadium and it showed.

"You practice year-round?" I asked him.

"It's more slack in the fall; training usually picks up again in the early spring, but the guys like to keep their bodies moving."

Cael was a natural at the talking part. He pointed out a few of the stadium highlights and made his way to a section in the back concealed by a mesh tunnel and led me to the rear.

Van Mitchell and Dean Tucker could be heard between loud cracks of wood and the sound of whooshing balls. A row of three batting cages lined the back of the stadium, all empty except for the one that housed the two men.

"Boys." Cael hooked his fingers into the chain fence.

"What's up, Cody?"

Van poked the end of his bat near the fence while Dean just stared at me like he wanted to say something. Neither of them bothered with shirts, showing rippling muscles that spanned over their arms and chests, soft stomachs, and tan skin. The bodies of baseball players work hard and play harder. I licked my bottom lip as I came to a stop next to Cael.

"Came down to show," he stopped short of calling me Clementine, "Ms. Matthews, what we really do..."

"You can't swing, Cael." Dean was the first to say it. "Ella's orders. If we let you in, she'll go full mom on us."

"Personally, I would love to see it, and it only makes me more tempted." Cael flashed his Cheshire smile. However, he stopped and leaned over to look at me. "I'm not getting in. Mary is."

"No." I shook my head. "I'm extremely opposed to having balls hurled at my face."

Cael snorted, and I glared at him.

"It's not as scary as it looks," Dean offered through a clenched jaw.

Cael lost it laughing that time.

"Am I the only person in the cage right now that hasn't had balls in my face?" Van looked between all of us and brushed his long, shaggy mullet under his ballcap. "I'll turn down the speed on it, and as long as Cael promises not to swing the bat, I'll play lookout and keep Ella busy."

"Keep this up you might get some balls in your face for good behavior," Dean teased and unlocked the cage, slipping out with his back turned to me. Something passed between him and Cael, who looked more tense than he had all day.

Van handed me the bat. "Do you think he's serious?" He asked me. "About the balls..." He scooted out of the way.

"You aren't my type, Van," Dean groaned from the end of the hall.

"No funny business, or I'm snitching." Van stared at us, tapping two fingers to his chest at Cael, who mirrored the motion before turning to me.

"In you go."

CODY

"*Be careful with that one.*"

That's what Dean whispered when he slid from the cage. It was low enough that Van and Clementine missed, but he made sure I heard it. I didn't know what to say to him. The defense caught in my throat.

Van's eyebrows shot up when he caught Dean's face and vacated as quickly as his legs would take him.

Clementine turned to look at me. "I'll make you a deal."

"A deal?" I looked down at her. I wanted to take her round face in my hands and pry the air from her lungs with my mouth. "I'm listening," I said instead.

"For each ball I hit, I get to ask you a question." She pulled a small recorder from her pocket and set it on the long thin ledge where we kept helmets.

"You would turn this into work—"

The arguement died on my lips when she batted her eye lashes at me and that bottom lip jutted out just a little more than usual. How could I deny that look?

"Fine," I said confidently. The bat felt so good in my hands that, for a split second, I was tempted just to try, to see how it would feel to take that swing but Clementine pried it from my fingers.

"You promised the giant chocolate Labrador you wouldn't."

"Actually I never promised Van, he just handed me the bat." I shrugged and she rolled her beautiful brown eyes at me. Her attitude drove me insane. "Loophole."

But she didn't laugh and her grip tightened on the bat.

"Alright." I lifted both hands into the air and backed against the cage.

"Each ball." She pointed the bat at my chest and smiled. My heart went up in flames like a bonfire. "One question."

"One answer." I nodded, constantly willing to push my luck. I asked, "how about a kiss to seal the deal?"

I leaned off the cage, looping my finger tightly around it. She didn't move as my lips ghosted over hers, my breath fanning over her. Her brown eyes looked up from my lips, a tiny raging fire dancing inside. She searched my gaze for a second, the longest second of my life. I unlocked one finger at a time, slowly falling forward more until I could feel the skin of her bottom lip brushing against my top one.

Seven years was an excruciatingly long time to wait to kiss her.

Another finger popped from the cage and I glided forward ready to be consumed by the bliss that one kiss from Clementine would surely provide.

Sharp pain dug into my rib cage in the form of the end of her baseball bat.

"Ow!" I yelped and pulled back.

"An answer for every hit ball," Clementine breathed out with a mischievous smirk on those pretty, pouty lips as I rubbed the spot she poked. "No kiss."

"You're a tease." I rolled my eyes at her and reluctantly held out my hand. "Ok, deal."

I grabbed a helmet from the ledge and settled it down over her head. "Just in case."

"I look like a dork." She laughed.

"You look adorable," I corrected her and brushed the loose strands of brown hair off her face. "Turn and listen," I said, taking her shoulders and angling her toward the pitching machine. "There's a whirring noise and then a pop. Keep your eye on the ball and swing."

I gripped her hands gently, showing her the movement. Her ass was pressed tightly to me and I swallowed, pushing my heels into the ground to keep from acting impulsively toward the friction. A deep groan settled in the base of my throat as she rolled her hips from left to right and swung the bat and connected sloppily with the first automated pitch.

"That's my girl." I stepped back, clapping for her.

She turned to me, eyebrow raised and on a mission, she pressed a record on her device. "Why shortstop?" She asked.

"That's cheating, I helped you hit that one," I argued.

"That wasn't stipulated in the rules, just that I hit the balls." She smiled at me and I crumbled like a house of cards. Smart woman.

"Dad...*Coach*," I corrected with a huff. "He drilled the fundamentals of baseball into me," I said, pointing to the machine with the remote to pause the pitches. I hated that she dug like this, asking questions she knew the answers to. It was like watching our life together on repeat and each question she asked left a new, heavy feeling in my stomach. What was she looking for? Something, somewhere. She believed there was a misstep. "I already understood everything. I just needed to be fast, and flexible." I smirked at her. "Which I am. Very fast and very *flexible*."

Tension rolled over me and hung in the air between us.

"There has to be more to shortstop than that." Clementine narrowed her eyes at me.

"It's all about communication. I'm only as good as the outfield, the first baseman, the pitcher." I shrugged.

"Arlo's gone now, who's primed to take his spot?" Clementine asked and I shook my head at her, starting the machine again.

"That's a question." I cocked my head to the side. "Better hit a ball, *Mary*." I sneered.

She steeled her gaze, jaw clenched, as she turned back to the machine that spat a ball out before she was ready for it. Her laughter filled the batting cages and injected my veins with pure serotonin. I just wanted to reach out and wrap her up in my arms.

I shoved my hands into the pockets of my jeans and counted to ten.

It didn't work to calm me down because, when the next ball came, she hit it without hesitation. It stuttered for a moment but bounced off the back of the cage with an echo of vibrating metal. Clementine threw her hands in the air, cheering for herself as she turned back to me. With rosy cheeks, and light flooding her eyes like it was coming from inside of her with all the power of the sun, she shook her hands.

"Who's primed to take Arlo's spot?" She asked without pause.

"No decision has been made, and if there has been," I leaned forward and lowered my voice, "I wasn't part of the conversation."

Clementine took a beat to consider my answer and turned back to swing before I even had time to pause the machine. The bat cracked against the ball. "What was your dynamic like with King, and why did it work?"

"That's two—"

Another ball smashed against the cage.

"Silas." I swallowed tightly. "Doctor Shore," the formality of his name was weird rolling off my lips, "once said it was like locking a rabid dog in a room with an alley cat. It shouldn't have worked."

Clementine laughed at that. It bubbled out of her like honey. Sweet and sticky, it clung to her lips and I wanted to steal the sound straight from her mouth.

"But it did because Arlo never tried to make a dog out of me," I finished. "He just let me be a cat I guess. We understand... *understood*," I ate the anxious emotion that threatened to derail me, "each other. It was always a give-and-take. We have each other's back and that's really what it boils down to. A pitcher needs his shortstop."

I tore my eyes away from her, feeling self-conscious under her gaze. I knew I had walked into a trap. She wanted to know more about Arlo leaving and how I felt about it and I had just given her exactly what she wanted.

But Clementine didn't say anything; she just readied herself for the next pitch, missing this time. The ball crashed to the back of the cage, rolling around by her feet until the next was thrown. She missed the next three, her hands too loose around the bat and frustration seeped in on her delicate features.

"Reset," I said.

Moving toward her, I felt her tense as I wrapped my hand under her arm and placed my palm flat on her chest. "Breathe," I whispered into her ear. "Feel it here," I instructed as her chest rose. "Push back on my hand."

She listened, filling her lungs until my hand lifted from her chest, over and over again. Rising and falling until she was relaxed and the tension was gone in her body.

"Try again," I said, stepping back and bringing that hand to my own chest. My fingers itched to hold the bat and my resolve was slowly crumbling.

I curled them against my heart, letting the racing rhythm of it ease me back from the ledge. Temptation chewed at the back of my head as she swung and hit the ball perfectly against the back of the cage.

I needed a meeting.

"Are you scared for next season?" She asked, but it didn't feel like her other questions. It felt personal.

I'm scared right now.

"Yes," I answered honestly. "Reworking a team after losing a star pitcher isn't easy. You and everyone else saw what happened to the Hornets when Nicholas King left. Arlo has always been the better pitcher, but the skill was mute. We hadn't figured out how to work together, it destroyed us."

"Given the explosive way the season ended, I'd say you still don't have it quite figured out, Cael."

She was more than right. I could barely keep it together long enough to heal my shoulder and keep my head in the game. Next season was going to be a war zone.

Clementine cocked her head to the side, ignoring the whirling of the machine. The ball lurched out of the pipe at her, unprepared for it she jumped back as I caught it in my bare hand with a strangled grunt. A flash of hot, tingly pain washed over my palm and down my wrist, as I took the ball in my hand. Van had turned it down but it had to have been going over fifty miles per hour coming out of the machine.

"Fuck," I grunted. All that mattered was that it hadn't hit her.

"Oh, God!" She dropped the bat to the ground, flipping the helmet from her head, and stepped toward me as I slipped the machine into off and wiggled out the stinging pain that vibrated across the palm of my hand.

"Are you hurt?" She grabbed my wrist and turned my palm over.

I wanted to tell her it barely stung, I've made the idiot mistake of catching a hurling ball with my bare hand before but never one coming from a machine. It didn't feel great but the sight of her fawning over my skin, her lips fanning cool air over my palm. She didn't need to know it was fine.

"It might be broken," I faked, groaning as I lazily wiggled my fingertips. I hiss playfully as she ran her fingers over mine. "You can kiss it better if you want?"

"Do you need ice? Should I get someone?" She asked not looking up at me. Her worry was too thick to entertain my flirtatious teasing. "I'm so sorry," she said.

It was cute to see her like this; there had been so much back and forth. Her walls surrounded her like a forcefield, preventing me from seeing the old Clementine. She was protecting the little girl inside her heart and, tragically, we had that in common.

Her brown eyes flickered up to mine, welling with tears, and I laughed gently.

"I'm alright, Plum," I hummed, the need to console her running rampant. "I just need some ice," I whispered, wrapping my other hand around the back of her head and raking my fingers through her hair. "I'm glad you didn't get hurt." I brushed my lips over her hair.

She apologized again, turning her face upward to look at me, and my breath hitched.

"There you are," I whispered.

Seventeen-year-old Clem stared up at me, innocent, heartbroken eyes gleaming under the lights of the batting cages. Hair stuck to her face and her cheeks were pink with worry. I knew I wasn't allowed to but the urge to kiss her never faded, like a dull roar at the back in the back of my mind it flared at the sight of her.

But I could do this. My self-control waning like a flag in a hurricane, I pressed my lips to her forehead and settled for the softness of her skin instead.

MATTHEWS

2015

The music blasting over the speakers was some form of techno-country that hurt my head. I had lost Cael an hour ago and, even though he promised not to stray too far, I could hear the gaggle of senior girls by the pool laughing at whatever jokes he was telling.

It had become a surefire way of finding him.

Follow the groupies.

"Hey, Clementine!" Andrea Fernsby wandered over to the small kitchen island, her eyes rolling over my outfit with disdain before a horrible smile curled on her lips. "I didn't think you'd be here, but I guess where Cael goes, *you go.*" Her eyes flickered to the crowd around him and back to me like it was an insult.

"Mm," I nodded, just trying to stay out of her way. "He said it was okay if I came," I said, barely audible over the music.

"Sorry, what was that?" Andrea leaned forward in her tiny tank top, her long dark hair spilling over onto the counter as she got closer. "I couldn't hear you, little mouse," she mocked.

"I said—" I opened my mouth and closed it again when I realized she was teasing me.

"It's just so loud in here!" She shrugged, a sick smile still plastered on her face. "Hey, just girl to girl, can we talk?" She asked.

"Sure." I swallowed the bile that rose in my throat. Even on a good day, Andrea would never be seen dead talking to me. It was suspicious enough that she was in proximity to me, but now she wanted to have a heart-to-heart? Something stank.

122

She looped her arm into mine and led me out to the deck, where the party was in full swing. Kids filled the lawn chairs and swam in the pool. It was a warm, June day and, with the school year practically over, everyone had entered summer vacation mode.

"What did you—" I slowed my pace as we approached a quiet corner.

"So, like..." Andrea smiled. "You're really close to Cael, and I was just wondering if you could put in a good word for me?" Her eyes flickered across the pool deck to where Cael sat with two girls from our Math class.

I tried to stifle the laugh that bubbled from my throat.

Andrea gave me a dirty look upon hearing the sound.

"Oh, you were serious?" I said quietly and awkwardly, avoiding her gaze.

"Of course I was serious, Clementine." She scowled at me. "Are you going to help me or not?"

"Why don't you just talk to him?" I asked her.

"If just talking to him worked, I would do that, but he's always surrounded," she groaned and took a sip of the liquid in her plastic cup. "You would know that," she turned her malice back to me, "always following him around but always on the outside of the circle. It's pathetic."

"Okay, well..." I buried down the feelings that rose at her words. "I could try. Cael doesn't really like being told what to do..." I trailed off, but Andrea wasn't even listening. She heard that I would try and perked up.

"Really? You'll do that for me?" She cooed her demeanor back to sweet. "You're such a good friend, Clemmy." The nickname left a bad taste in my mouth but I nodded as Andrea started fixing her skirt and brushing her hair with her fingertips.

"Oh, like right now?" I laughed nervously, and she stared at me like I had six heads. "Yeah, sure..."

I inhaled deeply, steadying my racing heart, and started across the deck to where he was. He looked over from one of the girls, and a smile spread across his face. I hated watching him flirt with other girls, not because of the action itself, but because it wasn't him. At least not the Cael I had grown up with. He projected someone louder and funnier around girls, like he needed to take up all the space or no one would pay attention to him.

But he couldn't be more wrong.

He looked handsome in a white tank top and jeans. His necklace hung from his throat and swung lazily as he shifted on the lawn chair to extend his hand to me. One of the girls beside him scoffed and stared me down for a long, very awkward moment. Cael was completely oblivious to how much they all hated me.

"Can I talk to you?" I asked him over the music, and he nodded, pushing the second girl from his lap. He stood and followed me back against the long fence.

"What's wrong? Are you not having fun?" He asked in a panic, his eyes searching around the party. He was already trying to problem-solve without an actual problem.

"No—I mean, yeah, I'm having fun," I lied. "But that's not why I came over here. You know Andrea Fernsby? She's in my English class."

"Uh," Cael pressed his lips together as he thought about it before shaking his head softly, "I don't think so?"

"Little, dark hair, well endowed..." My eyes widened, trying to get him to see her in his mind. "She always smells like cinnamon hearts?"

"Oh! Andrea!" Cael finally clued in.

"She seems really interested in chatting with you," I said to him, leaving out the part that Andrea would surely make my life a living hell if I didn't do this for her.

"Chatting?" Cael laughed. "What did she say to you?"

"The usual. She talked about how big your head was, how bad your jokes were, and then complained that if you were only a few inches taller—"

"Okay, okay!" Cael put both hands in the air, still laughing.

"She just wants a moment alone with you," I said, forcing a smile to my face. "I guess she couldn't break through the wall of cheerleaders to get her hands on you, so she sent reinforcements."

"You are the cutest wingman a best friend could ask for." He wrapped my face in both his hands and kissed my forehead. "Are you sure you're having fun?"

I nodded. "She just wanted me to put in a good word for her, so I did."

Cael's eyes narrowed on me. "Why would you do that?"

Because she would literally never let it go if I didn't.

"She's pretty." I shrugged. "She kind of looks like that actress you love."

"Sophia Bush?" Cael asked, turning around in a circle slowly until his eyes landed on Andrea across the deck. A small smile formed on his face when he caught her gaze, and she wiggled her long fingers in his direction.

"You sure, you're sure you're okay?" He asked me again, looking back before he walked away.

I nodded.

The reality of the situation was I wished he would search a crowd like that for me. I wanted Cael Cody to scan the faces until he found mine and watch his heart explode as a smile spread across his face. But I was always the one pointing out the girl he was searching for, never the one he found.

MATTHEWS

I found a group of players, including Cael and Dean, in the living room watching a university hockey game. They were strung around the furniture with bored looks on their faces. Van was hanging upside down on the living room chair with a camera over his face and clicked the trigger as I came into view.

"Who's playing?" I asked.

"St. Louis and Pittsburgh," Cael groaned, not looking over from the TV. Pittsburgh were up by three goals in the third period and it didn't look promising for the other team.

I shrugged and leaned against the archway with my arms crossed. "Is this what you guys do during off season? Lay around and watch hockey?"

"Pretty much." Dean shrugged. He had a binder open in his lap and he was scribbling notes from a textbook beside him on the floor. "Were you expecting grand parties every night?" He asked, looking up at me with his lips pressed into a thin line.

"No," I said, *but absolutely.* "Isn't that what university is about? Parties, drinking, girls."

Van snorted. "Cael's sober, I'm committed, both Todd and Jensen are on probation with Coach, and Dean has slept through most of the male sports teams."

Dean growled at Van and kicked his foot against the bar that controlled the foot rest of the chair he was sprawled across. The motion sent Van tumbling downward onto the floor, protecting his camera with lanky arms as he hit the ground.

"Ow," he grumbled and shoved a leg against Dean's binder.

The two of them lunged at each other on the living room floor rolling around in a ball of strong limbs and curse words as they wrestled. The rest of the boys either kept their eyes on the game or egged them on.

"Is there anything fun to do in Harbor other than hockey games and amateur wrestling?" I asked as Cael jabbed Van in the ribcage to give Dean the advantage. Seeing the opening, he flipped Van on his back and hooked his arm around his face, squeezing it between his forearm and bicep.

"Tap," Dean grunted as Van wiggled to get free. "Just tap, Mitchell," he said again when Van tried to pinch his way out of the hold, but Dean used his other hand to swat him away.

"I tap," Van coughed out and pushed away from the floor. "We could take her down to the stadium..." Van looked over at Cael as he straightened himself out. "You know..." He wiggled his eyebrows at him and Dean let his head fall backwards to stare at Cael upside down.

"Oh please, *Caely*," he whined. "It'll be so much fun and we haven't done it in so long."

"Caely?" I mocked and Dean gave me a dirty look.

Cael sighed, looking around at all of us. "Get Ella. If we do it without her she'll kill us."

"Yes!" Van pushed his giant body into motion and disappeared from the living room as Todd and Jensen started moving.

"We'll go get the stuff," they both chimed together and were gone without another word.

"Do dumb and dumber always finish each other's sentences?" I asked as the front door shut. Dean laughed as he collected his school work and nodded as he wandered by. Cael seemed unimpressed by all the shenanigans, which wasn't like him at all; usually he was the center of them.

"It gets worse when they're drunk," he said. "Just wait."

"Remember, when we get there," Cael sauntered over to me, the bored look on his face still solemn, "*you* wanted something fun to do."

"What's wrong with you?" I asked him quietly.

"Nothing." He looked at me, his eyes trailing down my body, taking in the light athletic sweater and tights. His eyes glimmered for a moment before the light died as he looked back up at me.

"You hate hockey." I poked him in the chest and he grabbed my wrist.

"You're right, *I do*." He kissed the inside of my wrist like he couldn't help himself and turned me toward the TV with a spin. "But I love watching *Hart* get kicked around by the Pittsburgh defense." He lowered his voice, his face brushing against mine as he nodded at the TV as Kiefer Hart was slammed into the boards.

My heart sank seeing his face as his helmet was spun off onto the ice, a gripping feeling like I had been planted in concrete planted me to the ground in front of the TV. His dark, sweaty hair stuck to a fresh cut on his forehead as he yelled in the face of the ref.

"Oooh tough. You're mocking an NHL player..." I tried to deflect the way I felt. The way it *made* me feel that Cael held that grudge even today, but the words came out shaky and a nasty, beautiful smirk formed on Cael's face.

"He's still a pussy," Cael whispered with malice. "Come on." He tugged me away from the TV as Dean came back down the stairs. "Where's Ella?"

I looked back at the TV. The puck had been dropped again and the image of Kiefer was gone but the feelings that surfaced upon seeing him after so long lingered. Sometimes when I closed my eyes I could still smell him, feel his hands, and it ran a chill down my spine.

"Here."

The sound of her voice snapped me from my nightmare and I turned just as she appeared from the kitchen with Van on her tail and Zoey on his back with a bright grin. "I heard we were hazing Mary." Ella beamed.

"What the hell does that mean?"

"I warned you," Cael said quietly, and wrapped his arm around me until his fingers were tucked into the pocket of my sweater.

"What fun can be had at the stadium that isn't the batting cages?" I asked Cael as we all walked the path down the hill. He was still glued to my side and I'd be lying if I said I didn't like the constant contact.

Everyone else had gotten further ahead of us; Zoey still on Van's back, as Dean and Ella laughed back and forth, locked in a conversation we couldn't hear.

"You'll see." Cael shook his head. "Impatient as always."

I didn't notice him drop back as we broke out from the path to the road, his quickened footsteps startling me as he slipped to the outside and held something out to me.

I looked down and between his fingertips was a flower with soft pink petals that could fit into the center of my palm. It was a cherry blossom. "Where did you find this?"

"There's a tree just before the path breaks, it's down off the ravine. It blooms twice a year," he said. "Do you still put petals in books?" He asked me, his eyes searching for answers I couldn't give him.

"I haven't in a long time..." My brows knitted together tightly. It was a wonder that he even remembered that, it was a silly hobby of a little girl who had too much time on her hands.

Something that mimicked anger flickered across his face. "Shame."

He didn't say anything else on the matter as I tucked the flower into my pocket. "What?" I asked him, catching up to match his long stride.

"Your books used to be littered with them." He stared straight ahead, watching the road and his friends with that same dark expression. I hated that, his eyes were so dark and void of the sparkle they usually had.

"People grow out of hobbies," I said with a small huff, the air cold enough outside that evening that it fogged the moment it left my lips.

"You're right, but it's a shame no one buys you flowers you *want* to last forever."

"That's a wild assumption, Cael." I brushed him off.

He turned his head to look at me. "You didn't grow out of the hobby or you wouldn't have put the blossom in your pocket. Which means either no one was buying you flowers, or *someone* was buying you flowers you hate."

I hated that he wasn't wrong.

Julien *always* sent red roses. Fickle ugly things, with delicate petals that died in a week.

"You sound jealous," I deflected with a smirk.

"Until the day I die, Clem," he grumbled as we got to the empty parking lot of the stadium. I could feel the heat rising on my cheeks from his words but I turned my head up to the sky to let the cool air bite at them as we walked.

I would never get away from how easily flustered he made me. How such simple honesty held such power over my emotions. The wind messed up his hair and forced pieces against his forehead as he turned to look at me over his shoulder.

"Come on, slow poke." He nodded toward the door which Ella scanned to unlock.

Dean grabbed it from her and held it open for all of us and we made our way through the dim stadium halls. He wandered ahead, saying something quiet to Ella as they rounded the corner toward the players entrance to the diamond.

I wanted to ask Cael what was wrong but it didn't really seem like the time or place until Dean cleared his throat beside me.

"This time of the year is hard because it's when she started to get really sick again. Cael has good days and bad days," he explained as we walked past Coach's office, the light still on but Ryan hidden behind all the boxes and clutter. "It's worse this year because he's sober."

The words were like a knife to my chest; how I hadn't noticed that he was sad long before today caused a guilty sensation to bubble up. But I nodded, listening carefully to Dean's warning, his caution clearly warranted and coming from a place of love.

"Baby gloves," I said quietly and he turned to nod at me before tapping two fingers to his chest. My whole body tightened at the sight of it but it wasn't uncomfortable. Just a gesture I hadn't expected to ever see again. It was warm and fond as the memory cascaded over my shoulders.

"It's ready." Jensen came crashing around the corner from the tunnel with a shit-eating grin on his dumb face and his feet tangled together like strings.

All the worry from the day seemed to fade away and Cael's smile returned to his face, although it was half-hearted and still full of grief, the light shimmered in his ocean eyes.

"Alright Plum." He turned to me, framed by Ella and Dean. "During the off-season we started having team building nights most of the time, that included us getting absolutely shit faced, until Silas scared all of us straight and demanded that at least one team building exercise was dry."

"We fought him on it," Dean added seamlessly.

"What we're about to show you we take very seriously. There are three rules and under no circumstances are you allowed to break any of them," Cael explained with a sly grin.

"What is this, Fight Club?" I asked and Ella snorted.

"We wouldn't be talking about it if it was," Dean quipped, clearly proud of himself for catching the reference, because Ella leaned over with a tiny enthusiastic thumbs up.

"No filming, you can't say no, and if 'Party in the USA' is played you finish your drink." Cael listed them off and I went to open my mouth about the drinking. "It's juice."

"You play drinking games with juice?" I laughed. A few pieces of my hair fell from the half bun it was pulled into and tickled my jaw as I moved my gaze between the three of them.

"One percent pure apple juice with no sugar added," Dean said, trying to keep a straight face as he crossed his massive arms over his chest.

"Do you agree to the terms, Plum?" Cael asked, extending his hand to me.

"Fine." I said, shaking it.

"Oh you're so fucked," Dean laughed as he and Ella turned on their heels out the tunnel.

CODY

Tweedle-dee and Tweedle-dumb had collected half the team, a few partners, and even some of the long term staff that hung around the stadium to help facilitate practices. As per usual the outfield had been made comfortable with pillows and blankets we kept in the storage locker on site.

"Wait, is it like a drive-in?" Clementine asked as we walked across the infield and onto the turf.

"Better," I said, as Jensen popped out from one of the service doors below the big screen used for games. It played replays, crowd reactions and kept the score. But on nights like this we used it for Karaoke.

"Cael," Clementine whined my name, and off her lips it sounded less like a plea for help and more like sin.

"You shook on it, Clem. There's no going back now." I smiled at her.

Today had been long, all I wanted to do was curl into bed and pray until my skin stopped itching and my head stopped pounding. But when she sauntered into the living room, all sass and tight pants, I couldn't deny that perfect pout a goddamn thing.

I missed Mama something fierce and I felt horrible but it made it hard to be around Clementine. She made me so happy, but then the guilt seeped in on these days when memories were darker than they should be and I'd rather be alone. Not because I was mad at her, but because it made it hard to control the urges, nearly impossible.

Even now I had my hands in my pockets, picking at the seams and pulling the threads loose to keep my mind busy. Clementine looked horrified but Karaoke had turned into a pastime that we all enjoyed. Maybe a little too much. It had been a lot more fun when Arlo would sneak in a flask of vodka, only to share it with us behind Silas' back.

"Alright." Van pulled a mug out. It was yellowed and the Hornets logo looked like it might be from the early years of the team, peeling and cracking on the side as he held it out to the group. "Everyone draws."

Inside was a series of popsicle sticks, some clearly had been chewed on, and I laughed as Clementine took notice with disgust on her face. She took it out and held it up.

"Three?" She said, angling it in the air so I could see it.

"The number on your stick is the order we go in," Mitchell explained, as the rest of the group drew sticks. Dean yipped with excitement as he drew one and the entire field lit up with groans.

"Get ready to drink," Ella laughed, as we all settled into the blankets.

"Will he really?" Clementine asked, her thigh brushing against mine as she sat between Ella and I.

"It's a rare occasion when Dean *doesn't* sing it." I pushed my hair back off my face and leaned back on my elbows to stare up at the big screen as it lit up brightly across the dark field. It took them a moment to get the song up but, as predicted, *Party in the USA* blasted over the field.

The sound scared Clementine, her whole body flinching next to mine, but I didn't mind because she leaned into my shoulder and tilted her head up in the cutest way possible. The lights from the screen twinkled in her eyes and mimicked the stars.

Her giggle echoed in the form of fireworks down my spine as Dean started to sing terribly out of tune only to be distracted by Van tapping my shoulder and handing me a cup of apple juice with a wink.

It was such a simple gesture but it created a wave of gratitude I wasn't prepared for. The expectation going into recovery was that none of them would want to be my friend if I wasn't that goofy guy they loved so much. The party animal with a lack of regard for his own safety and always dialed up to one hundred.

There had been a real fear when I returned from rehab that I wouldn't belong in the Nest anymore. It was ridiculous but, at the time, so sober and in so much pain, it was tangible to my twisted, fractured mind.

But I had been so far from right. They had hung stupid banners with their second grade printing skills and cleaned out all the fridges in the Nest of alcohol. Instead of disowning me or shunning me because of it, they embraced the sobriety and made it their lifestyle too.

Of course they all still drank outside of the Nest, birthdays and parties at Delta. I could handle myself and, when I couldn't, I searched out Ella or my sponsor and we handled it together. But recovery had looked a lot different than expected and I couldn't have been more grateful.

"Hey, Daydream," Clementine whispered to me and I shook from my thoughts to look over at her. "You alright?" She asked and I nodded because, for the first time today, I actually felt like I was.

I had spaced out through most of Dean's horrible rendition and came back to reality half way through Jensen belting out some Queen song that only he and Van knew word for word.

"You're next," I said to her with a tiny smirk.

"Switch me," she begged.

"Sorry that's against the rules," I laughed and looked at the scribbled five on my stick.

"You said there were only three rules and that wasn't one of them." Clementine poked me with her stick. "Trade me spots."

"What are you going to do for it?" I smiled up at her, offering her the chance. "Before you answer, I'll sing everyone's turn here for just one kiss."

"Shut up and let me think," she groaned.

Her eyes trailed over my body and it lit me up like a raging fire, heat licked every inch of my skin under that chocolate gaze. I could see her trying to come up with something that might be worthy of such a trade, her teeth sinking into her bottom lip and calling attention to how full it was.

She leaned down, her lips brushing against my ears.

"You can tie me up," she whispered, heat raging as her breath fanned over my skin. "Once, whenever you call it in."

My eyes flickered to meet hers as she pulled away and stared down at me through heavy lashes. Her nose scrunched up when I didn't answer but I loved to watch her squirm. For all her gained confidence she was still so easily rattled; it had taken everything in her to offer that. And now it was taking everything in me not to pick her up, carry her to the closest room with a lock, and make good on it.

"Fine," I said tightly, shifting to adjust myself. "But you can't say no when I come to collect." I pushed from the ground and walked over to Jensen.

"I swear to god, Cael!" Van groaned and Zoey instantly lost it in a fit of laughter as the first chords to Like A Prayer blasted over the speakers.

"We should add this song to the rules," Dean shouted over the sound of my voice as the first chorus rounded.

Strutting towards him I used my free hand to yank my shirt over my head and flicked it at him while I sang. He pushed it off his face and glared at me. I blew him a kiss and belted the next lyrics with both hands on the mic and my chin tilted to the sky.

"You sing it so much that I hear it in my nightmares!" He threw his empty juice cup at me as I sang in his face.

I jumped out of the way with a goofy grin on my face and wandered over to stand in front of Clementine in the grass, her eyes never leaving mine.

"*When you call my name, it's like a little prayer,*" I sang, and the blush crept to her full cheeks. With a smile I dropped to my knees before her. "*I'm down on my knees.*"

She shook her head at me and all the images of me on my knees for her flooded back, memories I never wanted to forget. Clementine mouthed the next line along with my obnoxiously loud voice with a smile on her face and a twinkle in her eyes.

There was something about this song that made me feel alive, like an adrenaline rush to the system. Maybe it was the act of singing it for them that did it because, as I spun around acting like a fool, I realized I didn't actually listen to this song unless I was singing it...

I dropped back to my knees in the turf and sang the last chorus as loudly as I could until their claps roared and I took my bow.

"Thank you, thank you," I said dramatically and winked at Clementine. Van rose to take his turn and I chucked the mic at him before settling back down against Clementine.

"Good luck following that up." I kissed her cheek before she could stop me and rolled back onto the blanket beneath me.

"You guys are so dramatic," she huffed, clearly nervous.

"Do you know what song you're going to pick?"

She fidgeted with the blanket under her butt and thought about it quietly with a small hum that wasn't much of an answer.

"It's harder than expected to just *pick* a song to sing." Clementine laughed. "Do I go nostalgic and do something I know?"

"Hah!" I barked. "Every song you know well enough to call nostalgic is a depressing country ballad, please don't do that." I put my hands up in mock surrender and fell back against the blanket, giving her the space to lean over my chest.

"Oh come on, they aren't all depressing. They're about love," she argued, with a small pout that begged for a kiss.

My will power waned under the sight but, no matter how badly I needed reprieve, I wouldn't break the intense eye contact we held.

"Love is *depressing*," I whispered to her and she pulled back, narrowing her eyes at me. We both knew I didn't believe it but, in the moment, unable to show her how much I did love her, it sure felt that way.

"Mary," Jensen sang into the mic as his song ended. "You're up."

She pushed off my chest and it took everything in me not to grab her and pull her back into my space. The world felt a little colder without her body pressed up against mine and I grumbled as I rolled to sit up, earning a small chuckle from Ella.

"She's good," Ella said quietly as Clementine whispered to Jensen and they scrolled through his phone looking for songs.

My face must have read as confused because Ella sighed.

"She pulls you out of your own head. It's like there's a string tied to both of you and one tug is enough to balance you out," she explained. "I can see why she's your *happy*, Misery.

MATTHEWS

I had been here almost three weeks longer than expected, but I was dragging my feet and taking my time. Tony had called repeatedly for updates, but I kept making excuses. *"I'm on to something. Give me an extension."* He had agreed, but I knew I was pushing my luck.

I selfishly needed more time with Cael.

The connection between us had shifted that day in the batting cages. Cael's apologies had gone from heated and physical to small gestures of attention that did more for my heart than I wanted to admit to anyone. Even Bobbi.

She had called for an update the day after, but I hadn't been able to give her an honest answer. One simple hug, so tender, it was a sedative to all my hardened edges and dangerous thoughts. I hated his ability to be both people at once. Crazy, free, and funny, but quiet, careful, and purposeful with his intention all at the same time. I was just a mess. I just wasn't sure if I could be what he needed.

I wasn't stupid. The second Silas had mentioned the accident, the look on his face gave away more than if he had even told me the truth. I had gone through six more interviews. I didn't need to do the second string members of the team, but I wanted more information and, in doing so, delayed my departure from Rhode Island. Not a single one of them gave me anything on Cael. I had to finish his interview and still needed to speak to Dean and his father, but I had a feeling they wouldn't be helpful.

So I went digging. Cael was a mess. Drugs, alcohol, experimentation. It seemed like he had done everything in his power to piss off his Dad over the last seven years. All while still pretending to be that sweet boy with his bright smile. An all-star athlete, on the baseball field and off, he was stumbling through the minefield of his own mind. I wanted to ask him about it, about why he did the drugs and drank himself into that state, but it really wasn't any of my business anymore.

"Knock knock." Ella's voice floated to me from the doorway.

She leaned against it, dressed in her navy shirt and jeans from work, blonde hair tucked up away from her face. I had looked closer at her as well, letting jealousy get the better of me, but only found more sadness and understood within three lines of the article why she and Cael had bonded. It wasn't romantic. Their souls were just missing a piece that the other was able to fill in ways that no one else could. Platonic in the heaviest sense. Ella had lost her brother, Cael had lost himself, and when they found each other, the scales became balanced again.

"Sorry." I pressed pause on my music. "Was it too loud?"

"No." Ella waved a hand in the air and stood up straight. "There's a Halloween party at Delta tonight. Arlo is away in Dallas, so I was wondering if you'd be my date?"

A Halloween party.

"Zoey and I are going to the thrift store to find something to wear," she added, when I didn't answer her immediately.

Old Clementine would have declined, Halloween was never my favorite, but the new Clementine was a different monster, so I nodded, and Ella went from nervous to excited in a millisecond. It was the perfect opportunity to remind Cael he wasn't courting the same seventeen-year-old by the creek.

"I have an idea." I smiled at her and she cocked her head to the side.

"Oh, I like the look in your eye." She laughed.

"Do you have a key for the equipment room?" I asked.

Delta was packed, making the party at Hilly's look like child's play. The entire house was dark, lit only by flashing white lights and hanging purple bulbs, which gave everything an eerie feeling.

"God, I hate the east coast, it's freezing outside." Zoey climbed from the car and tiptoed in her tennis shoes across the grass. "But, shit, we look so hot!"

She was right. We looked really good. Ella had done her part well. Sneaking down to the stadium, she'd lifted three specific Hornets jerseys from the locker room. Zoey had hers buttoned up, her legs bare except for her short spanks underneath the hem. Van's jersey was like a dress on her, but she looked amazing with her long brown hair in two high pigtails and a smear of dark makeup across her cheek.

Ella did a flirty spin, resting her baseball bat over her shoulders. Her blonde hair fell around her face in soft curls, which had matching markings to Zoey. Arlo's jersey rode up on her thighs, exposing the tight jean shorts beneath.

"Take a picture for me?" She handed me her phone and pulled at the undone buttons of Arlo's jersey to expose the white bra beneath, the long chain and ring dangling between the swell. "I *begged* him not to go to Dallas this weekend," she said, taking her phone back with a mischievous grin. "The least I can do is make him regret his very responsible adult decision."

"Looking good, ladies!" Jensen and Todd hung from the railing of Delta in matching mustard and ketchup outfits.

"They look like idiots," Zoey huffed, linking her arm to mine.

We walked up the steps of Delta and into the house to find Van arguing with Dean. Van was dressed as a pirate and his head snapped to where we were. I could have sworn a stream of drool dripped from his open mouth.

Dean looked cute in what might have been a toga but was definitely just a white sheet with a knot on his muscular shoulder. His eyes ran over me with a cautious look on his handsome face, a storm brewing, but he wasn't the attention I cared about. Cael, in all his half-naked glory, lay lazily over the staircase, with two girls chatting on either side of him. His blue eyes flickered over me and a wicked smile formed on his face at the sight.

Cael's jersey hung over my shoulders, buttoned in the middle by two small buttons that did nothing to hide the lacy, black, harnessed bra beneath it. Our eyes didn't leave each other's as Zoey pulled from my grip and slipped into Van's, or when the jersey slipped open and exposed my thighs, but I could see the restraint flickering over his sharp features. His fingers gripped tightly to the bottle he was holding, and the muscle in his jaw ticked.

"Hey." Zoey tugged gently on one of the two braids she had laced with navy ribbon, so we really looked at the part. "Come on." She dragged me through the house, that was crowded with people, to the kitchen, and Van handed me a solo cup full of what smelled like lighter fluid.

"Jungle Juice." He laughed and kissed Zoey on the cheek.

"It smells disgusting." I laughed back.

"It *is* disgusting, bottoms up." Van tapped two fingers to his chest and the rest of the men in the room followed.

"Drink the Kool-Aid, Mary." Ella giggled, pressing her fingers under my cup and lifting it to my lips. "It'll be good for you."

The entire college experience was foreign to me. I had gone, I had studied, and I had even participated in after-school activities, but nothing to the extent of how the students at Harbor University did. Their parties felt like a moving time capsule. It was as if they were dragged straight from a 90s slasher film. It was intoxicating.

"What are you supposed to be anyways?" Dean appeared from our left, his eyes on me as he sipped from his cup.

"We're *bat bunnies.*" Ella lifted herself onto the counter and leaned forward with her fingers curling around the edge.

"How degrading of you," Dean joked and slid in beside her, his height still eclipsing her as he leaned over and whispered something that brought a smile to her face.

"It was last minute," I said, defending the cleverness of our outfits. "And if you take the degradation of the term 'bat bunny' and use it against those who coined the term. Isn't that a shift of power?"

Dean's brows furrowed, and Van snorted.

"So, really, it's pretty empowering of us."

Ella watched the interaction with a funny look on her face.

"Sure," Dean licked the trace of booze off his bottom lip as his eyes darted up away from me to Cael, who had moved into the kitchen behind me.

I only knew he was there because I could smell the citrus cologne that mimicked that sweet gummy bear smell, it coated his skin and wafted through the stench of drunk college kids. Cael stood at my back, his hand hidden as his fingers rubbed the fabric of his jersey at the hem along the curve of my ass.

"If I had known a group costume was happening, I would have joined." He pouted. "I would have looked better in that than you. Everyone knows I'm Arlo's bat bunny." He pointed at Ella with a smile on his face and the bottle he was babying between his fingers.

Ella scowled at the liquid sloshing around inside.

"It's water, Peach." He tossed the bottle through the air at her, and she popped the lid, unashamed, and smelled it. I was slightly offended for Cael, but he didn't seem to care, catching it in his hand as she chucked it back to him.

"You though..." He turned to me, voice dropping in tone and eyes dragging down over my body. "I've never seen that jersey look so good."

"And you wear it every night," I cooed back. "So that's saying something."

Cael blushed, with red cheeks and dewy-looking eyes, as he exhaled.

I thought for a second he might do something brash in public, but he tossed his arm around me and smiled, tucking me into his side. "Let's give Mary," he choked out the name, "a true Harbor Hornets Halloween." He looked down at me, and the mischief in his smile made the tips of my fingers tingle.

"What exactly does that entail?" I asked as a few of them moved through the house to what might have been a dining room, but it was covered in silly string and fake skeletons. The music thumped through the walls from the living room on the other side, and it was hard to hear myself think.

"Poker." Van smiled.

"That feels underwhelming after stadium karaoke." I sat in the chair that Cael pulled out for me and took Ella's drink as she wandered around to my left.

"They always play for something," she whispered in my ear as she sat down. "They're also really fucking bad, none of them have poker faces."

"Not fair, because Ella hasn't lost a game since..." Cael waved his hand in the air and rolled his eyes dramatically. "Well, I've never seen her lose...so statistically her opinion is flawed."

Dean sat across the table from me, between Van and Zoey, while Cael took a spot beside me. "So what are we playing for, clothing?"

Strip poker was something I had never played, but I was certainly down to try.

"Nah." Van shook his head. "We've all seen each other naked. It's not fun anymore."

"It's always fun to see me naked," Cael chirped.

Ella dealt the cards with a smirk on her face.

Dean grunted and checked his hand with a scowl.

"So what then?" I asked. When Cael looked up at me over his cards, my body trembled in response, his lip between his teeth and fire behind his ocean eyes. "We play for keeps." He shrugged, and I watched his pupils flare. "We play for orgas—"

"Absolutely not," I said before he could finish. He was trying to wager our intimacy over a poker game, and I saw right through him.

He leaned in close, whispering against my skin, and said, "you can have anyone. It doesn't have to be *me*." His tongue ghosted over my ear lobe and my cunt throbbed from the sensation that flickered down over my skin. "You can pick any Hornet you want." His voice was hot against my neck. "But keep it inside the Nest. The prospects in the Delta pool are infested."

"Infested?" I asked, trying to hide my laughter.

"STIs." Zoey giggled. "They have a running line outside the doctor's office." She pointed to a group of six standing in a huddle. Three of the six had shifted uncomfortably, clearly itchy.

"All holes are goals with those guys," Van sighed like he had seen the horrors of Delta firsthand.

"So *any* Hornet I want?" I questioned Cael.

"Within reason." He shrugged. "Best to leave Van alone unless you wanna wrestle Sour Patch in the pudding pool outback."

"I mean, that could be—"A hard slap stifled Van's comment.

"Any Hornet."

My eyes widened as I pulled back to look at him. I hadn't expected that.

"Anyone?" I asked as my lips started to curl.

He nodded, and I picked up my hand, eyes lingering on Cael before I checked it.

"I want *him*." I looked up from my cards, eyes landing on Dean Tucker, and felt Cael tense beside me. He had expected me to pick him, but I had seen his hands all over that girl on the stairs. His mind and hands wandered. Why couldn't mine?

A punishment suited to the crime.

The question was, would Dean play with him as the stakes?

Cael looked over at him, all the color leaving his face for a second, as Dean continued to glare at me. The tension in the room rose the longer Dean remained silent, but Cael exhaled a heavy breath as he finally spoke.

"Fine," he bit back. "But don't get your hopes up."

MATTHEWS

I may have been terrible at hitting baseballs, but I could play a hand of poker if the stakes were good, and they had never been higher. We played six rounds. Every round came down to Dean and me, staring each other down, waiting for the card to drop. He had won two rounds, but I was up and, if I won this one, which I would, I would win the bargain. I could tell he wasn't amused, but it didn't matter.

Cael didn't question my decision. He had walked himself into a corner, and he was willing to sit like a good boy and watch the situation unfold. But he was fidgeting. His fingers traced lazy circles up and down my thigh, and I knew his hand was a bust by the way they paused as Ella dealt the next card.

Dean was harder to read, and Van had nothing; I could tell by the way he kept nervously shifting in his seat. Zoey, though, was his biggest tell. Leaning over his shoulder, she continuously brushed her fingers through his hair with a disappointed look on her face.

When I turned to look at Ella, she just raised an eyebrow at me, as if to say *this is why I don't play anymore*. It was like playing with a table of toddlers.

"Three of a kind," Dean laid his cards out, three eights.

I looked down at my cards, feigning disappointment as Van laid down his garbage hand, and Cael followed with nothing but a subtle groan.

Ella had dropped a ten on the table and won the round for me with the flick of her wrist.

"Does four tens beat three eights?" I tilted my head to the side. "I'm just a bat bunny so I'm not really good at math."

144

"There's math in poker?" Van asked, confused, and Zoey tugged on his mullet gently. "That would explain why I'm so bad at it."

"How drunk are you?" Zoey giggled and kissed the lines of his confused face as the rest of us sat waiting for someone to make a move.

Dean pushed his cards to the center of the table and stood. He then walked around to my side of the table, stopping beside Cael, who seemed to stop breathing.

"You won." He held out his hand to me. "You don't have a card up your sleeve, do you?"

"Do you wanna pat me down and check?" I asked, pulling open the front of my jersey to expose the swell of my breast in the bra.

Cael grunted, choking on his own spit.

All of a sudden the air shifted. Before it felt like I was in control, punishing Cael for being a shit head, but I could see that Dean had needed it more than I ever did. I licked my lip and winked. "No sleeves."

"Fair point." He linked his hand in mine. "You never specified what you wanted me for."

"A dance." I smiled and felt Cael deflate beside me with relief.

I just wanted to talk to Dean in a setting that made him more comfortable.

"Alright." He nodded and turned without another word.

I followed him through the house and could *feel* Cael on our heels as Dean pushed out into the dark, crowded dance floor and wrapped me up in his strong arms. Fake fog rose from the floor in suffocating clouds and turned the whole room into nothing but thumping music and grinding bodies beneath the purple lights. His chest was warm, and the fabric of his toga tickled the bare expanse of my thighs as he swung around in circles.

"I know who you are," he said to me, his lips pressed to my cheek. "I don't know if he's told anyone else but you, the *lavender girl*. You're nothing but *lore* in the Nest. A ghost story."

"Is that why you stare at me like I am one?" I asked him as his hand pressed against my lower back and ground our hips together.

"I don't stare," he huffed.

"You could burn a hole in a girl." I shook my head. "Cael's a big boy," I added.

"Cael is my best friend," he corrected, a vicious hush to his tone.

"I don't need a conversation about respecting him and what you'll do to me if I don't, Dean." I swallowed tightly as he started to laugh and swung me out wide.

"I'm not worried about *him*." Dean laughed, the first time I've ever heard him truly do it. His features lightened and the blue in his eyes sparkled against the dark, hazy purple of the living room. It felt like we were dancing through fairy dust when he pulled me back close and whispered in my ear. "It's *you* that's in trouble."

Dean was missing information. He knew only one side of the story.

Cael hadn't asked again, either. If he did now I might have told how many there have been. All meaning nothing, all forgettable. I wasn't the naive lavender girl they all thought I was.

I didn't have time to respond before a second set of hands wrapped around my thigh and dug into the tender inside pulling me back against him. Dean moved closer, pressing himself against my front while Cael danced from behind. Hands-on skin and lips to my throat, I felt like they were everywhere all at once. I couldn't get enough of the intense adrenaline rush that it gave me. The tingling sensation filled my veins and set my body on fire as Cael's hands raked over my stomach beneath his jersey.

"You can have it, you know," he whispered lightly. "You can have all of it. Dean will let you."

Dean smiled down at me, but his eyes flickered dangerously to Cael's, and it finally set in who they were to each other. *Cael is my best friend.* Cael was his lover.

The air shifted for a second time and suddenly I couldn't breathe.

"We've done it before." Dean dipped his lips against my throat, and I hummed against his touch as Cael's sultry laughter filled my ear. "We're a really good team," he said as he pulled back, hooking a finger into the top of my jersey and pulling me away from Cael, the warmth at my back dissipating for a split second as he spun me again to face the other direction.

"Ask him, Clem." Cael mouthed the words, but I could hear the order in his voice, and it made my toes curl.

Dean extended his hand around Cael, pulling us tightly together as the music became muted, and there was nothing else in the room but the three of us. His lusty gaze trailed over my skin to Dean behind me, with a mischievous smile on his face that stirred my gut and disturbed all the sleeping butterflies.

"I want it all." I tipped my chin to the sky, catching Dean's attention. "Will you do that? For me?" I asked him, and his tongue darted out over his bottom lip in response as he nodded. "Is there somewhere we can go?"

"The Nest," Dean said.

"That's so far," I pouted, and Cael flicked his thumb over my bottom lip.

"We aren't doing anything in this cesspool."

Cael turned, offering himself for a piggyback, and I obliged him. He wrapped his strong arms around his back and supported my ass as Dean led us from the frat house into the cold air. The walk back to the Nest seemed faster than the trip down the hill. Maybe it was because of their long legs or the mounting excitement. Cael's fingers dug into my skin and heat pooled between my legs with each passing second and stolen glance. We were crashing through the door of the house before I knew it, and Cael let me slide from his back.

I dodged his lips as he pulled me close and stared at him with fire in my eyes.

"Oh, come on," he growled low, and his eyes narrowed on my lips.

"Rules are rules, Loverboy." I kissed his sharp jaw to keep myself from instantly breaking all of them. It would be torture to have him like this and not kiss him, but I had to stand my ground. It was the last defense against becoming that girl again.

Feeling the tension, Dean's arms wrapped around my middle, and he scooped me into his arms, carrying me the rest of the way to Cael's room and throwing me on the bed. Both of them stood tall above him, Cael leaning over to flick on the lamp beside the bed as I kicked off my shoes and curled into the mattress.

I watched silently and impatiently as Dean flicked the snaps of Cael's ridiculous gladiator kilt and dropped it to the floor, exposing the tight boxers and the full length of Cael beneath. Heat licked at my core; it had been a long time since I felt that pressed against me, but my body trembled for it, begging him quietly with each clench. I pressed my thighs together, trying to hide the need as Cael kissed a line over Dean's bicep and unknotted the white fabric of his costume.

My teeth scraped against my bottom lip at the sight of them, tanned, toned bodies and big blue eyes. It was a dream I never wanted to wake from. Dean cupped Cael's neck with one hand and placed a line of slow, sloppy kisses to his throat as Cael raked his eyes down my body, his fingers reaching out for my ankle.

MATTHEWS

"**C**ome here," he growled, and I giggled as my ass slid across the bed. "You've been teasing us with this all night." He dropped to his knees between my legs, and Dean crawled onto the bed behind me.

He tugged roughly on the braid in my hair and exposed my neck to his lips as Cael snapped the buttons on his jersey, sending them flying through the dimly lit room. He laughed with a playful shrug and pushed the jersey down over my shoulders until it was hanging at my wrists.

"Are you nervous?" Dean asked, his chest leaning against my back and his mouth brushing over my ear.

"Should I be?" I swallowed tightly, but I wasn't. Only excitement coursed through me.

"I warned you, he bites." Cael kissed a line over my stomach as his fingers tickled the base of the black harness, looking for a way in.

Dean's teeth dug into my shoulder and my hips arched into Cael's grip. A delicious spike of pain ripped over my skin, and I wiggled for more attention. "So needy," Cael whispered. "Look at her."

His words were like lighter fluid igniting the kindling in my stomach, and heat exploded over my skin as his teeth grazed the fabric along the swell of my breast. Wetness pooled in my underwear as Cael's full length rubbed against my inner thigh, and Dean wrapped his arm around me to pull me back onto the bed.

With my head tilted, I could kiss Dean, his lips finding mine aggressively. It was hot but I could tell it was a show. Cael's growl was deep as his fingers traced the edges of my shorts and dipped between my thighs. I broke from the kiss to find him staring at us, a possessive snarl on his lips, waiting for *something*.

"Do you need an invitation, Loverboy?" I narrowed my eyes at him and let my leg fall open.

Dean's hand raked over my shoulder, massaging my skin until his fingers managed to work their way under the harness. My hips bucked as his fingers found my nipple and pinched hard enough to draw a low whine from my lips.

Cael watched for a moment longer, one hand half in my shorts and the other gripped tightly to Dean's massive thigh as he watched us. Blue eyes so bright they could have been mistaken for fire as a smile formed on his lips.

"Cat got your tongue?" I pushed harder.

"You're brave for being outnumbered," he said and dipped his fingers into me.

My core was wet and aching for his touch as he plunged two fingers deep without warning. Cael pulled away just as quickly, leaving me gasping for his touch as he shucked the shorts from my thighs and tossed them across the room. He sunk down against my thigh, dipping his head between them and taking my clit into his mouth as he pushed his fingers back inside.

A throaty moan left Dean as he snapped the strap of my bra.

"Ow," I whined, and he kissed my back where it had bit into my skin, working his way back to my throat only to replace it with his hand. He was more deliberate than Cael, moving slowly, taking his time to tease my skin as Cael lapped at my core and drove me to the edge.

"Fuck me, Cael!" I cried out as he hooked his fingers against me and bit down on my clit.

His face was covered in wetness as he climbed my body, his hands covering every inch of my skin as he went. There was no teasing or preparation when he pushed into me quickly.

I gripped his shoulder, and my nails dug into his skin as my body clenched around his massive cock. It pressed painfully against the walls of my overworked core, raking against the G-spot creating small waves of tingling pleasure. A tiny chuckle left his lips as he angled his chin upward toward Dean with wide, glassy eyes.

"Do you want a taste?" He whispered, and my body shuddered at the sound as Dean licked his lips and wrapped a big hand around Cael's face, bringing him in for a long, heated kiss.

Cael's hips rolled against me as he reached for Dean's embrace. They broke in a breathless huff, and the focus shifted again.

"Fuck, you're so tight," Cael groaned, his hand found my hip and pressed me roughly down into the bed. His tone was gentle as I lifted my leg and wrapped it around him to steady his rhythm.

Cael felt so damn good inside of me. My body ached for seven years for that feeling. My fingers raked into his hair, and I whined in his ear, telling him just how deep he was and how good it felt to be that full. My words lit a fire and his hips rocked harder against my ass as Dean managed to pop the second button on the harness, releasing my breasts from the fabric. They spilled into his hand, and his fingers brushed painfully over my sensitive nipples.

Cael's eyes widened, and he dipped his mouth over the unattended nipple quickly, his teeth grazing but never biting. They were surprisingly good at sharing as Cael continued to mindlessly fuck me against his best friend.

"I'm going to fuck you until you can't hold anymore of me." Cael growled against my ear, "I want you to scream my name, Plum, *beg me.*"

My head fell against Dean's chest as Cael's pace became brutal, and his grip on my hip grew tight enough to leave bruises, but I kept my mouth shut. He would have to work harder for that if he wanted it.

"I want the entire Nest to know exactly who you are," Cael demanded, slipping slowly from my center. His length ran against me at a torturous pace until his tip popped from my entrance, and he slipped through my folds. "Who you belong to."

I shuddered at his touch, and Dean chuckled against my skin. His lips and teeth praised my sweaty jawline. "You should listen to him." Dean gripped my throat gently and angled my face toward Cael.

"Scream my name." He hovered above us.

I wasn't going to break as easily as he wanted. Free of his cock, I tipped my foot over, knocking him off balance enough to flip on the bed and pushed Dean back against it. My mouth found him, and he tasted faintly of Cael and me all tangled together. I rolled my hips down against Dean's massive length, eyes wide at his size.

His eyes searched mine as his teeth nipped at my bottom lip, and his hands roamed over my ass roughly. Cael was out of sight and mind, and I knew it would drive him insane.

Dean knew. I could see it all over his face that he understood the assignment. Even though we normally weren't on the same side, tonight, we were. Before Cael could balance himself and take control, Dean's hands were around my hips, lifting me up and preparing to guide me down over him. But Dean wasn't hard for me, and we both knew it with shitty grins on our faces and mischief in Dean's eyes. Teasing him was leaving me soaked, and him going mad from the sight of us.

"Fuck that," Cael growled from behind me. Still perched over Dean, his hands replaced Dean's and tugged my ass back against him. "This is *mine*," he snapped, sinking without warning deep into my soaked core.

"Oh, God." I gripped Dean's chest, nails digging into his skin hard enough to leave marks as my walls throbbed around Cael's shaft, with his cock plunging deep inside of me, sparking nodes of pain that mixed dangerously with pleasure. I giggled gently, my body rocking forward against Dean's chest as Cael worked relentlessly.

Dean's hand found my ass again, gripping at the soft curves as Cael remained silent out of view. I could feel the burning gaze from him on my back as I rolled down to meet his hips over and over again. The pleasure licked at my stomach and warmed my core at an alarming pace, and if he continued his brutal rhythm, I wouldn't last much longer.

Dean's mouth found mine as his hand twisted around a braid, bringing me closer. His tongue swiped into my mouth, and Cael's hips thrust even faster than before. I moaned against him, my head fuzzy with desire. My pulse quickened as his fingers found my soaked clit and rubbed in tender circles, making every nerve in my body tingle. He pounded into me with reckless abandon.

Cael pulled out from me suddenly, leaving me gasping at the sudden chill. Only to appear beside us, his hand gripping Dean's chin and pulling him from our connection.

He wasn't very good at taking turns. I could feel it in his gaze and under Dean's grasp as Cael raked his hand through the shaggy blond curls roughly, tugging on the scalp until Dean's fingers dug into my hips, and he was gasping for air.

I dropped down further, angry at Cael for abandoning me. He was trying to rile me up, acting like making out with Dean was a punishment, but it only stoked the fire in my stomach further. I continued to sink down far enough until Dean's cock brushed the underside of my chin. His attention pulled to me for a split second as I wrapped my lips around Dean's massive erection, sucking until my cheeks hollowed out, and Dean's hips were stuttering beneath my touch. I peered up at the two of them, mouth full of cock, eyes watering from the size, and watched as they crashed against each other in a fury of teeth and tongue.

It didn't take long for Dean to come completely undone between the two of us. I sucked harder, swirling my tongue against his shaft delicately until his hand tangled in my hair, and I felt him tense. His cock pulsed deep within my throat as he filled me. It spilled from me as I looked up into Cael's stormy eyes. I felt exposed and electric as Dean lifted me by the arms back to him, brushing his thumb over my swollen lips as he worked to catch his breath.

But Cael was sick of sharing. He moved around us quietly, licking his lips as he crawled onto the bed behind me. His hands wrapped around my waist and pulled me away from Dean without a second thought.

"Enough," he moaned, the sound low in my ear as he pulled me against his chest and laid me on the bed.

There was a fervor in his eyes that wasn't there before, and I could feel the restraint as he fought internally over whether or not he should cross the lines we set.

"Do you want me?" He asked quietly as Dean recovered, his soft pants filling the room as he repositioned himself against my side.

"Answer him." Dean kissed my shoulder as his hand dipped between us and found my aching clit. The touch alone made my body shiver, and my hips rose to meet Cael's as he hovered above me, waiting for an answer.

I nodded, a tiny whimper leaving my lips.

"Out loud, Clementine," he said. "I want to hear you say it."

Cael knew what he was doing. It wasn't about the sex or fucking him. He wanted confirmation.

"I want you," I whispered.

A wicked grin formed, and he pushed in, dragging a tiny yelp from my lips as he rolled his hips until he was embedded to the hilt.

"That's my girl," he whispered, his teeth grazing my ear lobe before he turned his attention to Dean. He pressed tightly to my chest, his arms wrapping around me as his hips continued to roll against mine. Dean lifted to meet him. Kissing him softer than I had expected. It was surreal watching them interact so intimately while I fought against the shove of pleasure that built violently in the base of my stomach.

Cael was softer than Dean, like he was reminiscing.

"Don't stop," I whispered, because the present was tangled with the past, and small flickers of who Cael and I used to be kept flashing across my dizzied vision.

"Clem, you gotta talk to me, I don't want to hurt you."

I could hear his voice in my head and his hands on my hot skin without the ability to tell real from fake. My heart was racing in my chest as he broke the kiss with Dean and looked down at me, brushing the sweaty, loose strands of hair away from my face.

I could tell all he wanted to do was kiss me.

It was written all over his beautiful, sharp face.

Those bright, blue eyes filled with longing and sadness as his lips curled downward. How could something that started so fun and feral become so heartbreakingly painful?

"Buck up, Loverboy, and finish the job," I choked out, just trying to hold on to the Clementine I was now so as not to lose her to the shy, scared Clem I had been back then.

"Always so mouthy, aren't you?" He groaned and pounded into me faster than time. Each thrust shook the bed and forced my orgasm higher.

I was overstimulated, my core raw, but he didn't slow down even when Dean rolled into me and took one of my nipples into his mouth or when his fingers slid down to my clit.

Overwhelmed, Cael hammered into me faster while Dean circled my aching core relentlessly. The bed shook beneath me, caught between pushing myself into extreme pleasure and letting the heartbreaking memories of Cael Cody sweep me away.

I was fine.

Foggy almost, and ready to finish, until Cael opened his stupid, pretty mouth. His disheveled blond hair stuck to his strong neck, and his lips red from kissing Dean.

"You're so beautiful." The praise was too tender. I could feel the swell of butterflies as they rose through me. I needed the cocky boy. I couldn't handle this tangled version of grown Cael and the seventeen-year-old version of him that had been left branded to my skin after our first time.

"Shut up," I blurted out. "Just shut up and fuck me, Cael."

Dean pulled my chin toward him, capturing my lips in a rough kiss as Cael huffed, dipping down and kissing my neck.

"Cael," I whined loudly against Dean. The kiss was enough distraction for me as the orgasm tore through my body, and Cael stiffened on top of me. "Fuck!" I gripped tightly to his biceps as he rocked forward roughly, hitting every unstable, overworked nerve. His cock throbbed as he completed his promise of both of them taking turns to fill me to the brim. Dean's sticky orgasm was still clinging to my throat, and Cael's was dripping from between my thighs.

Cael silently rolled off of me, sandwiching me between their giant, sweaty bodies. Dean rubbed lazy circles against my thigh as I worked to catch my breath. Cael didn't say a word, his eyes plastered to the dark ceiling above us.

I had a feeling I had made a mistake.

Fucking him for the first time, since the first time. Doing it with his best friend hadn't been the plan, but they were hard to resist and, at the time, I thought it would push Cael further away.

Instead, it only reopened old wounds that I thought were healed.

And I had a feeling it opened wounds I didn't understand between the two of them.

Shit.

The adrenaline from the orgasm was wearing off, and the panic was seeping in.

"I should go," I pushed away from Dean, kissing his cheek. "This—"

"You stay, I'll go," Cael panted between shallow breaths, rolling his sweaty, tanned chest further away from me.

"No," I protested. Even if I felt welcome, this room, this space. It wasn't mine to invade. "Thank you," I hummed, my legs still wobbly from the orgasm as I found the floor and collected my shorts. "This was... fun..." I groaned and wrapped the buttonless jersey around my chest as best as I could to at least cover myself for the shameful exit.

I didn't look at Cael. I couldn't. Instead, I just backed away and closed the door behind me. It was only when I was safe in the guest room, the door locked behind me, that I sunk to the floor and cried.

Some wounds never heal.

MATTHEWS

I snuck out.

Me, Clementine Mary Matthews, snuck out of my house to go to a house party across town without my Daddy's permission and *without* Cael.

My hands shook at my side. Most of the walk over there was spent trying to convince myself of why I should turn back and go home. But Kiefer Hart, from my advanced Socials class, had told me specifically to come.

"It'll be fun, and all the girls that usually show up are all the same. Having some fresh faces around to talk to would be nice."

Kiefer was cute, *really cute*. A six-foot hockey player for our high school team. He had dark, wavy hair that he always shoved under a cowboy hat when we weren't in class and big, glassy green eyes that looked like the pine trees that grew along the highway leading into the city.

Cael hated him, from the tip of his black suede cowboy hat to the worn-out leather of his pointed cowboy boots. *'He's a showboat with a charming smile. There's nothing sweet or gentlemanly about that guy. All hockey players have an agenda, Plum.'*

It always sounded like Cael was jealous of him, but I still would go into the situation cautiously. Cael might have been jealous, but he wasn't usually wrong about people. The party was already pumping when I arrived in my jean shorts and *Brittany Spears* baggy t-shirt. I had tucked my long brown hair into a ponytail and put on a little bit of makeup.

For the first time in a long time, catching my reflection in the window didn't make me sad. I felt prettier than usual, which was enough of a win for me. Even if tonight was a bust, even if Kiefer was just being nice to the loner girl in class, I had taken what courage I had, dressed and came down here alone.

I pushed open the door into the crowded house, much bigger than mine, and it was going to be easy to get lost in a crowd of bodies. I stood by the door, picking at the frayed edges of my jean shorts, and a sudden sense of discomfort settled down over me.

Coming here alone might have been a mistake.

"Hey, Matthews!" A name called out to me as I turned to walk back out the front door. "Where are you going?" Kiefer slid into the space between me and the door, wearing an open Hawaiian shirt that exposed his muscular chest and a pair of low-cut jeans that showed off... *everything*.

"I—"

"In the time it took me to beeline from the living room to you, something changed up there." He tapped my temple. "You looked like you were going to bolt."

"Parties aren't really my..." I scrunched up my nose when he chuckled at my response.

"Give me twenty minutes," he said, stepping forward and creating distance between me and the doorknob. "If you still want to go, I'll walk you home."

I stared at him, my eyes flickering to the cup in his hand and back to his face.

"It's soda." He held it out for me to smell. "I don't drink, but the guys here partake in heavy peer pressure. It's my way of getting out of it."

"I don't know, Kiefer. I don't fit in here." I wrapped my arms around myself. He was sweet enough, charming in every aspect, but I couldn't see myself getting comfortable here.

"I think you fit in perfectly, Clementine. Twenty minutes."

He held out his elbow to me, and I wrapped my hand into its crook as he weaved us through the tightly packed dance floor and into the backyard. The air was sticky and warm on my skin, but Kiefer kept a tight hold on me as he led us over to where the rest of the hockey players were.

A few of them gave me looks but when Kiefer unlinked himself and threw his arm around my shoulder, they all turned their attention to other girls and issues.

"You look really pretty tonight," Kiefer said, leaning down to meet my ear. "I'm glad you came. The party was looking bleak without you."

"You're so full of it." I laughed at him and he mirrored my smile.

"No, really," he said softly. The lights from the paper lanterns that hung in limp strands around the backyard sparkled in his eyes.

"Thanks for inviting me," I said quietly, turning my face away from his as the blush crept up my neck to my cheeks.

"Can I get you a drink or..." he asked, and I shook my head. "Are you sure?" He stared at me like not needing anything was a crime, but I wasn't used to so much attention, and it was making my heart race in my chest.

He was too pretty.

Too close.

Smelled too nice.

A kid named Baxter, whom I knew from elementary school, wandered up to where we were all standing. Kiefer's attention was still on me as he whispered something else in my ear.

He made a face at me, and I tried to ignore it, but when he didn't stop staring, Kiefer turned on him. "What?"

"Nothing." Baxter raised his hands in the air. "I'm just surprised you got the..." he looked me over. "...recluse away from her journal. In elementary school, she used to pen the names of all the books she liked on the covers over and over. It was pathetic."

I swallowed tightly, waiting for Kiefer to laugh with him, but he just stared at Baxter.

"Even more surprising that you got her away from her guard dog," another hockey player chimed in.

"You got it wrong. She follows Cody around like a lost puppy and half the time he forgets she's even around until she makes a noise or something. I've seen him jump in the cafeteria when he remembers she's there."

The pit in my stomach grew. I knew eventually someone would call me out for the weird behavior, but no one outside of Kiefer had ever taken the time to talk to me. Cael wasn't in that class with us and, that day, someone had taken my seat and I was forced to sit beside Kiefer. It was just an accident. I tensed up beneath his arm and slipped away from his side.

"I should go," I said quietly and backed away from the group of laughing hockey players. Listening to them tell Kiefer how much better he could do, I brushed the back of my hand over my face and scooted through the crowd to the fence that led from the backyard.

The front street was quiet, with only the occasional street lamp to guide my way back to the path that led to my house. It was only a fifteen-minute walk, but the further I got down the street, the more apparent it became that Kiefer had listened to what they had to say and, yet again, I was alone.

"Aye, Matthews!" His voice echoed against the night sky, tangling with the breeze that pushed through the treetops. "Where are you going? My twenty minutes aren't up!"

I turned to see him jogging down the road. "It's been over," I said, shaking my head at him.

"Nope! You aren't allowed to count the two minutes those assholes wasted." He shrugged with a smile on his face that screamed *'I'm sorry.'*

"I told you I don't really fit in at parties like that, Kiefer. You tried, and the effort was noted. I'll see you in class next semester," I said with my arms wrapped around my body.

"No, hey." He shook his head. "That was my bad." He pulled off his hat, rubbing his hand over his neck, and looked up at me from the ground. "I should have asked you on a real date. I was just being a coward and thought having people around would make you more comfortable, but now..." He trailed off as he came to stand toe to toe with me. "I should have just listened to you."

My heart stopped at his confession. No boy had ever talked to me that way.

No boy except Cael.

"Are you cold?" He asked, brushing a finger down my arm. I shook my head. I just wanted to curl in on myself and become as small as possible at that moment. "Will you then?"

"Will I what?" I asked him.

"Let me take you on a date?" He laughed, hat still hanging from his fingertips as the wind tangled in his dark hair.

"Uh…" I opened and closed my mouth.

"Please?"

"I snuck out to come here tonight because my Daddy doesn't really let me… do fun teenager things?" I confessed, and my cheeks flushed.

"You go out with Cody all the time?" He questioned, and he wasn't wrong about his assumption.

"There's a rule that I'm not allowed to go out with anyone that my Daddy doesn't know."

"Then I'll come meet him." Kiefer shrugged. "I'll pick you up tomorrow in the afternoon. We can go to a movie. I'll have you home before the sun sets." He stared at me, his face begging me not to say no to him.

"Are you sure?" I asked in disbelief.

"Let me make up for tonight?" He pleaded. "One movie, and I'll meet your Daddy if that's the stipulation to get you out, pretty girl."

CODY

"You're more screwed than I thought." Dean was still lying in my bed, his hands under his head. The sun pushed through the curtains and bathed his naked torso in warmth, highlighting the spots where Clementine's nails had marked him the night before.

She hadn't been so inclined to stay.

"Are you sure you're not upset about last night?" I asked him, suddenly feeling too far away.

"It hasn't been easy, Cael." He looked up at me, and there was a pang of sadness that vibrated off of him. "But it was fun. I'm figuring things out about myself I didn't really understand. But I don't know," he swallowed, "seeing her with you yesterday, seeing..." He stopped and sat up so we were at eye level. "You've been different. Happier. We've all noticed. You haven't slipped, not once since she's been here."

"Don't do that, don't attach my recovery to her," I said lazily, putting my hand out. "I understand what you're saying, but I've been working hard before she got here."

"Yeah no, man, you have been. But she's made it *easier*," Dean said quietly, "and Cael." he scooted forward to take my face in his large hands, calloused from the bat. They scratch my skin in the best way as he lifts my chin to look at him. "It's alright that she has."

"Is it?" I narrowed my eyes at him because it didn't feel alright. "I enjoy the game we're playing, it's fun."

"But?" Dean asked, reading me like a book as I paused. A few tufts of his sweet blond hair fall against his forehead, and it takes everything in me not to be soft with him.

My heart aches. I wish I could love him the way he deserves.

"Do you know why she won't kiss me?"

She had kissed Dean because it meant nothing to her, because the kiss between them was nothing more than lustful attention. He shook his head.

"Because she's leaving," I said. My throat grew tight and the noose tightened with every thought I had about losing her again. "She's not staying at Harbor once this piece is done, and our past doesn't matter to her. She made that clear."

"What does a kiss have to do with that? She spent the half night screaming your name..." Dean looked at me, so pretty and so confused.

"That was *sex*." I explained. "It was fun. A kiss, a real kiss is—" I dug deep for the right word. "Intimate," I said. "It's a promise."

"A promise to stay."

"A promise to love each other." I nodded. "It's scary..."

"But you love her, right?" Dean asked, a shard of hurt flickered across his face.

I didn't answer him. I couldn't decide if I was upset or happy. The look on her face when I called her beautiful felt more like shards of glass embedding themselves in my heart and less like I had expected.

Clem had reacted like I'd slapped her.

But somewhere between losing her and finding her was this woman that I hadn't expected. She was everything that I wanted and I lost control of myself in the moment thinking I could have her. She read me like a book.

"Of course I do. I never stopped." I looked at the bed between us, trying to collect my thoughts, when Dean shoved me hard. I tumbled backward, smacking my head on the hardwood and scrambling to my feet.

"What the fuck?" I chucked a nearby shoe at him, but he caught it with a grin.

"Go get the girl." He made it seem so obvious, and his words chipped away at the reasoning I had not to. "Cael! You idiot," he barked, making me jump. "If you love her the way I know you do, you're making a fool of yourself standing here."

"I can't just go."

"Holy shit, man." Dean lifted to his knees, the sheets falling down around his thighs, and my mind wandered for a second. How easy it would be to sink back into bed with him, to forget everything and just be here.

"What do you need? A blessing? *I love you.*" He said it so profoundly I felt it in my soul. "I always have, but we've talked. I know that this doesn't end how I want it to. It was never the end game, and I still have a lot to learn about myself. I can't love you the way you need me to and I can't ask you to love me in the dark. You shine too bright to be stuck in a closet with me." There was pain lacing every word he spoke.

"Dean..." I shrunk in size as my heart broke.

"I'm okay," he said, "I'll be okay."

I shake my head. "I'm sorry," I choked out.

"So what is it that you need," He snapped, it broke into frustration.

"What if—"

"Not once in your life have you ever thought to pause and think something through. I've watched you jump off the bridge in town into the river in the middle of February on an impulsive thought. You've crashed more cars than anyone I know, you never back down from a fight and you literally run on nuclear waste as an energy source. Stop thinking about everything that can go wrong, and just *go!*" He exclaimed, a storm brewing behind his eyes as his lips pressed into a thin line.

I moved toward him, cupping his face in my hands and dragging a long kiss from his lips, lingering on our past and promising him quietly that no matter what, I'd always love him. He tapped two soft fingers to my chest as our foreheads came together.

"Go," he whispered, so softly that I could have imagined it. I turned to find shoes, but his fingers caught my wrist. "Get dressed first." He looked over my naked body, laughing wildly as he rolled his eyes and fell back on the bed.

I wanted to pause to ask him if he was really okay with this, but I had a feeling that if I did, I'd never leave the room. The nerve he had instilled in me was already starting to fade, and I hadn't even pulled on a clean shirt. My shoulder groaned as I slipped into my sleeve and over my head, but the pain was just a dull throbbing reminder of the mistakes I had made.

Taking the stairs two at a time, I slid down the hallway, praying that she was in her room, but found it empty. "Fuck." I slammed her door shut and moved through the house, checking all the spaces she was normally in.

Ella was sitting on the counter, her hair in a messy bun and eyes glazed over with a wicked hangover when I busted into the kitchen.

"Hey, tornado." She laughed when I nearly knocked over a pile of crap on the island.

"Have you seen Clem?" I stopped, catching myself before running into the door.

"I think she was going down to the stadium to interview a few of the staff and your Dad." Ella brought her coffee cup to her lips. "Do you want some coffee?"

No, I wanted Clementine.

"Maybe later, Peach." I tapped my chest.

"Not so fast." Ella's head fell to the side as she looked over at me. The mistake was in calling her Peach. It was too serious. She knew something was up.

"Not drunk, not high, just…"

"Abnormally flustered." Her bright smile pulled me from the dizzy thoughts swirling around in my head. "Cael," she cooed, reading me like a book she had written herself. "Do you think storming up on her is going to win her over?"

I stopped then, looking at Ella, and ran my hand over my face and then through my hair just trying to dissipate the feeling of anxiety under my skin.

"You boys are so dense." Ella shook her head as a breathing laugh fell from her. "Do you remember how scared I was when the Nest found out *who* I was and what I had done?"

I stared at her. Usually, I could place her thoughts and follow where she was going with a conversation, but I couldn't, not this time. My heart was still racing, chasing after Clementine on its own as time stood still.

"Yeah, of course." I scratched the back of my neck, watching her and waiting for her to tell me the point of her rehashing at an urgent time like this.

"Alright well…"

"Please for the love of God, get to the point, Peachy." I begged her.

"On a scale of one to ten, how big are your feelings right now?" She asked me, setting down the cup and wandering toward me. Her hands combed through my messy hair tenderly, a sister looking after her stupid little brother with cautious care in a way only Ella could.

"Eleven, twelve, maybe?" I mumbled and raised my eyebrows at her.

"I know how intense you can be about—*everything*," she paused, "but for Clementine's sake, take a moment to think about how she feels. Or Cael..." Ella fiddled with her necklace, and I knew she wanted to say something that would upset me. "Are you sure you aren't just substituting one drug for another?"

"That hurt." I scowled at her and looked away because it hit hard.

I understood where she came from, the suspicion of trading in and trading out one substance for another. Loving Clementine felt like drugs. It burned bright and made me feel like I was looking at the world through a kaleidoscope.

"The truth usually does." She pressed her lips into a thin line. "I'm not saying your feelings for her aren't real. I wouldn't. I just want you to consider hers before you blow up her life with a grand confession that you can't take back."

I raked my hands through my hair as my shoulders rolled forward and my gaze dropped to the floor. She wasn't wrong. As much as I wanted to burn in the heat of Clementine's love, it wasn't fair of me to blow up her life like that. I had done that once already, even though it hadn't been my fault, not entirely, but laying all of my feelings at her feet when the ground below us was shaky... It was selfish.

"Why do you always have to be so reasonable?"

"What are big sisters for?" Ella winked at me and straightened the hem of my t-shirt. "Start slow. Keep showing her how you feel at a pace that doesn't feel like you're driving down the freeway."

"I'm not even sure I have a slower speed." I shrugged, a tiny laugh falling from my lips.

"Figure it out." Ella slapped her hand against my face gently. "Don't screw this up."

"You sound like Arlo," I groaned lightly and inhaled once before slapping my hands over her shoulders.

"I was just trying to give you the full mom-and-dad treatment. How did I do? Mean enough?" She smiled up at me, and I rolled my eyes.

"Not nearly enough swear words," I laughed, "but close enough. If not full speed, what then?"

"Take her on a fucking date, Cael." Ella laughed like it was the most obvious option.

"Perfect...right..." I nodded.

"And stop playing 'poker for keeps'. That game is horrible." She shook her head and went back to her coffee. "Take her somewhere that'll mean something to the both of you, Cael." She looked at me over her shoulder, her glare icy as she said, "also, take a damn shower. You smell like *Dean*."

I leaned my nose into my shoulder and caught a good whiff of suntan lotion, which made my lips curl into a smile before I nodded. I needed a better plan than just '*go*'; it needed to be bulletproof so she couldn't possibly say no to me.

First, I needed to collect my thoughts. Dean and Ella had pulled every option tight from either side like a vicious tug-of-war. I needed the advice of someone who would tell me the truth even if I didn't want to hear it.

CODY

"I ordered you a water." Joshua Logan sat in the booth with his hand wrapped around a half-drunk soda.

"Thanks." I slid into the booth and our long legs bumped against each other beneath the yellowed table top. "And for meeting with me. I know you have a lot going on right now."

He pulled his attention from one of the cute employees who wandered around behind the main counter. It was easier to forget how handsome he was when he was being an asshole on the pitching mound. With his sharp jaw, covered in a thick layer of scruff that brushed against the collar of his team sweater, and his dark hair tucked under a dark red Lorette's hat that made it curl at his neck and behind his ears.

Josh smiled, but even curled at the corners it looked so serious, almost like it made him nauseous to do so.

"You don't call me often, Cody, so when you do I know it's important. You alright?" He asked me.

"Yeah, better than usual."

Josh's sable brown eyes rolled over me, quietly checking for signs. Any other person probably wouldn't notice; he was sneakier than everyone else about it. But he still checked, and it still stung.

The waitress brought my water, and Josh waited for me to explain. He was never one to pry something out of me. In the last few months, I'd learned a lot about him. In the beginning, there was pushback from both sides. Neither of us thought him being my sponsor was a wise decision, but I trusted the chair of our group, and I had destroyed any chance of asking Ella. She was tangled into my recovery now. She was a victim of my carnage.

It was only later I found out that Josh had been sober for almost four years and we had more in common than either of us could have imagined. The problem was we had both decided it would be better for everyone if *no one* knew he was my sponsor. The rivalry between the teams was too high, and it had to stay that way. It made for good baseball. So we met every couple of weeks in a shitty restaurant on the other end of town, a mid-way point for us both.

"I need some advice." I pushed the glass of water around nervously.

"Is this a short conversation or a long one because I'm starving," Josh asked, nodding his head and calling over the waitress when I shrugged.

Once we had burgers, I told him everything that was going on, and he stared at me with the same distant look he always had. He stuffed a few more French fries into his mouth as I finished telling him about the Halloween party.

"Is she affecting your sobriety?" Josh asked, cleaning his hands and taking a sip of soda.

"No," I said, without hesitation. It had been weeks since I even thought about drinking, months since I needed the drugs.

Josh nodded. "I get it man, it's scary when all of a sudden your thoughts aren't consumed by that next fix, and you think she's got something to do with it?"

"If she leaves…"

"Which it sounds like she's going to," he finished. "I'll tell you something my sponsor used to tell me: focusing on the past is a surefire way to walk yourself into the oncoming traffic that is the future."

"I came for advice, not riddles, Logan." I pushed my half-eaten plate of food away.

Josh pushed it back. "Finish, you weigh less than a feral kitten," he grumbled before continuing his sentence.

"It just means that, when the time comes, she goes home. We deal with it then, together. As much as I hate to admit it, you've got a good circle of friends and family, Cael. You're already on a better track than most before your first year, but slip-ups happen. You shouldn't weigh your recovery or your self-worth on a sexual relationship. *Ever*."

"So you're saying go for it?" I asked him.

"I've never met someone so dense," he hissed. "I'm saying use your common sense, don't let your judgment be clouded by anyone. How is your Dad in all of this?" He asked.

Dad had been a major topic during recovery.

He was a trigger point, meaning I had to talk about him, but it was a horrible feeling, even if I wasn't necessarily blaming him for things. I still hated it.

When I didn't answer, Josh sat forward and sighed.

"Have you talked to him about any of this?" He asked, and I watched him with a solemn expression as his eyes rolled back in his head. "Cael, come on, man!"

"Don't give me that shit." I shook my head, but if anyone was allowed to it was him; it was his main role in our relationship. He was there to call me on my shit, to help me manage it and work through it when it became too much and there wasn't anyone else that understood.

"You have to talk to him," he groaned, "especially right now. He was on your list."

"At the bottom and only because you thought it was a good idea to put him on there," I reminded him. I hated that list. It burned in my pocket every day, nipping at my skin and never letting me forget all of the names on it.

"If this girl is a part of your past, she's a part of his. And I mean, if you're going to screw around and fuck shit up again, he deserves a heads-up. It's about forming a line of trust with him."

"It's annoying when you're right," I scoffed.

Josh smiled at me., "It's the only reason I'm your sponsor, so I can see that stupid look on your face every time I am." He stood from the table. "You'll figure this out, just keep on that straight line. Thanks for lunch."

"Aye, Logan!" I waved the bill at him.

"Go see your Dad, Cody," he yelled, brushing me off as he left the restaurant.

CODY

"Where the hell are we going?" Clementine asked from the passenger seat in her plaid shirt and jeans. She looked extra pretty today with her hair down and cheeks pink from the fall wind that was rushing through Harbor.

"Into the city, Plum. Relax." I said turning onto the highway. "I want to take you on a date," I purred.

"Sorry, you have to ask my daddy permission for that," she said in a thick Texas accent that made my chest fuzzy.

"Mr. Matthews was my number one fan, remember?" I said. "Besides I've already fucked you silly, I don't think we're past order and formalities."

I watched her cheeks and neck turn an even dark shade of pink. *That's my girl.*

"We can pull over right now and do it again if you want," I suggested and she rolled her eyes. "Car is a little small for that, but I could make it work if you could..." I kept going and she clapped her hand over my mouth.

"Shut up and take me on the date, Cael." Clementine laughed.

"Ask me nicely," I kissed her palm before she pulled away, unable to resist myself.

Clementine glared at me with those soft brown eyes, unaware that she was incapable of looking mean but trying nonetheless.

"Come on, Plum. You better ask quick before we hit something," I said with a smile, rolling my hands over the steering wheel. I could tell it was making her uncomfortable that I wasn't watching the road.

"Are you seriously doing the *stare and drive* right now?" Clementine scoffed. "That barely worked in two fast, two furious. You'll kill us before I cave."

"You want to bet?" I cocked my head to the side, the road ahead was a straight shot for another two miles, no bends, no hills. One lane highway. And at this time of the night... we'd be lucky to see another car.

Clementine was starting to sweat.

"Cael," She warned as her tone lowered and she fidgeted in her seat.

"Clem," I retorted in a similar tone.

Her tongue darted out over her bottom lip, her eyes flickering to the road and back to me.

"Please," she said quickly.

"Please what?" I combated.

"Cael..." she growled and I smiled.

God I loved that sound.

"Yes, Clementine?" I purred, melting into the way she said my name when she was angry.

"Please take me on a date," she huffed, the panic clear in her tiny voice.

"Good girl," I praised, looking back to the road finally. Out of the corner of my eye, I watched the fear dissipate and the excitement rush in.

But she was prepared to get her revenge for my behavior, her hand slipping down between my thighs and passing over my cock with soft pressure from her palm. My eyes flickered down and I swallowed roughly as her fingers drifted higher and teased the metal buttons of my jeans.

She flicked the button free as she unbuckled her seatbelt and rose to her knees, leaning over the console it was hard not to notice the way her full breasts spilled from the flimsy tank top. I was so warm I could feel the sweat pooling between my shoulder blades just from the sight of her.

"That's dangerous, Plum," I warned.

"Didn't I tell you to shut up earlier?" She scrunched her nose up at me, and even the demand sounded sweet as she sunk lower. Her fingers made easy work to free my shaft from my jeans. It sprung free from the fabric of my boxers against my stomach and I huffed heartily knowing what was coming.

"Clem," I warned in a low tone. Her eyes flickered up to meet mine as they broke from the road for a split second, her tongue darting out over that bottom lip that I loved so much.

"Always so ready for me, aren't you?" She brushed the top of my leaking cock with her thumb.

I hated the way my body reacted to her teasing, it ached under the sound of her voice and the whisper of her touch. I fought my hardest to keep my hips in the driver's seat and my focus on the road as she leaned down and captured me between her lips.

A strangled moan dripped from me as she sunk over and the tip of my throbbing cock craved her touch. She took it without complaint and rocked herself into a slow, tortuous rhythm with her tongue pressed flat against me.

She looked fucking undone and messy as she sucked and bobbed her head up and down my shaft, the deeper I went the more unwound I became. I was losing my grip on the steering wheel and let one hand fall to tangle in her hair roughly as my head brushed against her throat.

"Shit Clem." My eyes rolled into the back of my head and I lifted off the gas as her teeth raked against my cock to the top before she dropped back down. Her cheeks hollowed out around me and the pressure was building too fast for me to even warn her before I came.

With my fingers curled into her hair, gently helping her motions as she sucked harder, spit pooling from her full, red lips. She took the full length of my erection I came hard, into the back of her mouth as she fought to keep herself balanced in the moving car.

I groaned, the sound vibrating through me as I pulled to a stop sign and fought to catch my breath and clear my vision. Ripples of pleasure shot through my muscles making my thighs tremble as my cock pumped out the warm liquid onto her ready tongue.

Spit dripped from her lips as she cleaned my shaft with her tongue and rocked back on her heels, shifting in the seat without a word but with a proud smile plastered on her pretty, flushed face. She buckled herself back up and kept her eyes straight forward with her bottom lip between her teeth as I adjusted myself back into my pants and pulled from the stop sign.

"Now take me on my date, Loverboy." She turned her head, resting it against the seat with the prettiest smile I had ever seen on her swollen lips. The urge to fuck her in the front seat of my car just to remind her who was in charge was unbridled and coursed through me like electricity.

"You're a fucking brat, Clementine," I growled.

"Mmm," she hummed and used the pad of her thumb to clean the corner of her mouth.

"There's an Asian horror fest in the city," I told her after a beat of silence, knowing she wouldn't ask again but was dying to know what the original plan was.

"Really? Luckily you can multi-task now we won't be late," she giggled, "I can't remember the last time I watched a good horror movie."

"You're the only person who loves them like I do," I said, "Dean's too much of a chicken and Arlo pulls them apart like it's a book report. It—"

"Takes the fun out of them." She finished my sentence. "Bobbi just sexualizes everyone. The newest Halloween?" She said, looking over at me with a small smile.

"Kills?"

"Ends," she corrected. "Bobbi spent the entire movie trying to convince me why Corey would make a good boyfriend based on his— and I quote, 'Feral ability' to protect his girlfriend."

I laughed, "I mean... he knew what he had to do."

"Cael, he killed half her friends." Clementine scowled.

"He also killed that aggressive pervert doctor, and that one mean girl..." I argued just to see her cheeks turn pink.

"Violence isn't a way to show love, Cael." She shook her head and turned in her seat. "He could have just left with her, they could have been happy somewhere else. Away from all that."

I turned to look at her for a second and my smile faded, *is that what she wanted? Was she trying to say something to me without out right confessing her feelings.*

"That feels like a secret, Plum." I said, my heart clenching in my chest tightly at the memory. I could always tell when she was packing her feelings away, bricking them up with wet cement.

"It's just an observation." She rolled her eyes as she countered.

"Sure..." I nodded, not believing her for a second. "Well they hold this festival every year, last year I went alone because no one wanted to be around me." I said, I had gotten way too high and slept on a park bench. Arlo found me three days later on a bender. I didn't even think I would make it to the next festival. Let alone do it sober and with Clementine in the passenger seat.

That grateful feeling bubbled back up pushing out the thoughts of relapse. *I could do this.* The city was busier than expected, the streets packed with people partaking in late Halloween festivities. I found a spot about a block from the small theater where the festival was being held and opened the door for Clementine.

"It smells like popcorn," she hummed and let her head fall back.

"We can get a big one and dump all our candy inside until it's a mess and doesn't resemble popcorn anymore." I linked my hand in hers and our bracelets rubbed together like they always did.

"Deal." She said and tucked in close to me as we wandered down the street.

"We can make out in during the movie too," I suggested knowing she'd shoot me down.

"In your dreams, Loverboy." She rolled her eyes and giggled.

"It was worth a shot," I nudged her as we made our way to the entrance. I bought the tickets and as promised supplied her with plenty of snacks as she fan-girled over the line up.

"Some of these films were never released in the States, how did they find copies?" She waved the pamphlet in my face as I carried the arm full of food.

"You can ask yourself," I said, waving down a friend. "Clem, this is Margie," I introduced her to a small redhead with freckles that covered her face and big blue eyes amplified by thick lensed glasses.

"Clem?" Margie put both hands out and wrapped them around Clementine's shaking with enthusiasm, "Cael's never brought a girl down here you must be special."

"Margie," I cleared my throat. "But she's right, for the purpose of brownie points."

"Mmhm," Clementine shook her head. "It's nice to meet you Margie."

"Big Mac Margie here is in charge of this whole night, she's an enthusiast." I laughed and could see Margie squirming to say more. "She also has this incessant need to talk."

"He's right, I never stop. It's like once I open my mouth all the words come out and I just can't stop myself. Half the time I make a fool of myself but by then people have stopped listening anyway so it usually doesn't even matter." She said in one massive breath. "And I'm not an enthusiast. I'm a specialist. I didn't spend four years studying film at university to have you belittle it with your lack of vocabulary Cael Cody."

"Breathe, Margie." I winked at her. "Why don't you sit with us and then you can run Clem's ear off about the feature film?" I asked her.

"Oh I couldn't do that, you two look like you're on a date and I'd hate to get in the middle of that with my yapping." She shifted in her black overalls and retro Ju-On shirt.

"He asked." Clementine said before I could reassure her. "Besides, he's barely educated on tonight's line up. I could use a professional."

I watched with a full heart as Clementine and Margie started in conversation. A third wheel wasn't exactly how I saw tonight going but I wanted to give Clementine one night out where we weren't worried about the pressure weighing down on our lives.

"Have you ever seen The Wailing?" Margie asked her as I followed close.

Clementine shook her head and smiled, "I could never find anywhere to stream it."

"The copy I got my hands on has the original subtitles, no dubbing." Margie said with excitement.

"Dubbing ruins the integrity of a foreign film, I swear. The translations never do it justice!" Clementine giggled and I leaned into the sound as we found our seats. Half the nonsense that came out of their mouths was indescribable and I couldn't have kept up even if I tried as they rambled about the movies.

I was just happy to be here.

In all honesty I had continued to watch horror movies because they had always been Clementine's favorite. She found a calm in them that she didn't in other movies. At first I thought there might be something wrong with her but as I got older and the distance between us grew I realized that it was the subject of the films.

It wasn't even really that she *liked* blood and guts.

It was that the worst possible outcome happened in horror movies, so bad that even the PG-13 ones made life seem not-so-bad all of a sudden. Leave it to Jason and Freddy to take the edge off every math exam I'd ever had.

"Save me a spot, I need to go make sure everything is set up." Margie pointed to her seat next to Clementine who threw her plaid over it for safekeeping.

"She's incredible," Clementine whispered as she took off running in her platform sneakers. "How the hell did you trick her into being your friend?"

"Ouch," I barked and clutched my heart, "I'll have you know that I was here every weekend after we moved here. It was one of the only places I felt close to you and Margie's parents own the place so she was always around." I pointed up to the projection box. "They live on the second floor, so eventually we just became friends."

The truth was Margie had found me crying more often than not at the movies but she never made fun of me, she never said a word about it. She just talked about the movies and the sound of her voice, the way she just genuinely enjoyed them...it made everything feel less urgent and heartbreaking.

Margie had been there when no one else could be.

"I really like her," Clementine rested her hand on my face, sensing the pause in my enthusiasm. "You did good."

"Mmm." I said quietly. "She was missing a Clementine though, I can't keep up with her half the time. She needed someone who knew as much as her."

"Oh so this wasn't a date, it was a gift that came with more strings." Clementine whispered, "it was sweet but you can't tie me down here Cael. I have to go home eventually." My heart clenched painfully.

"That wasn't my intention," I said truthfully. "I just wanted to do something nice with you, *for you.*"

"Mission accomplished," she purred as the lights went down and the movie started.

"Clementine," I whispered, wanting to get something out that didn't make me sound like a total idiot or have her running in the opposite direction when we had started to make so much progress. But her skin on my skin, it blurred my common sense and suddenly. "You know I love you right?" I said, swallowing bile that rose with the words.

She stared at me for a long while and, for a moment I was unsure she heard what I said as the previews blared through the speakers. But I could see her answer in her eyes, hear it in the unanswered silence. I could feel it thrumming through her fingertips that still lingered on my jaw as she turned to watch.

I knew she loved me back, with every fiber in my body I knew.

I just needed to figure out a way to remind her so that she'd stay in Harbor with me.

So she'd *want* to stay.

CODY

"Come in," Dad called from his desk, his scruff-covered face dropping into annoyance as I wandered through from the front office. "I don't have time for this today, Cael. King is a grown man, and I didn't make the decision for him. If you wanna fight someone, fight him."

The dirty black cap he always wore was flipped backward, and he was tucked down into a navy Hornet's hoodie that looked like it had never been washed.

"Over it," I sighed under my breath. I wasn't really, but there wasn't much else I could do about it. I wandered through the office and picked up one of the frames on the shelf, running my fingers over the old photo of him and Mama.

She looked so young, her long dark hair curled around her skinny little face. Big blue eyes so clear they might as well have been the sky.

"Sometimes I forget how pretty her smile was," I said, setting the frame down.

"Don't know how..." Dad grunted and flipped a paper over without looking up at me. "You carry it around with you."

I looked over at him, hoping maybe he had taken his attention off his work, but his pen scribbled across the paper mindlessly. I licked my bottom lip, frustrated and feeling forgotten moments after he'd reminded me that I had Mama's smile.

"Why do you do that?" I asked him, slumping down on the couch.

"What?"

"Pretend like you have any interest in me when in reality you can't even look at me for more than two minutes." I rolled my eyes and laid my head back against the couch. It smelled like two years of him sleeping on it, and it annoyed me.

"Cael," he said, low and warning, as if I was the problem. "What do you want? If you came to talk me into letting you play..."

"Not everything is about baseball, Dad," I hummed, trying to keep my cool as the sounds of his scratching pen echoed through his silence. I dug my fingers into the arm of the couch, trying to control the anxious frustrations that rolled through me like a tidal wave. Irritation grew tenfold every time the clock ticked forward a second.

"This was a mistake." I pushed off the couch.

"If it's not Arlo, and it's not baseball..." he started, and I laughed so loudly that it drowned out his huff as I cut him off.

"It's about Clem," I said finally, her name bubbling from my throat like a rock that had been lodged there.

Dad finally looked up from his work.

"What did you do?" He set the pen down as his green eyes traced over my body, looking for signs of drug use or anything that might suggest I was acting erratically.

"I didn't *do* anything." I rolled my eyes. "I just need some advice about something I *might* do."

"And what kind of advice do you think I can offer you?" Dad rubbed his hand over his face, never taking his eyes off me.

"I don't know... You know her better than anyone, and you and Mama—"

I watched him flinch at the mention of her.

"—You guys were in love for so long," I said.

I didn't remember a time when they weren't in love. They knew each other better than I've ever seen two people know. Sure, they fought, but they were never real fights. They were over which flowers to plant, or what movie to watch. I swear they fought for fun. Even when Dad was being an ass, Mama always had a way of making him smile.

"Whatever you think you have with Clementine," he said, "it's nothing close to that. When did you revert back to being that stupid kid chasing tail?"

"Chasing tail?" I huffed. "It's Clem..."

"Exactly. You've got yourself in knots over the same girl that ignored you just like she did all those years ago. Doing everything you can to get her attention

180

when she just doesn't care, Son. You will always be her past and letting her define your future based on foolish childhood memories is going to leave you right back where you started." Dad spoke slowly, with no malice in his voice, but it stung all the same.

He looked away for a moment, pressing his hands flat to his desk, before meeting my eyes again. "You have a career to think about, Cael."

"You're more worried about my career than I am." I shook my head.

"I noticed." His voice was tight when he spoke and, for a second, I thought he might be willing to help me figure this all out. "If not your career, focus on your recovery. What happens when she leaves and it..."

He was worried that I would sink back into that version of myself. Understandably so; that little monster inside me tore apart the Hornets from the inside out, and the lid on Pandora's box was taped closed at best, ready to explode at any second.

"All that work." He shook his head at me, and his brows came together. "When she leaves..."

"Stop saying when." I cut him off. "*If* she leaves."

"What's stopping her?" Dad snapped finally, his big, scary, father voice coming out.

"*Love*, I don't know—me?" I shrugged.

"Love isn't a superpower, Cael. It can't solve problems, it doesn't prevent bad things from happening." *Or people getting sick*, his green eyes blazed with unsaid words. "And you're just an out-of-control kid without any clue of what you want to do with your life. Get your head out of your ass." He rose from his seat in a display of dominance.

I stared at him, trying to figure out his motives, but coming up with nothing as he rounded the desk into my space. Stepping back and swallowing tightly, I tried to hold on to my feelings, tried to rein them in so as not to give him what he wanted.

A Cael Cody blow-up.

It would only prove his point, no matter how badly I wanted to right now.

"For a man that only ever knew the brightest love, you sure are a skeptical fucking asshole." I laughed, but it was hollow and angry. "I'm stronger than you want to give me credit for. I'm healing, I'm recovering. No thanks to you!"

"All it takes is one slip." Dad raised his finger in the air. "One wrong path, one bad decision, and you're right back where you started."

"Right back where you left me."

He closed his eyes and, for a moment, I was grateful to have a second without his dark green stare boring down on me. I could feel how angry he was, it radiated off him in waves, but I meant it, and there was no taking it back.

"You said once that *you wished it was me.*" I watched as he looked up at me, readying himself for the blow. "I've tried to give you that more than once, maybe in a sick attempt just to get your attention, but it never worked. It only ever hurts the people that actually give a shit about me. I wish I believed that you cared about my recovery, but you only love me when I'm measuring up to your standards."

"I'm not a bad dad, Cael." He cut me off.

"No, you never hit me or ran me into the ground with abuse, but you were never a good dad. You gave all your love to Mama, and she did her best to pass it on to me, but she died, and she took every little piece you had left with her. And that's fine. I understand your grief, Dad, but don't act like I'm the only problem between us. What I did, who I was, and who I am now is because I feel everything. Who you are is because you just don't give a shit anymore."

"Cael..." He sighed.

"And maybe feeling too much all the time is a curse, but at least it's better than building up my own personal purgatory and rotting away inside of it." I opened my arms wide and pointed around at the chaotic office, piled boxes, old blankets, and duffle bags stuffed with clothes. "You may have shut it off, Dad, but it doesn't mean I have. I'm sorry you don't understand why I love Clementine. I'll take solace in the idea that there was a time, a version of you, that would have. That version who sat in our living room on the weekends teaching Clementine every facet of baseball because I couldn't stand being the reason you didn't play anymore. That's why she's here. It's not just for me. I wasn't the only one who broke her heart that day. Even if it wasn't my fault, you dragged us here to chase *your* dream. The guise was never there for me. I knew you didn't love me, not like you loved baseball, but Clem, she believed you loved us, she believed you had the dream. Me, Mama, baseball on Sundays with her. You are just as much to blame."

"I warned you I wasn't going to fight you today," he huffed, but I could see the crack there underneath the surface. It ran deep. Maybe something I said had finally gotten through to him.

God, Mama, if there was ever a time to visit him in his sleep...

"I meant it." He nodded to the door, tempering his expression.

"That's it?" I laughed and nodded, just fighting to keep the tears at bay. "I thought maybe now that I wasn't an embarrassment to you, maybe you'd start treating me like a son again, but I was wrong. You never cared."

"Get out, Cael," Dad barked. "And I swear if you screw up this piece on the team..."

"You'll what?" I looked back at him from the doorframe, "Make me run laps? Bench me for the season? Disown me? You made it clear a long time ago we weren't family anymore. You'll have to come up with a better punishment."

I left the office, not bothering with the door, but heard it slam from the hallway as I sunk against the bricks and tried to compose myself. Everything he said made sense and pissed me off all the same. I shoved off the wall and stripped from my shirt before slamming into the empty workout room.

"Where are they..." I dug around in Silas's spare desk. "Got you...." I tugged out a pair of headphones that had been there for years and shoved them into my ears, playing my music as loud as it would go. I needed to silence the world. Too many voices were screaming at me, and I couldn't figure out exactly what I needed to do.

Maybe it was me that needed a visit from Mama.

CODY

2016

Sunday was quieter than usual. Clementine hadn't come over to keep Dad busy with baseball, so he was grumbling outside, helping Mama with a project as I weeded the garden for her. She kept looking over at me like she had something to tell me, but always went back to bossing Dad around instead.

When I was good and done with all the weeds I chucked them in the compost and wiped my hands on my jeans. "I'm going to go shower for dinner."

"Alright, Honeybug," Mama smiled at me softly, cupping my face in her hand as I passed by to excuse myself. The T.V. wasn't even on inside as I walked through the living room to the single bathroom in our house.

I checked my phone to see if Clementine had called from their house to bug me, but there were no missed calls, so I stripped my dirty garden clothes and climbed into the shower. The warm water did nothing to distract my thoughts from her. *Where the hell was she?* She always spent Sundays at our house.

When the water turned cold, I got out, running my fingers through my hair before changing into clean clothes and sitting on the edge of my bed. I stared at the wall covered in shitty horror movie posters and sighed. I couldn't imagine she had anything better to do... Mama hadn't said anything about the Matthews' plans.

Maybe she was sick? Or slept in?

No, Clementine had never slept in a day in her life.

I clicked on the TV and pulled out my summer school binder to try and get some of my homework done to the soundtrack of Halloween 2. As the sun started to drop in the sky through my window, I turned on my laptop and continued to work, having the frustrating realization that the school work was actually keeping me well distracted as I started another movie.

"Cael?" Mama knocked on the door and opened it a crack. "Dinner is ready, Honeybug. Wash your hands."

I nodded, closed my binder, and stretched out on the bed before standing up and doing what I was told. When Mrs. Matthews' laughter floated down the hallway, I picked up my sluggish pace and wandered into the kitchen to find only four of them. Mr. Matthews helped my Dad set the table as Mama set down a tray of her lasagna in the middle.

I helped her with the pitcher of iced tea and took my seat, staring across the table at Clementine's empty spot with confusion. "Where's Clem?" I finally asked, as Dad started to dish out salad onto his plate.

"She went to the movies." Mrs. Matthews smiled at me and handed the salad bowl in my direction.

"She didn't tell me she was going to the movies..." I said, taking the bowl slowly as Mr. Matthews chuckled.

"Clementine doesn't have to run everything by you, Cael," Mama said, scooping me a massive piece of steaming-hot lasagna. "She probably went with some friends."

"I'm her friend." It came out much angrier than I had wanted it to, but it was true. Where was Clementine if she wasn't with me?

"It was a nice boy," Mrs. Matthews said. "He came right down to the house to meet us before he took her out. What was his name again?"

"Kiefer," I answered before Mr. Matthews could.

Clementine had been lost in that hockey asshole's eyes for weeks, ever since he'd transferred into her class. When she told me he invited her to that end-of-the-year party, I told her not to go. Mainly because the other sports teams weren't allowed. It was hockey guys only, and those guys only ever had one thing on their minds.

"They went to the movies?" I asked, looking at her parents, who both nodded.

"The afternoon show," Mr. Matthews confirmed.

185

"It's seven. Shouldn't she be home by now?" I grumbled and picked at my salad.

"Cael," Dad hushed me from the end of the table, but my mind was swimming. I couldn't believe that a kid like Kiefer had conned them so badly that they just didn't give her curfew. Even if I took her out, we always had to be back by a certain time. It was stupid, and she didn't even have a phone to check on her.

I stood from the table. "I'm not hungry."

"Cael!" As I left the house through the back door with a huff, Mama's voice rang out.

I marched down to the creek and sat in the grass, staring at the farmland surrounding me. Clementine hadn't even bothered to tell me she was going on a date. The worst part was I didn't even know why it made me so angry. I should be happy for her, finding her footing. Flirting with guys? Did that make her happy?

Or was I jealous?

But of what? Kiefer got to take her to the movies, and we went to the movies all the time. No. It was the thought of him holding her hand, them sitting together, and him getting to wrap his arm around her. Kissing when the lights went down...

I ripped some grass out and inhaled slowly. Why did that make me so angry?

Those were more explosive feelings I wasn't necessarily ready for just yet.

"Cael Cody," Mama's voice called from behind me as she came down the hill. "What the hell was that all about?"

"I—" I opened my mouth only to shut it again. I was confused.

"Spit it out." She sat down in the grass with me and nudged my side.

"I don't like that Kiefer guy." I shrugged.

"And why's that, Honeybug?" She asked.

"He plays hockey. Those guys are all dicks."

"Oh." She paused, and a tiny sigh left her lips. I knew she could see right through me, and I hated it. If Mama could see through my lie, then she could see how much I was struggling with my realization. "Have you told Clementine how you feel?"

"I don't feel anything, Mama. I just don't want her dating guys that won't-" I stopped and picked at the grass some more as the sun started to sink in the sky over the hill.

"I don't know when you started to lie to me, but I don't like it when you do," she scolded.

I grumbled and looked away from her, knowing she could tell from my face that I was jealous and upset.

"I know that it's a scary thought. You've spent your entire life loving Clementine because she's always been there, and if that love is deeper than your sixteen-year-old heart imagined, it's okay. We all go through moments like that."

It's not a moment.

"You mean..." I turned to look at her. Her long dark hair was braided down, and she watched me with her soft blue eyes. Always so patient with me, even when I'm acting like a jerk.

"You have time to figure out what kind of way you want to love her," Mama said with a smile as she ran her fingers through my hair. "But you can't run around here with a sour mood blaming her when she explores other options waiting on you."

"I don't think Clementine likes me like that." I shook my head. "I don't even know if I like her like that..."

"Don't rush. Just enjoy the time you have with her. You're sixteen, Honeybug. You aren't figuring out your feelings on your deathbed. You'll get there." Mama laughed, and I leaned into her for a hug.

"Look," she pointed into the dusk at a set of headlights pulling up to the Matthews' house. "She's home."

MATTHEWS

The stadium was quiet as the evening dragged on. I had come down for video footage of the stadium to fill the gaps in the piece and to filter underneath certain interviews. I checked the time on my phone and cursed. I'd missed dinner at the Nest, and my stomach was rumbling. I was searching for a restaurant other than Hilly's on my phone when I heard the soft padding of feet. I followed the sound down the hall and found a long wall of windows that gave a view into a fully equipped workout center.

Pushing through the heavy door as quietly as I could, I wandered around the back side of the gym, watching Cael every step of the way.

Lean, tan muscle drenched in sweat. It pooled between his bare shoulder blades as he pushed himself at a grueling pace with the jump rope gripped between his hands. His gaze was straight ahead, completely lost in the moment as he bobbed his head to whatever music he was listening to. His biceps tightened as his pace quickened. Damp, blond hair stuck to his neck and temples. It took everything in my power not to stroll over there, but he seemed on edge about something, so I slid back on the desk and watched.

Cael hadn't noticed me as he started to sing along to Moulin Rouge that pumped through his head phones. He was actually pretty good as the words rolled off his tongue in time with his quick footsteps over the rope.

I watched as the sweats he wore hung low over his hips and shifted with each strenuous jump he took. His face was scrunched tightly, and I could tell from his angle that it was bothering his shoulder, but he didn't seem to have an off switch.

Wanting to ask what was wrong was like defusing a bomb with Cael. His demeanor was so different from the last time we had been here. Gone was the friendly, sweet boy with the bright smile and loud laugh.

The Cael in front of me was the one from his file.

The Cael beating himself into the ground five feet away was the one that was shown in all the news reports about the accident. The man I had been expecting to come face to face with when I arrived.

"Enjoying the show?" He asked breathlessly.

I hadn't even realized he'd stopped until he looked up at me through the mirror across the room with a warm gaze that flooded my nervous system and turned my cheeks pink.

"I am," I confessed. No sense in trying to hide it. "Do you jump rope to Moulin Rouge regularly?"

"It's a good song, has a good tempo..." He whispered.

Goosebumps ran the length of my arms at the sound. I needed him in every way, and position, possible before leaving Harbor. I wanted to map every inch of Cael Cody with my tongue.

"God, I love it when you get nervous." He licked his bottom lip and looked over his shoulder at me, tugging out the headphones from his ears.

"Why are you here so late?" I asked him, crossing my legs and gripping the edge of the table.

"Why are you?" Cael countered with a cheeky grin as he sauntered toward me.

"I was—" I stuttered slightly as his hand brushed my thigh. The smell of his cologne and sweat tangled together in the air, making me lean into him. "Getting B-reel for the production team," I barely finished.

"I was fighting with my Dad." He shrugged like it meant nothing, but his words weren't as light as they usually were and it made concern flicker across my face. "Don't do that, Plum. Look at me like you feel bad for me. It only makes me feel *little*."

You're still that boy.

I wanted to say it to him, whether or not I meant it. It felt like something he needed to hear, but maybe that was just my newfound knowledge of his past speaking out loud, not my logic.

"You are anything but *little*," I hooked my finger into the band of his sweat-pants and dipped my hand inside, changing the mood with the soft caress of my fingertips over him.

"Brave." He leaned into my touch as my thumb brushed over the tip of his cock. "We're in public." His breath stuttered and fanned over my cheek as my fingers wrapped tightly around him.

"I've been up and down the concourse three times tonight. There's no one here but us," I whispered back and pumped over his shaft until he grew impossibly hard in my palm. I kicked off my shoes as his fingers worked the button on my jeans, tugging them down off my hips and leaving me in my underwear and t-shirt.

It was just us now.

"You better hope you're right, Plum." He swooped forward before I could stop him, and his lips were on my neck, tracing a sloppy line to my jaw, but he paused, stopping himself before he reached my lips and lifted me from the desk into his arms. "Because I'm sick of sharing."

A tiny yelp left my lips, heat surging through me at his strength as he walked me across the room to the wall directly across from the row of mirrors. He watched me carefully, gauging my reaction to his every touch with blown out pupils as the adrenaline from his workout coursed through his muscles.

"Stay," he whispered as he lowered me to the ground.

I didn't even flinch at the demand as he kissed a line down my arm to my wrist.

"What are you doing?" I asked him.

"Tying you up." His eyes flickered up to mine through heavy lashes as his lips tickled the palm of my hand before he wrapped the black plastic jump rope around my wrist.

"Cael," I warned. A shaky breath left my lips when I understood what he was doing, the rope wrapping around my second wrist gently and tugging them

190

together in a tight bundle I couldn't escape. "You can't do that here," I said to him.

"Sure I can, you didn't place stipulations on our trade. I get to tie you up, that was the deal," he all but purred. "Are you nervous?" He asked.

"No," I lied as my heart raced.

Cael's tongue pressed against his bottom lip as it curled into a devilish smirk.

"If you want to stop, Clem, we can," he whispered.

"Scared of getting caught, Loverboy?" I bit back, my toes curling in my socks at the thought of someone walking in on us.

He lifted my hands over my head, his lips ghosting over mine but landing on my nose as he walked us backward until my back hit the wall. The muscles in his back tightened and flexed as he tossed the rope over the chin-up bar above my head.

As he tightened the rope so I couldn't wiggle free, I laughed. "I can't move my hands at all," I huffed, the memory slipping from me without effort, and Cael paused for a second. His cocky persona cracking as he met my gaze with fire behind his beautiful, slate-blue eyes.

"Good," he said. "*I don't want you covering up,*" he whispered back under his breath like it was instinct. Like he had memorized every second of that night.

"Stop doing that," I demanded and wiggled against the ropes, drunk on the dizzy lust but running from those feelings in our past.

"No." Cael laughed. "I like how nervous it makes you to think about that day. It's the only time I see *her.*"

He was talking about the weak, insecure, quiet Clementine. The one without real-world experience or a new attitude. He was talking about that little girl he used to know.

"She's gone." I shuddered as his fingers tickled down my arms and danced across my collarbone.

"She's not gone." He leaned in close, the smell of sweat and the remnants of his cologne filling my nose. "There's nothing wrong with protecting her. We all do it, tuck vulnerable pieces of ourselves away," he whispered in my ear. "But I promise not to hurt her."

You already have.

I stared at him as he backed up, blue eyes burning into my skin. Swallowing tightly, I pushed aside the urge to fight him, to remind him of all the ways he had let that girl down, so I forced a smirk to my face and leaned into the sharp pain of the jump rope biting into my wrists.

"You talk too much," I purred at him.

Cael narrowed his eyes, but a wild smile formed on his lips.

"Yeah, maybe I do." His smile grew, his thick erection straining against his sweatpants as he wrapped his arm around my waist and pulled my hips forward. The motion forced me to my tiptoes with my hands restrained. There wasn't anywhere for me to go as Cael shoved down his sweat pants and stepped between my legs.

He wrapped my leg around his hip, lifting me off the ground and sliding past my underwear and into my entrance without warning.

"But you're always soaking wet." His eyes fluttered close as his hips rocked forward, and he filled me completely. "So I must be doing something right," he hummed and dragged his teeth along my jaw as he started to find a pace that suited us both.

I intertwined my hands around the ropes and tightened my leg, pressing into his ass with my heel to keep him close as he thrust relentlessly into me. His fingers dug into my skin hard enough to form little crescent shapes with his fingernails as he buried his face into my neck.

Cael's pace buckled out as his heart started to take over again. I could feel it in his kisses on my skin and the way his hips rocked to a more tender rhythm. Within moments, the heat building in my stomach was raging with every lick from his tongue and grasp of his fingers.

"Don't stop," I begged as he relaxed at the sound of my strangled whimpers in his ear.

He pulled back, chest glistening with sweat that coated his hard, tan muscles. It rolled down his neck in salty drops that I wanted on my tongue, but he was glazed over. I had lost him to the memories again.

"Don't be gentle," I warned him, but he didn't listen. I was standing in front of him, begging for it, but all he could see and hear was *her*. "Quit fucking me like you know me, Cael, you don't."

A growl vibrated from him, his expression shifting from a haunting, heart-breaking stare to something angry as he picked up the pace. We melted into one another as he shoved deeper and harder than before.

I didn't need him to protect me anymore. I wanted the pain and all the pleasure that came with each brutal thrust. Cael sucked at my skin as I used what was left of my strength to lift and drop myself into his ragged thrusts. My aching walls throbbed around him, aching for release as the coil in my stomach wound so tight it was ready to snap.

"I don't care who you think you are," Cael growled breathlessly as his teeth found my ear. "You'll always be mine." His final thrust broke the walls down inside of me, and the pleasure crashed over my muscles like a tidal wave. My leg tightened around him, and my toes curled into the mat below. My nerves were shot, and my head was dizzy from the intense orgasm that filled me to the brim.

Cael stuttered in his step as his body tensed, and he fell over the edge shortly after me, his lips peppering my throat gently as he rocked himself through the downfall of pleasure.

His chest was ragged as he tried to catch his breath, his eyes trained on my lips. There would be nothing I could do if he decided that was his chance, but they flickered back to my eyes, and his jaw clenched tightly as he stepped forward and worked the knot loose on my wrists.

As Cael brought them down between us, his eyes widened at the marks the plastic had left. Even worse, he saw that stupid frayed pink friendship bracelet, limp and torn from me, in his palm.

He said nothing as he curled my fingers around it and brought the raised red skin to his lips, kissing it gently with his eyes closed. "Sorry," he sighed and started on the other. "I didn't think it was that tight."

My breath hitched in my chest at the idea that, after all this time, the bracelet had finally broken and, stupidly enough, it nearly made me cry. I swallowed tightly, trying to control myself as he delicately cared for each wrist, blaming himself quietly, no doubt.

I hooked a finger under his chin and lifted his gaze to mine. "It didn't hurt me, Cael." I shook my head, ignoring the fact that he wasn't talking about my skin.

He was upset about the stupid pieces of thread. "I liked it, and you obviously needed an outlet."

That dark look flickered across his face, unsure if he should believe me or if I was just trying to make him feel better. I rubbed my hand over his shoulder, the scars still pink from his surgery months before. It would be a little while longer before they faded into white, and the pain subsided enough for him to play baseball again.

"How bad is it?" I asked him under my breath.

"Are you asking as Mary or Clementine?" He swallowed tightly.

"I'm only Mary now." I sighed. "Clementine never left her room, Cael. I became Mary because I was protecting myself, not to punish you."

He let go of his breath and looked up from where my fingertips still traced the thin, delicate scar.

"Don't lie to me." Cael chuckled under his breath. "It's not like I don't deserve it." He smiled, but it didn't reach his eyes as he shook his head softly and he looked away from me.

"Maybe your mistake was thinking this was about you."

"Why do you hate me so much?" Cael's shoulders straightened like he was trying to hold himself together.

"I never hated you," I said, so quietly that the sound of Cael trying to catch his breath was louder than my words. "I hate the way you make me feel, and I hate that you do it with such ease."

MATTHEWS

"Hello?" I answered the phone, already annoyed, and I put him on speaker.

"Clemmy." Julien's voice flitted through the other end.

"Hi, Julien," I said, curbing my tone with him.

"I've been trying to get a hold of you," he purred.

"Service in Rhode Island isn't great." I lay back against the deck and groaned softly.

"When are you coming home?" He asked.

If my heart had its way, never.

"Soon, I'm almost finished. Couple of weeks at most."

"Weeks?" Julien's voice raised. "You should have been *home* weeks ago, not needing a few more to finish!"

He said home like he was it.

"This is my job, Julien." I reminded him and myself as my mind wandered to Cael's naked, sweaty chest. "I have to get this right."

"It's a newspaper, Clemmy. If it falls through, I'll take care of you," he said. That was the problem with him, it was never encouraging and constantly suffocating. *'I'll take care of you, we can get married, I'll buy you a big house, you can have kids. Stay home, be a mom'...* I stifled the groan that bubbled up.

"I'll be home as soon as I finish," I deflected. "I should go. It was nice to hear from you." The lie came out half-strangled.

"I miss you, Baby," he whined.

"The space has been good for us, Julien. Give me some time," I repeated myself for the thousandth time. "I'll call you when I'm coming in. You can pick me up from the airport, and we can talk."

"I love you," he said.

"Goodbye, Julien."

I set the phone beside me on the deck and sat up.

Everything had been peaceful until he decided to call, or at least not plagued with more decisions about my future and what I needed to do with it.

I stayed out there behind the Nest, soaking up whatever sunshine November had to offer, with my laptop propped on my legs, trying to figure out how to write this paper in a way that made sense. The air was starting to get chilly but it cleared my head and made it easier to think. The first four times I had started I made it seem like I was writing a human interest piece on Cael. The paper needed to be about all the Hornets, not just the handsome, cocky, irritating shortstop.

Cael's words played back in my mind on repeat like a broken record. *Why do you hate me?* I had walked away from him, knowing that it didn't solve anything but it had felt good to be the one that left for once. A power struggle I hadn't realized I was fighting with had snapped that day.

But I missed him, and I hated that.

Seven years ago, I missed him.

But as the years went on, the urge to miss him faded. I was left in the dark without a word from him—no letters, no phone calls, no visits. Missing him had turned to resentment and bitterness.

All the while, I could never shake the feeling of his lips on my skin. I hated that it made me dizzy even remembering how I'd felt. I ran my finger over my wrist where the twisted, pale pink threads used to be and chewed on my lip. *If you hate him so much, why are you so upset about that stupid bracelet?*

I'm convinced this is what whiplash felt like.

"Daydreaming about me again, Plum?" His voice was soft as he lowered himself onto the deck beside me.

"No," I lied.

He wore a hat turned backward over his shaggy hair and a dark shirt layered over another white one. He angled his head back, the veins in his throat rolling to the surface as he smiled at me with all his teeth.

"You've always been a terrible liar," he hummed and shut his eyes as the sun tickled his skin.

"You keep saying that, and yet..." I trailed off. It was easier to keep secrets with my mouth shut, but Cael had a way of prying every single thought from me without even trying.

"You keep lying to my face, knowing I don't believe you." He laughed. "Who's Julien?"

"No one," I answered too quickly and received an eyebrow raised in response.

"That feels like a secret," he said, and my heart skipped a beat.

He stared at me for a long time, maybe hoping I would give in, but he didn't need information on Julien. It wasn't worth the time it would take to explain that I had left my boyfriend-turned-fiancé in Texas because I couldn't get the way Cael's lips felt on mine out of my head.

"Clemmy is a cute nickname," he teased, breaking the silence.

"God, don't!" I groaned, covering my face as laughter filled my chest. For a split second, the air was lighter between us. "You know I hate when people call me that."

"He sounds super nice." Cael's tone was soft as he rotated the ring on his pinky finger.

"You sound super jealous," I teased.

"I am."

All of the air was sucked from my lungs as he turned his head to look at me. There was no maliciousness in the statement, only misery. Those big, sad, blue eyes would be the end of me.

"What are you doing?" Cael asked the question as if I hadn't left him standing there in the gym a few nights prior. As if I didn't continue to shut down every attempt he made at rebuilding the bridge between us. He seemed so relaxed, at ease, even though I was most certainly fighting with my own inner monologue over him. Over what I should do.

"Working on the piece. The sooner I finish, the sooner I can leave."

That struck a chord. His lips flickered downward into a deep pout as he stared out over the rolling back half of the property.

"Can you take a break?" He asked, as if the sentence didn't bother him.

It bothered me though, how easily he brushed past things.

"Depends," I said, but closed my laptop in preparation.

"I want to take you somewhere." He hopped off the deck into the grass about three feet below with a graceful thud. "Come." He held out his hands for me, rings sparkling in the sunlight as I slipped into them. He lowered me down beside him.

"That would be?" I asked as he linked his hand into mine like it belonged there. My heart flinched at how perfectly it did.

"Surprise." He brought us around the side of the Nest to his car and opened the passenger door for me. The seats were low to the ground and it was funny to watch his tall body slink into the driver's side. The engine rumbled to life, and he pulled us from the driveway with a speed that couldn't be safe and one that he continued to push as he drove down the hill and out of town.

The sun silhouetted Cael's sharp jaw in a warm glow as he turned down a path away from the highway. His tongue brushed out over his bottom lip, and his eyes focused on the road ahead. Blue like the ocean after a brutal storm, catching the light and sparkling like sea glass.

The soft swoop of his nose, the cute imperfections of his ears, and shaggy blond hair. From my spot in the passenger seat, I couldn't see his freckles but, like muscle memory, I could count every single one and trace them across his sun-kissed skin with my eyes.

He was unbearably beautiful.

It was like he glowed the prettiest shade of violet.

Sad, lost, and beautiful. Maybe Cael Cody wasn't that little boy anymore, and it settled against my chest in the most painful possible way.

Heartbreak was a weird thing. One moment, I wanted nothing to do with him, but the next, I wanted to be as close to that lavender haze as I could. I just wish he could see himself the way I saw him—fragile and free.

Cael turned to look at me with a soft smile on his face. "What?" He purred.

I shook my head. "Nothing."

"You don't get car sick, do you?" He teased.

"Not usually," I responded and looked away from him finally, eyes focusing on the single-lane road he was speeding down. "But you drive like a lunatic, so there's still time."

"I do not," Cael laughed and shifted gears, pushing the car faster.

"Now, who's lying?" I teased and looked out the window. "You aren't taking me out to the woods to kill me, are you?"

Cael's wild laughter filled the space. "Tempting, but I enjoy the idea of people hearing you scream my name too much."

Heat licked at my cheeks.

Before I could stop him, he was slipping beneath my defenses again. Making himself at home in all the darkest cavities of my heart. Back where he belonged.

Cael pulled the car to a stop off the side of the road where the grass was worn down and led into the trees. He hopped from the car, digging through the trunk as I stepped out into the cool air. He had a backpack on and extended his hand to me.

"Watch your step." He smiled and helped me over the roots and down onto the path.

He kept his long fingers tangled lazily into mine as his arm hooked around his back, and he led us down the path deeper into the woods.

"Cael Cody." My finger squeezed his as I stumbled over loose rock. "I haven't hiked since graduation, and I didn't plan on doing it today."

"It's worth it, Plum. Just keep that pretty mouth of yours shut for two more minutes, and I'll prove it." Cael laughed, and it echoed softly around us, almost harmonizing with the birds in the treetops.

And God, was it ever.

The trees opened to a small hill that kissed the shore of a long winding creek that rumbled down and out of view to our left.

"I found this place a month after we moved." Cael stopped and loosened his grip on my hand so I could walk out in front of him.

"It looks so much like home," I whispered under my breath.

"It was like my little piece of Texas but it's always been missing *something*." His words were carried by the wind that brushed through my hair, and I turned to look at him. Cael nodded his head to the side, and his brows scrunched together tightly as he looked at me. "Sorry." He mouthed an apology as his blue eyes watered and stared at me against the backdrop of his safe haven. His throat bobbed, and he looked up into the sun away from me, squinting at the brightness as the tears rolled down his cheeks.

"I'm a mess, Clem," he grumbled and wiped the tears on the back of his hand. "I thought I was gonna be able to handle that, but..." He looked back at me and exhaled shakily. "I've been seeing you in my dreams for seven years and, knowing this is real, it's overwhelming."

I didn't know what to say to him short of giving him false comfort that everything was going to be alright, but I couldn't do that because I didn't know. Closing my eyes, I let the breeze wrap around my senses, brushing my skin and dulling the sounds of my tangled thoughts. All I could hear was the birds, the creek, and trees all working in tandem as they stitched together an old memory that Cael and I had shared a thousand times growing up.

Eyes still closed, I felt him closing the distance between us. His breath fanned over my face as his finger traced over my eyebrows and then rubbed down the length of my nose. Cupping my jaw with his fingers, the pad of his thumb ghosted my bottom lip. His forehead met mine as his thumb paused, tugging gently against my pout.

My hands tangled into his shirt at the hem as I inhaled his breath, drinking it down like I hadn't taken one in seven years. I could feel his lips hovering there, waiting for me to tell him it was okay. To ask him to kiss me.

"Cael." I forced my eyes open, ripping myself from the memory and facing the blue fire behind his eyes. "I can't."

"Fuck." Cael stepped back in the grass, putting a good foot between us and rolling his shoulders out.

"I'm sorry," I said. I wanted to, God, I wanted nothing more, but it would mean too much to him and to me. I couldn't suffer through the heartbreak again.

"It's fine, Clem," he said, but I knew it wasn't.

He inhaled tightly, his neck straining as he fought to hold back what he really wanted to say to me. Kneeling down in the grass, he dug into his backpack and pulled out a blanket. He laid it flat in the long grass and sprawled out on it like nothing had passed between us.

"I hate that you do that," I said, settling down next to him.

"What?" He rolled his head back and let it hang between his shoulders.

"Move on so fast." I kicked off my shoes and wiggled my toes as I rested back against the blanket. "When someone expresses frustration toward you, it's like you absorb it and forget about it. Don't you..." I stopped, baffled that he didn't seem to trip up over anything. I huffed out my inability to express myself. "You're allowed to get mad at people!"

He stared at me for a moment, his lips curling into a smirk. "Mama would hate that."

"Hate what?"

"Wasting time on being upset." Cael shrugged his strong shoulders and rolled back off his elbows into the blanket to stare at the sky. "I can't control how you feel, Clem," he said as I watched him. "But how would screaming and fighting against your feelings work?"

Cael raised an eyebrow at me as his head rolled to the side, "it would only make us both feel shitter than we already do about all of this. I'm trying to make more time with you, Clementine. If you want to spend it fighting, we can, but you have to promise we spend the other half of the time fucking."

"You're insufferable." I shake my head.

"You missed me." He smiled with his eyes closed. The words buried their way into my heart and stung; he had no idea just how much. "I have something for you," he said.

"See." I laughed and rolled onto my stomach as he dug into his jeans pocket.

"Holding on to every hard feeling for everyone else is what got me into this mess in the first place, Plum. I can't do that again." There was a deeper meaning to what he said, but I was sick of being the one who started the fights.

"Close your eyes," he instructed, and I did.

"If your surprise is trying to kiss me..."

"Shh," he whispered. "Hold up your arm."

I felt the string hit my wrist and before I even opened my eyes the tears stung at the corners from his gift.

"Different girl, different bracelet."

Gone were the faded, ratty shades of pink. Wrapped around my wrist was a thin braided bracelet of purples, the same as before, but different and new. He had gotten better at the knots... I supposed he would have. Expecting a thirteen year old boy to thread a perfect bracelet had been a silly expectation. It was precious and heartwarming, but it felt like a thousand tiny paper cuts as his fingers brushed my wrist and pulled away.

"Thank you, Cael." I smiled. "But now yours is old, and mine is new," I teased through the sadness.

"*Same boy, same bracelet.*" He held up his wrist to show off the tattered bracelet, still somehow hanging on strong. But I didn't think that was true anymore. He was different. He just refused to admit it, so he was determined to hide in our past.

CODY

"Do me a solid?" I slid onto Silas's desk, almost knocking over his cup of coffee.

"No." Silas put his hand over the cup to stop it from spilling on his things as he turned his eyes up to me. His hair was pushed back off his face in waves of chestnut and streaks of gray and he was wearing a pair of glasses that I had never seen before, and that I would most certainly tease him about later, but right now I needed a favor.

"Oh come on, you owe me!" I said.

"For what?" Silas didn't laugh, he didn't even smile. He pulled off his glasses and tucked them to the side and his brows pinched together in the center as his annoyance with my presence grew.

"Probably...for... *something*." I shrugged and started to fiddle with the pens on his desk until two fell to the floor and he tossed me another dirty look. "Sorry." I scooped them off the floor and set them right. "Just one thing, please?"

"What do you want?" He set down his pen and turned in his chair to look up at me with his arms crossed together.

"You have the best sleuthing skills I've ever seen, and I need to find someone."

"Cael." he chuckled. "Did you interrupt my actual adult job with real adult issues to help you internet *stalk* someone?"

"Yeah." I nodded.

"*Someone*?" He asked.

"Yeah," I repeated.

"Who's it for?"

"No one important." I shrugged and crossed my arms.

"Right," Silas groaned, closing his eyes, turning away from me, and picking his pen back up. "Get out of my office." He shooed me away.

"Come on, Grandpa, it'll take two seconds but I couldn't find him and I need to know what's making her so determined to go back to Texas!"

"There it is." Silas set down the pen again. "This is about Mary."

"Her name isn't—" I started but it didn't matter.

"Please tell me this isn't a trade-in situation, Cael," Silas said. "You need to stop using people as distractions when you get itchy for drugs."

"Aye!" I raised my voice and stepped back. "I've been clean since the accident and I'm not trading *in* anyone, this isn't a distraction."

Silas cocked his head to the side; it wasn't often I raised my voice to anyone, especially not him or Arlo. Dad was the only one who ever heard that bitter, cold and angry side of me. When I argued with Silas or Arlo, it was playful, it was stupid, but never serious.

Well unless I was *high*. "I'm not high," I said quickly, and pressed two fingers to my chest. "Promise."

"Were you high the other night when you took Dean and Mary back to the Nest?" He asked me and I suddenly felt like I was being scolded.

"Sober as can be." I smirked.

"Did you stop to think about how that might affect Dean?" He asked me.

"We talked the morning after, he was fine. He doesn't care anymore, he sent me on my way and went back to bed."

"Back up." Silas shook his head. "You're telling me that Dean Tucker, the Dean Tucker that takes *everything* personally, was hunky dory about you running off the morning after... whatever the hell you three did. And I don't need details."

"Shit." Maybe I should have doubled back. "I fucked up."

"Have you spoken to him since?" Silas asked in a pensive voice that only made me feel more guilty for not checking in.

"No, I've been...distracted." I chewed down on my lip.

"Listen, I'll help, but you're going to have to explain this history to me, your Dad is a brick wall and Mary puffed up like a cornered animal when I confronted her about knowing you both." Silas shook his head. "So if you want me to start looking into someone, you need to explain to me what's going on, and after, you go find Dean and make sure he's actually okay with everything happening. He's only got you, Cael," he warned gently, encouraging me in the right direction like he always did. Effortlessly and more like a father than my Dad had ever been. "Don't leave him in the cold for your new toy."

"She's not a toy," I warned, my voice skirting that line of playfulness and anger again.

Silas narrowed his eyes on me.

"I'll talk to him." I tapped my fingers to my chest to promise.

"Good, now spill."

I cleared my throat and started from the beginning. "It's been seven years, my Mom is dead, and she showed up here without so much as a word. The first time I saw her since that night was two months ago."

"Seven years, no contact? You two know phones exist right?" Silas questioned in awe.

"I called but...she wanted letters, I sent letters," I said, knowing how stupid it sounded. "I sent a letter every week for seven years."

"You still send them?" Silas's brows pinched together. "And she never responded?"

"Never. I used to put them in the basket with Susanna in the morning before school so she'd mail them." I had taken a spot on the floor and picked at the laces of my shoes. Part of me had always suspected that the letters had never left Rhode Island, but it was never worth the argument. Writing them was what made me feel better, whether or not she had gotten them was something I refused to dwell on. It was heartbreak no matter the outcome because she had never written one to me.

Silas scowled. I could see the gears turning behind his eyes.

"So why aren't *you* more upset?" Silas asked me.

I wasn't really sure.

"Because..." I rubbed my hands over my face and straightened up. "Because we grew up together, attached at the hip, it was always Cael and Clem," I said to him, "There was never a moment for her to just be Clem, on her own. She spent her entire life keeping me alive, keeping me on the right track and protected from the world, and I thought maybe…" The idea of her alone made my heart clench tightly.

"She told me that day that she was just my shadow. She believed that if I left, she'd just fade into the sunlight, and that broke something inside of me." I hadn't meant for the day to become therapy and Silas was taking it like a champ, but I missed Arlo. He would tell me to shut up and figure it out. *Two steps at time.*

Except he wasn't there to walk with me, so that felt useless and only made me upset.

"I thought maybe she'd find herself and be grateful that I left her, and even if she wasn't grateful, even if she came back spiteful and mad, then at least she had figured out who she was without me. I just held onto the hope that she was able to spread her wings. It was the least she deserved for everything she ever did in sacrifice for me."

"That's stupid, Cael." Arlo's voice fell on my shoulders and I turned to the door. He leaned against the frame with his duffle curled into his fingers. Black hoodie, dark jeans, and a Dallas Ranger's ball cap pulled down over his dark hair.

"You're back." I pushed to my feet, not realizing how sad I had gotten. Before he could protest, I wrapped my arms around him and, despite our size difference, I buried my face against his shoulder.

"You've made a mess while I was gone, Kitten." It took him a moment, but eventually he hugged me back, tight and welcoming.

"Turns out I have the ability to destroy everything, sober or drunk." I pulled away and looked at him for a second. "You look dumb in that hat," I added with a sad smile and flicked the brim up off his browline.

"You haven't destroyed anything." Arlo grabbed the back of my neck roughly. "Nothing that can't be fixed."

"You're early," Silas said, standing from his desk. "We weren't expecting you until Thanksgiving."

I stepped back so Silas could find his space in the circle and wiped my damp cheeks with my shoulder before breathing out a slow shaky breath.

"Blondie called." Arlo looked over at me. "Said we had an F4 on our hands."

"It's not that bad." I shook my head.

"He had a threesome with his ex-boyfriend and his ex-girlfriend," Silas corrected.

"She was never my girlfriend." I scowled.

"Sorry, I'll elaborate better," Silas snapped and looked at me. "He had a threesome with his ex-boyfriend, who is having an identity crisis about who he is, and his childhood best friend, who he fucked once and then never saw again for seven years until..."

"Two months ago," I finished for him.

"Two months ago." Silas sighed, rubbing a hand over his beard and closing his eyes to take a moment before saying, "you're a liability."

"Awe thanks, Grandpa," I cooed at him and Silas shook his head, disappointed and completely over it.

"So where does that leave us?" Arlo asked, setting down his duffle bag and wandering into the office.

"Cael here wants me to search for a man named Julien."

Arlo turned to me. "Why?"

"Clem was talking to him on the deck the other day. He called her *Clemmy.*"

"So she has a boyfriend?" Arlo narrowed his eyes on me.

"Maybe?" I shrugged. There was something off in her voice when spoke to him, and she hadn't responded to any of his flirting, just brushed him off. "But she sounded weird on the phone with him. I just want to know who he is."

"She sounded weird on the phone because she's been sleeping with you the entire time she's been in Rhode Island." Silas rolled his eyes. "If I look this guy up, will you drop it?"

Arlo laughed at the answer before it even formed on my lips.

"Not a chance."

Silas looked him up anyways, first searching through Clementine's business profiles until he found her personal Instagram and then from there he found one single tagged photo of Clem that wasn't even posted by her. It was posted by an account named *Bobbicantbebothered,* and it was of Clementine smiling up at a tall, goofy-looking, asshole in a fitted suit, who was laughing at something behind the camera.

Her big brown eyes glimmered in the bar light. Her hair was long around her face, the picture was old, from two years before. She was in a black dress that fitted to her perfect, round curves and breasts. She took my breath away.

"Look," Silas pointed to the caption.

Congrats M&J, to life well lived.

"Shit," Arlo swore under his breath as his eyes dragged to her left hand.

An engagement ring sparkled on her finger like it was mocking me.

MATTHEWS

Thanksgiving came faster than expected.

I had everyone breathing down my neck about the timeline. When are you coming home? When will I have that piece? Are you finished yet? Stop wasting my time.

I had two interviews left.

The two I had been avoiding.

Dean Tucker and Ryan Cody.

Julien had called fifteen times in three days because I had missed his birthday and Bobbi had even reminded me but I just didn't care anymore. I didn't want to hurt him, but my heart hadn't been Julien's, ever. I knew that even before coming to Rhode Island, but Cael just reminded me that life didn't have to be hard.

I hated him for it.

It was going to make it harder to leave.

"Mary." Dean appeared from the side of the living room with two coffees in his massive hands and handed one to me. "Black," he said, settling down onto the couch across from me in a pair of black shorts and a Hornet's shirt that looked a size too small across his broad chest and round biceps.

"Morning," I said, setting the coffee on the table and flipping open my binder.

The tension between the two of us had started to fizzle, but sometimes I caught him looking at me like I might spontaneously combust and take the Nest with me. The jury was still out on that one.

"How are you?" I asked him when the silence stretched too tight.

"Fine." Dean sipped his coffee and laughed. "Probably shouldn't do that, act like I haven't uh…" he swallowed.

"I feel like I'm back in highschool." I sighed.

"If it makes you feel better, I feel like that everyday." He grimaced.

"I'm sorry. We can get this done quickly, I'm sure you have a lot to do."

"Offseason has its perks. Take your time," he said with the shake of his head.

He had his curls tucked neatly back and they curled at his neck. He really was handsome, glassy sea-green eyes and a big genuine smile that was full of teeth.

I asked him a few questions about his career and the team, sticking close to home and trying not to stray when he talked about moments that were definitely involving Cael. I couldn't help it though, it was infuriating how easily distracted I could become at even the idea of him.

I wasn't that girl anymore, I promised myself I wasn't before coming down here, and yet… When I closed my eyes I could see Cael coming down the step behind his house, in that dumb blue shirt, a smile bright on his face and we were sixteen again. Happy again.

"Dean, do you believe the team can survive without Arlo King?" I asked him.

"I believe in the team, I believe that Arlo did everything he could to make us much more than that. We're a family, and if anything is going to help us get through this adjustment period it's that," he answered smoothly.

"Do you think the reason for King's departure from Harbor is because of the post-season accident."

His eyes narrowed and a tiny chuckle left his lips.

"*No*," he answered with conviction. "If anything, that accident is the only thing holding Arlo back. We play NCAA ball, there's the expectation that eventually our time with a team will come to an end. He graduated, we knew he'd look for a new team."

"Even though he's been offered a position with the Hornets?" I assumed so. I couldn't be sure but I needed more from Dean than just a surface interview. He was the next closest to the situation after Silas, who only reprimanded me for digging.

"That's speculation," Dean smiled tightly, "and if Arlo was offered some-thing better," he said, leaning forward and rolling his huge shoulders out. "Then

I'm glad, he deserves it. *We* all know it and believe it. He was the best pitcher we've seen come through Harbor in fifteen years."

"You'd damn the King legacy?" I laughed.

"Line up the brothers, I'll tell them to their faces. Arlo is the best player to come out of that family."

"Bold." I nodded with a fond smile. "I like it."

He watched me carefully as I scribbled some things down and prepared myself to ask the next question. "And Cael Cody, can he recover without the backing of King?"

"Do you want the truth or do you want what Cael would want me to say?" Dean said smoothly and my heart flinched and how serious his tone was.

I had to make a decision now. If I wanted to know the truth then I would have to risk not having anything to use from Dean other than drabble like most of the other players gave me or risk my relationship with Cael, what little we had repaired, for my career.

It just all depended on how attached my stupid, foolish heart had grown.

I leaned forward and pressed pause on the recording.

"I want the truth."

"The truth is Cael has no idea what he wants ever. He's a mess, he's unpredictable but he's loud about all of it. More honest than any person I've ever met," Dean said, without hesitation. "He's had a hard time here from the beginning. I met him when we were nineteen years old and he's always had a hard time in Rhode Island, but he's always been authentic to himself, he's never bent himself over for anyone. He's always just been Cael, messy or not. He loves everyone with every bit of his heart and I—" he stopped himself. "I always appreciated that about him."

"Until you didn't?" I asked.

"Until he stopped appreciating that about himself," Dean corrected me. "After Mrs. Cody died..." Those sharp teal eyes glassed over. "He felt more trapped than ever and his drinking got worse until that wasn't enough for him and then he turned to drugs. He didn't want to feel anymore, he wanted to be numb because suddenly feeling was the enemy. Mrs. Cody dying changed him."

It changed us all.

"The only thing that's kept him sane is his '*lavender girl.*'" Dean stared at me. "You are a ghost story in the Nest, but you have always been his anchor to reality and you don't even understand him." Dean shrugged, I could tell he was getting frustrated with me.

"I didn't know it was like that, I just thought it was a joke you all had..." My voice was barely a whisper.

"That accident was a catalyst for Cael," Dean said, his hands gripping the cup so tight it buckled slightly in his grasp. "It scared him bad and he's been clean since but—"

"I'm not here to stand in the way of his recovery," I said quietly, my heart racing so fast it felt like it was trying to escape from my chest. I knew the facts about what had happened to Cael that night, but it was hard to hear that it wasn't a one time thing. That he had been on a path of destruction since leaving Texas.

"It's not you being here that scares us all." Dean stood, breaking me from my thoughts, clearly done talking to me. "It's you leaving."

I watched him leave the living room and fell back against the couch.

The tears started before I could even stop them, streaming down my face.

All this time I had thought he was thriving here.

When in reality he was just trying to survive.

A sob tore from me and that stupid friendship bracelet rubbed against my cheek as I brushed my tears away, only making me cry harder. He was just so generous and thoughtful and it bubbled up inside of me violently.

"Clementine?" Mr. Cody's voice snapped me from my tears as he entered the living room. "Are you okay?"

"Fine," I stuttered through my tears and dabbed away the ones that clung to my cheeks.

"You sure?" He asked, and settled down on the couch next to me.

He looked more put together than the last couple times I saw him. A clean pressed Hornet's polo and jeans, his hair was brushed back off his sharp features and his graying beard was trimmed neatly against his jaw.

"Not really..." I sniffled and met his sad green eyes. "Do you remember that bird?"

"We lived on a farm, Clementine, there were a lot of birds." He gave me a weak smile and reached across the table for a tissue, handing it to me.

"No, we were only ten I think. It flew into the back window at your place. Hurt its wing." I tried to help him remember.

"Oh yeah, that little barn swallow." He nodded, his brows coming together in confusion. "Cael hounded me until I made that stupid box and sat up with it for weeks in his room until he nursed it back to health. Woke up crying one morning because the bird had found its strength and flew away out the bedroom window."

"What?" I stopped and looked up at Mr. Cody. "No that bird died."

"No," he shook his head with a sigh. "It squawked nonstop in his room for three weeks, I remember because no one got any sleep and he woke us up at five am sobbing because he didn't know how to tell you he lost it."

"Lost it?" I said. For the last thirteen years I thought Cael had let the bird die.

Mr. Cody sighed and tried to remember, his tongue brushing over his bottom lip. "He was determined to help the bird because it made you sad, Clementine. He was miserable for weeks stressing about it, telling Rae that seeing you crying was the saddest he's ever been and he had to fix the bird to make you happy."

"You told me it died," I whispered. "Momma told me it died."

"We did that to protect the both of you. I'm just surprised Mary never told you the real story..."

I had believed all this time that Cael wasn't capable of loving me.

Believing that he got bored of me and let the memory of us die.

Cruelty had come so easily because I was angry.

But Dean, and now Mr. Cody, had shattered the thin crust of resentment and left my heart raw to the truth that Cael Cody had never stopped loving me.

I had let him down because I let my anger get in the way.

The bird had flown again.

Love had been enough.

CODY

"Hey, Plum." I wandered into the kitchen where she was hunched over her laptop, drinking coffee and typing away. I stared at her hand, the information we had found eating me alive from the inside.

But I shook it away, it wasn't my story to tell and if she didn't want to tell me who Julien was, I wouldn't push it. Instead I dared kiss her cheek in passing and felt her body relax from my touch. A soft tingling feeling spread across my chest at the reaction only fueling the urge to do it more but I stopped myself.

Next weekend was Thanksgiving and, with Arlo home, I was starting to feel better about everything going on. He had filled Silas and me in on everything that was happening in Dallas, but he didn't seem convinced he fit in there.

"There's something weird about them," Arlo said with a tight shrug like he was *uncomfortable in his own skin for the first time in his life.*

"Like what?" Silas leaned back against his chair, shoving french fries into his mouth.

"They don't like each other?" Arlo laughed when Silas made a face, twisted and surprised. Arlo was painfully aware he didn't sound like himself because he had looked over to me with a sigh.

"It's a job, a professional baseball team." Silas brushed it off.

"Yeah, but so are the Hornets. We might play college ball, but we still take it seriously. We live together, we eat together, we're a family. Those guys go home from practice and ignore each other on the weekends?" Arlo explained. *"I just don't think Dallas is where I belong."*

"So you're coming home?" I blurted out between bites of hamburger.

"We'll see." He sighed. "I have to ride out pre-season with them, I owe them that for giving me the chance."

"You don't owe them anything," I grumbled.

"Enough," Silas warned, hand out to silence my grumbling before he turned his gaze back to Arlo. "Take what you can get while you can."

I hadn't asked about Julien again since the porch, scared to hear her answer, so instead we danced around each other for the week.

"How did your interview with Dad go this morning?" I asked her and her eyes shot up from behind the laptop. "That bad?"

"No." She shook her head but I didn't quite believe her. "It went really well. I got some good footage."

I watched her for a second more, taking in her closed-up demeanor before grabbing a water bottle from the fridge.

"We're going down to Hilly's for dinner, did you want to come?"

"Yeah, I could use a break."

I narrowed my eyes at her. Surprisingly, she did not fight or suspect me. I could see the gears turning behind her soft eyes. I was doing that thing she hated so much: ghosting the problems we had in favor of enjoying the time we had together. I didn't care. I just wanted to be around her as much as possible.

Trying to cram seven years of distance into four months of unexpected togetherness. It was painful to think about her leaving, so I just opted for ignorance. Had it hurt when she asked me why I don't fight her on things? Sure, but Clementine had spent enough of those seven years fighting with my ghost, I could see it every time she looked at me.

I'd been lucky, blessed even. Absolutely ignorant. I spent seven years hiding in the good memories of her, fucking, and laughing. I just wanted to give her that now that we were together. No matter how little time I might get to do it.

"Alright, go get changed. I'll meet you out front."

Arlo was home, Clementine was smiling, Thanksgiving was in a week, and life seemed okay for once. There was no itch to fill the spaces with drugs or need to get drunk; I had everything I wanted.

Within five minutes, she was sitting in the passenger seat, wearing dark, tight jeans and a white cropped tank top that showed off the smallest strip of skin along her hips and stomach. It was taking everything in me not to pull over on the side of the road.

It didn't help when her head lolled to the side, and she stared up at me with those beautiful chocolate eyes. I wanted to live in the look she gave me, soft and careful, with a delicate curl to her pouty lips.

Seven years of wishing for this and it still didn't feel real.

"What?" Clementine asked me.

"Nothing, you're just beautiful," I answered and turned into the parking lot of Hilly's. She didn't respond but the blush on her cheeks told me enough as we climbed from the car and made our way inside.

Everyone upstairs hovered around one of the booth tables, chatting with Arlo as Ella laughed with Zoey, and Van threw darts with Dean.

"Hey," Silas called out to me with a handful of glasses. "Help." He handed me a couple. "You're still here?" He narrowed his eyes on Clementine.

"I sure am." She smiled and held her hand out to help.

"You should join us for Thanksgiving next weekend," he said to her.

I could see her declining before she even opened her mouth to speak. "Oh, come on, Plum. One last dinner, and then you can leave us."

Hurt flickered across her face, but she shrugged. "Sure... why not."

"Cody," Silas said before walking away. "We need to sit down and plan out the exhibition game; I've got a hundred people up my ass, and you said you'd help so..."

I tapped two fingers to my chest. "I'll get on it tomorrow."

"What's that for?" Clementine asked as I ushered her toward the table with mugs in my hand.

"Every offseason, we do an exhibition game with the Lorettes just to keep the rivalry alive going into the season. It amps up the fans and the players. It's a big deal this year." I shrugged.

"Because you won." She smiled up at me, and I could feel my chest tighten.

"Exactly." I handed a beer to Van and offered Clementine a seat at the booth as I leaned over the side. "Are you going to be home for that?" I asked Arlo, who looked over at us as we settled into the group.

"The exhibition game?" He sighed, and Ella watched him for a moment. He knew the answer. He was just scared to say it out loud. "I'm hoping to be, but no promises."

"Damn, man, the fans are going to show up at the stadium with pitchforks." Dean scoffed at him and leaned over Clementine to grab his cup. The awkward tension between them was still thick, but neither of them seemed to notice. Silas watched the interaction carefully, gray eyes scanning up to mine with a parental scowl on his face.

"Has there been a decision by Coach who will take over as Captain?" Van asked the question we had all been thinking about for weeks.

Arlo's eyes flashed to Clementine's. "Probably not the best time to talk about it."

Ever since we found out that she had been hiding a fiancé, Arlo had been making tight remarks about Clementine, insinuating that she might be lying about more than just her life back home.

"I'm off the clock, promise." She raised her hands in the air.

Arlo didn't seem convinced and turned to whisper something to Ella, who rolled her eyes at him. He laughed gently, rubbing his thumb along her jaw, and whispered a soft please that had Silas shaking his head at the interaction.

"Do you play pool?" She turned, breaking the kiss Arlo had started, and asked Clementine.

"Not very well," Clementine shrugged.

"A new victim." Zoey clapped her hands together, slid from the booth, and extended her hands to Clementine.

Brown eyes met, one set suspicious and skeptical, the other curious and intelligent. She understood what Arlo had done, but she took Zoey's hand regardless of his intentions to get rid of her.

"What the hell was that?" Silas said the minute the girls were out of earshot. "And why the hell did Miele go along with it?"

"She's still a reporter." Arlo shook his head and leaned across the table. "We don't need her writing rumors into that paper."

Dean looked over at me, waiting for me to lose my shit, and by all means I should have but I inhaled, slowing the anger that coursed its way to my heart, and sat down.

"There's been nothing from Coach on who he wants as Captain, he hasn't even spoken to me about it," Silas said. "Not that I have a say... I'm just the medical staff, but has he really said nothing to you?"

Arlo shook his head. "He's keeping the decision close to his chest. I'll be surprised if he announces it beforehand."

"Do you think he'll pick someone outside our circle?" Dean asked, worry lines forming on his face.

"If he picks anyone, it should be you," Arlo said with a hard nod.

Van and I don't flinch. "I agree." I added.

I never had a chance at Captain. Even if I was ready for it, even if I had been a model player my entire career, Dad would never stoop as low as handing it to his son. Van had one more season before he was either drafted or focused on his career. Dean getting it made the most sense. Out of all of us, he had the most potential to go pro.

"There's no one better for it." Van slapped him on the shoulder.

"Enough shop talk," Ella groaned loudly from the pool table across the loft. "Either come make things interesting or go home."

Zoey laughed and leaned on the pool cue that was basically the same size as her, her eyes bright and full as Clementine shook her head in amusement.

"That's my middle name!" I slipped from the booth.

"Shop talk?" Dean asked, confused as he followed.

"No, you dumbass, *interesting*." I looked back at him and laughed. "It's a damn good thing that you're so handsome," I teased and cooed at him like he was a dog, ruffling my hand through his blond curls as he scowled at me.

"You called for fun, and here I am. We playing teams?" I asked as I leaned over the pool table to come eye to eye with Ella.

"Me and Mary," she pointed, "against you and Dean."

"That's a bad—" Clementine started, but Ella shushed her.

"Losers streak through the campus library."

Dean's face turned pale.

218

"Hell no."

"Scared to lose?" Ella arched her brow at him. "Didn't take you for a coward, *Franklin.*"

"Don't call me that." Dean laughed as he shook his head. "Fine, but in underwear. No full frontal! The last time this happened, Cael and I were put on a twenty-four-hour hold and missed a game."

"Good thing it's off-season." Ella shrugged and held out her hand.

Clementine scooted in beside her and whispered, "are you sure you don't want Zoey as a partner?"

"I want you." Ella didn't take her eyes off of me. "We won't lose."

God, I loved it when Ella got that look in her eye. We walked into this game at a loss but it didn't mean I wasn't going to mess with Clementine's focus.

"You better hope you wore your pretty bra, Plum."

Clementine turned bright red as I extended my hand, full of shit, and shook Ella's to seal the deal. She groaned and tugged her short brown hair up into a tiny, messy ponytail as Zoey handed her the pool cue along with a rant of advice.

"She's going to kick our asses, isn't she?" Dean sighed as we turned around to figure out our strategy.

"Probably with her eyes closed." Arlo didn't miss a beat, laughing from his spot at the table where he watched proudly.

"It's disgusting to see how in love you are. Put it away, man." I turned away from the table and back to Dean. "She's got a disadvantage playing with Clem, but it means nothing. She's too smart to make a bet she can't win."

"So why the hell did you agree to it?" Dean asked, fear in those big sea-glass eyes.

"Because *I'm bored.*" I smiled so hard it hurt my cheeks. Most days, it was hard to feel that fire that drugs helped ignite but, for once, I finally felt like myself.

"Fuck sakes! *That* should be your middle name. The phrase *'I'm bored'* gets us all in more trouble than anything!" Dean groaned dramatically and thrust a cue at me before helping Zoey rack the balls. I wasn't very good at pool. The last four games we played for keeps, I lost. But Dean wasn't half bad when he was sober.

"Give me that." I took the beer from his lips as he aimed to down it and shoved it at Van. "I need you sober if we're going to have a chance."

"Seriously?" He rolled his eyes and pouted.

"Do you want to streak through the library?" I asked him, turning my hat backward on my head. "Because I don't."

"Yes, you do." Dean laughed. "It's like your favorite activity next to skinny dipping and taking shelter dogs for walks."

"True." I shrugged. "Well, for your sake, you'd better win."

"Rock, paper, scissors for start." I held out my hand to Clementine.

It was a game we played as kids when we wanted to shaft our chores off on each other. Clementine never won and, thinking back on it, I think she might have *let* me win... I scowled. All the times I had her do my chores so I could sneak off with girls, leaving her alone, she had let me do that.

"What, no ladies first?" She tilted her head to the side, breaking my thoughts.

I wanted to kiss her so bad my breath hitched in my throat.

"I don't see a single lady here," I said instead, looking around the table. "Except maybe, sweet, innocent, Sour Patch." I winked at Zoey, who smiled and framed her face with her tiny hands.

"Stop fucking flirting with my girlfriend, Cody," Van growled from his stool and threw a straw at me.

"One day," I teased and blew Zoey a kiss, narrowly avoiding the fork Van threw next. "Best two out of three," I said, turning my focus back to Clementine and raising my hand.

She wins the first one with paper.

"Ready?" I asked, but she was already saying the words. "Hah!" I yelled, "Rock beats scissors." I playfully crush her hand with my rock.

When we go the next time, I pause as she claims rock and split my fingers into makeshift scissors, letting her win. She smiles, biting down on her bottom lip, and looks up at me with excitement swimming around in her eyes.

"You let me win, Loverboy," she cooed.

"I would never, Plum," I mocked, outraged and clutched my chest, backing away from her.

MATTHEWS

"**Y**ou got this." Ella instructed me through the break and, surprisingly, I did a really good job. I lined up for my second shot, aiming for any ball I could sink, when Ella stopped me.

"Wait," she said with mischief flickering across her face. "The dare is covered, but each ball sank is a truth you have to answer."

"Oh come on, El!" Dean groaned and leaned over on the table like he was in physical pain. "You didn't say this was truth or dare, you just made a bet!"

I watched Cael staring at Ella, something passing between them. Whatever game Ella was playing beyond the pool table was *cerebral*; she was playing a mind game. She was more subtle than Arlo, who played with his ears pinned back. There was no secret that Cael's faux-older brother was a protective doberman-type alpha male but seeing the look in his eyes today. Something had shifted.

He stiffened his shoulders in the loose gray t-shirt and shook his head, admitting a silent defeat.

"Fine, each ball sank is a truth answered."

"Why do you play these stupid games with her? She always wins!" Dean groaned and paced in a loose circle as Zoey laughed.

"Less complaining, more... *pool shark-doing*." Cael waved his hands around at Dean, who responded with a strained and terrified, "you think I'm a pool shark? We're screwed!"

I laughed and Ella leaned close to me. "Take that pocket, really slow, inhale, and shoot."

Her voice was so calm and I followed her every word, watching the orange ball bounce off the left pocket. Ella didn't flinch. She was calm as Cael leaned over the table and sunk the first ball he laid eyes on. As he straightened out his eyes met mine, sparkling like they were made of ocean waves.

"Favorite color?" He asked me.

"Juvenile," Dean scoffed.

"Spell that." Cael laughed at him, attention breaking just for a moment, but Dean just shrugged. "Don't use words you can't spell, Tucker."

"Green."

It was purple, but I wasn't going to give Cael an inch of satisfaction. No matter how simple things had become between us, the urge to remind him how horrible it could be lingered.

Cael looked back at me and smiled because he understood the game. Without breaking eye contact, he sank another ball.

"Is there a surface in the Nest you prefer, Ella?" He turned his head slowly to her.

Arlo lost it laughing, wild and loud, breaking the hardened persona for a brief second to enjoy that teasing. It was a hard feeling to swallow, standing on the outside of their circle, watching them laugh and treat each other like family. I had Bobbi, and in moments like that, witnessing the magical entanglement of an unbreakable thread that strung the Hornets together, I missed her.

"It's at least twelve inches long." She laughed and winked at Arlo, whose laughter stopped, and a blush spread across his cheeks.

"Is that medically safe?" Zoey asked, her eyes bouncing between Ella and Arlo's crotch with a horrified look on her face. Van scoffed like she had personally insulted his penis. "Aw. Baby, you're perfect," she cooed at him. "I don't need twelve inches."

Arlo lost it laughing again, this time Silas joined him in a chorus of taunts that faded out as Cael lined up to take his next shot but missed. He watched me from across the table as he handed the pool cue to Dean.

Ella wasted no time taking her shot and landed a double ball in the far right pocket.

"That's my girl," Arlo praised.

"Have you been using the batting cages?" She asked Cael without remorse.

He chuckled, and I watched as the lie flickered across his features.

"Of course, I have been, Peachy."

But he doesn't lie like I expect him to, and it rattles me a little because it proves just how unafraid he is to get in trouble. Maybe it was how honest he was even when playing a kids' game that scared me, but our lives weren't a game and he had never lied to me.

My heart raced at the thought.

Ella didn't say much else, but she turned to me. "I sunk two balls, ask a question," she whispered to me.

"That's not the rules," Cael groaned.

"You wouldn't follow them even if they were, shithead," Ella hissed, clearly upset with him but finding other ways to punish him for his secret activities.

Cael looked to Arlo for help but his friend just shrugged him off.

"She has a point," Arlo said. He might have been on Cael Cody protection detail, but Ella was meddling and she was the boss.

"First time," I ask him and the grin falls from his face.

He had been mine, despite everything that happened, *he had been mine.*

I could see the gears turning behind his eyes, the storm passing as he faked a smile and leaned over the table at me. "Her name was Clementine," he whispered, his eyes flickering to the bracelet around my wrist. "Waste of a question."

Dean looked on quietly, and Ella watched the two of us with a smile on her face that could only mean trouble. Cael was pissed off. Outraged that I would even ask him, I could see it in his shoulders and jaw. The huffy little smile that formed on his lips was a tell-tale sign that the question upset him. It brought his morals into question and rattled the walls around the memory we both held onto so desperately from that night.

Ella took another shot and sunk another ball.

"What about you?" Ella poked Dean in the chest with her finger and smiled at him. "First time?"

A blush crept on his cheeks, he scanned the room and leaned closer to her, lowering his voice. "Patrick Harvey." He shrugged, "In the back of Van's truck after we won the season opener two years ago."

"That was your first time?" Cael looked at him surprised. "In College?"

Dean looked at him. "It's not like I could bring guys home."

"You fucked a Pittsburgh player in the back of my truck?" Van hollered. "You could have at least picked a piece of ass from a good team! Or screwed around with someone on our team. Now there's bad juju in my truck."

"That was two years ago, Van, I don't fuck where I play," Dean said.

"Yes, you do," Cael and Arlo said in unison.

"I didn't back then." He rolled his eyes. "And can you all stop yelling, please? There are other people in the diner."

"Take your shot," Cael said to Ella. "Get this beating over with."

"Dean," Arlo called over to him and the first baseman wandered to the table.

He leaned over the table and Arlo whispered something to him that made Dean groan as he returned to the pool table and watched Ella miss her shot, which was strange because she was perfectly aligned. He surveyed the table before taking his own, sinking a ball without much thought.

"Who's Julien?" Dean asked.

My heart seemed to sink into my stomach. I should have expected Cael to get curious. He had heard more of that conversation that I had wanted, and now... I looked at Cael, hoping that he'd give me an out, but he wasn't on my side.

He was just as invested in the question as Arlo was.

"If you wanted to know, you should have offered to play," I called out to him, my body leaning around Cael to make eye contact with Arlo. "He's my ex."

Arlo's dark, judgemental eyes narrowed and he pushed to the edge of the booth. "Why's the picture still up then?"

"That's a question, King." I rolled my eyes.

Dean missed his next shot.

I tried to shake off the adrenaline that rushed through me when I didn't miss mine.

"Why were you stalking my social media?" I asked Cael, ignoring the heat that radiated off Arlo.

"Cause I'm a jealous idiot." Cael shrugged and leaned his head back to stare at the ceiling. "I had to know."

Cael watched me, his eyes burning blue and his jaw tight with unsaid upset.

"And you were keeping secrets again."

He said again like we were back in my bedroom and he was pleading with me to tell him why I was crying. *"I made you sad."* His voice broke in my head like it had done that day.

"It wasn't your business, Cael." I swallowed and turned away from him back to the table.

"Take a beat," Ella whispered, forcing me to breathe before taking my next shot. I sank that too.

"All yours, I'm sick of the truth," I said.

"What's with the bracelet?" Ella pointed to his wrist.

Cael looked down at the fraying threads and smiled. "Clementine made it for me in the sixth grade out of string she stole from the corner store in town." His eyes caught mine and sparkled under the pool table bulbs.

"Sixth grade?" Ella's brows pinched together. "How is that thing still on?"

Cael shrugged. "Willpower..." He searched for the word. "Stubborn determination."

I smiled at him as my chest filled up with warmth and I leaned over the table to shoot again. I missed my second shot, my hands were shaking with adrenaline as his silent affection poured over me.

Cael moved around the table, brushing up against me as he lined up his shot and missed.

"You're distracted!" Dean groaned as his eyes counted the balls still left in play. "We're going to lose."

"We were never going to win, big guy." Cael slipped back into his typical cotton candy demeanor. Fluffy and sweet.

I backed away from the table so Ella could sink the last four balls. One at a time they plunked into their respective corners and Arlo's grin took on a new brightness. Beaming with pride, Ella straightened out and surveyed her work.

"Have you shown Mary the calendar?" Ella asked and Dean went beet red while Cael just started laughing. "She hasn't seen it has she? You should use it in your piece, it's a work of art."

Zoey giggled from her side.

"Don't worry boys, I burned every copy of that calendar she's gotten her hands on," Arlo said with confidence as he crossed his arms and stared at his fiancée.

"Hey Kelly," Ella walked to the banister and yelled from over the loft, her head turning to Arlo with a sly smile. "You still have that copy?"

"What?" Arlo straightened out, his body growing tense. "Oh, Blondie..." He sighed. "You're in so much trouble."

"Yeah, yeah..." She waved him off as the hostess came up the stairs with a Harbor Hornets Fundraiser Calendar in her hands. "Remind me how much trouble I'm in later when we're alone," Ella hummed, kissing him but keeping the calendar out of the reach of his grabby hands.

She tossed it on the pool table, flipping it open to November.

Dean was squatted on first base in a pair of tight ball pants and no shirt, his skin glistening from sunscreen and sweat. Navy blue face paint smeared beneath his eyes complimented the green-blue color of his burning gaze. His hair wet and curled around his ears with a serious look on his face as he stared out past the camera.

"Mr. November," Zoey swooned. "Always a favorite."

Van choked on his beer.

"But Mr. June..." Ella flipped the calendar back to Cael's month.

"Oh my God." I covered my mouth and looked down at it. "How did you even get up there?"

Cael was standing with his feet wide, balanced on the massive block letter sign that lit up the front of the Harbor stadium with a bat carefully positioned between his legs and his hands wrapped around the top in such a way that he perfectly covered himself.

"A ladder." He shrugged, clearly very proud of himself.

The hazy blue light of the sign kissed his naked skin and complimented his stupid grin.

"You climbed that ladder naked?" Zoey giggled.

"I'll tell you something, there's nothing as freeing as the wind kissing your balls twenty feet in the air with the looming threat of death on the horizon." Cael smiled.

I dug my phone out of my pocket and snapped a photo of Mr. June and saved it.

"I have more, I'll mail you a copy," Ella said and Arlo practically hissed from his spot at the table.

"Oh relax, Cap," Ella waved him off. "I pulled Mr. January out of all of them. Your ass in those baseball pants are for my eyes only."

He cocked his head and the lightness returned to his features as he rose from his chair.

"One last question." She stared at Cael as Arlo rounded the table and hung himself around her, kissing her face just below her scar. "I asked about your past, but what do you see for your future?"

MATTHEWS

"You stink." I laughed as Kiefer came off the ice. He had invited me down to watch practice but I'd spent most of my time with my nose in my journal. It was fun to watch them play but hockey had never been my favorite sport.

"Yeah, I do." He smiled and kissed my cheek.

"Did you have fun?" I asked.

"Uh, yeah... There were a lot of drills today, I'm just kind of exhausted now," he said, running his fingers through damp hair.

I nodded, not really sure what to say. I had barely even watched practice.

"I'm going to go shower, and then I'll drive you home, yeah?" He said after a beat of awkward silence, backing up from me on his skates.

Sometimes there was this flutter in my chest that reminded me just how lucky I was that a guy like Kiefer Hart had even given me the time of day. And when he smiled at me, the way he was now, with his sweaty hair and flushed cheeks, that feeling ran rampant.

I nodded. "Go!" I shooed him off and went back to collect my things from the empty stands. There were a few parents around, and a girlfriend or two but, for the most part, the arena was quiet.

"Looks like Cael Cody's shadow got a boyfriend." Andrea sauntered up behind me with one of her many plastic-looking lackeys and smiled. "Surprising, I figured you would follow him around until you died. Do you like...have a chair you sit in to watch him make out with other girls or..."

228

She was bitter because things hadn't worked out between her and Cael. He'd said something like, *'she's probably the most vapid person I've ever spoken to,'* which had ended with us laughing so hard we were crying.

But Cael wasn't here now to protect me from her petty wrath.

"Did you need something, Andrea?" I politely asked her.

"Oh, I just came over to tell you that you're still pathetic, even with Kiefer Hart on your arm. It's a giant cry for help. He just got out of a relationship with someone and is clearly heartbroken enough to date the likes of... well you." Andrea giggled and looked me over. "Have a good day, Clemmy."

I stared at her back as she wandered away with her friends, pushing down the bile that rose as I battled the insecurities swirling around in the pit of my stomach. I sat on the bench for another twenty minutes, waiting for Kiefer and, when he finally appeared, laughing with his teammates, I was more than ready to go home.

Andrea was right. *Who did I think I was? Dating a hockey player?* Acting like I was one of those girls who could get away with that. I didn't even know he had an ex-girlfriend. She was probably gorgeous and tall. My mind tangled with negative thoughts.

"Earth to Clementine..." Kiefer's voice floated down around me and broke me from my existential thoughts. "Are you alright?" He asked as I stood up. He took my bag from me and slung it over his shoulder, tangling his hand into mine. When I didn't answer he just tugged me along slowly.

"Come on, let's get you home."

The drive home was quiet; I wasn't really sure what to say to fill the silence that had settled between us. It wasn't his fault my insecurities were eating me alive. His interest in me seemed genuine but now, with Andrea chirping in the back of my mind...

"You've been quiet," he said as he pulled up the driveway. My parents had gone to the city for the weekend and I was just looking forward to curling up on the couch alone and writing. "You sure everything is alright?" Kiefer asked again.

"Yeah."

"I know your parents are gone. Do you want me to stay and keep you company?" He asked, brushing a piece of hair behind my ear as I looked over to the empty car park. "No funny business, I promise. We can watch a movie."

I was going to say no but he smiled at me and all my resolve melted away. "That would be nice."

"We can order pizza?" He asked.

I nodded even though pizza was my least favorite of all the takeout spots in our small town. But he wouldn't know that because I never told him. Afraid to seem picky, so I would eat pizza with a smile on my face. Just for him.

He shut off the engine and helped me from the car, waiting patiently for me to unlock the front door before I led him inside. Kiefer ordered the pizza right away while I picked a movie. He complained when I grabbed *Thirteen Ghosts* and asked if we could watch something a little more interesting with less gore, so I conceded and grabbed *George of the Jungle* before I pulled out some blankets. It wasn't long before we were sitting side by side beneath one, full of our pizza and almost finished the movie.

"I don't see how you could hate this movie; Brendan Fraser's physique should be studied."

I rolled my eyes and laughed gently. "I don't hate him. *George of the Jungle* just isn't my favorite."

"You definitely hated every second of this," Kiefer teased.

"Not every second." I shook my head and leaned into him playfully. He looked down at me, his expression softening as he leaned closer. I opened my mouth to tell him I wasn't really ready for that, but he collided with me before I could protest.

Kiefer's lips were so soft it distracted me from his hand raking into my hair and his arm wrapping around my waist. He continued to kiss me as he lifted me from the sofa and laid me back. He pulled back momentarily, hovering over me before crashing down again and sliding his tongue into my mouth.

His hands were everywhere all at once and I was overwhelmed with excitement and—guilty? I pulled back from Kiefer and tried to catch my breath but he just came back for more. My hands were trapped awkwardly beneath his giant body and anytime I wiggled he took it as enjoyment.

"Kie—" He silenced my next plea with another kiss. "Kiefer stop!" I pulled back and shouted, prying my arms free and pushing on his chest.

"Oh come on, Clem, it's just making out." He laughed, dipping back against me. His frame was too heavy and wide for me to fight back against the full weight of his body.

"I don't—" I turned my face away from him and he caught it in his hand roughly bringing me back to his lips. The more he forced it the more panicked I became and the more I fought against him.

"Just lay back and enjoy it, Clementine," Kiefer snapped at me and shoved me back against the couch. "You should be grateful." He smirked but that warm feeling was gone and it was replaced with nausea that rolled violently up my throat.

He gripped my hands tightly and lowered again. "Kiefer stop!" I pleaded and shut my eyes tightly to block out what was happening. My throat was so tight I didn't think I could beg him again no matter how hard I tried. His other hand pressed to my stomach beneath my sweater, his palm sticky and hot on my skin as his tongue slipped into my mouth again, silencing my pleas.

"Stop," I cried. "Please."

The weight on my chest felt like a thousand stones and then it was just gone.

"Get the hell out of here." Cael's voice echoed through the living room as my eyes blinked open and adjusted to my surroundings.

I scrambled up from the couch, tumbling back over the side and wrapping my arms around myself as Cael shoved Kiefer back again.

"She invited me in, man. Back the fuck off!" Kiefer pushed back.

Adrenaline and shame coursed through my veins as Cael laughed in disbelief. "I could *hear* her telling you to stop!" Cael stepped forward, matching size for size, but Kiefer wasn't ready to give in.

"She was all over me, she was enjoying it, man. Wait your fucking turn—" Kiefer's next insult was silenced with a simple, deafening crack. Cael's hand crossed through the air and collided with his face, instantly causing the skin to flush with color.

Kiefer swung back, hitting Cael hard. He stumbled for a second but went back for more with a snarl only for Kiefer to step back and put his hands out to grab his shirt.

"Fuck you, Cody, she's not worth breaking my stick hand for." He shoved him back as Cael regained his balance and swung the front door open.

"Pussy," Cael growled and kicked it shut behind Kiefer before he turned to look at me. When he stepped forward I flinched and he stopped instantly. "Clem—" his voice was soft, too soft, and the sound of it made my eyes well.

I couldn't breathe and, as he stepped closer, the room came crashing down on me. Cael followed me down as I sank to the floor, sitting on his knees across from me he reached his hand out and wiggled his fingers.

"I'm here Clementine," he said quietly as I cried, "I'm here as long as you need me."

CODY

C lementine.

Loving her.

Holding her.

Spending hours making her laugh until we couldn't breathe.

Kissing her every night until she fell asleep in my arms.

I wanted every small win, every massive failure, and I wanted it with her.

The future I saw for myself was simply Clementine.

I looked at her, knowing that my cheeks were pink but not being able to stop myself from catching her gaze. Her. She was my future. She always had been.

But she's leaving. *You can't do that to her...it's unfair.*

"Thanksgiving," I teased lightly. It wasn't a lie, but it wasn't exactly the truth. Thinking about my future made me sick to my stomach. I lifted the hem of my shirt over my head and threw it at Clementine.

The one that had been tucked under her pillow had been missing from my floor for weeks. A selfish pride had filled me when I saw it there, where she slept every night. She shouldn't be embarrassed about it. I had spent the last seven years chasing around the smell of lavender just to feel her in my veins. My shirt had to smell like her now; she was due for a new one.

Clementine rubbed it between her fingers, her eyes flickering up to meet mine. I winked as I tossed my arms up and yelled.

"Now, who's driving us over to the library?"

She was still staring, her brown eyes glittering with excitement. She understood, and it made my heart skip a beat as Dean chucked his shirt at Ella. Arlo caught it in his hand before it hit her face. His dark eyes watched me carefully as he balled it up and set it on the table. I had known he would take the chance to push the conversation toward Julien; I just wished he hadn't put her on the spot like that.

It wasn't any of my business, or theirs, who she was dating. I did enjoy the conviction in her voice when she claimed he was an ex. Whether or not Arlo believed her was a different story and I could tell by the way he was studying my face that he didn't.

Clementine watched the interaction carefully, picking up on the tense energy that flooded the space as I flicked the button on my jeans. "Well?" I asked, looking over at a fully dressed Dean. "You too." My eyes dragged down his enormous frame.

"Stop making bets against Ella," he snapped each word at me as he shucked from his jeans and stood uncomfortably in a pair of tight boxers.

"You can run to the library," Ella cocked her head to the side. "Consider it payback for using the batting cages behind my back and before you argue." She wiggled from Arlo's grasp and leaned on the table. "I know you sneak him in there." She narrowed her eyes at Dean.

"Get moving, boys." Arlo cracked a smile.

I kicked off my sneakers and dropped my jeans to the floor, declaring, "I'm keeping my socks."

"Whatever," Ella barked as both Dean and I backed away from the table toward the stairs. She pulled out her phone, and I swore Dean yelped.

"Don't you dare!" He pointed at her. "If my Dad sees this..." Dean's voice trailed off.

"Your dad is definitely going to see this," Van laughed, his was hung around Zoey with a bright smile on his face.

"*Run!*" Arlo clapped his hands together and both of us took off down the stairs.

Dean shoved his way past me through the door. It was a fifteen minute run to campus, and if we managed to get picked up between Hilly's and the library, it would be a blessing. If we got caught in the library... *again*... who knew what would happen.

"You're out of shape, Cody!" Dean called to me as he rounded the corner to the base of the hill where the bar sat. "If you get caught, you're on your own!"

I wasn't out of shape, he was just pushing a brutal pace. The wind nipped at my bare calves and my chest started to burn from the intake of cold air but I pushed myself forward to catch up with Dean.

"How are you even that fast?" I huffed, with barely enough breath to ask the question. "You've got to...weigh like... two hundred pounds."

"Two fifty-seven," Dean said with pride and picked up his pace. "Shit, here comes the parade."

Four cars came up behind us, including Arlo's fastback and my car, Clem behind the wheel with a goofy smile on her face as they drove past up the hill. She slowed down as she passed, rolling the window down and blowing a kiss.

"Nice ass," she called out.

I winked at her but was instantly humbled.

"I was talking to Tucker." She burst into laughter and sped off.

"She's gonna kill my tires," I groaned and kept running, the cold air shrinking every impressive body part by the second.

"She drives like you." Dean lost it laughing.

"She's crashed way more cars than I have!" I called out to him as he sprinted up the rest of the hill. Once the land evened out, it was easier to keep up with his excruciating pace. "This is why I don't run with you." I was completely out of breath. "You're like... the Terminator! Do you even feel pain?" I cried out.

He stalled as we rounded the corner to the library to see the crowd that had formed, Ella had graciously stopped recording the dare and instead called the entire team down to the parking lot.

"Fuck," he swore and turned to run backward so I could see the anger on his face. "Stop betting against Miele. She's too good at party games."

"Never." I laughed loudly and kept running. "There's no fun in playing it safe, Tucker!" I stopped short of the doors, Dean's face scrunching up as a smile flooded my face.

"Don't," he warned. "If you do it, I have to do it, and I'm *not* doing it."

"Coward." I licked my lips and flicked my fingers into the elastic of my boxers, shucking them from my body and tossing them behind me. A chorus of cheering and whistling came from behind me.

"God damnit," Dean growled and kicked his own boxers off.

Someone yelled, *'Now that's twelve inches!'* as he undressed completely.

"I hate you!" He threw them at me.

"No, you don't," I said.

Bare assed, we both darted into the library. The crowd followed, if only to watch us get arrested by campus security. Dean and I had cuddled more than once behind campus bars and I had a feeling today would be no different. Dad would be pissed, causing such a scene with a reporter around, but Mary hadn't come to Hilly's, Clementine had.

"Hey!" The librarian yelled as we darted in the doors. "Not again!"

"*Again*," Dean hollered back at her, beet red and a huge smile on his face. "I'm sorry, just like, cover your eyes." He made the motion, laughing hard as he narrowly avoided smashing into a desk full of girls. "Ladies." He bowed, his hands slapping down to his dick and doing nothing to conceal how naked he really was as he dashed to the left.

The security guards came out of nowhere, from either side of the library, forcing us down the center aisle. "Bet you I can last longer," I yelled out as Dean spun around a guy just trying to find a book, side-swiping him. The book went flying, but before it could drop to the ground, I scooped it from the air and handed it back to him.

"I know you can't last longer." Dean looked back at me.

I missed that grin, I thought. Smile wide, the playfulness of who Dean Tucker truly was flooded in and puffed out his chest.

"Deal." He stuck his head out around the aisle. "Hey! Darcy!" He yelled at someone I couldn't see but dread washed over me.

"You're a dirty, fucking, cheating liar! Anyone but Darcy!"I started to panic, looking around for exit strategies. The random dude beside me just shrugged his shoulders, doing everything he could to focus on my face and not my junk.

"I know you want him!" Dean yelled.

Darcy Matheson was the fastest campus security and *my mortal enemy.*

"You're such an ass!" I chucked a book at Dean but he dodged it.

"Don't throw books, Cael." Dean threw his head back in laughter, eyes growing wide as he caught sight of someone. "He's over here!"

Darcy hated my guts after the impromptu karaoke in the auditorium during a graduation. One that had ended with me in handcuffs and on the news. The incident that had almost gotten me suspended from Harbor.

"Cael Cody." Darcy rounded the aisle as Dean slipped from his grasp. His eyes narrowed on me, trapped in the cramped aisle. "Don't move."

"Can we talk about this?" I darted to the next aisle and he followed, blocking my exit. "I had no idea those girls were your daughters, or I would have never kissed them during that Queen song! I mean, what are the chances that your twins were up there during that rendition of Under Pressure?" I backed up a step and Darcy's fingers flickered to the taser on his belt.

I cocked my head to the side, the tingle of adrenaline coursing through me.

"Oooh, Darcy. Are you going to tase me?" I gasped in fake outrage, it might actually be a little fun to be tased.

"More than once," he huffed.

"Will it tickle?" I purred and ran a nervous hand through my hair as I scoped for an exit.

"Sure, kid," he snapped and ran toward me.

But I was faster. I spun on my heels before he could unbutton the taser and took off down the next aisle and up the stairs to the second floor of the library. A crowd had formed inside, cheering on Dean as he darted in and out of the aisles, hands over his junk as Cole, affectionately known as 'mall cop', and Lionel, who was so old he should be in a wheelchair, chased him. Ella and Clem watched on from where they leaned against the help desk with wide smiles on their faces as Dean wiggled free from between the two guards' grasps.

I needed to distract him if I was going to win. Darcy was playing fast and dirty with volts of electricity, and eventually, I was going to go down hard.

Whistling loudly, fingers between my lips, Dean almost tripped over a rogue book bag on the floor. Lionel closed in on him again but Dean managed to juke him and climbed over a chair and across a row of tables. The students were screaming and clapping as he darted back toward the entrance of the library. It wasn't a matter of whether we'd be caught, we would; it was just about who would go down first.

"If you get caught before me, you take dinner duties for a month!" I holler down, gripping the railing and leaning over it. He lifted his hand in the air, flipping me the middle finger and launching himself from the tabletop, landing on the floor with a thud, twirling away from Cole and into a crowd of people.

"Mr. Cody, get your genitals off my glass!" The librarian screamed from the main floor and I stepped back in laughter, seeing the print I left.

"It's art," I said as Darcy appeared at the top of the stairs, out of breath. His red hair was sticking to the back of his neck, and sweat was building around his collar and armpits. "You agree with me, right?" I pointed to the smudge, but he wasn't amused.

"Just stop running," he huffed.

"Sorry, sugartits, I have a bet to win!"

"Cody!" He yelled as I jumped back from the railing. Weaving through the tables of studying students, I made for the emergency exit along the back wall.

"Excuse me." I sneaked through a group of guys, not daring to look over my shoulder for Darcy as I focused on my only exit strategy. "Shit." My shoulders slumped when I saw it, the door was padlocked.

"Now, Darcy, I'm pretty sure that's illegal!" I turned with my hands covering myself, knowing he was there. "That's a fire exit!"

"And your favorite escape route," he added. There was a sick grin of accomplishment on his pudgy face as he popped the button on his campus-issued holster. "Don't lecture me on rules when you've partaken in public nudity on campus more than once a year." He stared at me as he said it, his fingers sliding over the handle of the taser.

"We're even after this Darcy, alright?" I put my hands out to the side. "Wait!" I hollered and put my hand up to him as he aimed. "If I pee, don't tell anyone?"

Amusement flickered across his face. "I'm framing the picture I'm about to take and putting it in the trophy case in the main office."

"There's no way the Dean approves–" My words were silenced by the sound of snapping electricity soaring through the air.

The muscle cramping was the worst as the prongs of the gun dug into my stomach and sent shock waves through me. I dropped to my knees, my body shaking as the electricity wreaked havoc on my nervous system and turned my vision hazy. It was the worst feeling I had ever experienced and quite possibly the most exhilarating.

Darcy knelt beside my head. "Truce?" He stared at me as I curled into a ball to ride out the aftershocks. Even if I wanted to make a snide remark, I couldn't feel my tongue or my lips to use them. Darcy laughed at my suffering. "Good. Stay out of my library."

CODY

"Can you carry that?" I asked Ella as she shifted the crate of beer on her hip up the cabin stairs with the Thanksgiving air whipping through her hair.

"I'm fine, grab that." She flicked her fingers toward two more large boxes of food that were heavy but not horrible to haul up the stairs. My shoulder pinched uncomfortably, but I clenched my jaw and followed her into the noisy house.

She had worked my shoulder harder than ever in the week since the bet at Hilly's, and I had earned it. Sneaking into the bat cages, even if I was being careful...was stupid. But not any more foolish than believing that somewhere, tucked between all the good times Clementine was having, was the possibility that I convinced her to stay.

I didn't want her to leave and, with the weekend finally here, this was my last chance to prove that she belonged with me. I would follow her if she asked. It wasn't the first time I had thought about it, it plagued me a lot after we moved and I had come up with a lot of plans, but then she never responded to my calls or letters, so I just let her move on because it was what I thought she wanted.

But seeing her now, that day in my Dad's office, I knew instantly that's never what she wanted. We still had that connection, and I think she was finally aware of it.

"How is..." Ella set the crate down on the counter and lowered her voice, "the *Clementine* thing?"

The cabin was already packed with people. Sawyer and Lucas had come in and Arlo was talking to them on the deck as Nicholas hovered inside. The relationship between the four of them was still pulled pretty tightly, with Arlo not quite ready to forgive Nick and nobody blamed him. But he was trying.

Silas, with his messy, dark hair and beard that had grown less patchy recently, was forearm-deep in turkey, his soft-spoken mother giving him pointers as he shoved more garlic inside. Family weekend was nice, but most of the parents didn't really come anymore. The younger guys, sure, but the older players' family weekend was just a nuisance for them to all come out. Thanksgiving, though, everyone showed up when the Shores invited them.

The entire house smelled like baked goods, sweet potatoes, green beans, and stuffing. It was my favorite holiday, hands down. Professor Tucker helped Mr. Shore set up more tables, Van and his sister, Cosy, wrestled playfully as they laid out place settings, and Dean stood uncomfortably in the corner with his siblings and their significant others.

"Emergency services are needed," I said to Ella.

"Hey!" She whined as I dropped the boxes of food and kissed her cheek.

I was avoiding her interrogation, mostly because I wasn't even sure how to answer her. I wasn't going to lie and tell her it was going great because it wasn't, we were a mess but it was *our* mess. And that counted for something.

"Mmm." I heard her groan as I brushed through a crowd of loudly laughing, drunk dads, past the gaggle of moms bringing up old embarrassing stories of their sons.

"Oh, hello." I nearly tripped over a small child stumbling across the floor and scooped her up in my arms as I continued on. Her little fingers wrapped around mine, spinning the rings in amazement. "Well, aren't you adorable," I whispered against her curly blonde hair and scanned the room.

"I'd recognize those eyes anywhere." She giggled as I bounced her in my arms and spun around another group of bodies in my way.

"Who the hell gave you a baby?" Dean laughed as I approached.

There was a quick moment of her and I looking at each other, confused, before I looked back at Dean. "It was just lying around here... you know it kind of looks like you," I said, leaning back to inspect it and only making her giggle more.

Dean shook his head. "Her name is Josie," he said. They shared the same big teal sea-glass eyes and curly blonde hair.

Honestly, everyone in that family did. Anna's was longer but curly and her eyes were framed by pounds of mascara. His brother, Harvey, was taller and skinnier than Dean, exhausted-looking as he sighed. They hated me and God damn did I love it. Seeing their scowls gave me a rush of adrenaline.

"You didn't tell me you had kids!" I teased, brushing my nose against the baby's to make her laugh.

Anna scowled. "Give me my daughter."

"Sorry, we bonded." I held her tighter and she cooed in response. "I'm keeping her." I was joking, but the baby laughed and Anna grew more impatient with me every passing second.

"Cael," Harvey first named me.

"What, *Harvey*?" I sneered. "If Anna is anything like you, she'll have ten. She won't even miss one, and you like Uncle Cael don't you? Don't you..." The end of my sentence turned into baby talk as I tickled her belly. Harvey didn't like that joke, his hand rolling tightly around his beer. "Do you even give them names, at that point? Or are they just numbers?" I asked, never getting an answer as Anna took the baby by force.

"Ooh alright, not in the mood I see. Fine...a baby for a baby," I announced, snatching Dean by the collar of his dress shirt and dragging him from his corner.

I threw my arm over him and walked with him back to the stairs. "Come on." I nodded to the rooms, and he didn't argue with me. Soon the sound was blocked out by the door of our room, I put on one of Van's old records and sank down on the floor next to the hulking frame of my best friend.

Dean peeled at the label of his beer.

"I'd offer you one but—" He said. "You're doing really good."

"I've been seeing my sponsor a lot," I admitted.

I had gone to lunch with Josh yesterday. After everything I could feel the walls bowing in on me and it was getting harder to say no. I was fully aware that I was relying on my interactions with Clementine to keep me steady and it scared me even more.

Pretending came naturally to me. I would fake a smile or force a laugh. The louder I was, the less likely anyone was to notice that I was breaking down inside. It was simple math, and it had worked for the last seven years.

But my brain and my heart knew that this was the last weekend with her.

They were pleading for comfort.

The only problem was the kind of comfort they wanted was found in the bottom of a bottle of vodka, or the purse of one of those rich moms sitting in the living room. Every single one of them probably had something to numb the itch.

I hadn't realized how tense Dean was until the sound of everyone downstairs faded and it was just the two of us again, sitting to the soft, sad melody of some random Beach Boys song. We had spent so many of the nights here, stashed away from the world because it was the only place Dean could find peace while he fought a silent war with his family.

"You're on my official list, you know." I kicked my foot out and knocked into his outstretched leg as I turned toward him with my legs crossed against his side.

"What kind of list, assassinations?" He joked, but it was empty and almost sad.

"People that I owe apologies to, I guess." I flipped my hat off my head and set it down to run my fingers through my hair. It was getting too long and curled at my nape in sweaty bundles. "I've put you through a lot of shit over the years." I wanted to get close to him but settled for tucking my hands into my lap. "And you just took it even though you shouldn't have. It made me no better than your siblings, and I'm sorry that I did that to you when you were already dealing with them."

"You weren't all bad, Cael..." Dean said, but I cut him off before he could keep going.

"This isn't about me, and it's not about making me feel better. It's about all the shit I did that hurt you, that I shouldn't have done. And I'm sorry."

He looked up from the bottle with those devastatingly blue eyes and gave me a tight nod.

"But listen, I need you to take one more round of shit," I said and he shook his head, his body instinctively turning toward me. Ready to walk me back from the ledge I was on. But it wasn't my turn to be led; it was his. "Not for me," I added and finally closed the gap between us. "I need you to do this for yourself, and I'll be there to back you up when you're ready. But you need to stop hiding from them."

"I don't know; it's working out pretty good for me." He curled one of his long legs around me as I settled between his legs.

The connection and the closeness made us both feel less tense and awkward. But something settled; it didn't feel romantic, or the start of something like it normally would have. It felt light and platonic. It made me a little sad but I swallowed it down and focused on Dean.

"Is it?" I asked him.

Dean had always been like this. Sturdy and quiet. He was reliable and charming. His stupid soft, blond curls and pretty, perfect smile had me sold the moment he introduced himself. It was a surprise when he cornered me in the locker room after practice, our lips meeting for the first time. That make-out ignited a three-year-long, on-and-off-and-on-again, twisted relationship that hurt us both in the end.

I sank into Dean to distract from my sadness, and Dean used me as a safe haven when the pressures of his family got too heavy or too hard. We were bound to go up in flames at some point but, through that fire, our friendship grew stronger every day and I could tell that hiding was really starting to eat at him.

"This isn't me pressuring you to do it." I rubbed my hands over my face. "Come out to them when you're ready, don't at all if that's what you really want, but I just hate seeing you sad at these things. The gala, the exhibition games. Don't you want to celebrate with someone when we win or go home to someone when we don't?" I asked. "And don't say me because I mean someone who will really be there for *you*."

I just wanted him to be able to have those moments the same way all the other guys did without the worry that he was upsetting his family.

"Of course I do," he answered after a long break.

"You deserve to have it, Dean," I added. "More than anyone here, *you've earned that*."

A knock at the door silenced whatever he was going to say next, and Silas popped his head in. "I didn't mean to interrupt, but she actually showed," he said and my heart leaped.

"Go." Dean smiled at me and slapped the side of my face. "Hey, Cael," he said as I stood and looked down at him. "Thank you for loving me the way I needed, even when it was hard to hide. You're my best friend."

"And then some." I kicked his shoe, leaning over and kissing the top of his shaggy hair.

With one final look at him I made my way out into the loft and leaned over the banister to find her in the chaos below. A smile spread across my face as I found her, dark, soft curls around her beautiful round face and a small blush to her cheeks as she realized where I was. It had been nearly twenty-three years of knowing her, but Clementine Matthews had been stealing the air from my lungs every second of every day since the day we were born.

I had never needed a breath to live; I had only needed her.

MATTHEWS

Cael stared at me from the banister that hung above the giant, very crowded living room with the biggest smile on his face, and it made my heart race. The beige dress shirt he wore was unbuttoned around the collar, showing off his light layer of chest hair, and the thin necklace was fancier than I'd expected. His jaw was covered in scruff, making him look so much older. I wanted to know how it felt on the skin between my thighs. I smiled back at him; for once he looked relaxed and happy. The darker blue flecks in his eyes vibrant as he leaned back from the banister on his heels and showed off the swell of his biceps beneath the loose sleeves of the shirt that rolled at his forearms.

"You can put your bags in here." Zoey wrapped her hand into the crook of my elbow and led me back to a second set of rooms that had a few beds each. "Most guests share, so Ella and I thought it would be fun to have a mini girls' weekend. We're going to stay in here with you so that you don't have to bunk with any of the parents."

Zoey smiled at me in her yellow tank top and jeans. Her long brown hair was pulled into a loose bun at the back of her neck, and she had a sweet little dimple on her cheek.

"That sounds wonderful." I inhaled, and the breath came back out a little shaky.

"Are you okay?" She asked me.

"If I'm honest..." Which I wasn't sure I could be with someone I barely knew but I slipped my feet into Cael's shoes and tried.

"Nervous?" She scrunched her nose up and sat down on one of the beds, patting the mattress so I would join her. "Cael has been keeping the information close to his chest, but I think it's pretty obvious you mean a lot to him."

I nodded and joined her, not realizing how much I missed Bobbi until I was trauma-dumping in her lap and close to tears. I told her everything, from our past until now, and Zoey just listened. The suspicious feeling that she did that often, for a lot of people, crept up my spine with warmth.

"Wow." She sighed lightly and absorbed everything. "So you and Cael were practically born to be together in some capacity? I love a fated lovers trope," she gasped with a smile.

"Or this is the universe's idea of a cruel joke."

"No." Zoey shook her head. "It's a test."

"A test?"

She swallowed tightly. "Van and I aren't perfect, you know? Everyone thinks we are because we've never had one of those really big fights that couples have, but it's because we have all the tiny ones. We don't let it get to us, we just tell each other everything no matter how bad."

"That's surprisingly healthy." A small, feeble laugh left my lips.

"It never feels like it in the moment when we're hashing things out. It feels wrong and tense, but it's always worth it, and Van is worth it to me. I guess you just need to decide if Cael is worth it to you."

"Easier said than done." I resisted rolling my eyes, but Zoey stopped me with a tiny shake of her head.

"It's actually easier than you think." Zoey shrugged, sensing my discomfort. "It's that feeling in your chest that you can't tell if it's pain or excitement. It's the butterflies in your stomach you mistake for nausea. It's the relief you get from a cold breeze on a really hot day. And if your first and last thought is him..." She scrunched her nose up at me, her eyes flickering like she was in on a secret I didn't know yet. "Give this weekend a chance, give yourself a chance."

She rose from the bed and fixed the tiny rolls of her shirt before leaving the room and me with more questions that I had come in with. I looked at myself in the mirror, a question posed that old Clementine would have had an answer to almost instantly, but one I couldn't quite figure out.

When I finally found the courage to make my way out to the living room, it felt like the number of people in the cabin had doubled and the sound alone was overwhelming. Zoey's laughter rang out from the kitchen, where she laughed with Ella and an older lady with soft, graying-brown hair and big eyes lined with crinkles when she smiled.

"Mary," Ella called me over. "This is Mrs. Shore."

She held her hand out to me, and I introduced myself.

"So you're the reporter that had my husband in knots." She laughed, but there was a hint of pride in her voice. "I like you. I've never seen that man so riled up before. I hope that piece you're writing makes waves."

It already was.

"I'm having a lot of fun working on it. Harbor has been so generous to me." I smiled.

"Well, we're very grateful to have you for dinner." She smiled back. "Did you not have any family waiting for you back in Texas?" She asked.

"My Mom," I said quietly. "But she understands that this is important."

"Well, she sounds like a wise woman." Mrs. Shore winked at me but her eyes dragged behind me, and what could only be described as a motherly scowl formed on her face. "Cael Cody, get your dirty little fingers out of that!"

The towel snapped as we all turned to see Cael rubbing the back of his hand, mere inches from the frozen bowl of whipped cream on the counter behind us. He popped the cream covered finger into his mouth with a smile and reached out the other hand to me, palm up, possibilities endless.

The rescue was imminent.

I could have sworn Zoey giggled with pride when I took the invitation and Cael pulled me from the kitchen.

"Thank you." I laughed.

It was weird that after all this time talking to people for my job, it was still so hard to make small talk. I wanted deep conversations with everyone all of the time.

"Where have you been?" He asked, and led me outside.

"Getting settled," I shrugged.

"You were missing for like half an hour," he groaned and led me down the back stairs of the porch. He looked back at me for a second, blue eyes watching me carefully. "*And* you've been crying."

I ignored his comment as my feet hit loose gravel, but Cael didn't stop moving. He was taking me somewhere.

"Maybe you weren't looking hard enough."

His head snapped around as he scoffed, fake outrage shining brightly as he smiled with his entire face. When the sun hit him, my breath caught in my throat and, for a split second, I forgot how to breathe as he seamlessly transitioned back into that seventeen-year-old boy. His hair was longer, his shirt a different color, and his eyes a little older, but... there he was.

"You okay, Plum?" He asked, squeezing my hand as my steps slowed.

"Yeah, just déjà vu..." I forced a tiny smile to my face. "Where are we going?" I asked him.

It was his turn to have his smile falter.

"To see Mama."

Confused and nervous, I let him lead us away from the house, past a massive homegrown baseball field, down toward the lake. It was public knowledge just how rich the Shores were, but seeing the field put it into perspective. Homegrown was lowballing all the trimmed grass and freshly painted bleachers.

As we got closer to the lake, the trees grew taller and knotted together to create a dark canopy over the winding path. When the trees finally broke, I could have cried.

A small rickety dock extended out from the shore, swaying gently over the calm body of water. In the distance, the trees broke in the prettiest way on the horizon, just enough for the sun to nestle between them and turn the sky purple. The ground around the dock was blanketed in a thick field of lavender that stretched around and grew so tall it rocked in the breeze, practically dancing under the sunset.

It reminded me of a specific spot back home where the properties met, and Mr. Cody had built a small dock for Mrs. Cody where she could read and be alone for a while. She called it her own little Heaven after her and Momma spent a long weekend planting bushes and bushes of lavender along the path that led to it and the surrounding area.

"Lavender always was her favorite." I brushed my fingers over the tops of the petals and smiled softly, a lump forming in my throat.

"Yours too." Cael looked back at me, the purple sky dancing in his big, sad eyes as he spoke.

"Only because of her." My voice cracked a little. "She used to make us bundles from all those bushes and hang them above the doorways."

He nodded and looked out over the lake.

"It's beautiful," I whispered.

"The week after she died was the roughest time any of us had ever had. Not just Dad and I, but everyone at the Nest," he said and lowered himself to the dock. "You knew Mama. They were all her kids. She had been there for so long, doing everything for all of us." A tiny whimper bubbled from him. "Dad didn't give a shit. The minute the funeral was over, he disappeared into his office and never came out again. Silas was the only reason we survived. He collected us one at a time and shoved us on that damn bus, drove us up here, and put us all to work. It rained in sheets... pouring practically the entire time. It was like the sky was sobbing. Everyone was miserable, half of them still in their dress clothes from the funeral."

I watched him pick at the grass, it had always been his tell that he was holding back.

"We didn't argue, but we didn't understand either. Mama loved the Nest. It was where she belonged, and I fought against him every step of the way." He pointed up to the hill without looking. "Crying up there in my black suit like a brat as they built this dock and planted those flowers."

He sniffled, and I realized he had tears streaming down his face.

"I cried for three days while they did that. I don't even remember eating or sleeping. I just wanted to fight everyone, and it was the first time in my life I really felt angry. I was pissed off at everything, questioning why anyone would want to take her when she was the thread that held us all together."

My heart swelled at his story, it had been hard in the isolation when Lorraine died. Hard for me, but even worse for my own Momma. But we'd had each other. Cael had been hung out to dry by Ryan in the most heartbreaking moment of their lives.

"Arlo did his best to control the fallout but was just as sad. She had been his Mom, too, after he lost his own. He was 2-0 in that department, but I just couldn't find the space to care for anyone but myself. It was so selfish of me. She would have been so fucking mad at me for not picking Arlo up and walking through that anger together. I failed her that day. I've been failing her since, but Silas was right. He just didn't know how to explain it without sounding insane. On that third day, the sky cleared and, one by one, every player settled down on this stupid fucking hill beside me, as close as they could get, dirty hands, puffy eyes, and the sun dropped from the sky, exploding in purples, and I realized this is where Mama laid herself to rest."

Cael scratched at his chest with two fingers mindlessly as he stared out over the water, and the sun slowly disappeared behind the lake.

"She never even came up here." He laughed. "She said this was a place just for us, that we didn't need her up here. We needed her at home, at the Nest."

"And now she sleeps in the one place you can always find her." I nodded. "I miss her a lot," I said, thinking back on how wonderful she was. I scooted closer to him.

"She used to call me, you know?" I stopped when Cael looked over at me. "She'd never tell me what was going on with you. She'd say 'Little Lovebug, I called to know how *you're* doing'. She had a way of making everyone feel seen."

"I don't know how she did it." Cael shrugged those broad shoulders and wiped what tears remained from his cheeks on the shoulder of his shirt.

"Effortlessly." I smiled, tucked my arm into his, and leaned my head on him, *just like you.*

He had no idea how much of her was ingrained in him, and it broke my heart to hear him talk about himself like that. I closed my eyes as every repressed feeling from the past seven years rushed through me at once—all the anger and frustration dancing dangerously with the want and regret.

Sitting there in the quiet with him felt normal. It was comfortable again, and I hadn't realized just how much I missed that... How much I missed feeling like Cael and Clementine.

251

"You're right. She'd be livid with us, you know," I said. "All this fighting and for what?"

"You're the one fighting, Plum." Cael sighed. "I'm just a punching bag at this point."

"Well, I'm sorry. Maybe I should try making you feel seen instead of trying to drag some fight from you that you don't have."

"I have plenty of fight." He chuckled. "I'm just navigating seven years of feelings that I thought I'd never get to act on. I used to dream about you, more often than not. It was easier when my sheets smelled like you." He stopped, cheeks flushed with color. "So I started buying soap that reminded me of you. The guys teased me, but it was worth it because I got you back, even briefly."

My heart raced so fast it pained me as he talked about it.

All this time, believing that he had just moved on, but he hadn't, at least not from us.

"You were the majority of my life, Clementine, and I couldn't live it properly without you," Cael admitted. "Maybe that's insane, but I've done some pretty stupid things in my life. Loving you, unapologetically, was not one of them."

"I laid in bed for two weeks after you left," I confessed. "Everything hurt like I had been hit by a truck. I missed you so bad, but Momma would bring me warm french fries home every day on her way back from work, and she'd never say anything or scold me for lying around crying. She'd just set the fries on my desk and tidy up before leaving me until the next day. She still does that because you did that, bringing me french fries when you made me mad, upset, or cry."

"I hate when you cry." Cael's words were tight.

"I know." I sighed, thinking about that bird. "But she kept that alive because she knew I needed it. Eventually, I crawled from that cave and managed to find my feet again. Joined the newsletter club at school and found out I was pretty good at making news out of nothing. I slipped a little when Dad left, maybe a lot..."

It had never been our fault.

It had never been Cael's fault.

"Your Dad left?" Cael seemed surprised.

"Your Mama kept a lot more together than we ever knew." I clenched my jaw. "I was... I am..." I corrected myself, "angry because all of a sudden, every ounce of love had been stripped from my life. Everything I knew about endless love crumbled. Lorraine died, Daddy fell out of love with Momma. It felt like we had been lied to our entire lives."

"You know that's not true," he quietly argued.

"Do I?" I countered. "I've been here for weeks, and it feels like all we've done is run in circles, blaming each other for situations outside of our control."

"*You*," he corrected. "You've been running circles around me, blaming me, not listening to me. *Not kissing me.*"

"For a damn good reason," I fought. "The last time I let you do that, it crippled me so badly I couldn't leave my room, Cael!"

"So that's what it's about. You're scared."

"No, I'm not scared."

I was terrified.

"It doesn't matter. After this weekend is over, I'm gone. I'm not sticking around to find out how a heart shatters twice."

Cael stared at me like I had slapped him and suddenly, we were back on that hill behind my house, naive and angry at the world for all the same reasons.

CODY

2016

"You didn't need to hit him, Cael Cody." Mama pressed the ice to my face and I hissed in pain as she gripped the back of my head in anger.

"Yeah, I did," I said with conviction.

He deserved more.

My skin was crawling.

Mama had sent me up to drop off a crate of vegetables and I heard her crying from the porch. Anger flared inside of me like I had never felt before in my entire life and I saw red. Kiefer's hands were all over her and she was begging him to stop.

You should be grateful.

Tears streamed down my cheeks and Mama's hold loosened on my hair.

That asshole had hurt my Clementine and who knows what he would have done–

"He's lucky I only hit him once," I choked out.

Dad went to stay at the Matthews' house until they got back from the city, but Clementine had gotten off the floor without saying a word to me and marched to her room. I sat at the bottom of the stairs and listened to the shower run for nearly an hour before I called Mama. She rushed over and, the second she saw my face, she called Dad.

Mama got Clementine out of the shower and tucked in bed, but I could still hear the haunting sobs that echoed from the loft. I would never scrub the sound from my memory.

All I wanted to do was find that asshole and hit him again, over and over, until he begged me to stop, and then hit him again. My hands curled into fists at my side as the nausea built in the pit of my stomach.

"Violence isn't ever the answer," she gripped my chin, "but *I'm sorry* you were right about that boy; you shouldn't have to carry that guilt."

"I don't feel guilty, I feel angry," I snapped at her, and her brows pinched together.

"My boy is never angry," she whispered. "You don't even know how to feel that way. Dig deeper, Honeybug, 'cause it's something else eating at you." She tapped her finger once beneath my chin.

"Alright, maybe I feel a little guilty or sad, but what was I supposed to do? She was already spending less time with me, and if I spent all that time talking about how horrible Kiefer was..."

"She would have fought you on it," she finished my sentence.

"So what was I supposed to do?" I practically whined. "Make her sad?"

"You did your best and you protected her when it mattered, Honeybug," Mama reassured me. Truck lights flashed at the Matthews' house and my heart shattered as we watched them both hurry into the house.

"I don't know what to do now. Do I go see her?" I asked, stumbling through unknown territory.

"Give her the night," Mama suggested. "We can go over in the morning."

I nodded, excusing myself, and went to sit in the chair that faced the front windows to watch her house. I wasn't going to get any sleep anyways so I would wait until the sun came up to make sure Clementine was okay.

CODY

I stretched out my sore muscles, groaning into the pillow to stifle my annoyance that I was awake. It didn't matter how many times we slept in these bunks; it never got easier. My shoulder itched, the pain still a constant thrum after bad sleep. I rolled over carefully so as not to wake Dean; old habits dying hard in the form of both of us needing comfort.

Ella had snuck into our room again, tangled against Arlo's chest on the top bunk. Van was butt naked, with his blanket around his head blocking out the sunlight. It was insane how much I loved my little family, and it was indescribable how thankful I was for them.

The smell of coffee and pancakes filled my nose, and I knew Dad was awake and cooking breakfast. Thanksgiving was important but, even more so, the only tradition that stood strong was him cooking breakfast the day after.

He had done it at home, he had done it here, and he continued to do it for Mrs. Shore even after Mama died. She insisted that he didn't but he seemed to enjoy the tradition. I snuck from bed, slipping on a clean loose sweatshirt and a pair of sweats. I looked back at Dean for a moment, so peaceful in his sleep, and I took the chance to be grateful for him, to appreciate the person he helped me become despite my constant pushback. All the times I proved that bad luck and bad karma were real and dragged him down with me and he did it with a smile on his face.

I loved him, and I knew I always would. Now it was my turn to help him become someone who could love himself above everyone else.

It was obvious that the next weeks would be hell, wading through losing Clementine all over again, but I was finally in a place where I could extend my love and focus to other people. For once, I didn't feel like I was going to self-destruct in the face of stress and disappointment.

And I owed everything to Dean and I'd walk through fire to prove it.

I inhaled a deep breath before saving Ella from the show of Van's ass and covered him with a blanket. Arlo stirred against Ella, his eyes opening to see me as I backed away. To my surprise, there was no scowl as I stared at him, hoping that he'd understand that even if it ended in disaster, I still had to try.

He nodded and curled back into Ella, closing his eyes as I closed the door behind me.

Clementine had said Zoey put her up in a room on the main level, so that's the first place I'd look. I sauntered by the bathroom, stopping to check my appearance in the mirror and using my hands to fix the blond flyaways that had formed during my sleep. From the top of the stairs, I could hear Clementine laughing, and the sound made my heart explode. A sweet melody that I had become so attached to that the thought of losing it again only made me sad.

I took the stairs two at a time, excitement rushing through my sleepy muscles as I rounded the corner. My feet tripped over each other just to see her, but she wasn't alone. My Dad stood with his hand around a coffee cup, leaning against the counter as the pancakes cooked, and with a smile on his face talking to... Julien.

What the fuck?

My heart sank.

Every single muscle in my neck and shoulders tightened as I composed all the anger and shock that stirred around; swirling so fast beneath my chest that it formed a tornado that threatened to destroy everything in its path. *Why the fuck was that guy even here?* This was a weekend for the family, and he wasn't Clementine's.

His entire demeanor annoyed me. Tall with dark hair, thin lips, and a thick nose that took over all his other features; Julien had the face of a dopey-looking dog and brown eyes that drooped with the shape of his limp eyebrows. Never in my life had I wanted to hit someone more than in that moment. I forced the nausea down as he wrapped a hand around her waist and dug his fingers into the side of Clementine. *My Clem.*

"Morning, Cael." Dad was the first to notice my presence.

Clementine tensed against Julien before she turned with a heartbreaking look on her face that was quickly replaced with a tight, professional smile.

"Dad." I nodded. "Clem." I looked over at her as I made my way through the kitchen.

"Julien Hearst." He held out a hand to me with a crooked smile on his paper-thin lips that felt insincere. His voice was a grating, low-grade Philadelphia accent that curled at the end and forced the R in his name to roll away. It annoyed me even more than I already had been.

"Cael Cody," I said, extending my hand because I could be polite. "He's shorter than I expected," I said, looking down at Clementine.

My Dad groaned from behind me; a warning to behave.

Well... I *could*, it didn't mean I would be.

"Clemmy can make anyone look taller," he teased and kissed the top of her head.

That was stupid. Clementine wasn't short by any means, she was nearly five-nine. Annoyance flickered over my face, but I shoved it down, resisting the urge to roll my eyes.

"This is a surprise," I said, grabbing a mug of coffee and sliding up onto the counter. There was no reason for me to hover, Julien's handshake had been weaker than mine after major surgery and, frankly... He didn't threaten me.

Dad could tell because his body relaxed a touch as I got comfortable.

"I figured Clem would want some comforts from home for the weekend, so I invited Julien to join us for a few days," Dad said.

"How kind of you." I didn't take my eyes off Julien.

Clementine silently begged me to look at her, but I couldn't.

Being blindsided by her ex-fiancé wasn't on my bingo card for the weekend. The emotions that snowballed were laced and volatile and, given her silence, she wasn't entirely into him being here either. Looking at her, seeing her big, apologetic brown eyes, would kill any willpower I had to not beat the shit out of that guy.

"I've been missing her so much." Julien shook his arm around her and laughed as Clementine was jostled in his arms. "Jealous you lot have gotten to spend so much time with her. When Ryan called, I was surprised," Julien said, looking between the three of us as irritation weighed down his fake smile. "She's never talked about either of you." His dejected beady brown eyes stared at me. "Not a *single* mention."

I had so much I wanted to say, but my eyes slipped from Julien to Clementine.

Please don't, she mouthed and forced a smile to her face.

"Just old family friends," I said. "It's been nice to catch up with her." I slid off the counter, hovering over Julien by a good four inches with a cocky smile on my face. "I have to go set up for later," I said, my lips pressing into a thin line. "Do you play baseball, Jeremy?"

"Julien," he corrected me.

"Right, sorry, it's a forgettable name." I smirked when Clementine dipped her head to hide her expression.

"I play a little," he finally answered, his chest rattled with shallow breaths, like a peacock ready to fight for its mate, but I didn't need flashy colors to win Clementine back.

I had never lost her.

"Awesome." I pointed to the circle of them in the kitchen and clapped my hands together. "I'll see you on the field, Johnathan."

"Julien." He sighed.

"*Clemmy.*" I looked at her, and she nearly snorted at my use of the disgusting nickname. "Enjoy your pancakes." I winked. "Dad, make sure she gets extra whipped cream?"

Julien practically growled, his grip tightening on her side.

She shook her head but smiled at me, clearly amused with my nonsense, and it filled my chest with heat just knowing that she was entertained.

He'd have to work harder than that.

I could tell by the sparkle in her eye. Clementine was still mine.

Grabbing a sweater from the hook by the back door, I slipped it over my head and wandered out onto the deck. It was misting, but the rain felt good on my hot skin as I made my way down to the diamond and made sure everything was ready for the parents and players game we ran every year. I swiped a bat from the shed and tossed a ball in the air, swinging as hard as I could; letting the pain from my shoulder wash out all the jealous thoughts that plagued me.

It was better than letting them eat away at me.

For a man I just met, I had never hated anyone more.

And for Dad to bring him here, to rub that in my face... I wasn't sure what he was playing at, but it wouldn't work. I wouldn't let him blow up my happiness for a second time. I couldn't. It would kill me. I hit the ball over and over again until my shoulder screamed at me to stop.

"Fuck!" I screamed at the top of my lungs and threw the bat as hard as I could against the backstop. The light rain plastered my hair to my forehead and dripped from my nose as I sank on my haunches and caught my breath.

Dig deeper, Honeybug. Something else is eating at you.

The itch clawed between my shoulder blades, begging me to give in.

"You alright, Kitten?" Arlo called from behind me. His dark hair was damp and his tank top was clinging to his chest.

I looked over my shoulder at him, the build up of water dripping into my eyes as I found him leaning against one of the dugouts with his arms crossed. I contemplated lying to him, telling him that I was fine just so he wouldn't come down on me with his older-brother-bullshit, but he stared right through my thoughts.

"No," I said, defeated, and used my hands on my thighs to shove off the ground. "But I'm not—"

"Bad?" He finished for me as I got closer and nodded. Arlo watched me with dark eyes. Concern flickering behind them as he evaluated the situation. "Do you need to go home?"

"No." I shook my head. "I can manage."

"Ah. You out here pushing your shoulder to extremes and screaming in the rain suggests otherwise." He cocked an eyebrow at me.

"Healthy outlet."

"Until it's not." Arlo scowled.

"I promise if I can't, you can drive me back to Harbor." I tapped my fingers to my chest, my shoulder protesting from the movement, but I couldn't let him win every aspect of the argument.

I could tell he wasn't convinced even as we walked back up to the cabin, and he poured more coffee for me and one for himself. Everyone had gotten up and, one by one, were greeted in the kitchen by our new guest. Arlo and Silas nearly died drinking their coffees when Julien introduced himself to them without prompt. He just sat down at their table like they were old friends. The only thing breaking me free of the tightly twisted frustration was Ella removing the knife and the fork from his vicinity.

Once the dishes were done and the awkwardness faded away, whatever family wanted to play baseball flooded down the path to the diamond. The rest either spent the day locked away from the chill of the mid-November air or bundled up in the bleachers, ready to watch us all.

"That's him?" Van tied his shoes beside me on the bench.

Julien hung around Clementine in a constant, half-assed piggy-back formation, and it looked uncomfortable. The rain had stopped but the field was still soft and the game today would get messy. Everyone was in long pants and hoodies to shield themselves from the chilly air. I tugged a beanie down over my hair to keep my ears warm, leaning against the fence with my back to the love birds.

"Oh my God." Ella slapped Zoey playfully on the other side of Van. "Do you know who he looks like? It's been bothering me all morning."

Zoey looked from her own shoes to the diamond and narrowed her eyes as her head cocked to the side. "Scott Eastwood?" She said, "Just brunet."

"No!" Ella laughed. "Wait until he does the thing with his lip," she said, and everyone leaned forward to watch him like he was an animal in the zoo. "Right there! Do you see it?"

Zoey giggled, "Oh fuck, that's why you're so wound up. He looks like a dollar-store version of Miles Teller."

She nearly fell from the bench laughing as the rest of us surveyed Clem's ex-fiance from a distance. Dean's fingers were wrapped in the dugout fence, turning back to look at us with his brows knitted together.

"I didn't think the man could get uglier... but here we are." Ella scowled and it flooded me with a playfulness I had been forgetting about all morning.

"She's got a point." He nodded. "He's got something wrong with his face."

"Yeah..." I scoffed, wandering past in a fit of laughter. "His *entire* face."

Silas hovered in the family dugout with Luc, both watching Julien closely as he chatted with Nicholas in the outfield.

"What do you guys think?" I asked as I approached.

"If he likes Nicholas, there might be something wrong with him." Luc was the first to answer. "You should keep an eye on him."

"See." I stared at Silas, who had his arms crossed over his chest and a hat pulled over his brows. "If Luc doesn't like him, then I'm doing the right thing."

"I didn't say I didn't like him, Cody," he grumbled, low and stern like Arlo always does. "But there's something about him that's off-putting."

I rolled my eyes and moved on. "You guys ready?"

Mrs. Shore, Mr. Tucker, Robert, and Sawyer all nodded along with the other family members and double-checked their equipment. Ella appeared from behind us and wrapped an arm around my middle as I laid mine across her shoulders. She was tucked into Arlo's sweater, and her hair was pulled back into the cutest little blonde braids.

"How do we separate the teams for Thanksgiving?" She asked.

"The hat." Arlo said it like it was obvious as he walked through the dugout, pulling his hat down and calling out to Zoey. "Baby, it's *always* the hat."

"Do you guys like to pre-plan that when no one is looking or...?" Ella laughed, clearly suffering from déjà vu. Her gaze flickered back and forth between her best friend and fiancé. "I just imagine Zoey scribbling names in the closet while you handle the safety scissors...is that how that goes, or what?"

Arlo chuckled, kissing her cheek in passing, and held the hat out to Zoey. "Wouldn't you like to know what we talk about when you aren't around?"

"I mean, yeah?" Ella followed him back to the group of players at center field.

"Before we get started, does everyone know the rules of recreation baseball?" Arlo asked loudly as Zoey dumped a bunch of pieces of paper into the hat. No one said anything. Most people had played in this game for years. My eyes wandered to Julien, who wasn't even paying attention.

"Johnny boy, did you hear him?" I asked loudly and crossed my arms.

"Yeah, I heard him. I know the rules." Julien turned his dopey-looking face toward me and rolled his eyes. I had to stifle the laughter that bubbled from me when he answered to the wrong name.

I could feel Dean's chest brush against my back as I pinned my shoulders back and tried to control the urge to beat the hell out of him as an early Christmas present to myself.

"Embarrass him on the field." Dean pushed forward against me and clapped his hand over my shoulder.

"You can guarantee it." I smiled brightly but my eyes had moved to where Clementine watched me cautiously, waiting for the storm.

MATTHEWS

"God I missed you," Julien cooed and the sound of his voice was like an ice pick to my spinal cord.

His hands wrapped around me and I hadn't realized that, at one point, six or maybe seven months ago, Julien had touched me and it was the last time I had ever enjoyed it.

Now, every time he touched me, I forced down the urge to shudder.

"I'm still surprised you came down here," I said. More surprised his mother had let him. She was not a kind woman and, after meeting her, it became apparent where Julien had gotten his passive-aggressive behavior from.

I hated everything about the situation, but causing a scene wouldn't do any of us any good and, if I forced Julien to leave, he'd make it everyone's problem. It would be best to talk to him at home where he could flip out on me in private.

"When Ryan called I was surprised, but it's incredibly generous of them to invite me and I'd do anything for my Clemmy." His lips pressed to my neck and I forced myself to lean into it.

The teams were called quickly, and I knew instantly that Cael was going to cause trouble.

"Cael and Jensen are captains this year."

I felt every important set of eyes turn on me.

"I want Mary." He pointed at me.

"Idiot," Arlo groaned under his breath as I unlinked from Julien's grasp and made my way through the crowd to stand beside Cael.

"You could have at least picked me after a few *actual* players," I whispered without looking over at him as Jensen chose Arlo.

HONEY POT

"What happened to choosing him last?" Ella scoffed with her hands in the air.

"Thanksgiving rules, Blondie." Arlo shrugged. "You're just mad I got picked first."

"You're damn right." She rolled her eyes.

"Dean," Cael called out. "You know more about baseball than most of these idiots, you were a good pick."

"I was a selfish pick," I said under my breath.

"Prove me wrong." Cael shrugged as Dean settled in on the other side of me.

I missed whoever Jensen picked next because I was too nervous that they'd pick Julien last and start a fight. Cael had been good all morning, as good as he could be without outright insulting him, but he was riding a line. Julien had made a remark about Cael being rude when we went to get changed into warmer clothes.

"He's just protective," I said.

"Possessive," Julien corrected.

Cael scanned over the crowd. "Silas," he picked, which was received with a chorus of groans. "You can't have Arlo *and* Doc, Jensen, shut up." He shook his head.

Jensen narrowed his eyes on Cael. "Fine, I want Ella."

"Fine." Cael shrugged with a cocky smile on his face.

"Why the hell are you happy about that? She'll pitch and we'll be screwed," Dean growled, but it had been purely strategy and it became clear as Arlo started whispering to Ella in their group, her face twisted into a scowl and she shook her head at them.

"She got picked sixth, she's already pissed off," Silas laughed.

"That'll only make her play harder," Dean said.

"Ella and Arlo play their best when they're in competition with each other, putting them on the same team creates discontent *within* the team." Silas nodded like he was proud of Cael. "Smart. They'll spend the whole time fighting each other instead of playing."

"Not just a pretty face," Cael declared with a clap and chose Van.

"I see what you're doing," Silas mumbled to Cael, catching on to his game play before anyone else. I watched them pick people one by one, creating a team that might actually stand a chance to win.

"Lucas," Cael chose next.

"Sawyer," Jensen scooped up the next King sibling.

It was strange how much they all looked alike, with dark hair, tawny skin, almond eyes, and that signature scowl. Sawyer clapped Arlo on the back, his brown eyes flickering toward our group with a smirk, and Arlo gave him a quiet, tight laugh before turning to Ella. Cael had miss-stepped somewhere and they had picked up on it faster than us, but what was it?

"What are they whispering about?" I asked Dean who was watching them as well.

"Luc hurt his pitching arm in his final season, he hasn't played baseball since. It was an odd pick to take him over Sawyer," Dean explained.

"Sawyer plays shortstop." Cael shook his head. "But not better than I do, I wasn't going to lobby for a position on my own team."

I couldn't stop the laugh that bubbled from me. They took the game much more seriously than I had expected them to. "Isn't this supposed to be fun?" I asked.

"That went out the window when your ex showed up." Dean nodded to Julien.

"Cael's not going to do something stupid is he?" I turned to look at Dean who just smiled down at me.

"Nicky." He chose his next pick, and I felt Dean tense beside me. Even with a smile on his face, he couldn't hide the nervousness that coursed through him.

"He's in the middle of doing something stupid. The best you can do now is find something to hold on to. Wait out the storm. This is going to be a long day." Dean looked over at Cael, who seemed even more focused than before.

Endless ocean eyes focused far from where we stood, with determination staining his boyish features. The sun licked at the tips of his dirty blond hair that escaped the dark green beanie he wore, and the breath caught in my throat at his beauty. His sharp jaw was tilted proudly forward as he scanned over the remaining players, including Julien and Ryan Cody.

"Todd," Jensen picked.

Leaving Zoey, Julien, and Ryan.

"Zoey," Cael chose over either of them, and Dean sighed under his breath.

Both men stared at me like I was responsible and it felt like I had an anvil sitting on my chest.

"I'll take Texas," Jensen pointed to my ex.

"You're with us, Coach," Cael said with a tight huff of air. "Mrs. Shore," Cael turned and cupped his hands around his mouth, yelling for her. "Will you be our Ump?"

"Of course, Darling." She stepped out of the dugout with her long, dusty-brown hair in a high ponytail that pulled all her features tight. She was stunning, the kind that was terrifying, and I admired her for it. It was no wonder why Silas was handsome, his Mom was ethereal and she floated across the pitch toward the two teams.

"Quite the team," she noted and turned her slender frame around the field. "Picked last," she turned to Ryan with a smile. "That must be new for you."

"Happens more often than you think." Ryan squared his shoulders and crossed his arms over his chest as he bantered with her.

"You sure you can keep up with these youngins?" Mrs. Shore smiled at him.

"I think I'll be alright, Ma'am, I'm not as out of shape as I look." He chuckled.

"You don't look out of shape, Ryan," she hummed and moved around him as some color filled his usually pale cheeks. "Keep it as clean as you can, no funny business," she warned everyone. "I'm not calling for a helicopter to take any of you to the hospital."

"She has a helicopter?" I looked up at Cael to my left.

"She has two," Silas scoffed, his eyes darting between his Mom and Ryan as he walked backward into the dugout.

The game started, Cael lost the coin flip, and we ended up in the field first. I could tell that it pissed Cael off because he stomped back to the dugout like a toddler, with Ella on his heels.

"Cael." She grabbed him by the hem of his sweater and pulled him back so she'd look at him. "Don't push it," she warned him, saying a string of words I couldn't hear but the look on her face was tight and serious as she spoke to him.

It only made his mood worse because when he turned around the light was gone from his usually bright blue eyes and was replaced by storm clouds. His hand found my back as he guided me to the edge of the dugout for privacy.

"Where do you want to play?" He asked me, his eyes never leaving the field.

"It doesn't matter, I may know the rules but I can't play..." I laughed. "Your weird passive-aggressive way of stealing me away from Julien is ridiculous and it's going to lose you the game. You could have had anyone. You messed up picking me first."

"*No*. I didn't," he said in a low tone that sent a current of electricity down my spine and curled my toes. One that meant *I'll always pick you first*. "Where do you want to play, Clem?" He asked me again.

"Catcher." I shrugged, somewhere safe and relatively unimportant.

"Alright." He scanned the field and nodded, handing out positions to everyone else. Dean was on first, Sawyer on second, Cael would take shortstop and Silas on third.

"Nick, I need you to pitch." He turned on him.

"Are you high?" Nicholas scoffed, carding his fingers through his thick brown hair and everyone froze. "I didn't mean..." He stopped and sighed. "That's a stupid plan if you want to win."

"Yeah everyone keeps using that word this morning." Cael let go of a cold, tight laugh and walked toward him. "You're pitching. As much as I hate you, which, by the way, I definitely still do and will continue to do so long after Arlo forgives you."

Dean pushed off the fence ready to get between them. Cael was taller than Nicholas by nearly six inches and he towered over him with his hands behind his back, inking them together with white knuckles as if they had a mind of their own and would lash out given the chance.

"Which... eventually he will forgive you and you will *never* deserve it," Cael snapped in a tone I had only heard from him twice before.

At the family dinner the first night in the nest, and the night he found Kiefer on top of me. I shrank in size watching him as the memory flickered across my vision.

"You'll get under their skin and more than I need you to disappear, we need to win this game," Cael said.

"You sound like your Dad." Nicholas smirked but gave in with a simple nod as Cael scowled at him. "Fine."

Dean relaxed as Nicholas shoved his hand into a glove and walked toward the field. I watched him go, his shoulders tense as he took the mound and flexed his fingers around the ball. More interesting was Arlo's reaction to it. His eyes flickered from his older brother to our dugout and back again before turning to his own team.

MATTHEWS

"Hand," Cael instructed from beside me with a glove turned toward me. "It should fit, it's my old one," he said quietly. So quickly his demeanor changed.

A hundred faces, one for each person in his life.

"How's that?" He asked as his thumb traced a soft line along the inside of my wrist.

"It's fine," I snapped.

"Can you close it okay, feels too big..." He mumbled to himself.

"You're being ridiculous," I whispered to him as he checked the laces and my finger placements by massaging over the glove. He didn't answer me but his eyes darted over to where Ella talked to Julien with a tense but pleasant smile on her lips.

"Answer the question, I don't need you breaking your wrist," he ordered.

I nodded with my lips pressed into a thin line. "Cael." I turned my eyes up toward him and he met my gaze. "Promise me you'll behave?" I asked him.

"I don't make promises I can't keep, Plum." He leaned in like he wanted to kiss my forehead but stopped himself when he realized we were being watched. "Keep your eyes up, and ears open." He grabbed Dean by the shirt as he passed. "Only listen to me or Dean, do you understand? Drown everyone else out."

"Alright," I said.

"*Everyone,*" he repeated.

"I heard you, Loverboy," I grumbled.

But it was easier said than done with Ryan Cody drilling holes into me with those judgmental green eyes and Julien watching my every move. I felt like I was wandering around Harbor with a scarlet A pinned to my heart; punished for a crime that didn't feel worthy of scrutiny.

I had just fallen in love.

Again.

I looked up at Cael, painfully aware of my thoughts and feelings. He watched me for a second longer and the urge to curl against him was *so* violent.

But Ryan cleared his throat and Cael took off like an abused dog to the outfield. I was so confused as to why he'd thought it would be a good idea to bring Julien here. What in his right mind made him so brave? After the conversation about the bird, Ryan seemed to pull back from what little progress we had made in our relationship and I couldn't figure out why. He wasn't a bad person, I'd never once thought that about him. Even after he stole away the one person who saw me, even when no one was looking. I never hated him for that, but now... this felt like an act of hostility. Like we were fighting and I had no clue until the knife was buried deep in my back.

"If they foul out, let me take the flies." Dean knocked me from my trance. "He'll get through this today, just let him do it his way."

"I'm afraid his way will end in bloodshed." I sighed.

"Most likely but, knowing Cael, it'll be his blood," Dean said. He hooked an arm around me and walked us out to the pitch. "When the ball comes to you, throw it straight to me, don't worry about second and third. We'll cut them off at first base if we work together."

"Together, hey?" I cracked a smile.

"You heard me, come on."

The air around the field was instantly tense as Ryan played spare on a team he created. Watching from center as his son gave instructions to everyone in earshot. Arlo was the first to bat and as predicted, he seized up when he finally faced Nicholas on the mound.

"That was Cael's idea wasn't it?" He turned a set of dark eyes on me and I nodded. "Little rat," Arlo huffed and went back to his focus, gripping the bat tightly between his hands.

He crushed it out over Van's head into the trees with a cocky grin on his face and his shoulders pinned back as he took the base slowly and triumphantly.

They went through their order one by one, Nicholas shaking off the cobwebs that encased his pitching arm.

Ella was next, her swing was sturdy and, even with Cael chirping from shortstop, she managed to rip the ball just out of his reach. It rebounded off his fingertips and bounced down between Zoey's feet as Ella took her spot at second next to Silas.

Julien was last to bat and it was apparent that it annoyed him as he wandered up to the batter's box.

"Looking cute, Princess." He winked at me and Cael slapped his mit loudly to interrupt.

"Keep your eye on the ball, Joseph," he cracked, with a tight look on his handsome face; all business and no play as he figured out how to make a fool of my ex. It had been stupid of me to even think he'd behave today.

"He's an asshole." Julien took his eyes off the ball for a fraction of a second and it whipped by him into my glove.

It stung my palm as I pulled it from my glove and chucked it back to Nicholas.

I couldn't help but notice Cael staring, his nose scrunching up at me with that proud smile back on his face.

"I wasn't ready," Julien argued with Nicholas.

"Quit flirting then." He shrugged and settled down on his feet to pitch again. He fired off another ball, so fast it crashed into the backstop after bouncing wildly off the corner of the mound.

"Ball," Mrs. Shore called.

"Oh come on," Nicholas grumbled loudly as I went to find the ball where it had rolled.

"Nicholas King, are you arguing with me?" She used her Mom's voice and Nick clammed up with the shake of his head.

"No Ma'am!" He grumbled and reset.

Julien whistled at me like I was a dog when I bent over to scoop it up. A sound that irritated me worse than nails on a chalkboard and one I hadn't missed in the last few months. "I swear that ass gets bigger every time I see it."

I tensed, pausing long enough to compose myself before turning back and throwing the ball. I tugged my sweater over my hips, not cold but uncomfortable with his comment, and did my best to not look over at Cael.

Julien managed to catch the last ball on the tip of his bat and sent it up into the air over our heads in the infield.

"Pop fly," Silas yelled.

Ella, hesitated on her base for a beat as I squinted into the sunlight and tried to get my sights on the ball. Everyone was screaming and the moment felt as though it was thirty minutes instead of seconds. I couldn't concentrate as Julien left the batter's box in the dust.

"Two steps back." Cael's voice broke through the noise and I listened, *one...two.* Raising my glove into the air blindly and just like that the ball dropped into my outstretched hand.

"Second base!" Dean hollered and, instinctively, I threw the ball as hard as I could, getting Ella out as Silas tapped her across the shoulder in her ill-fated attempt to return to her base.

"That was a nice throw, Mary!" Ella hollered, with a disgruntled look on her face.

A smile formed on my face, my breathing ragged, and my heart beating faster than it ever had. Adrenaline pumped through my veins as my eyes dragged across the field to Cael.

The sun beat down on him, hat gone and tucked into his pocket, his hair was messy in the wind and his smile was infectious.

"That's my girl," he mouthed with a proud nod.

My hands shook from the excitement.

"Why the hell did you catch it?" Julien's voice shattered the illusion. "You could have let it drop and given me first base, Babe. I thought this was supposed to be fun."

He approached from my side and his voice was low but angry as his hand wrapped around my bicep roughly. I looked up at him, squirming in his grasp, and met his dark eyes with a scowl. His voice low, he growled so only I could hear him. "You did that on purpose to embarrass me in front of your new friends."

I opened my mouth to tell him to back up but it wasn't my voice that came out.

"Get your hand off of her," Cael demanded.

In the commotion, I hadn't even heard him come up beside me, but his chest pressed against my opposite shoulder, towering over me and Julien at the same time. Warmth filled my chest as I leaned into Cael's chest, my heart choosing for me before my mind could even catch up.

"This is none of your business." Julien didn't look away from me. "Is it, Clementine?" He snapped loudly at me and bared his teeth as his grip tightened.

"Andre Davey," Cael said, breaking Julien's vicious stare by confusing him, but, for me, it clicked instantly.

I knew that name and knew what Cael was about to do as I ripped my arm away and took two steps back, leaving the space between them empty. Cael's knee came up as his hands wrapped around Julien's face pulling him into what looked like a hug but Julien groaned loudly as Cael's knee connected with his nuts.

"Andre. Davey," Cael repeated himself, holding Julien up as he tried to catch his breath from having his genitals shoved up in his stomach. "Middle school winter formal, he pinched Clem in line for the punch. I remember the sad little sound she made but what I remember more is the horrific sound of his ballsack turning into dust when she kneed him for it."

"Cael," Mrs. Shore warned him with a soft, authoritative voice but Cael had tunnel vision and ignored her.

"She got a two-week suspension." Cael laughed and he looked over to me with a proud smile. "She kneed him *so* hard Andre walked funny after. I warned you to take your hand off her and now that I have your attention."

"You're a piece of work," Julien choked up.

"Yeah, I know. Are you even listening?" Cael's Cheshire cat grin remained wide as he raised his eyebrows at Julien's comment like it was something Cael took pride in. "This is an assumption, but you were a hockey guy, weren't you?"

"What the hell does that have to do with you being a possessive asshole, she's not even yours, man," Julien huffed and put his arm out in my direction, suddenly causing me to flinch.

Embarrassed, I shrunk into myself and backed up a step. *Worse*, Cael noticed. His eyes darkened as he looked me over with concern before stifling down the emotions that sparked and turned back to Julien.

"I'm just trying to get to know you. I want to understand what she saw in you, but I think I figured it out," Cael quipped. *They were polar opposites, in every way. There wasn't a trace of Cael in Julien.*

Cael's bottom lip jutted out in thought. "You know all the rules of baseball. So you clearly know how *outs* work?" He asked him, and Julien nodded sluggishly.

No one seemed to want to intervene, Silas and Arlo had moved closer but Ryan had stayed in the outfield and far away from the interaction.

I stared between the two of them as Cael backed off, brushing fake dirt from Julien's shoulders and making sure he could stand. I held my breath as the tension came to a boiling point, and the impression Julien left on my arm stopped stinging.

"Now I let the whistle slide, that was strike one," Cael explained. "We don't catcall women at Harbor."

I wanted to speak up but couldn't find my voice, so I shamefully enjoyed this version of Cael that had shown up. Possessive and confident, he was radiating in the same way he had the day I realized I loved him—brighter than the sun.

"And the ass comment. I *almost* flipped a switch because that made her uncomfortable, and if I know anything about Clem, which," he smiled and tipped his head side to side, "I know everything about her. Making her uncomfortable is a hard task. *That* was strike two. So you were already in hot water."

"Do you ever shut up?" Julien groaned and tried to get out of Cael's hold, but it didn't work. His grip was too tight, and he wasn't finished yet.

"You could have walked off the field like a man, taken your out with grace, but instead you decided to act like a coward. Strike three, Jamie."

"You know my fucking name." Julien shoved again. His anger was bubbling to the surface and he was ready to lash out, but Cael dug his fingers into his shoulder muscle.

The Cael in front of everyone was someone he kept shoved down deep inside of him, that angry little kid I hadn't seen in seven years and hadn't seen until that day, and it seemed he only came out when I really needed him to.

I stood up a little straighter, rolling out the shame and shook off the sticky feeling of Julien's fingerprints on my skin. I wasn't that seventeen year old girl anymore, and Cael wasn't that boy. It was suddenly clear.

"If you *ever* touch her like that again," Cael lowered his voice and made sure Julien was listening. "If you even *look* at her with those dopey shit-brown eyes maliciously... you'll wish the only thing I did was knock the wind out of you for thirty seconds. Do you understand me?" His tone shifted again broaching sing-song territory as a smile formed on his face.

"Answer me, Jeff," Cael ordered him with a laugh.

"Yeah, I heard you." Julien shoved him off and took a few steps back before he looked at me. Disgust, anger, and maliciousness surged from every inch of him.

Cael reached out and slapped his palm against Julien's face who had finally caught his breath and found his footing. Julien put his hand up but thought better than to retaliate as Cael spoke again.

"See, that's the look I'm talking about," he tsked. "Pop flies are impossible to catch in the sun even for experienced players, you should be praising her." Cael smirked. "Like this."

"You did amazing, Plum. You did exactly what I told you to do." He turned to me, lowering his voice into a husky purr that curled my toes in my sneakers. *"Such a good girl."*

Julien practically hissed, but Cael shushed him without looking away from me. I turned red under his bright blue eyes and filled my lungs with cold air to satiate the burning in my chest. Julien's stare had scared me, but Cael's... it made me feel invincible.

"Cael." I shook my head. "Everyone is listening."

"Sorry." He winked at me. "Alright then, do you see how easy it is to be kind to her?"

I stifled the giggle that rose from me and turned my face away from them.

"Now, let's get back to the game," Cael announced, clapping his hand on Julien's shoulder. "I really wanna see how angry I can make my physical therapists."

"Fuck your game, I'm going home," Julien announced. "Are you coming?" He turned to me.

"I—" I didn't have an answer for him. "I'll be home soon."

Julien looked like he wanted to say something more but kept his mouth shut, and it was a damn good thing he had because Cael was just itching for a real fight. There might have been an adorable smile on his face and a lightness to his step but it was written all over the rest of his body. How tight his fingers were curled into his palms and how the muscles in his jaw and neck flexed in restraint.

"Whatever." Julien shook his head and stormed off the field.

I already knew that this altercation, no matter how one-sided it may have been, would cause a lot of trouble. Julien would raise hell, and I'd have to talk him down. Cael was innocent and valiant in his intentions but... he had successfully forced my hand. I would have to go home to fix the mess that it caused.

It took a moment to sink in, but I trailed my eyes across the field to where Cael sauntered away without another word. Chasing after him, I called out.

"It was only a week," I said to him, and he turned to walk backward to the dugout.

I could hear everyone finally moving after the initial shock of the confrontation wore off, the familiar heavy footsteps of Dean coming up behind me.

"What?" Cael stopped with his brows furrowed together.

"I was only suspended for a week," I corrected him and his wide smile returned. It was a silent, secret thank you meant only for the two of us.

"You're welcome, Plum," he mouthed and returned his focus to winning the game.

My heart throbbed painfully in my chest as he stared at me. The sun-brushed over his high, chiseled cheekbones and illuminated the bow of his lip as he smiled at me. He was in there, that boy. From the day my heart first leapt at the sight of him, I could see him. I could feel him. My skin was even warm from the sun in the same way it had been but the wind bit at my cheeks and reminded me that we were not those kids. That we weren't under the Texas sun, running off into the field, abandoning chores in favor of dips in the creek and bonfires so large the sparks danced with the stars.

My head wasn't straight anymore. I needed to figure out exactly what I wanted, and I needed to do it fast because I didn't want the adrenaline rush that was Cael Cody to ever end.

MATTHEWS

2016

"*Clem, come on, just come out and show me?*" *Cael's voice echoed over the heavy curtain of the dressing room door.* We were looking for homecoming outfits at Dandy's, but everything we pulled off the racks was either ugly or too tight on my curves.

"No," I groaned. I hated everything about shopping for clothes. It only made me feel worse about myself, but Cael insisted we get something new for the dance. "I look stupid!"

Cael's head peeked through the curtain, blond strands of hair sticking every which way as I flinched and covered anything that wasn't concealed by clothes the best I could. "Cael!" I hollered and swatted at him.

"You didn't want to come out, I came in. Problem solved." Cael slinked into the changing room and scrunched his nose up. The bruise on his jaw was still healing from his fight with Kiefer, and I felt bad that it was festering in an ugly dark purple.

It had taken me two days to finally leave my room and, when I did, he was sitting at the bottom of the stairs. Momma had said he'd been there since it happened and that broke my heart all over again. I was stupid to trust a boy, especially one that Cael had warned me against. What had happened wasn't his fault, I had gotten myself into the mess. I would have to get myself out.

There was a meeting set for my parents and Kiefer's, because Cael had called his Mama, the incident was reported, and now we had to figure out how to

279

proceed. Kiefer had called a few times to apologize, but Daddy had picked up the phone and hung it up after the first sob session.

He doesn't deserve forgiveness. That's what Daddy had said but it didn't make me feel any better. After a week of sulking, Cael decided that getting out of the house was necessary. My parents were hovering, and I felt like I couldn't breathe. I had sent out a S.O.S. in the form of a flashlight call into his bedroom window and he showed up the next morning with a plan.

"We're going to homecoming," he'd declared.

I responded with, *"absolutely not."*

And then we drove to Dandy's and Cael pulled thirty dresses off the racks. He chewed on his lip.

"That's horrible."

"No kidding!" I slapped his shoulder and groaned. The dress I had somehow wiggled into pinched my stomach with dark blue scratchy sequins and rolled around my thighs. I couldn't even get it zipped up properly with the fabric bunching up.

"This store sucks. Why did we come in here?" Cael asked, staring over me. Blue eyes were always so quick and curious, sometimes making me feel even more insecure than I already was.

"Eyes up here," I barked, and he snapped them up to meet mine with a soft smile. "It's the only store that carries my sizes."

"That can't be true. What about at the mall?" He asked.

"That's a two-hour drive into the city." I shook my head.

"So?" He shrugged in the dark sleeveless tank he was wearing, his eyes glittering under the fluorescents. "You're forgetting your boy has a license now!"

"There's no way Daddy is going to let you drive me into the city without a parent. Especially not after you got in trouble!" I laughed at him, shoving him back until he was practically out of the changing room.

"Let me deal with Mr. Matthews." Cael winked and let the curtain fall over.

Let me make this right. He didn't say it but his glossy blue eyes gave him away. He still felt terrible for what happened, but he was treating me like I was made of glass now and it made me feel small.

Cael was gone all of ten minutes, leaving me waiting for him at the front of the store with my cardigan folded over my arms. He had a cell phone, I didn't. Something about it being too expensive and not worth the money if Cael had one and we were always together.

I suppose it made sense to our parents, but it became another reason I depended on him constantly. I couldn't leave the house unless my parents could reach me, which meant I wasn't allowed to leave the house without Cael.

Although it was his idea to attend homecoming in the first place, I couldn't have cared less. I'd rather spend that time in my room or by the creek, listening to the birds and writing in my journal about their songs; but he had preached the need for a proper high school experience, and, like the naive idiot I was, I followed him step for step into the unknown.

I hated how easily he convinced me to do the things I feared most.

When Cael appeared around the corner with a cheesy grin and a twinkle in his eyes, I knew that whatever plan he had devised had worked. "Mr. Matthews is a chump." He winked and linked his arm with mine.

"*Turns out the supplies we need to put together our science project can only be bought in the city. Yes, Sir, of course, Sir, I'll have her back before dark,*" he mocked my Dad's voice.

"He's going to expect a science project, you know that, right?" I laughed at Cael.

"That's later Cael's problem," he snorted and pushed open the door for me.

The truck was parked in the back row of the small parking lot, but from the door to the truck, my nerves bubbled violently, and I stopped in my tracks. Pressing my heels down into the cracked, sun-worn pavement with a shaky breath.

"Clem?" Cael turned to look at me, only realizing I'd stopped when he reached his truck.

"We don't need to go into the city," I shook my head and adjusted my small bag on my back. "I don't need to go to homecoming."

"What do you mean?" He closed his door and sauntered the few steps back to me.

"It's too much fuss over..." I stopped talking and started to fiddle with the straps with my fingers.

"Now I know you didn't just say that to me." Cael chortled. "It's not a fuss to find you a pretty dress for our first homecoming, Clementine, so what if we have to drive into the city? We can turn the music up real loud and drive too fast on the highway!"

Cael had this way of making everything sound fun, even when I was sad.

"I hate that we have to do that," I argued, but Cael just scoffed. "You don't get it, you're–"

"I'm what, Clem?" He stepped forward and waited.

"Average!" I grumbled. "You fit everything, and trying on dresses that I'm too big for makes me sad!"

"Trying on dresses that don't fit *you*," he corrected me. "You're not too big for them." He closed the distance between us and pulled the bag away from me. "So you're saying because you don't fit the Polly Pocket plastic Dandy's is selling, you don't deserve to go to homecoming?"

"None of the other girls have to go into the city for a dress they'll wear once, Cael. It's not–"

"*Fair*, I know," he said, picking my chin up with his finger. "That's why I lied to your Daddy, so that I could level the playing field."

"Cael," I groaned.

"You don't deserve anything less than going to homecoming and feeling as pretty as I know you are," he said, and I could feel the blush creeping up my neck. "You're worth more than a hundred girls dressed in the same cheap dress on any day, Clementine. Let me prove it to you."

He held out his hand to me, wiggling his fingers until I pressed my palm into his.

"And I am *anything* but average," he scoffed as he opened my door for me. "Clem," he said before closing it.

"What?"

"Promise me something?" He asked. The sun kissed his tan cheeks, and I watched his throat bob slightly as he danced around saying what he wanted. He was painfully handsome, and sometimes it was easier to forget just how so but, illuminated in the sun like he was today, it was clear he stood above everyone in this god-forsaken town.

However, no matter how beautiful Cael may have been, whatever he was about to ask was sure to be ridiculous. Gathering my courage, I nodded for him to continue.

"Try to stop bending yourself to fit into a box not made for you." He squinted in the sunlight and grimaced. "I hate watching you contort to what you expect people want from you, and I know me telling you what you want to hear won't help, but try being nicer to yourself for my sake?"

I know he wanted to say more, he wanted to talk to me about Kiefer, but I couldn't do it. It just hurt too much. There was so much wrong and there was not a single word that would quell my twisted, dark feelings. We both understood the risks of going to homecoming, and yet the look in his eye gave me confidence that maybe it could be fun.

But then the idea of coming face to face with Kiefer caught in my throat like a cotton ball.

"I'll try," I said but, deep down, that was a lot harder of a task than he made it sound.

CODY

Staring at the top of my bunk was going to kill me.

The ticking clock in the room only made the early morning time drag out. Clanging in my ear, I could hear the time being cut away. At some point, both Ella and Zoey had snuck in to find comfort with their people and I was jealous because it was easy for them. It was the third night I'd woken with them all surrounding me, accidentally rubbing their easy, warm love in my lonely face.

Even Dean had retreated to his own bunk.

I was cold and could feel her heart beating in the room below mine like I was lying beside her. She was calling out to me, and I was sick of being alone. I flipped back the sheets and went to find my comfort, padding down the stairs to the guest room on the main floor. I pushed the door open to find her curled up in the sheets, staring up at the moon through the unlatched window.

She had been crying, and there was nothing worse than the sight of her red, sore eyes searching the silence for answers that would never come. I didn't say a word as I pressed against her back, and my arms wrapping around her. My fingers found the hem of her tank top and climbed up beneath it to feel her skin. Clem was so soft and warm that I couldn't help myself but bury my face between her shoulder blades as her arms engulfed mine.

"Why are you awake?" She asked me.

"Because you are," I whispered, kissing a line across her back. "I could hear your heart racing from upstairs."

"That's ridiculous," she scoffed, but pressed into me because she couldn't help herself. It was the comfort we had both been craving.

"Mmm," I hummed, "maybe, but something brought me down here."

284

Your thoughts are loud, Plum, I wanted to say.

They screamed for me.

"Thank you for today," she finally said after some time. The sound of our breathing filled the space and scared away all the shadows. "He's not usually like that."

"What is he like?" I asked.

I knew exactly how we ended. Clementine would get on a plane tomorrow, no matter how hard I fought tonight, but if I was going to let her go, despite my heart shattering into tiny shards that littered my bloodstream, I needed to know she was taken care of.

No matter how much I hated him; if she loved him, I would swallow the shards and let them tear me apart in silence.

"He's intelligent, loyal," she said. "He takes care of me."

"I never took you for a dog person," I teased. "Does he wag his tail when you call him a good boy?" I tried to make light of it, but my chest was tight, and soon my ability to breathe would become strained.

"Oh, so funny!" She didn't laugh, though, because she was battling all the things she wanted to say the same way I was. "He's sturdy, Cael. He wants to build a life with me."

And I didn't know what my future looked like.

"Ouch," I mumble.

"You asked the question," she reminded me. I didn't want to have this conversation with her or about him. But...I had to make sure that I was doing the right thing by letting her go.

"Do you love him?" I asked next.

Selfishly and foolishly, I wanted her to say no. *Please say no.*

I let my hand wander over her heart and could feel how fast it was racing beneath my touch, and it threatened to drag tears from me.

Please.

"I did." She let out a breath, and it knocked me back like a force of wind. "I do..."

"Did you kiss him this weekend?" A question I could tell she wasn't expecting, because her body tensed beneath mine, but I had to know.

"No."

"That feels like a secret," I said quietly.

"It's not, I didn't even want him here this weekend but..." she didn't hesitate to respond as her words trailed off. "I haven't kissed him since I gave the ring back."

"You gave it back?" I must have sounded confused because she laughed.

"*Yes*, I'm just as confused about Julien as I am about you," she confessed.

"Do you love me?" I asked her.

"I've never loved someone the way I love you," she whispered, so quietly I barely heard the words.

"You're still going to leave me, aren't you?" I asked, even though it broke my heart.

"I think I have to," she answered. "You were very valiant and protective today," she said, and I could tell she was trying to avoid hurting my feelings.

"But?" I asked.

"But, that doesn't change the fact that I have real adult problems waiting for me outside of Rhode Island. I can't stay here and play make-believe with you."

Ow.

"If I could figure out a way to give you the world I would, Clem, but I don't have that to offer. I just have me." I sounded so defeated, but she had knocked out the will to fight.

"I don't want the world, Cael. I never have." She wriggled deeper against me. "We just never had enough time."

"We have time now," I grumbled, upset that she was so flippant about it all.

"Not enough, it's never enough," she whispered with a shaky voice.

"It can be. Why are you fighting this so hard!" I didn't mean to, but my voice raised, and my fingers dug into her side. Not hard enough to hurt her but hard enough for her to feel *my* hurt. "You're giving up on us."

"You gave up first," she said and stopped rubbing circles against the top of my hand. "I don't belong here, Cael. This is your home. I'm a ghost story."

"I hate that they call you that." I shook my head. "You were never a ghost to me."

"Maybe I should have been. That would have made all of this so much easier. If I hadn't come here, you would have been happy and forgotten about me, but you've always loved too hard, Cael." Her breath stuttered. "It's crushing me."

"I'm sorry." I couldn't figure out how to make it better for her.

She pulled away from me, rolling over in the bed and sitting up to face me. Her body looked so tiny as she folded down into her arms. Brown strands of hair stuck to her damp cheeks, and her bottom lip jutted out as she fought back the urge to cry.

"Do you remember the bird?" Her brows pinched together, and sadness pooled in her eyes wetly.

"That stupid bird broke your heart," I said, while my own seized in my chest.

Clementine smiled at me softly, processing my response before she spoke again. "Until last week, I thought that bird died," she said. "Everyone lied to me for *you*."

I sat up next to her. "What?" I was lost.

"They told me the bird died to protect your emotions," she said in the saddest tone.

"I didn't know that. I thought you knew it flew away..." I dropped my gaze from hers and scrunched up my nose to stop the stinging that formed in defense of tears.

"But you never mentioned it, and I never asked."

The common problem we've been having since day one.

"Secrets and shadows. That's the life I've lived, Cael, and it wasn't until you left that I finally was able to figure out who I was."

It was a shot to the heart, but one I should have seen coming. It's a tired argument we'd had before and it never got any better because I didn't know how to be anything but the center of attention.

"We were seventeen and I loved you so much I couldn't breathe." She shrugged one shoulder and tucked her knees up against her chest. "It wasn't healthy."

"You sound like my Dad." I sucked in a breath.

"Look at the effect that love had on us both. Open your eyes Cael." Her arms rested on her knees and she played with the bracelet around her wrist.

"When I'm around you for too long, I feel like the little bird in that box."

The laughter that left me felt hollow and was a hair away from turning into a sob. All that time was spent making sure she flew, keeping my distance, never pushing back on the silence. I had given up on proving myself to her because that's what I thought she wanted, just to find out that she felt suffocated.

"You're not the bird stuck in the box, Clementine!" I dropped my voice and moved back from her on the bed. I had never felt anger toward her, but it simmered below the surface. My eyes were brimming with hot tears.

"I made sure you weren't the bird!" I ran my hands through my hair and turned away from her. "For seven years, you went without contact, and I just hoped that you got what you needed without me in the way. I gave you space, I made sure that bird flew even if it killed me." I said, and there was no stopping the feelings that presented, whispering to her, "and it almost did."

MATTHEWS

"You're blaming the accident on me?" I stared at him for a long moment. My heart was in agony over the back and forth, the realization that our entire lives were a disaster. Could the two of us even co-exist anymore without destruction?

"No, Plum. Never." He grabbed my face roughly in his hands and stared at me with the most painful look in his stunning ocean eyes. "Not that," he said. "Without you, I was left to find joy while fighting for my sanity against every stern correction Dad could hurl my way. It was never enough for him, but I held on to the fact that I had been enough for *you*."

Ryan had done whatever he could to shove that bright, beautiful boy back into a box too small to contain his light because he didn't know how else to handle his son.

"So I found outlets that made me feel alive. I traded spots with you. I lived in that box, where I was put, a tiny injured bird without the ability to fly because I gave my wings to you. Then drugs changed that. I felt alive. People enjoyed my company. I was the center of attention. I could fly again."

He turned to look at me then. "But no matter how high I fly, it's never far enough away from him and never close enough to you."

"You can't blame me for this!" I scowled, heartbroken and frustrated.

"I can't help it." His voice cracked under the emotion. "You're the only person that just loved *me*. Dad always wanted baseball. Mama wanted kindness, the boys wanted a party boy, Ella wanted sobriety, Arlo wanted a brother, and Silas wanted a leader. But, Clem, all you've ever wanted is *me*."

289

"So what? We're in this mess because I didn't expect anything from you. Because *I* loved you too hard?"

"Why can't it just be love? Why does it have to be *too much?*" He asked, anger building between us.

"You aren't in love; it's infatuation! We had our time and it's gone. What we're doing is just fun, it's a distraction. We're different people with different lives," I practically cried out the last part.

"You keep saying that," he huffed and released me from his grasp, rolling on top of me in the bed and pinning my arms to the mattress. "You're wrong. I know what *way* I want to love you, Clem." He dropped his chin so our lips hovered inches from each other. "Infatuation is a flash in the pan, it's a firework or a lightning strike. The way I love you is the erosion of rock, it's the tide coming in every night, it's the way the trees lose their leaves every fall. It's slow, it's consistent and natural." Cael's voice rolled into a tight whisper.

"Picture day," he said. I followed the twinkle in his baby-blue eyes. The gaze I so desperately wanted to be angry with. "You got bubblegum stuck in your hair, and your Momma had to cut it out and you cried the entire bike ride to school. But you sat in front of that camera, and Dad still carries that picture of you and your crooked little bangs in his wallet. I loved you so much that day I thought my heart would explode from my chest. We *were* nine."

Our entire life was memories.

He was trying to remind me just how much he loved me.

But I knew, and it was already so painful.

"Christmas, years later, you gifted me the ugliest bracelet I've ever seen in my entire life. I swear you made it from the thread you pulled off your sweaters. But it was from you, and that's all that mattered. You had *thought* of me."

"This bracelet outlasted every single feeling either of us had ever had. The one that still clings to my wrist is the last bit of you I still carry around with me. My heart on my sleeve," he cooed.

"We were thirteen when I kissed my first girl." He stared at me. Hailey Lancaster cornered me after Science in the back building. "It was horrible, and all I could think about was how badly I wanted it to be you. How guilty I felt that it hadn't been? But then, when I told you..." He stopped, swallowing the overwhelming feeling that formed.

I remembered that day and how empty I felt when he stumbled over his words and told me he'd had his first kiss with her, the head cheerleader.

"I left out the secret, and you were so brave and happy for me we ended up going for ice cream. On the way home, you tripped and ripped the jeans your Mama had just bought you. You cried the entire walk home and I knew that I hated you being sad, but I was so young I didn't really know how to prevent it."

"Cael." I opened my mouth to stop him, but he hushed me.

"I need you to understand that I never forgot a single memory you gave me, Clem." His grip shifted on my wrists.

"Winter formal, you wore that fluffy purple dress your Daddy hated, that was too short with those platform shoes. That was the night Andre Davey pinched you next to the punch bowl, and you spent the rest of the night waiting for your Dad in the principal's office, but that dress..." He licked his lips. "It's burned into my memories. It hit that curve of your thighs, and *I* spent the entire night trying to keep my hands busy because I couldn't touch them. I found out that day I could love you even more than I already did."

I opened my mouth to protest, I hated these stories, all these moments. They felt sticky and hot against my skin, and I wriggled beneath him, but he wasn't finished.

He stopped, closing his eyes for a moment and centering himself. "When we were sixteen, Kiefer Hart–" He paused. "Hurt you, and I'll never forget the sound of you crying in your room, but *that* was the day I decided never to let you be that sad again. It was the day I learned how to be angry, I had never felt like that before."

Hurt flickered across his face.

"But I broke that promise to myself and have spent every day since avoiding making them with anyone because the last one I broke was the worst."

"Cael, stop." I pushed on his chest, all while my heart was beating out of mine.

"*Listen,*" he said. His voice wasn't loud but harsher than I'd ever heard from him as he rubbed his thumb against my wrist and stared at me.

"The next dance I had a plan, after we shopped for outfits. I knew you'd say yes if I asked, so I came to your house to ask if you would go with me and your Momma told me you weren't home. I knew that was a lie, because where would you go if you weren't with me? I should have climbed the stupid, broken terrace that night and forced you to talk to me. That would have been my only chance to dance with you that day."

A month later, Ryan found out about the coaching position. They were gone before people even started thinking about prom invitations.

"I cried the entire way to Rhode Island in the back of the truck, just praying that maybe Dad would change his mind and turn around. That we could go home, and I could feel you again. But my prayers went unanswered, and they continued to be ignored as my Mama withered away and my Dad became cold."

His words were like ice.

"You want to know why I don't fight people? Why I move on from shit so easily? Because my heart never left Texas. I'm too busy living in our memories to worry about what people want to argue about now. Everyone is always trying to fill up that hole in my chest with something other than *you*. You wanna pretend like our time is up, but it never ended for me."

"It's too late to pretend like you always loved me," I whispered, my chin tilted upward, and watched his restraint crumble with my lips so close.

"No, I've let you get away with a lot while you've been here, Clementine. But not that. You can't win this one. Time can be found, time can be made." He flinched, desperately wanting to close the distance between us, but he wouldn't—not until I asked him. It was my line, and he'd respect it. "Why can't you see how much I love you—how much I have *loved* you?"

"I wanted today to be fun and normal, but that's not us. We can't do that together anymore! It's too hard," I protested.

"Says who?" He huffed. "I was having fun until your fiancé walked into my house!" He shook his head at me. "*We* were having fun," he corrected himself. "I just want to love you."

"I don't want to fight with you." My voice cracked. "I don't."

"But you're still leaving?" He asked, and it broke my heart.

"You know I have to. Texas is home, Cael."

"Is it, though?" He asked me.

I had never experienced anything as visceral and painful as the way my heart shattered when he pointed to his chest. Two fingers over his heart, he tapped it.

"This is your home, Clementine," he said. "I didn't have a choice back then. I was seventeen, I didn't..." I had never seen Cael trip over words.

"Cael..."

"You have a choice. Please don't choose to leave me," he begged, tears pooling in his glassy blue eyes. The silence dragged as he stared at me. "Will you at least kiss me before you leave?" he asked.

"If I do that, I'll never go." I sighed.

I watched the selfish thought cross his features as he contemplated breaking the rule.

"You'll always have a home here," he said quietly, pressing his hand to his chest.

Every swirling thought wanted me to give in to him but I still wasn't sure I could.

"You make it impossible to think straight," I said, not wanting to give him hope because we both knew I'd get on that plane. The conversation didn't change that.

"We don't have to think anymore tonight." Cael collected himself, tears streaming down his face as he kissed my jaw. "We can just be Cael and Clementine one more time before you leave."

Sex wouldn't fix what was broken, but at least we'd have the memory.

"Please," my voice broke as I begged him.

Cael's hand slipped from under my shirt and pulled it over my shoulders, kissing the bare skin as he lifted himself over me and framed me in with his body on the bed. He leaned back, staring down at me as I carded my hands through his hair. The moonlight streamed through the window and bathed his toned, tanned body in a hazy white light that made him look ethereal. It danced across his lusty blue eyes, making them sparkle as a tiny smirk formed.

He came down on me, his lips carefully marking my skin, all while respecting my rule, even knowing that it might be the last chance he had to break it. His hand cupped my breast, kneading it gently as his tongue licked a warm stripe down my throat that pulled a tiny whimper from my lip.

"You have to keep quiet," he whispered.

I cocked my head at him. "Afraid to get caught, Loverboy?"

"Yes." His lip trembled as his eyes flickered up to mine. "I don't want to be interrupted. Just you and..." He kissed the underside of my chin. "Me," he breathed against my hot skin and sent a shiver down my spine. "So, stay quiet for me?" He asked.

"Alright." I pressed my hand against his cheek, and he leaned into it with his eyes closed, his chest expanding against my body as he felt it all.

"Good girl." he kissed the inside of my wrist and went back to his primary focus as his hand slipped beneath the band of my shorts into the wetness that awaited him between my legs. "Does he make you wet like this?" Cael asked me.

I shook my head no, and a grin spread across his face.

"It's just for you," I said quietly, my hips bucking as his tongue slowly lapped between me. His hands squeezed around my thigh, fingertips digging deep to hold me still as he licked and sucked on my clit in a torturous pattern.

Cael worked until my vision went dizzy and then teased me further as his fingers pushed deep inside of my aching walls, throbbing around him as he curled them against me. I shoved my hand between my teeth to keep from moaning his name and pressed myself back into the pillow. I could feel the smile on his face as he kissed my inner thigh with his damp mouth.

"I'm not going to last." I curled my toes into the mattress.

"I've dreamed this moment a thousand times over the last seven years," he confessed, his nose brushing against my clit as he moved his fingers faster. "And if I'm never going to have it again, I want it all right now," he demanded, sitting back to watch as he pumped his hand relentlessly into the wetness. He spread my legs on the bed, his pupils blown and hair messy from getting lost between my thighs. "You're beautiful," he praised from his perch.

My body screamed out when he added his thumb and began methodical circles against my aching clit until I couldn't focus on anything but my senses begging for release.

"Let go for me, Plum," he whispered and dropped to kiss my stomach as I spiraled down through my orgasm. It was soft and sweet as he relaxed his pace and walked me through the dizzying feelings that overtook my body. "That's my girl."

The sound of his praises flooded me with the need for more. I grabbed him by the waist of his pants, shucking the sweats over his hips and helping him as he kicked out of them. There was no hesitation as I fell back against the bed and fell open for him. He rested between me and thrust forward, sliding inside of me without pause. The feeling was instant euphoria. He packed me full and rolled his hips into me as slowly as he could manage as I kissed a pattern into his chest.

Cael's sweat was salty on my tongue as I licked his throat and tangled my fingers into his hair as he rocked us at a steady pace. He took his time with it, savoring every thrust with a quick nip of my skin or pinch of his fingers on my thighs. I needed it all. It was reminiscent of falling through time with him, tangling our souls together as we tumbled back to the present.

It was moments of breathless panting and soft, purposeful moans before both of us came together and fell into a tangle of sweaty skin and heaving chests. With my head dizzy, I never wanted this moment to end. The moment I pressed my head against his chest and heard the sound of his beautiful, big heart, I knew he was right. His heart would forever be my home. I closed my eyes and tried to sleep, but my head was still too conflicted to let me try.

"You'll have an extraordinary life, Clementine," Cael whispered against my hair after he thought I'd fallen asleep.

CODY

"Are you okay?" Josh's groggy voice echoed through the phone pressed to my face.

"I don't know," I answered him honestly, because what else was there to do or say?

Clem had left that morning and, for a moment there, I thought she might stay, that she'd figure it out in her sleep but she had slipped away without even waking me. Part of me knows the reason. It's the exact same reason why I had snuck away that first night, because saying goodbye hurt. It hurt like having your heart ripped from your chest, still beating, and watching the one person you trust with it walk away from you.

It made it impossible to breathe.

Hard to think.

I came out here because I didn't want to do any of that, but my head was spinning and my fingers had grown itchy with the need to stop feeling it all. My phone burned in my pocket and, in a haze, I had dialed his number.

"It's five am, Cody," he said with an exhausted groan. After a long beat, a few grumbled swears and him shifting in his bed on the other end of the phone he said, "She left didn't she?"

"Yeah." My eyes stung.

Josh sighed. "Alright, listen. We both knew this day was coming and there's not anything I'm going to say that's going to make you feel better. But we both know exactly what you're thinking about, and it won't make you feel better in the long run." *Drugs.* He didn't say it but the implications were there. It's why I'd called him in the first place.

I gripped the phone tighter.

"I know you're overwhelmed right now and the easiest thing to do is to find a source that will dull all those feelings wreaking havoc on you, but I want you to sit in the feelings," he said. "It's time you start feeling that shit because if you can't you're always going to turn back to the drugs."

"I called you, didn't I?" I said through gritted teeth.

"This time," Josh noted. "How close were you to calling someone else, someone who might be nicer to you for a couple of bucks."

I had called an old dealer and hung up.

"Don't bullshit me, Cody, feel it. Let it consume you just like you do with drugs," Josh said.

"I don't want to feel it," I groaned.

"I don't give a shit what you want, you called me before the sun came up and you're whining in my ear about your long-lost ex-girlfriend leaving you. So guess what, I'm now your problem. You're a time bomb, Cael," he snapped. "Let it out."

I closed my eyes and let the feelings rise in my chest. The agony of grief, guilt, and shame drowning out the rough beating of my heart and the painful constriction of my lungs. It pushed through my nervous system and flooded my veins until all I could feel was the overwhelming need to scream and cry.

It felt like drowning and flying all at once. The breeze was beneath my feet, but the water in my lungs burned. I tried to catch my breath, but relief never came. My skin itched, and my collar was too tight around my throat, but I was feeling it all.

I wanted my Mama back.

I needed my Clementine.

I hated my Dad.

I hated myself even more.

A hiccup exploded from me, tearing a sob from my chest, and it was only then that I realized I was wailing. It cascaded out of me in waves, my head throbbed, and my T-shirt became soaked as the sun rose over the lake. *Mama.* The sun-kissed my cheeks, and the breeze blew through the lavender, knocking petals around in the air. I could feel her fingertips against my cheek like she was standing there, telling me to feel it all.

"You look pretty today Mama," I cooed and closed the door behind me as Van left to get dinner started. *"How are you feeling?"* I sunk down into the chair beside her bed.

"Like I'm dying, handsome," she cooed, her accent still as thick as the day we left Texas.

I smiled at her joke even though it felt like a horse had kicked me in the chest.

"I didn't know we were doing fake smiles today," she teased.

"I'm doing my best, Mama, but this is hard," I said quietly. *"I'm sorry."*

There was some uncomfortable need to be happy for her. Like if she couldn't do it for herself because of the pain she was in, at least I could try. But sometimes it was just too hard and she never cared if the mask dropped. She was just grateful I was being honest with her.

"I don't know when you got so soft, Honeybug." She poked me with a frail finger.

"I'm not soft." I rolled my eyes, trying to push away the memories.

"You certainly didn't inherit that giant heart," she teased.

"Alright, Mama." I wrapped my hand around hers and laid it in her lap. *"We should revisit moving you into a nicer space. This room has no windows."* I looked around the guest room of the Nest and scowled. It was nothing but a storage room waiting to happen. It was dark and small.

"I get to see everything I need to when you boys come to visit," she hummed and the sound was wet and painful.

She couldn't even see the stars in here and it hurt my feelings I think, more than hers.

"That's not what I meant. You should be somewhere a real doctor can take care of you, somewhere that gives you what you need," I argued. We had the same fight once a week.

"I have everything I need right here." She pressed a cold hand to my hot cheeks. *"Dean is going to pass his Mathematics class, and Jensen finally asked out that girl in his sociology."* She smiled. *"Arlo is going to make Captain,"* she hummed. *"I left the recipe for the muffins in the drawer beside the fridge."*

"The one that sticks," I said with a nod. That drawer was the bane of my existence, it never opened, no matter how hard I yanked on it, but Mama could always slide it open like nothing was stuck.

"Make sure you double the chocolate chips when you make them for him." She narrowed her eyes on me.

"He's going to be a really good captain." I cleared my throat.

"He has an amazing team to lead," she reminded me.

Her brown hair had grayed and thinned, but Zoey had taught me how to braid, so I did my best to keep it braided and brushed for her. Even so sick her smile remained bright and it ate away at my resolve. I blocked out the feelings that seeing her like that produced. She had weeks left. That's what the doctor had said, soon she'd die in this shitty little room without windows and she wouldn't let me do anything about it.

I hated the idea of her dying in the Nest.

I shook my head. "Mama. You need to be—"

"Don't Mama me. I'm dying. I can do whatever I want. And what I want is to be here, taking care of you all. So let me," she scolded me.

I wouldn't win the argument anyway. Mama knew what she wanted and what she wanted she would get. She was never alone; someone was always in here with her. Jensen and Dean were both being tutored in their advanced Mathematics. Van read to her during his free periods; she would run through the old games with some of the other boys. She was teaching Silas to cook on the days she could get around, and he checked on her when he could, relaying with the hospital and a care nurse once a week. If I wasn't here, Arlo was.

Dad never visited.

Or if he did, I never saw him.

I was tired of trying to convince him that she wanted him around, but he just shut down. I know it's because he doesn't want to remember her like this and part of me understands, but if there was ever a time for him to be a Dad, it was now.

"Honeybug," she whispered to me and broke me from the trance I had fallen into. "Where'd you go?" She asked me quietly.

Somewhere, you weren't sick and frail.

"Nowhere Mama, I'm always right here."

I tended to keep her hidden away in my mind, far away from where she could creep in and help me. She felt safe there and if I didn't think about her then she couldn't ever tell me how stupid I was being. But maybe I wasn't keeping her safe, maybe I was only protecting myself. She'd hate the numb person I'd become, and maybe it was easier to keep her locked away so she couldn't encourage me to feel it. I pressed my hand into the cold, damp grass to steady myself, the phone still pressed to my wet cheek.

"Atta boy," Josh said softly from the other end. "Feels shitty doesn't it?"

"Yeah, this sucks."

Both crying and finding comfort in Joshua Logan's stupid voice.

"It makes it worse that you're a giant cry baby," he joked and I offered a weak laugh in return. "I have training today, but I'll keep my phone loud and in my pocket. But if you call and get me fined, you're paying it," he warned. It was his way of saying he'd answer no matter what, that he was here for me.

"Deal," I choked out.

"Promise me, Cody," he said before we hung up. "Call me if you need me."

I hated promises. "I promise, Logan," I said, and I meant it.

The phone went dead before I could thank him, but he knew.

The breeze kicked up again making my face cold and my nose run but thick flakes of snow started to fall around me in the grass. It felt poetic that the sky had decided to open up and cry with me.

CODY

"Cut those pieces a little smaller, Sawyer." Mama pointed to the cutting board and picked out a small piece of pepper. "Like this size," she instructed him. I sat at the island trying to concentrate on my Biology homework as Silas ran through my notes, and Mama taught the King brothers how to make lasagna.

"Fix that, and then you're done," Silas said, pointing to a sentence. I tore my eyes away from the commotion in the kitchen.

Arlo and Nicholas pushed back and forth for dominance over the steaming pot of meat sauce that Mama had started before she turned her attention to mixing up ricotta cheese.

"Hey, don't." Nicholas shoved Arlo, causing him to lose his balance. A splash of sauce painted the kitchen walls.

"Boys, if you can't figure out how to share, I'll make you go do laundry," Mama said without looking up from her bowl. A smile formed on her face as the two of them groaned and started behaving.

Laundry day after a long week of practice was a chore none of them ever wanted to do. When we'd moved to Rhode Island, I hadn't expected to be thrown into such strange dynamics.

The King brothers and Silas seemed to have their own little dysfunctional relationship. Arlo was in his first year of University, his brother Nicholas was a year ahead, and then Sawyer was two years older and coming to the end of his

301

schooling. They had an older brother Luc, who I had only met once and who never really came around much after he graduated.

Silas landed somewhere in the middle. I'm pretty sure he was the same age as Nicholas but they couldn't be more different. Silas was undergoing intense medical schooling to become a doctor. They all played for the Hornets baseball team and lived under the roof of the Nest.

It was a strange adjustment when Mama started spending more time here, helping them out with basic tasks. She had become the Hornets' house mother, and no one seemed to question it. For a little while, here and there, I forgot that I was missing a piece of myself.

Silas had offered to tutor me in Biology, but it wasn't the same as having Clementine there to help me with my notes. He was always grumpy and tired from his long hours and the endless practices my Dad had them run. There were no funny jokes, wiggled fingers, or escape plans. Just scowls and polite encouragement.

"Is Dad coming for dinner?" I asked Mama as I closed my binder and finished with my work. She inhaled slowly, looked up from her bowl, and shook her head.

"We'll bring him leftovers." She winked at me.

I couldn't help but think that maybe it was my fault he never came for dinner. Lately, the two of us had been at each other's throats more often than not. I was forced to live in a state miles away from the only person who ever saw me for me. At least Dad had Mama. I had nothing, not without Clementine.

He wanted me to stop being foolish, focus on the last few months of High School, and finish my application for Harbor... He had found a few applications for school in Texas and then told me that my grades would never be good enough, so the point was moot.

"Yeah, whatever. Keep letting him hole up in that office. You know, the more you cater to his shitty behavior, the worse he'll get."

"Bringing him dinner isn't going to make anything worse." She laughed at me, which only enraged me more.

"He can't even be bothered to come home half the time, so you moved Sunday dinners into this fucking frat house so that maybe, just maybe, he'd take the time out of his exhausting day training wannabe baseball stars to spend some time with us?" I raised my voice, and I knew everyone in the kitchen had stopped to watch my outburst, but it was too late to reel myself in.

"Watch your language with me." She scowled.

"He's too busy chasing a dead dream to love us anymore, Mama. Stop making excuses for him," I argued.

"Cael Cody." Mama hissed at me.

I shook my head and pushed away from the island, almost knocking the stool over. I wandered out to the front porch, which was quiet for a few minutes before the sound of footsteps interrupted what little peace I found.

"You shouldn't be so hard on her." Arlo's voice came from behind me as he lowered to the porch beside me. I turned to look at him and for a moment, wanted nothing more than to tell him off, but he wasn't looking at me. He was looking out at the gray sky that hung over the Nest.

"I don't need some bullshit talk about how to treat my parents. Thanks though," I grumbled.

"You really are a brat, you know that?" Arlo said. "You've got two parents that give a shit about you, and all you wanna do is fight back against them?"

"You don't know me or my parents, King. Not really." I scoffed. "How about *you* go back in and play family with her? That's all this is. A fucking endless sitcom."

Arlo stared at me for a moment, his heavy brows paired with dark eyes that felt like they were burning holes through me.

"What?" I snapped when he didn't answer.

"I know they don't beat you. They don't punish you. I've never met a mother so patient and filled with love, and you just walk all over her." Arlo slapped me with his judgment. "Maybe your Dad can't figure out how to manage work and his family, but that's not your Mom's fault."

"She lets him get away with it," I argued.

"God damn it, kid, you're like a cornered alley cat," he growled. "Maybe she's choosing to let the fight go because it makes your Dad happy, and maybe she's too busy fighting you at every corner to have the energy to fight your Dad." Arlo offered, and I turned to look at him in defeat.

"Wow, thank you for your sage advice," I said, pushing off the step. "Mind your business, Arlo."

"Pick and choose your battles, Cael," he said, "but make sure whatever battle you decide to fight, it's worth it."

CODY

"The boys said you were out here."

Dad's voice interrupted the ending of the golden sunset that was falling over the dock. Snow had started to fall faster, thick enough to coat the leaves of the lavender bushes that would soon be barren from the cold.

"The *boys* are chatty at all the wrong times." I rolled my eyes. "What do you want?"

"Watch your tone," Dad snapped and sank down in the grass behind me at a distance.

"Answer my question," I responded, keeping my eyes trained on the horizon.

"I came to make sure you were alright," he said.

I couldn't stop the laughter that exploded from me. "Are you serious?"

"Cael."

"Dad."

He groaned, a loud huff of air leaving his lips. "Dean said Ella drove Clementine back to town. I'm sorry."

"Are you?" I turned to look at him finally. "You're the reason she left."

"That's not true." Dad shook his head, and a few pieces of his graying blond hair fell against his forehead. "She left because she has a job to do."

"Recycling a seven-year-old excuse," I groaned and rubbed the back of my neck. "Classy."

"Adults have responsibilities," he responded.

"It's different, Dad. You dragged us across the country because you wanted to chase your dream. You didn't care what it meant for us. but we followed. Sure, I dragged my heels and made it your problem, but I was just a kid."

305

"You were seventeen years old," he corrected me.

"Yeah, Dad, I was." I stared at him for a long time, his tired green eyes screaming back at me. "I was seventeen when Mama collapsed in the kitchen of our brand new sparkly house while she unpacked dishes. You were at the stadium. I was seventeen when I broke my arm climbing up on the roof to put up the Christmas lights for her because she couldn't climb the ladder."

"You never broke your arm..." Dad said.

"In two places. There's still a pin in my wrist." I held up my arm to show him the scar. His face twisted in confusion and hurt.

"You weren't there, you were training Nicholas after hours on a Sunday."

I didn't want to be angry, I hated the feeling but, where Mama could pull out all the soft, saddest feelings, Dad only formed the most hateful, bitter ones. It felt like all I did anymore was hash out the old memories with the people in my life. I was fucking sick of it.

"I was just a kid when Arlo and I helped Mama paint the kitchen in the Nest. Silas sat in your spot at my fucking High School graduation." I held up my hand as he opened his mouth with an excuse. "I thought maybe there was something important going on, a valid reason you didn't show up, but the guys on the team were louder than anyone in the crowd. So if they were there with *me*, where were you?" I raised my voice as I posed the question.

"I was nineteen when Dean and I found her on the living room floor." I bit back the tears. "Nineteen, answering the questions my Dad should have been doing when I found my Mom passed out. I went to the doctor's appointments, I kept her spirits up. I read to her, I fed her, I bathed her. Just because you couldn't bear to see her like that. I was just a kid."

Dad stared at me, his jaw tight as he nodded. He listened to everything I was saying, but I couldn't be sure he was actually processing it.

"You aren't a kid anymore," he said after a tense moment of silence, his arms crossed over his chest and his eyes dropping to the grass. "Clementine can't erase all of the bad things you suffered, Cael–and I am sorry that you had to do those things. That's my fault."

"You're damn right it is," I snapped.

306

"But," he raised a hand, stopping me, "you were also a kid when you fell in love with her. You were six, nine, thirteen, fifteen, seventeen." He listed off the ages like they meant nothing, but I had a memory for each year I had loved her.

"You were young. You didn't know what love was," Dad said. "Leaving Texas was what was best for all of us."

"No, it was what was best for *you*," I snarled.

"You ever stop to think what would have happened to your Mama?" he stopped, stumbling over his words. His eyes shifted to the sky for a split second. "If we had been alone in Texas?"

"It would have been better than dying in a room without windows, begging for you to come see her. She begged, did you know that? She begged us all, all she wanted was you. All I wanted was you. At least in Texas, she would have had Mary and Clementine."

I watched a flicker of secret cross his face, an angry, deep-rooted secret, and I hated him for it, the ability to just shove it all down and ignore the pain he was in. I wanted to scream at him.

"Your mother's death destroyed the boy you were."

"You didn't know the boy I was," I hissed at him.

"What do you think it would have done to Clementine?" He asked.

The knife to my throat pinched, I could feel the blood dripping from each tiny cut he created with his questions. I couldn't answer because I knew that he had pushed me into a corner. Mama's death would have hurt Clementine more than anything; it had, and she wasn't even around for it.

"You spent your entire life protecting that girl, Cael." Dad pushed from the grass. "I was just trying to protect *you*. Loving her through grief would have broken you beyond repair. It would've broken her, and she didn't deserve that. You can't love someone like that without resenting them."

"I don't believe that." I shook my head. "You want to blame us, blame the way we loved each other, but I know deep down that there's nothing wrong with the way I love her and there has never been a second in my entire fucking life where I questioned the way she loves me," I snapped at him. "The grief broke me because you didn't care as long as I was playing baseball and keeping my head down. But I couldn't handle it alone, so I did drugs to feel alive and to keep putting on the mask you wanted me to wear!"

"Blaming me for your addiction, I thought we were over that. Isn't that what your sessions are for?" Dad asked.

"You wouldn't know," I said each word with frustration. "You haven't asked me a single question about my recovery. You go through Silas, who tells me by the way. He makes sure I know that you care, but you're too much of a coward to ask me yourself because you don't want to have this conversation."

"Maybe you're right." Dad nodded after a long beat of silence. Silas had always been more of a Dad to me than he would ever be. The wind ripped around us and the smell of damp lavender kicked up in the air.

Stop fighting.

Mama's voice floated between us and made me want to cry.

"I have this for you. I should have given it to you a long time ago, but I never thought you deserved to have it." He held a letter out to me, Honeybug scribbled across it in Mama's pretty handwriting.

Anger was the first to the party and it seemed that was the new normal but I shoved it down and took the envelope from him.

"I'm going back to Harbor this morning," he said, backing away. "I'll be at the office."

I watched him go, eyes trained on his back as he disappeared down the path.

The paper was old and light in my palm, and it wasn't clear how long it had been in his possession, but the fear of opening it was still so real. I folded back the flap and sunk back down into the snow-kissed grass, my knees against my chest as I read it.

My sweet boy, my Honeybug.

I bit into my lip and stopped reading to stare upward until the tears dried out of the corners of my eyes. I fucking hated everything about the moment. I had lost Clementine that morning, and now I was sitting alone, about to lose Mama all over again too.

Pay attention, I know this is hard and I know you don't want to read this.

If I know anything, you stopped the second you started and are contemplating folding up these words, shoving them in your pocket and never reading them. So much like your Dad and still refusing to acknowledge it. But don't you dare ignore me, little boy. You read this letter, you ingrain what I have to say in your bones, and you carry it around for the rest of your life.

Never let the compassion that thrives in your tender heart die. Stoke the fire until it burns bright so that it can lead others out of the darkness. You are the sun, Cael. You are my sun. So fierce and loud that sometimes it may be too much for others to share the space with you. But that doesn't mean they don't love you, everyone needs a little darkness every once in a while and, as impossible as it seems, one day you will need the moon too. I need you to remember that. That there will come a day when all you crave is the blue haze of the night, and you'll need to remind your Dad of his job.

You're currently angry at him. But, Baby, you've never known how to be angry. Not really. Dig deeper, it's something else.

I scoffed. I'm trying Mama.

And before you argue with the sky, lose the attitude. I'm not finished.

I laughed through the trickle of tears that coated my cheeks and lips.

You have every right to be angry, if that's what it is. But... we both know it's your grief tangled with guilt. That's always what it is because you always think it's your fault. But it's not. Not this time.

Your father is mean, he's grumpy, he's overprotective about all the wrong things. He's elusive and, to the untrained eye, he might seem cold and uninterested. But he is anything but. He has loved me his entire life, since the moment he saw me. I know because he told me so, every day since. Your father was the love of my life, and I was his since we were seventeen. He has changed over the years; he has hardened and grayed.

No one has ever known Ryan Cody the way I do.

Since the day you were born, everyone always said that you were your Mama's boy. But they were wrong. From the day you looked up at me with those big blue eyes, given they are mine, you have been your father's son. The one I know. He was funny and beautiful, his laughter made people smile, and his eyes were the greenest shade with flecks of gold that danced when he looked at me for too long.

Okay, Mama... I rolled my eyes.

309

I'm gushing, but you'll read every word because if you don't, I'll come down there and haunt you, Honeybug. Your Dad was the kind of spirit that couldn't be contained, he gave me every adventure even the ones I never asked for. He filled my heart and home with so much love he had nothing left to give. The problem never lied in how much he loved me, because no matter what troubles found us, we had each other. You are your father's son. Love and light.

It was my mistake. All the discourse between the two of you is my doing.

I've been sick since the day we fell in love. I knew that one day it would catch up to me, it was inevitable. It didn't bother me as much as it bothered him. I had made my peace with the monster to come but to help him cope I used to tell your father that it was his love that kept me healthy. That there was no room in my heart for sickness because of the way he loved me.

It's true that after I had you, the illness returned. My immune system was compromised and my body drained. I do not for a moment regret bringing you into this world, my sweet boy, so if there is a shred of doubt in your mind that I did, please know it's not true.

But you must understand your father is the way he is. It's not that he's cold or uninterested, Cael. He's tired and he is suffocated by his own guilt of loving you more than he ever loved me.

I choked out a sob that hit me like a moving truck and knocked the air from my lungs.

He believes that because he loves you more, he left gaps inside of me that allowed the sickness to return. But that's silly. I'm sick because of science and the cruel reality of life. He avoided me and you because he thinks that he failed us. That he failed me.

He doesn't know what's inside of this letter and, if I know your father, he waited years to give it to you like the stubborn jackass he is. But I also know that he never opened it because it was between you and me. And, right now, it may feel silly or frivolous because I am clearly long gone, but if you're still with me, I need you to do something for me.

"I'm always right here, Mama."

"I need you to find your Dad, and I need you to show him that it's okay to love you. That he doesn't have to feel guilty for doing so because I brought you

310

into this world for each other." Her voice washed over me like she was standing in front of me with both her warm hands around my face and our heads pressed together. "You have to show him, Honeybug."

The sun and moon cannot survive without each other, Cael. I am simply just the stars between the two of you.

MATTHEWS

There was a knock on the door of the Nest as I shoved the rest of my clothes into my suitcase for the airport. I'd have the rest of my equipment shipped back.

"Clementine." Ryan's voice made me pause, and I turned to find him standing in a sweater and jeans in the door frame.

"What can I do for you, Mr. Cody?" I asked him, turning completely and crossing my arms over my chest.

Even seeing him made my heart hurt. I'd missed Cael the second I crawled from bed, my heart screaming at me as I got dressed and let Ella drive me back into the city.

Ryan had the same boy-next-door features. The curved jaw, sloped nose, high cheekbones, and big, bright eyes. I used to swoon over the photos in Mrs. Cody's living room of Ryan when he was young, but now, remembering those and having him standing here, I couldn't breathe.

"Do you love him?"

Déjà vu.

"I've loved Cael from the moment I figured out how to love." I don't hesitate.

Ryan smiled with a soft nod. "I was asking about the other guy."

"Of course you were." I sighed and sat down on my bed, completely defeated.

He entered the room and grabbed the chair from the desk, spinning it around and sitting on it in front of me.

"I need you to understand that everything I've done up to this point in Cael's life has been to protect him."

My brows raised in question. From everything I've heard, their relationship was tense at best, and Ryan floated in and out of the picture without caring about who Cael was or what he did outside of baseball.

"Rae and I." He offered me a sad smile when he mentioned Lorraine's nickname. "We fell in love at a young age, and it dictated my entire life," he explained. "I don't regret a second of it, but I wanted Cael to make his own decisions."

"And he couldn't, not with me around."

I was starting to understand where the conversation was headed.

"He *wouldn't*. I tried repeatedly, but every decision he made, he did so with you in mind. He never chose himself, Clementine." Ryan said. "I knew that leaving Texas wouldn't be enough space. I knew that no matter where he was, he would always find his way back to you, for better or for worse."

I pressed my lips into a thin line as the puzzle pieces came together.

It had all started with the bird. The miscommunication hadn't been our fault.

Ryan had shoved the wedge between us.

"I knew it the moment he sacrificed his sleep and food to keep that bird alive for you." The confirmation was deafening. I pushed off the bed and stepped back from Ryan until my back was pressed against the dresser, and there still wasn't enough space. "You were both in too deep after–"

"Don't." I stared at him. I didn't want to talk about that day.

"He was glued to you, Clementine. He would have followed you no matter where you went, and you needed space from each other."

Shock clawed at my throat. Realization heavily weighted against my chest.

"Was my Momma in on it?" I asked him. "Did she have the same views on the situation? Did she not want us together?"

"No, she had nothing to do with this. If anything, that woman believed in true love more than anyone I've ever met." Ryan shook his head. "She hated that you were pulled apart."

"But you thought it was for our own good?" I furrowed my brows at him in anger.

"It was. Look at you, Clementine! You're a journalist, you did it. You're so intelligent and sassy. There are tiny pieces of not only your own mother but

Lorraine in you and I've never been so grateful for your time here... I'm proud of you." Ryan didn't move from his chair. "You thrived without him. No longer following him around like a puppy, you found yourself, and you wouldn't have done that waiting by the phone for him to call, and we both know it."

"You don't get to decide our fate!" I raised my voice. "You should be proud of *him*."

"I–" He paused with a curt nod, wanting to argue but something stopped him. "That's why I'm here," Ryan said, digging out something from his sweater pocket. It was a stack of letters in all assortments of colors. "He wrote to you once a week, every day. For seven years, Clementine. This is only a portion of them. The rest are in my truck."

"What?" I stuttered, my body in shock as he held it out to me.

My hands shook as I took them from him. An elastic band held together what looked like close to forty letters.

"Every week until the week you showed up here. He used to drop them in the mail collection for the secretary, and I would take them out before she mailed them," Ryan confessed. "You needed a complete disconnect. I couldn't let him believe there was still hope."

"But he did, even without a response from me." I shook the bundle of letters. "He believed for seven years, and I thought he had forgotten about me. I thought he didn't care about me anymore, and he sat here, writing these letters to my ghost. And you let him?" I practically snarled at him. "How dare you!"

"Clementine," Ryan started. "I've made a thousand and one mistakes over the last seven years. The biggest one was thinking I could stop you two from getting back to one another. I can't control fate, and I've never been able to control my son."

"So why bring Julien here?" I snapped. "That was juvenile."

"One last ditch effort to push you back where you belong." Ryan licked his bottom lip. "Mary sends me all your articles, I read every one. You're fucking good at it, kid. You have a gift, and you shouldn't blow that up."

"Who says I'm blowing it up?" I laughed, the letters weighing down my arm and reminded me that I had zero clue as to what had happened to Cael over the last seven years.

"*Me*," Ryan said. "You can love him. You can need him and want him, Clementine. But he's twisted, he's figuring himself out again..."

"You don't want me screwing up that recovery on ifs and maybes."

"No," he stopped me. "I don't want him blaming himself when he trips or has moments. I don't want you risking your future for that."

"How do you know he will?" I asked him. I understood the concern. What I didn't understand was the lack of faith and loyalty.

"Because I know he will. It's inevitable, but not unexpected. Riona said that he's bound to slip up, but the best thing that I can do for him is be there, and I've been taking the blame for years. I can handle it. What I don't want is for him to blame you."

"He won't." I smiled at Ryan. "He wouldn't." My thoughts wander to Cael, that perfect smile of his so loud in my memory. "He's never had it in him to blame me for anything. I could smash my car into the front of the Nest, and he'd find a way to make it his fault." I sighed.

"It's not that simple, Clementine." Ryan shook his head.

"It really is, Ryan," I said without hesitation. "I understand what you're saying. I hate it and don't accept it, but if you think what's best for Cael is leaving, then that's what I'll do. Because all I've ever wanted is for him to be happy."

He watched me carefully as I turned to my laptop bag, pulled out a handful of paper held together by a clip, and held it up.

"Will you do something for me, though?"

"I owe you that much," Ryan stood from the chair.

"This is the rough copy of the article. Will you give it to him so he understands why I left?" I asked him.

"Of course." He took the papers, looked down at them for a tense moment, and then up at me. "Rae loved you like you were hers, and I'm sorry that I didn't know how to tell you both when she died. It was a moment of cowardice that never should have happened." He licked his bottom lip. "You should have been offered the chance to say goodbye."

Ryan Cody had been swallowed whole by sadness but, unlike him and his son, I never believed she was gone. I looked for her in my melancholy, where she would celebrate every moment no matter how sad, because Lorainne Cody could find joy in anything.

"I got to say goodbye, Mr. Cody. In my own way. I didn't need your permission." A genuine smile spread across my face.

"No." He nodded. "You never did."

"It's time for me to go, Mr. Cody." I pressed my lips into a thin line. "Take care of him for me?" I asked, my eyes drifting to the bracelet on my wrist.

"I'll do better than I have been." He nodded and disappeared from the room, leaving me to finish packing to the sound of my own crying.

MATTHEWS

2020

"That's perfect," Bobbi sank onto the shitty dorm mattress with a moan.

"You think?" I asked her, looking down over the short plaid skirt and black long sleeve. I felt... exposed but sexy. I turned away from her to look in the mirror again. My hair was getting so long that, even pulled into a sleek ponytail, it cascaded down my back in chestnut waves.

"We're so ready to rush," Bobbi giggled. She had gone with a velvet green dress that complimented her warm skin and perfected spirals of dark black hair. She had brushed gold eyeshadow across her eyes and it made her shimmer.

We had been stuck in our dorms for weeks on lockdown and it had been lifted only that morning when all the parties started to pop up around campus.

"I don't know about ready, but we'll look good doing it," I mumbled and grabbed my cell before pulling Bobbi to her feet.

"What are these parties even like?" I asked her as we waited for the cab.

"Insanely fun, my brother tells war stories about them. If we're lucky, we'll both *get lucky*." Bobbi said as the cab pulled up and she hopped in.

The drive to the row wasn't long, ten minutes at the most, but the closer we got the more nervous I got. I couldn't even remember the last party I had attended and they had never been my thing. Too many people, everyone drunk off their faces being idiots. Blurred lines and even worse entitlement. I shuddered as the cab stopped in front of a massive building overflowing with bodies.

"There are guys here..." I said to Bobbi as we stood on the front lawn.

317

"Yeah?" Bobbi turned her head to me. "Some of the popular sororities will do co-ed parties for rush. You'll be okay, just stay close and try to have fun."

Bobbi had been a life saver, literally. The first day of University had been mortifying, and for a little while there I was convinced that I should just go home. She was working at the small coffee shop on campus and the first time we had met she asked my name and never forgot it. After that day, for at least two months, I struggled with my own shortcomings. *I didn't know how to make friends.*

Everytime I opened my mouth to talk to her, nonsense came out and I just embarrassed myself, but she didn't seem to care. She started getting my coffee ready before I arrived and tossed in small pastries because *'you don't eat enough.'*

Turned out we had three classes together and she had never once seen me in the cafeteria. But that was because I avoided it. It reminded me too much of high school and I couldn't stand eating in front of everyone, so I usually found a quiet spot on the back lawn and nibbled on the snacks I brought.

Eventually, we just started being friends.

I couldn't actually put a finger on when it happened but she'd come over to watch movies and I show her how to fix lines in her media homework. Bobbi was my best friend but never once did I feel eclipsed by her. It was equal.

The music thumping into my veins brought me back to reality as we climbed the stairs inside. It looked like any other party I had ever been to; girls in short dresses, guys double fisting whatever drinks they could find, and everyone blissfully unaware of the mistakes they would make in the dark.

"I'll go get us a drink." Bobbi smiled and her hand left mine without a second thought. I tried to follow but the crowd closed around her and I was stuck with my back against the door.

"Matthews." His voice raked down my spine and left goosebumps in its wake. Appearing like a nightmare from my left in a tight black shirt and a pair of jeans. He was taller, but his hair was still tucked beneath a faded cowboy hat and his smile was just as bright.

"Kiefer." I swallowed tightly and stepped back from him.

"I didn't know you went to AU," he said, those green eyes rolling over me and stopping at my hips before snapping back up to my chest.

318

"Eyes up here," I said and the comment made him flinch. His eyes darkened on mine but his smile widened.

"Easy, Matthews. I come in peace." He put both hands in the air and some of his drink spilled.

"I thought you didn't drink," I said as the tequila wafted into what little space he left between us. At one point the smell of his cologne was a turn on, I sought it out. On his clothes, in class, on dates. Now it made me gag.

"I'm a grown up now, juice doesn't cut it."

"Does the tequila make you a better person?" I stared at the cup, raising my eyebrow at it.

The laugh that dripped from him was hollow and full of malice. "Oh come on Clemmy, we were kids, I was dumb. You're being a little rude," he said, his tone dropping. "That's not like you."

"What were you expecting?" I tilted my chin up at him, my body filling with adrenaline. I wasn't that little girl that he had taken advantage of. He'd killed her that day and made me harder, and more aware of the dangers boys like him presented.

"Maybe a little nostalgia," he jabbed. "The least you could do is be civil."

I cocked my head to the side and, even though he towered over me, I stepped forward and brought us chest to chest.

"Why would you ever think I'd want to be civil with you?" I asked him with disgust, lacing every word. My hands shook at my side and my heart was in my throat but god it felt good to let myself get angry. I had been leaving it to fester for so long, mad at him, at Cael, at myself and the world. But lashing out here, at him. It made me feel alive again.

"We had fun and you're letting a small mistake get in the way of us doing that again." Kiefer didn't budge on his dominant stance to appear friendly or harmless, not even for a second.

"In the way of doing what again? *Sexual assault?*" I watched his entire body tighten at the words, almost like he had forgotten the term used for what he had done.

"We were dating, you–"

"I'm not insecure enough to fall for that again, Kiefer, but it seems you're still stupid enough to try it." I cut him off quickly before he could say something he'd regret. I waited patiently, unafraid but still coursing with adrenaline as he stepped back out of my space and gave me room to make an exit.

Before I got too far I turned and looked at him one last time.

"Kiefer?" His head popped up from its hung position with an angry but hurt expression plastered across it. "If I find out you hurt any girl on this campus, I'll go public and make sure the world knows exactly who you are."

All the color drained from his face as the crowd closed around me and I was lost to a sea of bodies and music, drowning in the rush of finally standing up for myself.

"Hey!" Bobbi's voice called out and her fingers found my arm. "You alright?" She looked me over, noticing the flush to my cheeks and how tightly my hands were clenched before looking around for the culprit.

"Yeah, never better." I hollered over the music and took the cup from her.

CODY

"You're on my list."

I found Dad in his office exactly where he said he would be hours later.

"You're going to have to elaborate, Cael," he said without looking up at me.

"Not until you look at me," I demanded.

"Curse your Mama for whatever she said in that letter. It only made your attitude worse," he huffed but pushed up from his seat and raised his eyes to meet mine.

"My sponsor made me put you there. It's for my recovery. I'm supposed to apologize to all of the people that I hurt. You're on it and, until now, I didn't actually understand what I had to apologize for. I was pissed off at you. For everything. For taking me away from Clem and then for not being there when Mama died. The anger overtook the logical reasoning in the back of my mind. You said loving her through the grief would have broken me."

I stepped forward, my fingers flicking against the envelope in my pocket as I worked on slowing my breathing and calming my racing heart.

"It took me a moment to get back to myself, Dad. Back to that kid, you wished I was. I'm sorry that the man I am today isn't what you expected. Most of all, I'm sorry that you never got to say goodbye to her, and I'm sorry that I expected you to love me through the grief." I towered over Dad but not intimidating him in any way.

"Cael." He put his hands on his hips and stared at me.

I took a moment and searched for the man that Mama had described. Digging for that love she talked about and behind the sadness, hidden safely beneath all that guilt and anger. The gold flecks danced across his evergreen gaze and Mama crept into the back of my mind.

The anger dissipated, slipping from me like it was never even there, and I could breathe again. I wrapped my arms around him and tucked against his chest like a little kid. When his arms tangled around me and squeezed, it was like a wrecking ball had been smashed through every wall we had built between one another. A shaky breath filled my chest as he sank into the hug and buried his face atop my head, his cheeks damp against my hair.

"I love you, Dad," I said, pushing off his chest. "She loved you too."

I dug out the letter and held it out to him.

"You should read this."

"No, she wrote that for you." He paused for a second, a scowl on his face, before he grabbed the back of my head and pulled our foreheads together. "I'm sorry that I fucked up the last few years. You should have never had to remember her like that, not on your own. I just couldn't figure out how to be there for you and myself at the same time."

"It's okay, we can figure it out now. Together." I said with a small hiccup. "I need you to know I'm letting her go. Clementine."

On the drive from the cabin back to Harbor, I had done nothing but listen to the silence as my brain tumbled around with itself. I had to choose, just as much as Clementine did. I couldn't fix everything, and I realized that. I needed to focus on repairing my life here and invest in myself and in my Dad. My career, Dean. There was so much in my present to be looked after. I had spent too much time living in the past and the Clementine I had loved wasn't even there anymore. *Different bracelet, different girl.*

I bothered the bracelet on my wrist and swallowed the second round of tears that threatened to fall. I would let her fly the way I had intended her to, train my own wings, and maybe, over time, find her again in the clouds. I swallowed the need to cry and sniffled back what remained from before as I shoved the letter into my pocket.

"Son of a bitch. You two have been love-sick idiots since you could walk. I swear you came out of that hospital tied together by a string," he grumbled, clearly conflicted about something. "I can't believe I'm going to do this," Dad swore under his breath. "It's my fault she left, but...she gave me something, and I think you should see it before you give up. "

"What?" My brows furrowed as he reached into his drawer beside him and handed me what looked like an essay. "Did you just admit you were... you know what nevermind," I said gently and reached out.

"It's her piece on the team." Dad looked down at it. "You should read it, but you should do it fast because her flight leaves and she thinks you've given up. *Again.*"

"I never gave up the first time," I said, taking the paper from him.

"There are things I have to apologize for, but there's no time for it. Go." He waved me off.

I shouldn't do this. She was happy. She was living her dream in Texas. She would be okay without me, and I couldn't ask her to risk all of that. I wouldn't.

She was going to thrive.

No longer in my shadow, but free to fly.

But I gripped the paper in my hand, staring at the title.

The Heart of the Hornets

I swear the world tipped off balance, and every small thing I loved about her came rushing back in, every memory, every fight. It was all there. *Would she even want me to chase her? After everything that's happened, would Clementine even want me?*

"*Fuck it,*" I swore.

My heart pounded in my chest with each step toward the hallway.

"Cael," he said as I rounded the door to leave on anxious feet. I paused, my head turning up to look at him still standing behind his desk. "I love you too."

I didn't look down at the paper again until I pushed through the front doors of the stadium into the parking lot. It felt so heavy in my hands as if it weighed more than three pages. I would have assumed she'd use a picture of us from the winning game. The one with the streamers and confetti, I could see it in my mind...

Instead, she had attached a photo of the dining table from the Nest. Empty except for one place setting in front of Mama's chair. The tear that left me was singular and salty as it hit my lips.

323

"Hey, Kitten," Arlo's voice called to me, and I lifted my head. "I heard you needed a ride to the airport." He leaned against the fastback with his arms across his chest.

"Shouldn't you be halfway to Dallas?" I asked him.

"A little Blondie told me that you needed me." Arlo smiled. Of course, Ella had sent him.

"Last time I was in that car, you punched me." I laughed, letting my head fall to the side as I walked toward him.

"Wasn't the first time, won't be the last." He shrugged and opened the passenger-side door for me. "Move your ass, we have a flight to catch."

He slammed the door behind me and, before I could even read the first line of the article, the fastback was peeling from the parking lot.

"What's that?" He asked as he turned down the music and gripped the wheel.

"The piece that Clementine wrote." My brows scrunched up.

"Why do you look like you're going to puke?" His fingers tightened around the wheel, "I swear to god, Cael, if you puke in my car..." Arlo took his eyes off the road to give me a dirty look.

"I'm not going to puke." I laughed. Well, when I thought about it, I might. "It's just not what I expected." The more I read, the more my heart swelled and the less I doubted my insane decision to chase her to Texas.

"The suspense is killing me." Arlo took a corner fast, and the fastback fishtailed with an overwhelming roar before straightening out on the highway toward the city. "If I get a ticket, you're paying for it," he grumbled, picking up his speed.

He'd never make me pay for the ticket, but the threat was adorable.

"I arrived at Harbor with the intent of interviewing each player on their specific position within the Hornet's Baseball team and how that led to their first championship in three seasons. A team that was previously record-breaking, in a slump, and in desperate need of a win. My expectations were set the moment I landed in Rhode Island. I was ushered to the main offices to speak with managers and owners. Suit after suit, I was given a rehearsed set of sound bites that some poor intern must have spent hours grueling over in her tiny office. While the quotes are exceptional and will be used in uplifting personality pieces that will air on the local news, they felt empty and disconnected from the sport and from the players."

"Fuck, she tore them apart," Arlo huffed and took a glance at me.

Smiling like an idiot

CODY

Clementine didn't stop there, the berating of the higher-ups, the ones that funded everything that went in and out of Harbor didn't cease. If this piece ever found its way to the public, *which it should,* all the men mentioned would have her job, but she wrote it like she didn't give a shit. I couldn't help but love her even more for it.

"Unfortunately my expectations were cemented by a group of old men in suits that had never stepped foot in the Harbor Stadium." I read as my heart swelled with pride. "These interactions set a precedent. Within my first twenty-four hours of being on Hornet soil, I had been mistreated, verbally abused, thrown out, and taunted. All by a group of suits who never stepped foot on the diamond. Meanwhile, the well-oiled machine that the owners painted a picture of was nowhere to be found. In its place, was a dysfunctional, loud, and chaotic group of young men enjoying the freedom of their off-season."

"Your girl has an attitude," Arlo snapped as his brows furrowed. "This better get good, or I'm turning this car around." He smiled as he lay on the empty threat.

"It took less than a day, fully immersed in the Hornet's Nest, to realize what all of the suits were missing. Living under the roof of Dansby House, affectionately known as the Nest. The elegant group home is a Victorian-era mansion perched upon the hill that overlooks the stadium. They yell, they curse, and fight one another. They cook meals together, go to class, and train together. The team wasn't well-oiled or well-behaved. The Hornets are simply a family."

"We aren't dysfunctional..." Arlo grumbled.

"Yes, we are." I shook my head and flipped the page. "Just shut up and let me finish."

"I was serious about turning this car around. I don't need anyone who doesn't believe in *us* or in Harbor."

"Did you say us?" I set the papers down in my lap and shove his shoulder. "Arlo!"

"I rejected the offer from Dallas." He steadied the car and looked over at me with a smirk on his face. "You're looking at Harbor's new assistant pitching coach."

"Seriously?" My heart raced in my chest, my family had been torn apart, but slowly the pieces had started to drift back together and fall into place.

"Yeah, Kitten. There was something off about Dallas that I couldn't put my finger on, but I had sixteen missed calls over Thanksgiving wondering why I wasn't at camp with the rest of the team. They just don't value each other, and I just..."

"...Needed your little dysfunctional family." I finished for him, and he tapped two fingers to his chest in time with me.

"Finish reading." Arlo nudged me. "At this rate, I'll have us at the airport before you get to the point of this article."

"Originally this was meant to be an inspirational fluff piece, however, the further I dug into the past relationships of the Hornets, the clearer it became that it wasn't baseball that brought them together. On the surface, the spectators and fans of the team see a team full of bright smiles and incredible, timeless skills, no thanks to their gloomy but charismatic head coach, Ryan Cody, but very few or any were aware of who made them a family."

A knot formed in my chest.

"There's a path that leads past the concrete and turf, tucked beneath the sounds of screaming fans and confetti cannons that winds up the hill back to the Nest. That's where you'll find the heart of the Hornets."

Arlo hummed, and I could tell that he knew what she meant before I even read the rest. The entire article was a eulogy to Mama. A proper one, like she was never given.

"Keep going, Cody," he encouraged me.

"Lorainne Cody had the Nest thrust upon her, but she didn't shy away from the challenge of being a surrogate mother to nearly twenty-eight men. She took a group of childish misfits and gave them a routine. She helped them pass classes, eat well, and form relationships with one another that you will never have within other teams' dynamics. The Hornets are a family because she taught a group of rowdy baseball players how to love each other sitting at the dinner table every Sunday evening stuffing their faces full of lasagna."

"Do you love me?" I turned to Arlo, fighting back the tears, and smiled.

"I love your Mom's lasagna," he deflected, but I knew he did. "Shut up and read."

"She spent her days preparing them for the hardest challenge they could ever face as a family, one all the players knew was inevitable. In turn, she created an unstoppable force. A wall so tall and strong that it seemed impossible for anyone to break through their defenses. But Lorainne Cody was sick. She had been since the day she stepped into the nest. All she could do was prepare them. Even ready for the end, guarded from the grief, the day the Nest's heart stopped beating, there was a misstep."

It felt like the grief from everything had caught in my throat.

"The Hornets stumbled, losing their way in the dark but the heart was still there; they just needed to take a closer look. Bundled beneath the core four, Arlo King, Dean Tucker, Van Mitchell, and the chief medical officer, Silas Shore, was Cael Cody. An unlikely and misrepresented hero in the story. The Hornet's star shortstop, lost in the dark, seemingly forever, needed help getting home. Cael had slipped through the cracks in the foundation that had been rattled the day his mother died. So there he hid, his heart beating loud enough to replace the echoed sounds of his mother's, so that the team could continue to survive. But a heart can only live beneath the floor for so long before it withers away."

Arlo looked over at me with dark eyes and a tight jaw, but I could see the softness in his gaze, the concern of an older brother who had been there for every single moment she was describing. Maybe guilty, but he shouldn't be.

"*Stop*, don't look at me like that. It's not your fault either," I said, before I continued to read.

"We needed the reminder," Arlo said, instead of leaving it alone, and I nodded in agreement.

"All anyone wants to talk about is the accident that predated the Harbor Hornet's winning the Supers. The accident nearly ended the careers and lives of Cael Cody and his captain, Arlo King. What happened in that car is none of our business, frankly, but it has *everything* to do with the reason they won. It was a catalyst for a team teetering on the edge of a three-year losing drought begging for a reason to fight harder."

I inhaled tightly, taking a second to compose myself as Arlo sped down the off-ramp toward the airport. He laughed under his breath as his hands rolled over the wheel.

"The Hornets had fallen apart without Lorainne but suddenly had a reason to band together, to put all the knowledge and compassion they had learned from their surrogate to save their shortstop. With the heart beating loudly in their ears once again, the Hornets found their courage, their drive, and their will to win."

Arlo sucked in a harsh breath through his teeth.

"I was sent here to interview their players on the win, on their skills and tactics, and I could have written this article with a slurry of facts and numbers that would bore you and force you to skim to the bottom. But the facts are tired, and the numbers that exist don't matter. I expected to spend my time here in the stadium, in an office, dragging information out of players who didn't have time for me. Instead, I was welcomed into the family. We spent more time outside of the stadium than we did inside. With family dinners, birthday parties, and cabin retreats, I was spoiled by the Hornets in the form of quality time. And when we did find the chance to visit the stadium, it was lively and light. There's not an unfriendly voice to be heard within the concrete walls. My time with the Hornets reminded me what baseball was meant to be, how it felt to be alive."

"For a second there, I thought I was going to have a serious conversation with you about that girl..." Arlo's voice trailed off beneath the sound of my own.

"What I was looking for in Harbor was a scandal. What I found in Harbor was my love of the game and *my* heart. In the words of their former Captain, Arlo King, *"we all separate the game from the emotion, when in reality, the emo-*

tions drive the game." The Hornets have cracked a formula that so many other teams overlook in the form of family dinners and formed sibling connections. A formula I'm affectionately dubbing the *Lorraine Method*."

"That's clever," Arlo said as he pulled into the airport parking lot. It took him seconds to find a spot, but when the car engine died and I didn't move, he looked at me. "What are you waiting for?"

"What if..." I stopped when Arlo grabbed the papers from me.

"What I found in Harbor was *my* heart," Arlo said in a tight tone before he turned to stare at me. "You're an idiot, and if you don't get out of my car right now, that next punch is going to creep up on you faster than you think."

"Alright, alright!" I put my hands in the air as he reached around me and popped the handle on the glove compartment.

"This is a ticket to Pittsburgh. It'll get you through security." He handed me a ticket. "Now, get out of my fucking car, Cael, and go get your girl."

I snatched it from him and nearly fell from the passenger seat onto the asphalt before picking up my feet. I ran through the parking lot, tripping more than once as I dodged bodies and emptied my pockets in line for security.

"Traveling light," the man behind the machine said with a smile as the other guard swiped me for metal and let me through. I didn't have time to respond as I scooped my belongings up and tossed my hat over my head while I ran toward the closest departures and arrivals board.

I stood there, scanning the board for her flight, and finally found it with a tiny, strangled whimper.

"Are you looking for your gate?" An older lady with a pretty smile and a soft voice stood next to me and looked up at the flashing times. She was wearing an official airport vest and clearly was just trying to be polite when she asked. "Did you miss your flight?"

I stared at the red letters that blinked Dallas and tried not to fall apart.

Departed.

"I guess I did."

CODY

"*Happy Birthday Clem.*"

I look down at the stupid cupcake and brush the tears back off my face before setting it on the floor of my new bedroom. The walls were so plain, it smelled too clean, and the alarm clock mocked me as it flickered to midnight.

It was the first birthday we had ever spent apart and, as predicted, it felt like the world was coming apart at the seams.

MATTHEWS

NEW YEARS DAY 2018

"Happy eighteenth birthday, Cael."

I looked down at my watch as the clock turned to twelve-oh-one and sighed. The small candle flickered in the breeze as I stretched out my legs in the grass beside the creek. I looked up at the stars and made one last wish.

"Take care of him for me?" I whispered and cried, unable to bear the weight of my sadness.

MATTHEWS

I spent the entire flight staring at the letters, never pulling the elastic band off, but playing with the corners of the stack. I wasn't sure I wanted to know what was inside of them. If there was any hope of me moving on from Cael, for good this time, knowing what was inside wouldn't change anything.

"Hey, there's my sad baby." Bobbi stood against a wall just beyond the arrivals gate in a silky orange sundress, her hair loose around her face. Brown eyes watched my every move as I strolled toward. "I missed that heavenly face." She scrunched her cute little nose up against me and wrapped me up in a hug. "Are you hungry?" She asked me, and kicked my sneakers with her white cowboy boots.

"I'm starving," I whined and fell into her arms.

The ride to the restaurant wasn't long, but I had been uncomfortable since leaving Harbor, and I didn't expect the guilt to subside anytime soon.

"Earth to M." Bobbi waved a ring-laden hand in my face. "I have a surprise for you."

"I don't know if I can handle any surprises today, Bobbi." I squeezed her hand as she led me toward the restaurant. But my opinions changed when I slid into the booth across from my Momma. "I warned you I couldn't handle it..." I switched sides and tucked into her arms. I let her smell engulf me for a long hug, not wanting or not being able to be the one that pulled away first.

"You drove all the way up here for me?" I asked when I could finally stop crying.

"Bobbi said you'd need me, Lovebug." she kissed my temple and stared across the table at my best friend.

"Well, Bobbi is never wrong." I admitted defeat quickly and painlessly, reaching out to take her hand in my own. "I definitely needed you." Tears stung at my eyes.

"Tell us everything," Momma said. We ordered martinis and fell into our natural rhythm of conversation. I explained everything that happened in detail, skimming over the ridiculous number of times we nearly got buried in each other.

"And then Julien showed up for Thanksgiving," I groaned and leaned against the booth.

"Ryan has never known when to keep his nose out of something; he's still just a loudmouth, meddling teenager," Momma cursed him.

Bobbi giggled. "Did Cael lose his mind?"

"I wish... he would have given me a reason to hate him," I said.

"Why are you looking for reasons?" Bobbi scoffed. "There is no timeline of our friendship that exists where you didn't love Cael. Even under all that bitterness, you still could never find it in you to hate him."

"What do I even pay my therapist for?" I rolled my eyes.

"So, you just left?" Momma asked. "It sounds like to me you had made up your mind long before Thanksgiving."

"I had, but it didn't mean what I wanted was what Cael needed. The decision to stay felt selfish with everything he's going through. Ryan confirmed as much," I said and yipped when Momma pinched my underarm. "That hurt."

"Good, will you stop listening to that man? He hasn't been right in the head since the day Rainey got sick, and he's not the authority on your heart or Cael's," Momma scolded me with a huff of air. "I raised you better than that."

"Don't piss off Momma Matthews." Bobbi put both her hands in the air, and I was met with a wink.

"Do you have any Advil?" Momma asked, and I pointed to my purse without taking my focus off Bobbi.

"Ryan's sheer stupidity aside, what do you want?" She asked, but before I could answer, I was smacked on the shoulder.

"Stop it, I'm emotionally traumatized. I don't need you beating me up too." I laughed and shoved her away playfully, my eyes trailing down to what she had hit me with.

"What are these?" Momma asked, holding the stack of letters up.

"Forty of the three hundred and something letters Cael has sent me over the last seven years," I said without breathing.

"What?" Bobbi leaned across the table, snatched them out of her hands and pulled the elastic back without the careful hesitation I had.

"Wait," I yelped like she had snapped me with it and she looked up with concern across her face. "I haven't looked at them," I blurted out.

"That boy went full *romance novel* on you, and you haven't read the letters?" Bobbi scoffed, "Are you serious, right now?"

"I–" The words were silenced by the sound of ripping paper. "Whatever is in those will just break my heart more than it already is. They won't change anything."

"The hell, they won't. *I'm* still confused about the details and why you're sitting here and not in Rhode Island with knockoff Nick Carter." Bobbi pulled the first letter out and unfolded it, her eyes scanning the pages. She looked up at me and back down with a giggle. "Did you really?" She gasped under her breath. "Clementine Mary Matthews."

"Bobbi!" I tried to snatch the letter from her.

"I'm just kidding." She handed the letter over.

I smiled at his chicken scratch and ran my fingers over the messy ink.

Clem,

I can't decide if writing these first thing in the morning or after a tortuous day of school is better. English class is hell without you doing my homework, and I swear the teacher can't understand a damn thing I'm saying to her half the time. The accent isn't that thick, but everyone seems to tease me about it anyway. The gym teacher calls

me Cowboy... I don't even own a cowboy hat. Every time I
think I'm getting the hang of things I picture you lying in
the grass, bathing in the sun with your bottom lip between
your teeth as you concentrate on your homework. You
derail every thought I have. I miss you.
Cael.

"*You derail every thought I have,*" Bobbi swooned, pretending to faint and sinking against the table as she wrapped her fingers around the stem of her martini glass. "That boy was down bad."

"Open another, Lovebug," my Momma encouraged me with love in her eyes.

Dear Clem,
Six months of sliding these letters in the mail bin with
Susanna every morning and coming home to them gone.
I just hope you're getting them. Every time the phone
rings, I race Mama to it just hoping to hear you on the
other end. Dad says I need to start my life here, that
chasing your ghost around is affecting my school work.
He's wrong, he always is, but arguing doesn't help me or
him. He'll never understand how hard this is. He wasn't
the one ripped away from the one person who loved him.
No, he dragged her across the country to this hell hole.
Graduation is in a few weeks. I had some girls ask me to
prom, but there's only one girl I ever wanted to take, and
she won't even call me back. That was mean, I'm sorry.
I hope you still wear purple. It makes your eyes soft.
Cael.

"I don't think you've worn purple in years," Momma said softly.

"That's because he likes it when I do..." I rubbed the paper between my hands. Every ounce of my new personality was still attached to him, just in spite of him, and I hated the realization.

Clem,

I have something that feels like a secret: I met a boy today. His name is Dean, and he reminded me of you. His eyes might be blue, but I see you when he looks at me. It's hard to explain. He's funny and smells nice. He laughs with his whole body like you do and I don't know... when I'm around him, it's not so hard to be alive. I hope that maybe you found someone like that, even just a friend. I'm sorry I stopped calling. It got hard to hear the answering machine every time. I just wished you'd answer.
I love you.
Cael.

"*The* Dean?" Bobbi mouthed.

I nodded. I couldn't even believe he had even told me about that. But of course, he had. He was never one to keep secrets. My heart swelled knowing that the reason he'd grown so close to Dean was because he found the comforts of home with the first baseman.

"So Cael's bisexual?" Momma asked.

"Uh yeah," I confirmed, looking up from the table. "I met Dean. He's well-rounded and really sweet. It seemed like he got Cael through a lot the last couple of years."

"A heart made to love everyone," Momma smiled. "I always knew that boy was made of gold."

"This one smells pretty." Bobbi held up a purple piece of paper and a piece of dried lavender fell to the table. "Oh my God, it's the first one." She held it out of my reach before I could snatch it. God only knows what he put in it from that night.

"Dear Plum, You asked for letters, and I won't ever deny you." Bobbi's mouth fell open in shock. "Alright, if you don't go back for him, I will."

"He's not your type," I snapped at her and tried to take the letter again.

"I'll make an exception," Bobbi giggled and continued reading in a voice that was meant to mock his. "Here's number one. *We left early this morning before the sun came up, and all I could think about was your skin and how it felt to trace every inch of it beneath my fingertips. Maybe I'm still dreaming.*"

"Please stop." I covered my red cheeks with my hands.

"Woof. Rated N for naughty." Bobbi winked over the paper.

"Clementine Matthews." My name rolled from Momma's mouth in astonishment.

I just prayed it didn't get any worse because, knowing Bobbi, she'd read it regardless of its television rating.

"*Maybe I'll open my eyes, and you'll still be tucked against me, wrapped in my arms where we belong. I miss you already so much it feels like someone has carved a hole in my chest where my heart used to be. If you wake up and find it still in Texas with you, keep it safe. I'll mail this as soon as we reach Rhode Island. I love you, Clementine.*"

"God, he's even adorable in letters," Bobbi scoffed. "I can't get a girl to even flirt with me for more than five minutes, and he's been doing it in ink like some Elizabethan-era male escort for seven years! I need you to be so for real with me right now." She leaned over the table with a playful dip to her brows. "Why are you here?!"

"Because I'm an idiot," I groaned and rested my forehead against the table.

We continued to open the letters as the pizza came, and tears flowed. Some of them were heartbreaking, and I ached to rewind time so I could be there for him.

Mama died yesterday. We were in the middle of rereading The Outsiders.

And dated a week later.

I wish you were here. But I'm really glad you aren't.

The short letters were the worst of them. I could feel his agony through the pages, some of them stained and crumpled from previously being wet. I couldn't imagine being alone like that.

"Poor Honeybug." My Mom read one of the longer ones when I couldn't get past the first sentence. "*Mama collapsed yesterday. Dean and I found her. I don't know how long she had been there but she doesn't look good, and Dad isn't answering his phone. I thought about calling your Momma, but I don't even know what I should say.*"

Opening them out of order was torture. The next one was worse.

Clem, I don't know if I can do this. Mama keeps denying food and won't let me help her anymore. I'm so fucking angry all the time. She just keeps asking for Dad, and he won't leave his office. I don't know what to do. The doctor said she'll be gone by the weekend...

"I didn't realize he was all alone when Mrs. Cody died." I folded up the short letter announcing her death and leaned against her shoulder.

"It's funny how a little perspective can change everything," Momma cooed and ran her hand over my hair.

"How do I rewrite seven years of unanswered questions?" I asked them with tears in my eyes and both of them stared back at me without a solution.

CODY

C hristmas came and went, and with it went the stinging feeling in my chest and the regret that chewed away at the back of my mind. The locker room hummed with anticipation and enthusiasm as they prepared for the game, but my thoughts were lost somewhere in the mad rush, and they had taken my raw joy for the game with them.

It wasn't even a real game, there were no stakes here, and yet...

I was terrified to let them all down, head barely above the water, I'm treading water in the deep end while everyone waited and watched with life preservers for my head to slip beneath the surface.

"Brave face you got there, handsome." Ella sat on the bench beside me as I tied my shoes.

With a tiny nod to my head, I pressed my lips into a tight line and looked up at her.

"Are you sure you want to do this today?" She asked me.

"And disappoint everyone out there?" I dropped my head and finished tying my shoes but my gaze lingered on the floor. My thoughts were far away from where I was. "We've been preparing for this for months. If I don't go out there today..."

"No one would blame you," Ella finished the thought a little differently than I would have. "Misery." She reached out and pushed my chin up to look at her. "Make the call, I'll take the blame. It's as easy as me saying you aren't ready. But don't force yourself, it's not worth it."

340

Her fingers never left my chin as she held my eyes. It didn't feel as simple as just *deciding*. It had been nearly five weeks since I spoke to Clementine. I'd stood in the airport for so long staring at that departures board that Arlo bought a second ticket just to come to find me.

I had been arguing with myself over buying a ticket to Texas or just letting her go.

It ended with me silent in the passenger seat.

The article was posted two weeks later, exactly how she had written it, and everyone at Harbor had a field day. Dad had framed the front page and hung it up in his office next to the photo of us and Mama. The only other memory he had ever hung. Silas' father went nuclear, storming the halls of Harbor like it might solve a problem or fix the damage the article had caused. I wasn't sure why it was a big deal, it wasn't as if it slandered them in a way that the sports community hadn't seen before. It was common knowledge that the owners and committee members didn't care about anything but money.

Silas explained that it had nothing to do with the article. Apparently, a dinner had been held with his Grandfather that involved a two-hour berating about the meaning of baseball and how Silas's father had destroyed what Hornet's Baseball was intended to be. There was internal grief in the family and, given Silas's recent mood, it was about more than just business.

The television piece that aired was clearly pieced together by an outside source. It was professional and almost cold. Watching all the guys give sound bites from the couch at the Nest. No footage of me to be seen, we had never finished our interview. The lack of emotion in the TV interviews made my mind wander to Clementine; whether or not she had kept her job or was still with Julien . I had almost gotten on a plane for the second time in a month just to know, but I couldn't clear my head long enough to make a choice.

Decisions had never been my strong suit. Everything good in my life up to that point had always been chosen for me. All of the bad things that shaped me had been my own. But when I asked Arlo what I should do he told me that he couldn't make the choice for me.

So I stayed. I didn't call, I didn't bug her. Out of habit, I wrote five more letters. They never saw the mailbox; instead, I tucked them into the drawer in my room and pretended that I wasn't completely devastated without her.

But I could do this.

My focus shifted to helping Silas and much to my dismay, organizing the exhibition event had actually been interesting. I had learned a lot about what it took to throw such an extravagant game. It was more than just showing up in a fancy suit and flirting with old ladies to stuff the pockets of the owners. It was booking hotels, deciding on themes, creating schedules, and calling vendors.

Today was important.

It was a game that packed the seats no matter how bad the previous season had gone, a game that set the tone for spring training camp and the season ahead. Weaponizing spectators' needs for drama and giving back to the community. Every year all the ticket sales from the rival exhibition game went to a different foundation.

My only job was to step foot on the field; we had worked too hard for me to chicken out now.

It was also the first time I had played in a professional setting since the accident. Ella was nervous, but my shoulder had passed every test she put it through. I was physically ready. There was no pain, not even after a full team practice. Sure, I was sore, but it was the normal kind of sore—the good kind that made me feel accomplished when I finally rolled into bed at night.

Ella was waiting for an answer, so I tapped two fingers to her wrist, letting them hang lightly against her skin. "I can do it," I said.

"Say the word out there, and I'll pull you." She winked.

She dropped her hands and helped me off the bench, wrapping me up in a quick hug before fixing my jersey and checking the buttons.

"These are nice." She admired the new, rich navy, special edition jerseys, which had a championship patch on the shoulder. Ella straightened out the tiny lavender flower pin over my heart and smiled softly. "I wish I could have met her," she cooed, stepping back so I could tuck the hem of my jersey into my pants.

"Mama would have adored you, Peachy." I smiled. "It would have made her so happy to see Arlo go toe to toe with someone, but even more to find someone who loves him. She was always so worried he'd end up like Arthur."

"Luckily she left you to look after him until I showed up." Ella laughed, scooping up her medical bag from the bench and leading the way out of the locker room.

The hallway was packed with bodies, players, reporters, and parents. Dad stood at the head of it all locked in a conversation with Silas. He looked good. He had cut down the sides of his long hair and finally trimmed his beard. *Who knew a shower would do him some good?* He shifted in his dark Hornets' polo and flipped a hat up and over his head as Silas patted him on the back and took off down the hallway.

I slipped in front of Ella, feeling her fingers tangle into the jersey at my lower back as I pushed through the crowd and brought her to Arlo.

"He's got the green light," Ella hummed and tucked into Arlo's side. His dark hair was brushed off his face and he looked really happy for once as his arm wrapped around her, clinging to his clipboard with the other. His eyes narrowed on me.

"Does he *want* the green light?" Arlo cocked his head at me.

"Yeah," I hiccuped.

"Convincing."

"I'm ready."

The words came out, and I knew I could do it, but I don't think either of us was ready for the feelings that lingered below the surface. Tonight's game was the first that I would play without Arlo, *ever*. Since joining the team, Arlo had been to my left, always guarding and protecting the pitcher's mound. Protecting my stupid oversized heart too. Everything felt so exposed. Tonight we will introduce the new captain.

"I might actually puke this time." The words came out of me in a blunt projectile confession. "Can the light be yellow?" I suddenly felt itchy in the uniform and wiggled around.

"No, all or nothing." Arlo shook his head and put one hand on my shoulder, the clipboard digging into my skin as the other hand moved over my racing heart. "Two steps at a time."

"Except you aren't out there with me anymore. So that's irrelevant, and I'm walking alone." I stared at him.

"I'm out there, just not where you're used to having me. You'll just have to put in a little work, Kitten." He laughed and little lines formed around his eyes. "When you need me, you'll find me. I'm not going anywhere."

The next breath I took was long and shaky but I tapped the back of his hand over my heart with two fingers. *I'm ready.*

"Alright boys you know how this goes, every year you go out there, and you get your asses handed to you by the Lorrettes," Dad started loudly over my shoulder and I turned to scowl at him, *inspiring.* "This year you're regional champions. If you lose, you'll only be embarrassing yourself."

Arlo covered his mouth to stifle the laugh that left him.

But Dad smiled, a surprising chuckle echoing over the silence in the packed hallway. He was fumbling through the entire *happy* situation, but at least he was trying. We were a team just trying to heal from the last few years, but it felt like we were all ready to try. Everyone listened to Dad speak with bright eyes and concentrated faces.

"Remember that today is supposed to be fun, so have it. Get the crowd fired up, make good plays, and don't stress, there will be plenty of time for that at spring camp. Win or lose, dinner tonight at the Nest." He clapped and the rest of us followed suit as his eyes landed on me with a tight nod.

The huddle formed and, for the first time in months, my heart rate slowed to a normal pace as the guys started their chant. Wrapped in each other shoulder to shoulder, the huddle rocked side to side like a wave on the ocean. Electricity charged through all of us as we broke free and jogged to the entrance of the stadium. The sound of fans and music boomed into the air, echoing off the steel roof and vibrating down through the concrete.

"Cody." Silas wandered forward. I had half expected him to be in a suit and tie, but he was in his normal uniform. He patted me on the back, his fingers digging into my shoulder just to see if I would react. "You're with me," he said.

"Ella said I could play." I tensed and looked around for her to support my claims, but I had lost her in the crowd. "*I can play*. My shoulder is fine!"

Panic, raw and overwhelming, flooded my body.

"And you're going to." He shook his head at me as the announcer started to call player names. "I need you for something else," Silas said.

CODY

Together we waited as all the other players and staff flooded onto the field after the Lorettes were announced, even after the national anthem was played. I rocked back and forth on my heels as we waited in uncomfortable silence.

"Please put your hands together for Silas Shore and everyone's favorite shortstop, number nineteen–Cael Cody."

Silas led the charge as we jogged onto the field. The lights were bright and surged in hot waves against my skin as we made our way to the center. The roof to the stadium had been left cracked open to let in the crisp winter air and cool the crowd naturally, the sky pitch black above us.

The Hornets and Lorrettes hadn't broken their lines, still positioned on either side of the mound, most fidgeting with their hats or with their hands tucked behind their back staring up at the rowdy crowd. Noticeably missing from Lorettes' lineup was Joshua Logan. I scowled and wondered where he might have been to miss today's event. He loved the rival game more than anyone.

"Good evening," Silas spoke into the mic, gripping his papers in his left hand as he waved them around in the air. "Welcome to the seventh annual Rivals Exhibition game!"

The crowd cheered for him in excitement.

"We're excited, too," he confirmed. "Now, I know usually it's my father out here addressing you all, amping you up for the new season, and thanking you for being loyal Harbor fans, but he's busy so you get me."

I stiffened beside him but held my stupid grin and nodded as he fumbled through his speech without lines or direction. The panic seeped from his usually cool demeanor and gave me secondhand-heartburn.

"Like every season before, the profits from today's game go to a worthy charity or foundation that gives back to the Harbor community." Silas side-stepped, moving out of my space and held out the microphone to me. "Cael Cody, everyone." He led a thunderous chorus of cheers. "We missed him too." Silas smiled and looked up to the bright lights. "During the off-season between careful recovery and surgery, Cael's been working tirelessly with me to put this entire event together, it's only fair I let him tell you what foundation we're supporting this year."

A nervous laugh tumbled from my lips, and I cocked my head to the side in confusion.

"If there was ever a time for you to be well...*you*, it's now." He held the microphone out for me to take. "Don't get shy on me, Cody. Give them a show," he whispered, just for us, and I swallowed the nerves as my fingers wrapped around the microphone.

Silas tapped my shoulder and handed me a small piece of paper with a paragraph of script on it. My brows pinched together and the smile came back to me as I read what he wrote.

"Are you sure?" I asked him in shock.

He scowled at me and motioned for me to get on with it.

"Alright, alright." I shook out the crippling fear, found my footing, and stepped forward.

I filled my chest with air, my lungs stinging and my heart racing.

"Who thought it was a good idea to give me a mic?" I yelled with laughter in every word as the crowd cheered. "It's insane here tonight! Who's ready to see us kick the Lorette's asses?" I hollered and the stadium thrummed with anticipation. The small groups of students that had traveled down from Lorette chimed in with a few, dull boos. "I know I am!" I chuckled and took the time to inhale deeply before bringing the mic back to my lips.

"This little piece of paper that Doctor Shore just handed to me contains the announcement for the foundation. A cause close to my heart and something that will mean the world to the entire Nest." I turned to look at them all with a tight nod, gratitude surging through me as they all raised their hands in unison, tapping their chests and encouraging me.

Always together, *two steps at a time.*

I tripped over my words, choking up on the microphone with a hint of panic I had never experienced before. For all my flaws, public speaking was not something I was afraid of...but suddenly... I couldn't find my voice.

I turned to find Dad, maybe in a pitiful attempt for comfort but he wasn't there. The spot he had been previously filling was glaring back at me.

And then all the lights in the stadium turned off except for the hazy yellow that shone at my back, highlighting the field in a circle around me.

"*Up*, Cael!" Dad's voice echoed from the dugout. "Look up."

I listened, looking up through the cracked open stadium ceiling, my breathing strangled with panic as my eyes adjusted to the darkness and the stars shone back at me, dancing around the moon in the sky.

An apology in the best way Dad knew how to give one. Bringing us all together again. Sun, moon and stars.

Hey, Mama.

I inhaled one shaky breath, filling my lungs as I looked back down to the paper and finished the speech.

"Through the generosity of the Silas Shore and all of you tonight, we were able to create the Rainey Day Scholarship. A fund that will help students on the path to recovery looking to further their education and start fresh here at Harbor University. A scholarship named after my Mama–*our Mama*, that would last long after we were all gone from the walls of Harbor."

I paused to catch my breath and to keep from crying as Ella's bright smile caught my eye. A foundation for kids like us, struggling but trying. She nodded, silently encouraging me to continue.

"Funding that would honor her name and support students like me. Kids who needed a little more help to find themselves and give them the resources to get an education that would help keep them healthy." My heart swelled and tears stung at my eyes. I angled away from the crowd, and I pulled the microphone away from my face to let go of the shaky sigh as the cheering grew louder. "If I keep going you're all going to watch me cry and that's– I'll hand it back over to

Silas's now, but hey..." I shook out the sadness and plastered a smile on. "Let's kick some Lorette ass?" The horns blew loud and the crowd lost their minds as I turned back to Silas.

"Good job kid." He pressed his shoulder into mine, praising over the air horns and screaming.

"This is...Thank you." I nodded at him.

"Unnecessary." His tone was stern. "It's about time we start doing some good around here. It's what she would have wanted." Silas swallowed roughly. I hadn't missed the fact that it wasn't the Shore family behind the foundation. Only Silas's name was in the announcement. He rolled back his shoulders and forced a smile to his face as he took the microphone back from me.

"Now for the bad news." Silas straightened out but gave me a proud smile, and my Dad approached from behind us to stand on the other side.

His green eyes narrowed under the lights, and for a second, I could have sworn they were glossy as he excused me back to the line-up. "One more time for Cael Cody," his rough and strangled voice said over the mic.

I fell back in line between Dean and Van. Mitchell nudged my shoulder with a smile and Dean's hand found my wrist with a tiny squeeze I hadn't expected from him. I watched as my Dad discussed the game, nearly boring the crowd into a coma.

"As you all know, Arlo King is moving on from starting pitcher and captain of the Hornets, we're fortunate enough to announce that he's staying in Harbor and will work with Nicholas King as our new assistant pitching coach."

Everyone cheered as Arlo stepped forward with his award-winning fake smile and waved.

"He was an incredible captain and we're sad to lose him at the helm of the Hornets team. After much discussion, and a few sleepless nights we have decided to name Dean Tucker as the new captain of the Harbor Hornet's baseball team."

Dean tensed beside me, all the slack excitement was quickly replaced with panic as Dad turned to him with his arm out. "Dean has consistently shown that he has what it takes to lead the Hornets into our next chapter and all of the players will agree that there is no one else we'd trust."

"This is the part where you step out and wave." I leaned over and pushed on his lower back with my hand. "Big smiles," I encouraged as he forced a bright, nervous smile. "You can do better than that," I whispered with a laugh and pinched his ass.

"Aye!" He swatted me away and turned the motion into a wave as he plastered on a confident smile for everyone.

It was clear to the team that Dean hadn't been warned before the announcement, but everyone huddled around him as he stepped back from the mound. They shoved him roughly around, laughing and smiling as they embraced their new captain. Congratulations filled the air and across the huddle, he caught my eye.

"I'm proud of you," I mouthed and he rolled his eyes.

Dean winked, and relief washed through me.

For all our trouble, we would figure it out.

We had to.

Dean took the coin toss with shaky hands and tense shoulders, but he won and we were set to bat first with a few tiny yips of eagerness. We flooded into the dugout, shoulder to shoulder, shoving each other around as we worked ourselves up for the game. God, I missed that adrenaline rush, the feeling that rushed through my bloodstream and got my heart pumping faster. I was home surrounded by the sounds of cheering and air horns, the smells of popcorn and sand.

For the first time in seven years.

I didn't want to be anywhere else.

There was no distance to count, no pain to measure. The grief subsided and the clouds opened up and the stars shone down on me. Even as the lights went back up I could feel her there in the stadium. Dad stood on the stairs, watching us with a smile on his face. Giving everyone a few moments longer to revel in the excitement and joy before he clapped his hands together and brought the focus back to the game.

I grabbed a bat and made my way back onto the field to stretch, looking out over the stadium as I swung my arm in a loose circle and let the weight of the bat gently pull the muscles. I could feel Ella watching my every move with her concerned brown eyes. She had given me the go-ahead, but I could tell she was still extremely nervous about today.

Weeks in the batting cages with her, proving her suspicions wrong, led to this moment. It was my first game back since the accident, and everything was on the line for my future, whatever that may be.

"You know," Ella leaned over the padded fence that separated the dugout from the field and squinted at me, "you did an amazing job putting this together."

"Silas did. I was just there to make sure Grandpa didn't die sitting at his computer." I ignored her soft smile and deflected her praise.

"Hey, grumpy!" A ball hit me in the shoulder, and I turned to see her with a scowl on her face. "I'm sick of this pity party. *It's boring,*" she mocked, her brows knitted together, and her jaw tensed. "You did this, so be proud of yourself."

The sight of her being mad made me laugh. I scooped the ball up from the sand and rolled it between my fingers until my skin felt gritty. I was trying, I really was. It was hard to navigate a twice-over heartbreak, but that time, being older and understanding the reasons why it was better this way...

Rolling out my neck, I stopped on her gaze and asked her, "Did you know about Dean?"

"Silas and I were asked a few things but that was before the decision was made," she said, "He earned it, and he's going to be a perfect fit for what comes next."

"I couldn't agree more, Peachy." I smiled at her. "I'm sorry I've been a downer recently," I apologized. "It did turn out pretty good." I looked up and over the stadium as the Ump called us to start.

"Something to remember for next semester." She winked at me. "I need to go grab some things, just breathe," she reminded me and slipped back into the dugout, leaving me to stew over her suggestion.

I finished my stretches, my mind skipping around in terrified circles. I had never been scared to play ball, but I was horrified to step back up to the box and swing the bat.

I sucked in a shaky breath, hopped the banister into my dugout, and beelined for the hulking frame of Tucker. "Dean." I grabbed his collar and threw my arm over his shoulder. "They need a *'this game doesn't matter'* pep talk."

I need it. I tossed him a pleading look.

"It does matter." Dean shook his head.

"No, it doesn't," I argued and forced a smile for him. "This game is for show. For everyone to have fun and make the crowd feel included. It's as stressful as the finals out here, Van has already devoured two canisters of chew, and Todd looks like he might die of heat stroke."

We looked back at the guy sweating bullets in the conditioned, temperature-controlled stadium. A genuine laugh exploded from me. "There's no reason for him to be that sweaty!"

"Alright," he groaned and turned to them, stepping up onto the step and getting their attention. "Guys." He put his hands up, and the request came out so soft half of them didn't even hear him at first until he repeated himself a little louder. "Stop worrying about the score, stop stressing about the outcome, the new reports, or the headlines. Clear your heads and remember why we do this."

He tapped two fingers to his chest, and the team followed.

"Play this game like we're at the cabin. It's just us out there on the field having fun. Don't do it for any other reason than the love of the game," Dean said.

Todd hollered first, cheering on Dean with a goofy grin as the rest of the team joined in and got themselves riled up for the second half of the innings.

"Not bad." Arlo patted Dean on the shoulder. "You're a natural."

Dean's face twisted into something between raw shock and overwhelming gratitude. "Did you hear that?" He shook his head, and a bright smile formed that made my chest warm. "Arlo complimented me."

"That's my boy." I clapped a hand on his cheek and absorbed his childish enthusiasm and wide smile into my bloodstream.

"Cael, you're up!" Dad barked, and I pushed away from the banister, gently pounding my fist against Dean's chest in passing. "There's an empty pocket in right field," Dad explained with his face turned toward me. *"Fill it."*

I went to step out, and he grabbed the collar of my jersey. "Take a breath, kid," he instructed. His voice shifted from scary Coach to my Dad. Hushed and careful, he looked at me with pride as a smile curled on his lips. "Feel everything."

He pushed me out onto the field. Adrenaline filled every aching, scared muscle in my body as I closed my eyes and took in the smells and sounds of the stadium. I walked across the line, the sand crunching with each shaky step closer to the box. I filled my chest with sweaty, clay-scented air and opened my eyes.

I could do it. The stadium thrummed in approval.

The Lorrettes relief pitcher, Yuri Fortuna, rolled the ball between his fingers and stared at me with his horrifyingly dark brown eyes. He was good, but he was no Joshua Logan. Yuri had ticks. Like the way his back leg shook when he was going to throw a slider. Or how he'd run his hand through his thick red hair before a curveball.

I adjusted my grip on the back, tilting my head in and waiting for the ball as I ran through my list. My shoulder didn't hurt, I hadn't touched drugs in months, and the itch to drink had faded out and never returned. I had been given more time with Clementine and finally repaired my relationship with my Dad.

I could hit this ball.

I know I could.

Feedback screeched over the PA system and caused the entire stadium to fall quiet.

"What the hell?" Yuri threw his hands in the air. "What kind of bullshit is your team pulling to win, Cody?" He asked in a threatening tone.

"This isn't us, you shit-for-brains." I rolled my eyes and stared at him like he was an idiot before searching around for the source of the interruption.

"Cael Cody." My name was hummed over the speakers in a shaky, sweet voice I never thought I would hear again. "We never finished our interview."

MATTHEWS

My hand shook around the microphone, but Bobbi and Ella both gave me an enthusiastic thumbs up. "You got this!" Bobbi mouthed with a big smile and love in her eyes.

God, did I want to believe that. Momma gave me a nod of encouragement.

The phone call that had gotten me to Rhode Island had come a week before Christmas.

"It's for you," Bobbi said, handing me the phone. She shoved her hands beneath the covers of my bed against my face.

"Make them go away," I whined and settled down into my sheets, wrapping my arms around myself and tucking my face against Cael's bunched-up shirt. It had been two weeks since I had left Harbor, one since I had gotten in a massive fight with Julien and kicked him out for good, and three days spent wallowing in my bedroom with takeout and bad television. Christmas was a week away and all I wanted to do was melt out of existence so the guilt and heartbreak would cease.

"Not this time, it's important." Bobbi ripped back the blankets, fighting against my grip but eventually winning out. "I swear," she growled and stared at me. Her lips pressed into a tight unimpressed line. "Stop acting like you're dying and answer this call."

I grumbled and snatched the phone from her as I struggled to sit up in bed and pressed the receiver to my ear. "Hello?" I snapped.

"Clementine?" Ella's voice was sweet as honey even over the phone.

Panic flooded me.

"Is he alright?" I asked, putting the phone on speaker, suddenly much more awake and aware.

"No," she said and then followed it up quickly with a "yeah, but no."

"Alright?" I said, confused about the reasoning for the phone call if everything was fine.

"Cael is…" I hadn't heard her stumble before. She was too quick-witted and eloquent for her to stutter her thoughts. "He's sad."

"He's a big boy, Ella," I said, tucking a strand of dirty hair away from my face and ignoring the twinge of pain that flickered through me at the thought of him being sad enough for Ella to reach out to me. And then like a tidal wave, his voice washed over me. 'I made you sad.' And I hated myself for doing that to him.

"I called because I need to know something. He won't talk about it, but I need to hear you say it so I can help him," she said.

"What?" My fingers found my wrist, rolling the threaded bracelet between them to keep my mind from spiraling to dark places.

Bobbi sank into the bed across from me listening and watching intently.

"Do you love him?" Ella asked.

Yes.

The silence stretched on. Bobbi groaned and leaned over pressing mute on the call.

"Don't you dare lie to her," she growled at me and unmuted it with a serious look on her face. She narrowed her eyes and pointed a finger at me.

"Clementine, are you still there?" Ella said softly.

"Yeah, I'm here," I responded, but I still wondered if I could tell her the truth.

I continued to stare at the phone, flipping the bracelet around on my wrist, trying to make a decision. I could smell him on my skin and in my hair, feel his fingertips on my body, and hear his voice in the back of my mind, but… was that enough?

"She does," Bobbi blurted. "She's sitting here like a deer in headlights, but I know she loves that bleach blond Ken doll more than anyone and anything she has ever loved in her entire life."

"Oh, sorry, I didn't realize you weren't alone." Ella quietly laughed.

"I'm Bobbi, her best friend and apparently the only honest person in the room," Bobbi snapped.

Ella laughed. "It's nice to meet you, Bobbi, I have one of you and, Clementine... if she's anything like Zoey. She's right."

Bobbi sat back triumphantly and held her arms out mocking me.

"I do," I finally said in a defeated voice, causing Bobbi to drop her arms and sigh gently, the confession lifting a weight off her shoulders. She gave me a sympathetic smile and brushed her hand over my cheek.

"Good, we have work to do," Ella said quickly in a hushed voice.

Ella had explained that something was wrong with Cael, like he was a shell of who he usually is. His recovery was still intact. He hadn't slipped when I left, which was a small mercy that had been consuming me. I had almost called a few times just to check in on him, but I knew the implications that would carry.

The work that followed wasn't as complicated as I expected.

Bobbi, my Momma, and I were booked on flights to Harbor for New Year's Day.

The day of the Rivals exhibition game.

I stood, my hands quivering in a pair of jeans and a t-shirt, my hair loose around my face just praying that I wasn't about to make a fool of myself as I started to walk down the stands toward the field.

"Keep going!" Bobbi grumbled under her breath and shooed me.

The dirty look I tossed over my shoulder had her backing up and raising her hands in surrender. I was doing okay until the cameras swung on me and my rosy cheeks and terrified expression showed up on the big screen. Stumbling on the step but quickly recovering. I was not that little Texan girl, seventeen and without confidence. Flightless and living in a shadow. Drawing in a long breath, I dug deep and pulled out that wild child, the confident woman who had found herself with wings.

Doing my best to ignore the crowd I spoke again.

"I'm assuming you know the rules of baseball, you know how outs work?" I asked into the mic, that time without the horrible squeal. Cael's eyes were on the screen and then his body was turning around on the batter's box as he searched for me. But he smiled, bright and goofy and nodded as he continued to search for me in the crowd.

I stopped in the two hundreds on a long concrete platform and stared down over the field. "I can do this," I whispered under my breath before bringing the mic up. "Moving seventeen hundred miles away was strike one," I said. "It may not have been your choice but every day after was."

Cael scowled, tossing the bat with his helmet against the cage before he rolled out his shoulders. He continued in a slow circle, time dragging painfully slowly until his eyes met mine, and he inhaled so deeply even from a distance I could see his chest rise and fall. My heart was racing so fast I thought it might explode from my chest as he looked at me.

"Strike two?" He called out to me. His voice carried over the stadium and ran a shiver down my spine.

"Strike two happened when you clipped your own wings," I said tightly just trying to control the shake in my voice. "Such a stupid, reckless thing to do! You were born to fly, Cael Cody!" The crowd cheered at that one, a lady standing from her seat next to me and screaming at the top of her lungs started a wave through the entire stadium.

I walked down another flight of stairs, resting against the navy banister that separated the lower bowl seats from the upper. Cael stared at me, the bright white lights glimmering across his shocked expression. With a single blink, he was there, that boy, big blue eyes shining bright as he came down off the porch with an infectious smile.

I couldn't help but smile back at him.

"You are the most insufferable, idiotic, feral, and stubborn..." I held up my wrist to show him the bracelet that I rebraided once again to include the all old threads. His eyes flickered from wrist to my eyes, "...person I know, and since the day you wrapped this stupid string around my wrist I knew I would never love anyone the way I love you. I'm sorry that you felt like you had to trade me spots in the box but you didn't. If you wanna fly, Cael, do it, I'll cheer you on and if you want to live in that stupid box forever, I'll live in that box with you."

Cael smiled with a little trembling nod, his eyes glassy as he ran his hands through his sweaty blond hair. He stepped forward and laced his fingers into the batting cage, the whole stadium lowering to a hush as I spoke.

"Is that strike three?" He asked, squinting up at me. "That I'm stubborn and stupid?" A laugh so wild and free bubbled from him that I felt that feeling through to my toes.

"No!" I shook my head. "Strike three is because you're still standing there like a fool, and I have waited seven years to be kissed again!"

The stadium erupted and my heart was pounding so fast I thought that it might explode from my chest when he didn't say anything or move from his spot on the field. No one had ever lived up to the feeling of that night, wrapped in Cael, knowing it was the first and last. I had spent seven years chasing that high only to be disappointed when I was left empty. Suddenly it was just us again, standing in my room, the sound was me blurting out that I wanted it to *be him*.

That little girl thrust back into reality so violently that it made my breath stutter and my hands shake harder. The longer he stood there, the louder the doubt grew in my head, echoing around in a haunting chorus of *he doesn't love you back*.

Cael's Cheshire grin faded at my words, his chest huffing out as he took one last look at me and took off running. With both hands on the railing, he hauled himself up into the stands and over the barrier. The crowd cheered and my heart raced so fast I forgot how to breathe.

He jogged up the final stairs taking two steps at a time with his long length, standing just below me completely out of breath, tilting his chin up to look up at me. "You gotta come down," he said with a small laugh.

"It's too far," I said nervously as I took in the small drop to the next platform. The barrier between us was too high and not meant to be crossed.

"It's not," he lowered his voice but his smile only grew, "I'll catch you, Clem."

I set the mic down and the crowd cheered louder as I climbed one foot at a time over the railing, sliding down so my legs hung over the edge, Cael reached out to me. I braced myself on his shoulders as his strong arms guided me down to my feet.

"It took you long enough." I scowled.

"I've been trying to kiss you since you got here." Cael shook his head and a strand of blond hair fell against his forehead.

"You've been trying to kiss *her*," I said. The old Clementine, the one that didn't exist anymore. He stared at me, blue eyes searching around for the meaning, and when he found it his lips curled into a brilliant smile.

The crowd's eyes turned upward around us as snow started to fall effortlessly in soft swirling patterns through the half open roof of the stadium. Everything was perfect. He was perfect.

"Cael if you don't—" I started to scowl but he moved so quickly I didn't have the time to.

He captured my lips in a tender, needy kiss, so warm and wanting that my hands tangled against his jersey and my toes curled in my shoes. Cael's hands cupped my face, fingers resting against my jaw and curling behind my ears as he tilted my chin to meet his. There was no one but us, the crowd faded away to nothing but an empty stadium. My fingers dug into the fabric and pulled Cael as close as I could get him.

Seven years of longing poured from him, deepening the kiss to impossible places as his grip grew tighter. I couldn't breathe, but I felt like I was flying. Clementine and Cael came crashing together again, new versions of ourselves. I could hear the thudding of our combined racing hearts as we melted together.

Cael grinned against my mouth, a smile so bright it spread warmth through my entire body as he pulled away, carding his hand through my hair and tucking my face against his chest. The overwhelming thunder of applause rushed back into my ears and the stadium came to life.

"I'm going to kill Ella." He laughed into my hair as I tilted my head up to the big screen at the far end of the field only to see our faces framed in a kiss cam heart. Embarrassment rushed to my cheeks, but his fingers found my wrist, brushing against the bracelet mindlessly as I hid my face and tried to catch my breath.

MATTHEWS

O nce the game was over, the Hornets taking it by one single run scored by Dean in the last inning, Cael dragged me by the hand down the packed corridors. Bobbi and Momma huddled near where Ryan Cody hovered, protecting them from the rush of players and parents pushing around in the small hall.

"Honeybug." Momma reached out to Cael, pressing her palm to his cheek and smiling at him. "You've gotten so big." She looked him over with tears in her eyes. "Rainey would be so proud of you," she whispered to keep from a full-on waterfall.

"I missed you too, Mrs. Matthews." Cael leaned into her touch and closed his eyes for a brief moment, like he could feel something the rest of us couldn't. "You'll come find me before you go home?" He asked her and she smiled at him with a small nose scrunch.

"Cael this is—" I went to introduce him to Bobbi.

"Bobbi." She held out her hand to him, which he gave her after he untangled his fingers from mine with a scowl. Bobbi stared him down for a long moment., "I'm the best friend who picked up the pieces you broke her into the first time so if you do it again..."

Cael put his hands in the air. "I promise."

Bobbi took that as enough, but I turned to look at him. Cael Cody had never made a promise he didn't keep. Even fighting against outside forces, he kept his promises. That was when he made them. His eyes caught mine for a moment, and I could see how serious he was, the feeling catching in my throat like a cotton ball.

"No one is going to object if I steal Clementine for a little while?" He asked, his hands wrapping around my waist and pulling me against him. No one said anything, and Cael took that as leave to move me along, only stopping to scold Ella for meddling but pulling her into the most weighted, caring hug I'd ever seen.

Cael kissed my temple as he spun me away from her before I could say anything and continued to take us further away from all the noise and celebrations.

"Don't do anything I wouldn't do," Ella called to us as Cael led me away from all the noise.

"That leaves so much room for activity, Peachy!" He yelled over his shoulder at her, and his grip tightened on my hand as he weaved through bodies unapologetically until he broke out of the pack of bodies into an empty hallway.

"Where are we going?" A burst of tiny nervous laughter left me but the answer was quick to come as he led us into his Dad's office and locked the door behind me.

His arms trapped me against the door, and his lips found mine for the second time. I curled my fingers into the band of his ball pants and tugged him flat against my body as his lips parted to allow room for my tongue. Cael smelled like sweat, sand, and gummy bears; it filled my nose and made me dizzy. A tiny vibration of pleasure left my throat as his teeth grazed my lip and my back arched into his touch. He groaned against my mouth as he lowered himself further into the kiss and wrapped an arm underneath me.

"Come closer," he grumbled as the kisses became sloppy as our noses brushed and tongues tangled together. I shook my head at his request when I was already melting against him, with no space to move.

"Cael." I kissed him again, trying to get him to come down from the clouds.

"Clem," he groaned back in protest.

My body lifted into his arms and I wrapped my leg around his waist as he walked through the office to the couch. Lowering carefully so I was in his lap, he pulled back and stared up at me with messy hair and kiss-bitten lips. Only a sliver of the sky was visible in his lusty blown pupils and his brows pinched together softly as he properly looked at me in private, just the two of us again.

"You came back," he said with a small voice as his hand brushed a piece of my hair behind my ear.

"I'm sorry it took me so long," I whispered and kissed his jaw tenderly, reveling in the way his body tensed under my delicate touches.

"No," Cael ran his hands over my hands. "No, no." His eyebrows scrunched together. "I'm glad you took your time, Clem, I would have waited forever. I told you once I would die loving you, I meant it."

"I would certainly hope not." I pouted, and he surged forward to take my bottom lip between his teeth. "I hated that I made you sad." It came out in a whisper as his eyes traced mine. "And for the stupidest reason. I never should have gone back to Texas. My home isn't there. It never has been."

I pressed my hand against his chest to feel his heart racing beneath my palm.

"It's right here. Wild as ever." I kissed him again.

"What about Julien?" He asked, his shoulders tense as he broke the kiss.

"He wasn't impressed but—" I laughed under my breath, pressing our foreheads together as his hands raked up my back and gripped me close to him. "There wasn't a single time when his kiss erased the memories of you. It wasn't fair to him, it wasn't fair to us."

He gave me a sweet, sympathetic smile. "Good to know my declaration left a lasting impression."

"Stop." I gripped his chin playfully. "I wasn't sure if you'd even want to see me again... It was so easy to crawl into bed and pretend like the world didn't exist. I was scared, Cael. I've never been so scared of anything in my entire life. I thought I would have time to adjust, and see you from a distance or something. But in true Cael fashion, you barrelled through that door and back into my life. I never stood a chance against you. Not then or now."

He watched me with those big blue eyes and listened so intently my heart wanted to claw its way out of my chest just to be closer to him.

"Loving you before felt like being in a tidal wave and no one could hear me screaming for help. Seeing you here, happy... It was a shock to the system and suddenly I was just that little girl again, wandering around in your shadow. I couldn't breathe around you but I figured out pretty quickly that I couldn't breathe without you either. Julien had been easy, comfortable—" I swallowed.

"But he never gave me that feeling of running in the grass barefoot under the sun, with the blades tickling my feet and fresh air burning my nose. He lacked the shock that tumbling down the hill into the frigid creek water provided. Cael... Julien never made me feel alive, he just kept me numb enough to not feel the absence of *you.*"

Cael watched me as I spoke, never taking his eyes off me as I explained my feelings. He made me feel like the entire world even at my most vulnerable. He brushed his nose against my jaw, a permanent smile on his lips.

"I thought I was doing right by you leaving. Your Dad came to see me, and the argument was sound." I tilted my head back to stop the tears that threatened the corners of my eyes, and Cael pressed an encouraging and delicate kiss to the base of my throat. I hummed and collected myself. "He had been taking the letters, Cael."

I had expected surprise, perhaps outrage or anger even from him but instead, he nodded softly and said, "I know."

"You knew he wasn't sending them?" I asked him, confused by the confession.

"Well I had a suspicion...It didn't matter if you got them or not, it wouldn't have changed anything. They would have just made you sad; he would have lied about keeping them but they kept me sane even sitting in my Dad's desk drawer for the last seven years," Cael explained with a light smile.

"I read them," I told him. "All of them, and you're right. They did make me sad, heartbroken and angry. I didn't know how to fix it, Cael, how to make up for seven years of silence." I chewed on my lip, but he brushed his thumb over it to stop me. "But then Ella called."

"Of course she did." Cael pushed into my grip and stole a kiss like he couldn't resist the urge any longer.

"She understands you," I said, and he nodded. "When she said you were sad, I—it triggered a memory of that day. How determined you were to make sure that I wasn't sad anymore, even though it wasn't your fault I was. I couldn't let *us* go until you knew that I loved you back. I'm just sorry I couldn't figure out how to love myself and you at the same time."

Cael covered the guilt I felt in quick little kisses that peppered my throat and jaw in fireworks that fizzled beneath my skin and lit a fire in my belly. His fingers trailed over my body, wrapping around my wrist and bringing it to his lips as his eyes burned the brightest shade of blue.

It made my heart ache.

"Don't apologize, Clem," he whispered against my skin. "I'm grateful for the time you took to become–" He filled his chest with air and a proud smirk formed on his lips as he looked me over. "*You*. Beautiful, brilliant, confident you. I should be the one groveling, I was so determined to hold true to the past out of fear of losing someone else the way I lost Mama, but you aren't her and I shouldn't want to live in the past. I should want a future, for myself, for us."

I smiled and took his face in my hands. "I like the sound of that."

"Yeah?" Cael let out a relieved sigh and wrapped himself around me in a tight hug that weighed down all my worries and fears. "But what about your job?"

"I quit and got fired I guess..." I laughed and leaned my head back. "One of the interns got a hold of *the* tape." I raised my eyebrows at him and smirked.

"Like *the tape?*" His eyes went wide when I nodded.

"Probably the most embarrassing conversation I've ever had. I swear he was barely eighteen and had never even used the word sex in his entire life." I laughed, turning beet red.

"Well I hope he had fun with it." Cael snapped his teeth at me, tugging on the collar of my shirt, exposing the skin so he could kiss a fuzzy line across my shoulder. "How did he get his hands on it?" Cael stopped and looked up at me.

"I might have left it in the box on purpose..." I shrugged, my confession turning into giggles as his fingers found my ribs and stomach.

"That's my girl," he praised as his hands roamed up my shirt, but I pushed him away. "Clementine," he purred my name.

"Not in your Dad's office." I licked my lips. "I'm not that wild."

"It was worth a shot." He kissed me with a smile.

I brushed back some of his messy blond hair, taking in the features of his face I had committed to memory. His short sloping nose, his hardened jaw, and his high cheekbones. And also the new ones that I never had the time to appreciate. The tiny scar above his cupid bow upper lip and the one that dug into the tail end of his right eyebrow. The lines around his eyes and the more recently sun-stained freckles that kissed the bridge of his nose.

He was even more beautiful than I had remembered.

"I do love you, you know that right?" He said in the silence as if he was uneasy by it.

"Every form of you, no matter how many times you change, you'll always be my Clementine."

"For better or worse?"

"I do," Cael teased with a Cheshire grin, his chin tipped to me and throat exposed.

"Save it, Loverboy." I kissed him and ignored how the words *I do* gave me butterflies. "Oh, and one more thing." I cupped his face and stared down at those big blue eyes. A wish had come true that day on my thirteenth birthday, I was as happy as I could ever be.

"Happy Birthday."

EPILOGUE

TWO MONTHS LATER

"What are you wearing?" I asked Clementine through the phone, with my feet propped up on the back of a stadium seat. My head hung back between my shoulders and I stared at the roof, bored to death and grumpy about being up before seven am.

"A mini skirt and no underwear," Clementine teased, her voice muffled. She said something on the other end that I couldn't hear. "The movers keep clapping everytime I bend over, no idea why..."

"They're in your apartment?" I grumbled thinking about her long legs in her skirt. When she didn't respond to my question a low whine left my throat before I could stop it. "Plum, please..." I hoped she could hear how pathetic I looked right now.

"Are you jealous of the movers, Cael?" Clementine laughed and it made my heart race.

"Yes," I said and sat up in the chair. "Are you really wearing a miniskirt?"

"No Cael, I'm packing." I listened as she switched the phone to her other ear. "I'm wearing sweatpants and I haven't washed my hair in a week, I must smell like a locker room."

"That's even worse!" I groaned loudly, my cock hardening at the thought of it. "Sweat and lavender..." I huffed, I could almost smell how delusional I'd become. "Your ass is mine Clementine, you should be charging extra for them to see it in those pants." I gripped the phone tightly, I could picture exactly what her butt looked like in those sweats and my entire body shivered in response. "And I miss your smell," I whined without meaning to, it just slipped out.

"It's only been a few weeks Cael, we've gone longer." She dropped her tone. "I'll be there soon."

"Don't shower until I get home from Spring Camp," I demanded.

"I'm showering the second I get to the Nest," she argued and I licked my lip at the thought of her rolling those annoyed, beautiful brown eyes at my request.

"You're not playing fair," I kicked my phone against the chair.

"*We've gone longer*," Clementine reminded me.

"Which is exactly why this is torture. It's not a daydream anymore. I can count down the days and time is laughing at me." I removed my hat and ran my hand over the fresh fuzz that had formed after my buzz cut. She was going to flip out when she found out I cut it. "I still can't believe you won't move into the Nest permanently."

"I'm not moving into the frat house, Cael," she said, before bossing someone around on the other end. I wanted her home, bossing me around. I clenched my jaw as I listened to her use that stern voice on the mover, shifting uncomfortably until finally just getting up from my seat and starting to pace. "Having my own apartment is what I need," she reminded me.

The conversation had begun rocky when we finally sat down to discuss what we both wanted, and the only thing we could agree on was her being closer. I had begged her to stay at the Nest, but she was bound and determined to have her own space and, as upset as the space made me, I understood. She was still scared of my shadow and I wouldn't force her to live in it. The apartment was a compromise, it was close to campus with controlled rent but still gave her independence.

"I left the keys on my dresser," I said to her in defeat, after I had made a copy that was currently burning a hole in my pocket.

"Thank you, *Baby*," she purred and, just like that, all the frustration melted away. "I'll be waiting for you when you get home from Spring Camp," Clementine reminded me. "You'll come see me?"

"My first and only stop," I confirmed. "I hope you don't have plans because we aren't leaving bed for a week," I warned her, dropping my tone. "I'll be starving by then."

"Two at least; if you're a good boy I'll wear the skirt." She giggled and every muscle in my body strained under the sound.

"No underwear?" I asked, the thought of her thighs creating a burning pressure in the pit of my stomach.

"Will you clap for me when I bend over?" She dropped her voice into the tiniest moan.

"Are the movers listening?" I asked her.

"No," she said.

"Put me on speaker, I want everyone in that god forsaken apartment to hear it."

"Bobbi is here," Clementine warned.

"She's going to love this. *Speakerphone*, Plum. Now," I ordered.

"You're on speaker." She laughed softly and I heard her set the phone on the counter.

Perfect.

"Good girl." I returned the praise, knowing the exact shade of pink the comment turned her cheeks. "When I get home I'm going to spend the first week fucking you until you can't form a real sentence on every surface in that fucking apartment. And then when we're done, I'm going to start all over again, marking your sweet little pussy with my tongue until you can't breathe. You'll beg me to stop."

I heard the strangled gasp that left Bobbi from the declaration alongside a few mumbled curse words and a '*that man is setting unrealistic expectations for society. He's a menace.*'

"Don't hold your breath," Clementine purred, the sound getting soft at the end as she said, "I love you."

"How much?" I asked her with a smile as I pushed into the main hallway of the stadium.

"A thousand lifetimes worth," Clementine finally answered, after thinking about it for a moment. "Say it back, I need to go," she ordered.

"I love you, Plum," I reminded her. "I'll see you in a couple weeks. Thanks for taking care of my girl, Bobbi."

"She's *my* girl, Lance Bass!" Bobbi yelled from the other end.

"Have fun, Loverboy," Clementine cooed and hung up the phone.

I stopped at the main offices, turning down the hall, my sneakers squeaking against the waxed floors. My phone buzzing in my hand halfway to my Dad's office, I smiled down at the screen. Clementine in her sweats hanging low on her hips, her soft stomach and beautiful skin on display in a lacy purple bra that barely contained the swell of her round breasts, both straps fallen off her shoulders. Her brown hair was messy and falling from two cute little buns at the nape of her perfect neck. I wanted to spend hours kissing every curve of her body. God I missed her. I swallowed tightly and texted her back.

> **Three weeks minimum, I want you bent over that counter at least twice and no tip for the movers, they should be thanking you for the religious experience.**

> **Plum: Deal. xx**

"Dad?" I knocked on his office door, shoving my phone away and adjusting myself in my pants before coming inside, stopping and looking around. "Did you clean?" All of the boxes were gone, as were the blankets that usually crowded his ugly couch and the duffle bags of dirty clothes that littered the floors. I tucked my hands into the pocket of my hoodie and wandered closer as I took in the organized space. I'm pretty sure I hadn't seen the floor in here since rookie year.

"It was Sylwia," he grumbled.

"Like, Mrs. Shore?" I said, and I must have sounded bewildered because Dad's green eyes glowered at me when I looked back at his desk. "At least someone organized, I guess." I shrugged and walked over to lean on the desk.

"When does Clementine get back to Harbor?" He asked me.

"Next week. Bobbi and she are packing up the apartment and driving. I'll be gone when she gets in, so try to make an effort at least until I get back," I said.

"What does that entail?" Dad grumbled.

"Help her move into her apartment? Take her for dinner? I don't know, Dad. Turn on the Cody charm and be polite for a few days." I sighed and ran my hand over my neck as I turned to sit on the desk. "Can you do that?"

"Sure," he huffed.

That was as much as he was going to give me, but it was more than usual.

"Silas said you had the roster?" I said, changing the conversation.

He handed me the clipboard without looking up.

"Promise me you'll behave at camp, Cael," he warned.

"I don't make promises I can't keep, Dad." I mocked and ran my eyes over the roster stopping at the new starting pitcher's name. "Is this real?" I asked him.

He nodded without looking up and repeated himself. "Behave."

I left him to whatever had his focus and wandered down the quiet halls of the stadium, saying hello to a few of the ladies in the office before pushing outside in the chilly spring air.

Silas looked stressed, his gray eyes scanning over a piece of paper as everyone moved around in the parking lot checking their gear. The buses had started loading for spring camp and his plate was full with not only our team starting our season but three other teams.

Ella shook her head at something he said and flipped the page to point to something else. Nick and Arlo stood with their arms crossed, looking more like brothers than ever but still tense in each other's company. It would be a little while before they found their way back to siblings, but for now, they were at least functioning as colleagues.

I leaned against Van's truck and looked over the roster again, my brows furrowing together. Silas broke off from Ella and made his way toward me with a scowl on his face as he reached out for the roster.

"I can tell from your expression that you've seen the newest addition to the team." He said, standing across from me in his Harbor hoodie and jeans.

"They're going to riot." I shook my head and looked over at them all happily chatting and getting ready. "This is going to ruin camp."

"This is the best time for him to bond with the team." Silas wasn't budging on the matter. "I need you to help this go smoothly."

"They're going to string him up on the flag pole and throw tomatoes at him." I laughed and tapped the clipboard.

"Sounds like bonding to me." He shrugged. "You cut your hair?" He raised an eyebrow at me, and rubbed his palm over the buzzcut. "Looks good."

"I think the school board calls it hazing..." I said, ignoring his observation. Silas didn't respond. "As long as you're aware of how badly this will end." I clapped him on the shoulder and wandered over to where most of the team was huddled up.

"You better tell them soon before he gets on that bus," Silas whispered in passing as he grabbed his bag from Ella and climbed onto the bus ahead of the team. She offered no sympathy and followed closely.

"Tell us what?" Van asked, crossing his arms over his chest as Dean joined the huddle in his sweatpants and backward hat.

"What's going on?" He asked me.

"Uh," I opened my mouth to speak but the sound of a duffle loudly dropping to the ground interrupted my explanation.

"Hey boys," Joshua Logan, former pitcher of the Lorrette's stood in a t-shirt, sweats, a cocky grin on his face and a twinkle in his eyes. "Who's ready for Spring Camp?"

TUCKER

A first look into Honeysuckle, book 3 in the Hornet's Nest Series

"No." I looked Josh over, "that's really funny, you guys."

No one moved; their eyes roamed over Joshua Logan like he was a wild animal, and they were trying to process how to make it out alive. There wasn't a chance in hell that Coach thought this was a smart decision.

Josh Logan, the irate asshole and former pitcher of the Lorettes, joining our team?

No.

"Sorry, Tuck, it's not a joke," Josh snapped. He watched me carefully with fire behind his dark brown eyes. His smile said 'glad to be here,' but his eyes held a pitch to them so dark that there was no telling what was going on behind them.

"Don't call me that." I stepped back from the huddle to put space between us all as some of the guys started toward the bus. Van and Cael stayed, hovering to ensure nothing happened as Josh adjusted his bag on his shoulder.

"I don't want to be here anymore than you do," Josh said.

"Then why are you here?" Van asked before I could get the words up and out.

"Lorrette didn't need me anymore; you needed a pitcher," He said in a matter-of-fact voice that grated against my skin.

"We don't need you," I said, and Cael huffed but put a smile on his face as he stepped between the two of us. His hand was going to rest on Josh's chest to push us apart.

373

"Don't touch me, Cody," Josh snarled, and the adrenaline spiked in my chest. I pushed forward, but Cael blocked my advance to keep me from the fight.

"Watch your tone," I warned him, my hands balling into fists at my side.

"I thought you were the soft one, Tuck?" Josh sneered.

I hated that fucking nickname.

"You wanna test that theory, Logan?" I snapped, surging forward, causing Cael to shuffle his feet to gain control as Van stepped forward, ready to assist in breaking up whatever started.

"Alright, boys, we can set up a pudding pool at camp, and you can work this out there, but for now, we have a bus to catch," Cael said, his eyes flickering from Josh to me. "And unfortunately, you have to promise to do it shirtless and no headshots. *You're* both too pretty for that." He tapped two fingers to my chest, drawing my attention downward.

"That's right, Tuck. Listen to your boyfriend and get on the bus. Tail between those legs," Josh snipped, and part of me wanted to lose my mind, but Cael stared at me, begging me to remember who I am now.

Van interjected with a smile, and the wind blew around his shaggy sheered mullet. "You know, Josh, this isn't the best way to start Spring Camp, out in the woods without anyone to hear you scream."

"You're annoyingly tall," Josh noted, gauging Van's size. "I can take care of myself, Mitchell. Thanks for the advice though."

That was the problem. Joshua Logan didn't know how to belong to a team he liked to win; he preferred to do it alone.

Cael pushed me back two steps.

"Get on the bus, Dean," He said quietly, "You can kick his ass in training, come on."

"Catch you later, Tuck." Josh smiled at me.

"It's Captain to you." I looked him up and down before climbing onto the bus in a huff.

"Take a beat before Arlo comes back here and kicks both our asses," Cael said to me as we found our seats.

"Is Coach serious?" I shoved my backpack between my legs and stripped from my sweater beside Cael, who looked mostly unbothered by the situation.

"Have you ever heard my Dad tell a joke?" He shrugged.

Cael shrugged at me.

"Are *you* fucking serious right now?" I hissed at him.

"What?" He turned to me like the enemy hadn't just invaded our team with a smile. I was missing something and wasn't a fan of being left out. I stared him down for a minute, knowing eventually he'd crack under the pressure. "Players transfer, Dean." He looked at me with those endless blue eyes, and his brows twitched.

"There's something else going on. There's no way he'd transfer *here*," I said, recognizing the tell of Cael Cody hiding information from me.

"Well, he did," Cael said like it was a matter of fact. "And you're the Captain, so you get to deal with the shit storm he brings."

"That's the other problem. Why the hell didn't Coach warn me?" I slumped back in my seat as more guys flooded onto the bus. Josh followed Arlo onto the bus, both tense as they sunk into the only empty seats at the front. Silas made space for Josh as Arlo found his place beside Ella without a word.

I hated this.

"He didn't warn anyone. He handed me the clipboard this morning and told me to deal with it five minutes before Josh arrived," Cael explained, his eyes forward. "I know it feels like the end of the world, but you can handle it, and we need a pitcher."

"Not that one," I grumbled. "If he calls me Tuck one more time..."

"You're taking this whole captain thing too seriously. You're turning into Arlo," Cael teased.

"Shut up," I groaned, closing my eyes as the bus started. "How do I captain a player I fucking hate?"

"Arlo's been doing it for three years," Cael laughed.

"Who the hell does he hate?" I asked.

"All of us," he snorted, and that was all it took to break the tension. "The only person on this bus he enjoys being around is Ella, and unless you wanna role play, I don't think you're getting in his good books any time soon." Cael teased. "You're also the size of a bear, and I don't think Arlo is into..." His eyes drifted down to my sweatpants.

I huffed, but a soft laugh came out as the bus lurched forward.

"At least the guys know you didn't sleep your way to the Captain position?" Cael laughed.

"Was that in question?" I turned to him in shock, and he laughed harder.

"It's a damn good thing you're handsome." Cael shook his head. "I'm going to nap now. Can we schedule the next mental breakdown for when I wake up?"

"Yeah...yeah, sorry," I said as he got comfortable. "Don't worry about me, I'll just be here, having an existential crisis."

"I don't think that's the term you're looking for..." Cael said in a sleepy voice.

As soon as Cael fell asleep, the worry seeped back in, and most of the bus ride was spent with me growing through a binder Arlo had given me.

"I kept this the entire time I was captain; it's all the guys' information, numbers, weaknesses, and strengths. Use it. Memorize it. Add to it." He stared at me with his hand on the top of it. *"You're more than capable of carrying this team, Tucker."*

He meant to be encouraging, but every bit of encouragement added weight to my already crumbling shoulders. There was so much expected of me now that I had the captain title attached to me. The binder was *extensive,* though. It had clippings from articles tucked into each of the players' sections and notes from games over the last three years. Arlo had watched us all and made some sort of endearing yet...sick scrapbook of all our accomplishments.

I hadn't found the courage to flip to my page yet, straying clear of the tab that said *Franklin*, knowing that whatever was inside would just add pressure or chip away at whatever confidence I had left.

Arlo's opinion of me, his real one, unseen and unspoken... I couldn't deal with that. Not right now. There was too much on my mind.

How to be a great Captain was at the forefront, quickly followed by the overwhelming smell of Cael's cologne and the scratchy fabric of the bus seats. The air felt like I was being suffocated, churning the contents of my stomach until they inched up my throat.

"I'm going to be sick." I climbed over Cael and hurried to the bathroom as the Bus made another jerky turn. I lost my step and slammed into the tiny bathroom. My shoulders were too big for the space, and the rocking motions of the bus made it feel so much smaller.

"I can't do this." I stared into the warped plastic mirror at my twisted reflection that did nothing but amplify my anxiety. "Why the fuck did they think I could do this?" I swore and leaned on the counter with all my weight.

"I'm not a Captain. I'm barely a human being." My shirt suddenly felt less like an extra large and more like a small. It constricted my throat and stuck to every muscle, drenched in sweat that I swore wasn't there a moment ago. "The only guy you've ever loved can't love you back. You can't tell your parents that you're gay, and now you have to pull the team together for the hardest season they'll face in the last six years."

I swallowed the vomit that rose.

"Why my season? Why Joshua Logan?" I bit down hard on my bottom lip and breathed through my nose to settle my stomach.

A knock came from the door, and I popped it open to find Silas staring at me.

"You alright, big boy?" He handed me a water bottle but didn't let go of it even as I nodded half-heartedly. The bus lurched forward, and I lost my balance again. "Try again," he said.

"I'm fine, just a little motion sick," I said, straightening out. I tried to roll out my shoulders, but the bus bathroom was not made for a six-four, two hundred-and-fifty-pound first baseman, and my shoulders brushed against the walls uncomfortably.

"First time for everything, I guess," He said, finally letting go of the bottle. He crossed his arms over his chest, and his head cocked to the side as he examined me with his stupid judgmental gray eyes.

"I'm fine, Doc." I lied.

"You're going to do fine," he offered, ignoring my answer. "Logan is a speedbump. You know how to Captain these guys. You were born a leader. If anyone can bring them together, it's you. Just..." Silas's eyes trailed up the bus to where Josh sat with his headphones over his ears. "Give him a chance."

I watched Silas's demeanor soften, just for a moment. Deep somewhere beneath all that hardened older brother nonsense, there was a heart he was just trying to safeguard.

"Alright." I nodded, taking another deep breath as the nausea settled slightly. "But making the team accept him is going to take a miracle."

"Better start brainstorming, Tucker. You've got three hours until they hit camp, and then it's martial law."

Spring camp was arguably the best part of pre-season. It was two weeks of pure team bonding out in the middle of the woods. We slept in cabins, played games, trained, and came together before the start of the season. It was typically players and a few staff members. Nicholas declared last year that he'd rather chew off his own arm than come to spring camp, but the moment Arlo volunteered to be a chaperone, suddenly Nicholas was ready to go.

Silas always came. I think he liked it out there, in the middle of nowhere, with no responsibilities other than hanging out with the team. But that was when there was no animosity amongst the players, and everyone got along.

Josh threw a wrench in the plans. He was a live wire—he always had been. Loud and obnoxious, he was always looking for a fight and would do anything to get one. He got under my skin quickly and with such ease, which was part of the problem. I couldn't stop the rage that bubbled up in his presence, and if I couldn't control my feelings about him, how was I supposed to expect that of the guys?

It was going to be a long two weeks.

Acknowledgements

Screaming from the rooftops with pride that book two is finally finished. This book was so incredibly hard to write and truly came out of a place of not only immense love but tremendous grief. I lost my Bubbe a few years ago and she was that person in my life (next to my wonderful husband) who always looked at me and with out a doubt loved me. For all the good and the bad, she didn't care. She also believed in this dream. She believed in my career long before I could figure out how to make it a reality she was pushing me to take the leap. So usually I thank Aaron first, but for Honey Pot, I thank my Bubbe. *Lorraine.*

Of course though it wouldn't be possible without the undying support of my sweet, loud husband who chases away the doubts and always keeps me laughing. He's the banter that fills these books and brings them to life. The stupid phases, the dumb nicknames, those are Aaron classics. Thank you for believing in me and making it possible for me to sit in my office for six plus hours typing away on my loud keyboard creating fictional standards for women that no man, except you could ever live up to. *You are the counterweight to all the bad things in my life.* I love you.

Twinkle Toes, who keeps me sane enough to keep writing and who talks me out of every hole I write myself into. Thank you for being my light even when it feels like were both sitting in the darkness together complaining in circles like it's the only thing we're good at. The Pauly to my Vinnie, I never want to write a book without your help and I'm so proud of all we did in 2024. We have work to do in 2025 but we are making our dreams come true and doing it together makes it extra special. I hope our lives are always, screaming over twitter posts, crying over tik tok edits and writing the most heart wrenching crap. I love you more than Dean Winchester loves pie.

And I can't go without mentioning all the other people who get ear fulls of plotting, planning and panic attacks (very important PPP) on a daily basis. My family, my friends— close and far. You guys bleed into the pages and help me create these found families that everyone adore so much. You showed me that family is whatever I make it. To my Holy Trinity who sit down and watch movies with me or forcing me to take breaks and relax my racing mind, my Golden Girls, the Treehouse, my Sugarclub, my Lil Fucks, Mom and Dad. The Hornets were born out of the love you show me.

To Bec, who quite literally keeps me running like a well oiled engine. Cleaning up the dumpster fires and helping my career succeed despite my boundaries. My UK Momma, she edits every word with love and has helped me grow so much as a writer over the last few books. I hope that I always make you proud and my work reflects how much you've taught me. I love you until the end of the line.

Everyone should be thanking her, but to Rory who took my cry for help and created five incredible covers for this series. You are so incredibly talented and everyday, each cover finalized, I grow more proud of you. I know that 2024 was hard, grief is all consuming but you made what you could of it and you did it on your terms. You will always be the Jesper to my Inej.

Honey Pot would be nothing without the Beta's that combed through it. You guys constantly show up and show out for me and I can't express how much that means to me. These books are nothing without your support for me and I'm glad I get to do this with you!

A special thank you to MK and Jas, my terror twins (affectionally) who constantly reminded me that I was doing a good job, who have not only been in Cael's corner but mine since this all started. Thank you for helping with the secret project that made this release so much fun for not only me but everyone else. I'm so grateful to have not one but two friends that see my protentional even when I can't. My Arlo and Ella. I love you both.

AND TO YOU Thank you for taking a chance on the Hornets, on me. Everyday I'm unbelievably grateful to be doing this as my career and I can't do it without you. So thank you for becoming Hornets, lets keep getting into trouble and lets keep our standards for relationships (romance and plutonic) high. If writing this series has taught me anything, it's that everyone is capable of love and that even in our darkest moments we deserve and are worthy of the love that finds us in the shadows. Keep reading your books, keep spending money on trinkets that bring you serotonin, take sick days from work and binge your favorite TV shows. Call your Mom, hug your pets and help a stranger in need. But don't stop living, even when it feels like the world is too heavy. We do this **two steps at a time,** together as always.

P.S MADI (MADI.LOVEBOOKS) **HAPPY BIRTHDAY LOVE.** (IF YOUR READING THIS ON JANUARY 2ND GO WISH HER A HAPPY BIRTHDAY) I HOPE THE GIFT OF CAEL CODY FOUND YOU, THANK YOU FOR YOUR ENDLESS SUPPORT AND I HOPE YOU HAVE THE BEST BIRTHDAY XX

Made in the USA
Columbia, SC
02 May 2025